ONE BY ONE

Also available by Sarah Cain

The 8th Circle

ONE BY ONE

A DANNY RYAN MYSTERY

Sarah Cain

CROOKED
LANE

NEW YORK

Copyright © 2017 by Sarah Cain.

Published in the United States by Crooked Lane Books, an imprint of The Quick Brown Fox & Company LLC.

Crooked Lane Books and its logo are trademarks of The Quick Brown Fox & Company LLC.

Library of Congress Catalog-in-Publication data available upon request.

ISBN (hardcover): 978-1-68331-087-7
ISBN (paperback): 978-1-68331-088-4
ISBN (ePub): 978-1-68331-089-1
ISBN (Kindle): 978-1-68331-090-7
ISBN (ePDF): 978-1-68331-091-4

Cover design by Melanie Sun.
Book design by Jennifer Canzone.

Printed in the United States.

www.crookedlanebooks.com

Crooked Lane Books
34 West 27th St., 10th Floor
New York, NY 10001

First Edition: March 2017

10 9 8 7 6 5 4 3 2 1

To
Howard, Alexandra, Michael, and Mary

Be sure your sin will find you out.
The Fourth Book of Moses,
called Numbers, 32:23

June 1992

The fireball shot up, shattering wood and splitting asphalt as it roared toward the heavens. The redbrick row house seemed to draw a breath, willing itself to retain a last moment of normality before exploding outward, glass shattering, flames bursting in streams of heat so intense that metal beams began to bend and curl. The houses on either side ignited, and the windows split apart, smoke and flames flaring out as the fire ferociously gulped oxygen.

"Jeez, what the hell was that?" Papa Joe said as he watched the flames shoot skyward. "Sounded like a bomb."

"It does sound close." The heavy woman in the turquoise dress paid for her groceries: a Diet Coke, a bag of Cheetos, and six packs of Tastykake Butterscotch Krimpets. She glanced out the window at the people running down the street. "I'd better get home." Collecting her change, she hurried to the door of Carlino's Deli. "Take care, Papa Joe."

She scuttled out the door and down the street, pushing through the crowd. Approaching sirens cut through the babbling voices of the people huddled together to watch the spectacle, and she took a minute to catch her breath when she saw the row of burning houses.

"Did ya see what happened?" a woman in a yellow sundress was saying.

"That house went boom, like a bomb hit it!" a young man in an Eagles T-shirt replied. "Jeez, I ain't never seen nothin' like it!"

"It's just like that other fire."

An older man stood at the corner waving. "Step back! Step back! Those houses are gonna take the whole block with 'em."

The fire trucks had made their way down Second Street, and the woman in the turquoise dress clutched her grocery bag in her sweating hand and ran to the end of the block. The fire captain shouted into his intercom, "Everyone, get back. Let the men do their work."

"My baby!" The woman burst through the crowd and grabbed the fire captain, pointing to the middle house, her voice barely audible over the wail of the sirens.

The fire captain was shaking his head, and she collapsed against him.

"You don't understand." Her voice rose to a high-pitched keen. "My daughter's in there. You have to save my daughter."

News helicopters were filling the sky, and on the ground, a tall man with a Leica snapped pictures as the fire raged.

*

The fireball shot up, shattering wood and splitting asphalt as it roared toward the heavens. For a moment, the sky over South Philadelphia glowed bright gold.

In an office four blocks down and several blocks to the west, a man looked up from his site plans when the explosion rocked the ground. He poured himself a whiskey and strolled to the window as the sirens blasted through the quiet afternoon. Even from here, he could see the fire leap from roof to roof as it roared through the adjoined homes.

"Here's to urban renewal," he said as he watched the dark smoke rise into the sky and obliterate the light.

Present Day

1

All the old familiar faces haunted sad, forgotten places.

The thought skittered through his mind as Danny Ryan stared at the "Going Out of Business" sign on the Shamrock. The old, familiar face he was meeting belonged to Greg Moss. Danny hadn't seen him since high school and found the sudden request for a get-together odd enough to be intriguing. They hadn't been old pals, more like acquaintances, but Greg had been a loyal customer back in Danny's days as a minor-league dope peddler.

He crossed the wide stretch of Oregon Avenue. A South Philly institution, the Shamrock was a neighborhood tappie, a cop bar where small celebrations took on a larger importance and sorrows were dulled, if not drowned, in a pint and rowdy camaraderie. It had been his father's refuge after a long shift, Detective Tommy Ryan's favorite place to tie one on before he came home to break a few teeth, if not bones.

A crooked yellow sign nailed to the side of the building announced that the Shamrock was the future home of Exxotic Eats, one of those restaurants that served up deep-fried crap with a side salad and perhaps a lap dance. A local wit had added "Shit" to the bottom of the sign in black spray paint. Danny smiled and took a couple of pictures with his phone.

Change crept up on you or slammed into you like an eighteen-wheeler, but you couldn't stop it.

Danny pushed through the door and was greeted by a blast of frigid air bathed in the aroma of stale beer. The glow of neon tinted the dim room emerald, and the silent television broadcasting ESPN cast a blue-white flicker over the bar. Photographs of dead cops lined the walls. His father. His oldest brother, Junior. Christ, there was Ollie Deacon. They'd gone to high school together. Ollie had dreamed of being a cop from the time he was three, but he'd gotten himself killed the first year on the job. Now he was a souvenir.

Some Irish dirge played loud enough to augment the gloom.

At the bar, three old men hunched over shots of whiskey with pints of Guinness beside them. They looked almost like triplets with their white short-sleeved shirts and shiny bald heads. A quartet of younger guys were shooting pool in the back, cursing and waving their bottles of Pabst. At a corner table, a great mound of a man with stubble blooming like gray moss over his triple chins slouched back with a glass of whiskey.

No sign of Greg.

"Yo, fella, how are ya?" the bartender called, his voice neither welcoming nor hostile. Tall, thin, with steel wool hair and narrow, hooded eyes, he had the stoic look of a man who'd witnessed more than his share of weird occurrences. In a cop bar, the ability to keep one's mouth shut and listen was an excellent survival skill.

Danny recognized him. Eddie Dougherty. His father, Sean, had owned the Shamrock for as long as Danny could remember, and Eddie had tended bar since he was eighteen.

"Yo," Danny said. "I haven't been in here for a long time. Thought I'd come pay my respects. My dad was a regular."

Eddie peered at him, his eyes squinting as though he was trying to get a handle on Danny's face. "Can't place you, fella."

Danny stepped closer to the bar. "Last time I was here, I was ten. I sat on the bar right there." He pointed to the space in front of the middle bald man.

"Jesus Christ. You're Tommy Ryan's boy." He waved Danny closer. "Sit down and have a drink on the house."

"No, I—" Danny started to explain his lack of drinking expertise but stopped. *One last round for the Shamrock. You might never be able to go home again, but you could never escape your past.* It sounded like something from a novel.

"Whatever you have on tap," he said.

Eddie set down a mug of beer in front of him and gave Danny a pained smile. "Your old man was one of our best customers."

"Why are you closing shop? You're still a young guy. Business dropping off?"

Eddie shrugged. "I'm not as young as you think. Got a good offer on the place."

"From Exxotic Eats?"

"The developer. Cromoca Partners. You ever heard of 'em? It's like that line from *The Godfather*, y'know? They made me an offer."

The door squeaked open, and Danny shifted in his seat. He would have recognized Greg Moss even if he hadn't bothered to look him up on Facebook. In twenty years, Greg hadn't changed much. He was the quintessential all-American quarterback. He'd put on some pounds and his features had softened, but he still had that leader-of-the-pack look about him.

"Dan Ryan. Long time, right?" Greg flashed a big shark grin, grabbed Danny's hand, and pumped it. He waved to Eddie as if they were old friends and ordered himself a beer.

"What's up, Greg?" Danny asked.

"I got this problem, and I thought maybe you could help." Greg pointed to a table in the corner.

"What kind of problem?"

"This is gonna sound strange, but I think someone's stalking me."

"Stalking you? And what? You want me to write a story about it? Don't you think that's a matter for the police?" It was possible that Greg believed Danny had followed his father and brothers to the Police Academy instead of the pages of the *Philadelphia*

Sentinel, but Danny figured Greg had taken the time to do some homework. He had arranged this reunion for a reason, and it had nothing to do with sentiment.

Greg picked up his beer, and Danny followed him to a table tucked into a corner near the glowing neon shamrock. Greg slouched down in the creaking oak chair and sighed. He drummed his fingers on the table. "I don't know that I'm ready for the police. Not yet. I been getting these text messages."

Danny pulled out his notebook. "What kind of messages? Threatening?"

"Kind of. Yes and no." Greg waved his hand, trying to seem dismissive. His mouth tightened, and he gripped the edge of the table. "Okay. It's gonna sound weird. I been getting these Bible quotes. Like this one." He pulled out his phone and squinted at it. "'It is better to go to the house of mourning than the house of feasting.' What the hell does that even mean?"

"I don't know, Greg. It sounds ominous. Are they all like that?"

Greg looked around and leaned closer. "Yeah, they're all kind of like that. Bible quotes. I'm not a preacher. I don't read the Bible. The most recent one was this one: 'Better is it that thou shouldest not vow, than that thou shouldest vow and not pay.' Freaked me out."

"When did they start?"

"I don't know. A while ago."

"What's a while ago? A week? A month? A few months?"

"I don't know. A few months. At first I thought it was some kind of prank, y'know? But now, I'm not so sure."

"Why aren't you so sure?"

Greg took a swig of his beer. He ran a hand through his hair and drummed his fingers on the table a few more times.

"Look, I'm a realtor, okay? I'm involved in a massive development project. Massive. It might be someone trying to fuck with me."

"And why would that be? What the hell are you into?"

"It's politics. A Jersey–Philly venture. That could be all this is."

"Or?"

Greg's face seemed to sag, and his vigorous charm deserted him. In that moment he seemed to age fifteen years. He leaned close. "Do you believe in ghosts?"

2

"You remember Ricky Farnasi?" Greg asked, and Danny tried to dredge up a face to go with the name. Ricky Farnasi played football in high school. If Danny tried hard enough, he might even remember what position.

"I remember the name, yeah."

"He moved to Boston, but we kept in touch—until a couple years ago. Now he's dead. Chris Soldano, the same."

"He was getting Bible texts?"

"They're dead. And so is Nate Pulaski. You gotta remember Nate. Huge guy. Offensive lineman. We called him Penis Head. What do they have in common?"

"Football, right? They were part of the, uh . . ."

"The Awesome Eleven. We all were."

Greg sighed, and for a moment his face went still. Danny knew he was remembering the glory days. The Awesome Eleven—the starting offense for the Furness Eagles led by none other than Greg himself.

"So you guys were all getting these Bible quotes?"

Greg's face hardened. "I guess. I don't know. Maybe."

"So is there a connection between high school and maybe your real estate deal?" Danny wondered what Greg wasn't telling him. "Because this makes no sense. You really should talk to the cops."

"I can't. I mean I just wondered if—for old time's sake—if you'd just look around. Maybe talk to your brother. Kevin's still a cop, right? I don't want a formal inquiry. I can't afford that. The publicity. Just—it might not be anything connected. But it might be. Look, Danny, you were always a good guy. Would you do it?"

Danny considered for a moment. Greg and he had never been best buddies. They had no "old time's sake" to consider, unless Greg figured that the bonds of dope ran deep.

"You know I'm a reporter, right?"

"You don't work for the *Sentinel* anymore."

"I still write freelance."

"I'm asking for a solid. I won't forget."

"What the hell am I looking into? What are you involved in?"

"Like I said, I've got this big deal. It's political. Lots of threads. You know how it is." Greg's voice insinuated that Danny enjoyed rolling in the dirt.

"No, Greg. I really don't know how it is. You haven't told me much of anything."

"Just ask some questions. Maybe check out what happened to Ricky and the others. I mean, maybe they were just coincidences, right?" Greg was pleading now. Like he wanted to convince himself as well as Danny.

"Just tell me a little more about this land deal."

"I'm just—it's a political thing. A Philly–Camden federal initiative with this group I've been working with. Cromoca Partners. Trying to bring new business to the area."

Danny felt a small niggle of unease as he wrote down "Cromoca." "They're the same people who bought this bar."

"Cromoca has bought some property in South Philly, yeah."

"You make some enemies along the way?"

"It's complicated. Danny, please. I'll send you all the info you want. Just say you'll look into it."

Every instinct was telling him to walk away, but Danny nodded. "All right, Greg. I'll ask around. I don't know what you think I'm going to find, but I'll ask around, and I'll talk to Kevin."

"Thanks, man. I owe you." Greg stood. "I'll send you info today, and next time you're bored, give me a call. If you're up for a party." He winked.

"I'll keep it in mind," Danny said. He didn't think he was up for one of Greg's parties, though he suspected that's where the story might be. He shook hands.

Danny watched Greg head out the door, brushing past a young guy in an Eagles hoodie who was sauntering into the bar. When Eddie nodded and asked for ID, the guy glanced at Danny and gave him a conspiratorial smirk.

The hair on the back of his neck prickled, and Danny looked away.

3

When he walked through his kitchen door, Kevin Ryan hadn't expected to find his brother Danny seated at his table, chatting away with Jean. Then again, he should have known when he saw the black BMW parked at the far end of the cul-de-sac. He was sweating and tired and feeling every one of his forty-four years, but he should have been paying attention.

"Jesus Christ," Kevin said. "Where did you come from?"

Danny saluted him. "Good to see you too, Kev. I was in the neighborhood and thought I'd stop by to chat with Jean. She invited me to dinner."

Kevin nodded to his wife, slung his blazer over the back of a chair, and slumped down. Before he could answer, Jean had sprung to her feet, kissed his head, and fetched a bottle of Yuengling. She set it on the wood table, and Kevin cringed a little at the sight of Danny's bemused smile. Of course, Danny's wife wouldn't have given you a goddamn sliver of bread if you were starving. Kevin never understood what Danny had seen in that stuck-up piece of work.

He almost blessed himself. Ma always said not to speak ill of the dearly departed.

"What I meant was, you didn't mention you were coming by. You okay?"

"Yeah. I was in South Philly today. I stopped at the Shamrock."

"Jesus Christ, why?" Just the mention of the Shamrock was enough to ruin Kevin's evening. *That fucking bar. Pop's watering hole.* He'd get himself tuned up real good there and then come home to play whack-a-mole with Danny's head.

"I was meeting someone," Danny said. "Do you recall Greg Moss? He went to Furness. He was in my class."

Kevin frowned. *Who wanted to remember high school?* "Should I?"

"He played football. Quarterback."

"Not when I was on the team." Kevin took a swig of beer and closed his eyes. *High school.* His final shining moments. When he opened his eyes, Danny was watching him intently, head tilted. Kevin could never tell whether it was real concern or something he put on, but Danny had that ability to look like he gave a shit, with the sympathetic eyes, the way he softened his voice and tilted his head. It was a skill.

Jean was puttering around the kitchen, checking whatever was baking in the oven, and Kevin wanted to tell her to sit down. Why the hell couldn't she just sit like a normal person, like she did with Danny? They'd been talking about some stupid thing or another when he walked in. She'd been laughing.

"Sit down, Jean," he said.

She patted his shoulder as if he were one of the kids. "I have to get dinner ready, sweetheart. You know that. Don't mind me."

Kevin frowned. "So uh, this Moss character? Who was he?"

"Greg Moss was quarterback my senior year," Danny said. "He was one of the Awesome Eleven. I know you graduated before they played but—"

"Oh, yeah, Greg Moss. Now I remember him. He was a backup my senior year. So what?"

"He thinks he's being stalked."

"He should call the police. That's what we're here for."

Danny shrugged. "That's what I told him, but he's involved in some big development deal and doesn't want the publicity."

Kevin frowned. He knew where this was heading. "You buy that?"

"No. There's definitely something bizarre about Greg Moss and his land deal, but according to him, three other members of the Awesome Eleven have died."

"Recently?" Kevin sat up straight and set down his beer. "Three in your class?"

"That's what he says. He asked me to look into it."

"And you're here because?"

Danny gave him a sheepish smile. "Maybe you could check out the murders? See if there's any connection? He says he's been getting text messages. Bible quotes. Maybe the other victims were, too."

"Do you have names?"

Danny handed him a paper with three names: Ricky Farnasi, Chris Soldano, and Nate Pulaski.

Kevin could have lectured Danny about getting involved in what seemed to be a bullshit case where a potential victim clearly wasn't telling everything he knew, but it wasn't worth it. He suspected Danny already knew this Greg Moss character had told him only a third of the story. It was easier to go along.

It wasn't that he minded helping Danny. This probably involved little more than a few phone calls. Though when Danny was involved, things had a way of mushrooming.

Kevin glanced at his wife, who was slicing tomatoes for a salad. Jean insisted on trying to force him to eat green shit when all he wanted was his steak and mashed potatoes. When Danny showed up, it was worse. She always tried to prove they were healthy eaters because Beth had always been such a food snob, with her seaweed-wrapped shitballs and wheatgrass crapola. Jean didn't understand that Danny was actually a human garbage pit.

"Where are the kids?" Kevin asked Jean.

"TJ's next door. Mike and Sean should be here soon, and I have to pick up Kelly in a half hour," she said.

"If you want, I'll get Kelly," Danny said.

Jean nodded. "That would be a big help."

Kevin ran his finger against the sweating bottle of beer. Sometimes he could feel his chest constrict at the sight of Danny's face when he chatted with Kelly or roughhoused with the boys. For a long time, he hadn't understood why his brother, who had a great deal more space of his own, wanted to crowd into this small twin house so often. Loneliness, certainly. But Danny was a young guy. He had the capacity to start over, if not the will.

Jean always said Danny needed to heal in his own way. His life had been twice broken. "Be kind," she'd say. "Healing takes time."

Kevin looked around the kitchen, at the battered oak cabinets with the dingy off-white paint next to the refrigerator that was covered with photographs of the kids. He sighed. Maybe Danny would never be whole again. He folded the paper with the three names and slipped it into his jacket.

"I'll check these out tomorrow," he said.

4

Greg Moss lived in Bellmawr, just outside of Camden, and worked at Carson Realtors out of an office in Haddon Heights. He was in the Golden Club at Carson for ten years running, which meant he was a man with good connections in the community.

The information on Cromoca Partners that Greg had sent Danny was useless. Just a puffy bit of public relations bullshit on the wonders of urban renewal Cromoca was proposing for the Camden–Philadelphia area. Danny found that the group had bought a good deal of land around Camden and South Jersey and was also busily scooping up parcels in Philadelphia. This new Camden–Philly initiative seemed to involve selling prime land to the cities at a fairly reduced price, which would be partially underwritten by state and federal grants. It also meant a decent commission for Greg Moss, which was interesting, though, on the surface, not illegal. So how did that tie in with three murders and Bible quotes?

The federal forces driving the deal were Congressman George Crossman from New Jersey and Senator Robert Harlan of Pennsylvania. *Christ.* Big Bob Harlan, his ex-father-in-law. Danny had thought he was going to retire, but he should have known better.

Bob Harlan held onto his office as if it were the key to life. Maybe for him it was. His power was a cloak of invincibility.

Crossman was someone Danny only knew from his press kit. The congressman was the majority whip. He enjoyed the spotlight and, with his Hollywood face, made the most of it.

Danny had been nosing around this business for a week and had nothing to show for it, though he had written a nice little piece on the Shamrock that the *Sentinel* bought as part of its "Lost Philadelphia" series. That was fitting. The Philadelphia Danny knew was disappearing. He wasn't sure if it was a good or bad thing.

Danny leaned back in his comfortable leather chair to observe the disorder in his office. Books crowded the built-in shelves, teetered in stacks on the burgundy leather sofa, and stood in piles on the floor. Unpacked boxes waited in the corner. He knew he should let Mrs. Kresinski in to clean this room next time she came, but that would require some attempt on his part to bring order to the disorder.

He'd intended to move into the city. He'd wanted an apartment, not another suburban home on the Main Line, until he'd stumbled upon Mr. Rebus's Rare Books. The store existed in a prerevolutionary stone house on two prime acres not far from the Devon Horse Show and Country Fair Grounds. Mr. Rebus, a gnome of a man with huge hairy ears, surrounded himself with first editions of Virginia Woolf and James Joyce and for a substantial fee could locate an exceptional volume of Blake or an extraordinary folio of Shakespeare. No questions asked.

"The developers are waiting for me to put this property up for sale so they can sweep in and shoehorn some ten-thousand-square-foot monstrosity onto the space. We've been selling rare books here for over one hundred fifty years," the little man had said.

After several more conversations, Danny had found himself striking a deal with Mr. Rebus to buy the house and not tear it down.

"It's only fitting that a writer buy this place," Mr. Rebus had told him at the settlement. "I've left you something, if you've the wit to find it."

Danny hadn't found the mystical "something." He decided either he lacked the correct amount of wit or Mr. Rebus had been lying. For the first time in his life, however, Danny felt like he'd found his real home.

Conor would have loved it.

These days, he could think about his son and remember the good times without that gut-piercing stab of white-hot agony. Conor still came to him at night, but Danny could deal with that. He welcomed Conor's ghost, especially since he was a benign spirit. It made up for those other nights. The uneasy ones. Those were the nights he appreciated insomnia.

Better to type until four than to lie in bed and dream of the monsters lurking in his subconscious. It had given him the motivation to start the novel that had germinated in his mind and was now sprouting in unexpected directions. His draft had grown from twenty-thousand words to fifty to ninety, and he was still writing. The problem was he wasn't sure where he was headed. He thought he was writing the fictionalized story of his life, but the more he wrote, the less he liked himself.

Maybe his old editor, Andy Cohen, was right. His best work was 99 percent fury, and right now, he just wasn't angry enough. He'd become comfortable, edging toward middle age. If he wasn't careful, he'd end up writing some sappy boyhood memories kind of thing, a golden-hued glimpse into a nostalgic never-never land. It would end in tragedy, of course. Hankies out, eyeballs watering. Christ, the thought made his teeth ache.

Danny's phone buzzed. He picked it up to read the text.

Do you remember me?

He dropped the phone.

Kate. It had to be Kate. She'd come into his life almost two years ago, broken his heart, and disappeared for almost eighteen months now, but he knew she'd come back. He was sure of it.

He didn't recognize the number. When he called back, it rang twice and clicked. No message. Nothing.

Danny set the phone down. He was an idiot. Kate was a memory, a wisp of lavender smoke. She'd worked for Bob Harlan when he'd met her almost a year after he'd lost Beth and Conor. He'd known her for too brief a time, but she'd rescued him, literally and figuratively. She'd been a flickering light in the darkness that had almost consumed him. When she'd gone, she'd left him with the fragile husk of his heart. Danny took a breath. He'd push her to the back of his mind, where she'd stay until those nights when he couldn't sleep, and then he'd drive himself crazy remembering. The phone vibrated again.

Do you remember me?

What the hell was the matter with him? Kate wouldn't send something like this. So who the hell would be texting him?

He was supposed to meet Greg this afternoon and report on his progress or lack thereof. He didn't need this shit.

Kevin had learned that the other three victims had been shot with a nine-millimeter bullet. The only similarity was that all of them sustained a shot to the heart, though Ricky Farnasi had also been shot in the back and Chris Soldano had taken an additional hit in the throat. No mention of any text messages. All the shootings appeared to be random, and none had been solved.

His phone vibrated. It was getting annoying.

June 1992? Remember? Remember? Remember?

5

Alex Burton steered her green Mini past the Whole Foods shopping center and swung left toward Danny Ryan's house. She'd been thrilled when he moved into the neighborhood. He was her only actual friend from the *Sentinel* (even if he didn't work there anymore), someone who understood that she really did love her job and wasn't pining for the joys of motherhood. At least not yet.

She'd spent an hour this morning at Senator Robert Harlan's press event. It wasn't much of an event, but it was weird to see the old bastard walking, even with a cane. He was using the occasion to announce his return to health, his plans to run for another term, and his involvement in a big new economic development initiative that would bring jobs to the region. The last was yet to be unveiled. But it was coming. Soon. Like the Rapture.

Over the past eighteen months, he'd made a miraculous recovery from the broken neck bestowed upon him when his wife clocked him with a wine bottle, and now he was walking. Danny was right. Robert Harlan was incapable of being destroyed. He'd stood smiling and nodding. His hair had turned paper white, but his eyebrows remained as black as his glittering eyes. He still had that sonorous baritone voice.

It had been a waste of her time. He'd taken no questions from the press, just made his announcement and said he was flying to DC. No comment about his wife, whom he'd stashed in some mental rehab hospital. No comment about his ex-business associate Bruce Delhomme, who currently resided in a rehab facility trying to put together the shattered pieces of his mind and body while the FBI rubbed their collective hands together and waited for him to become lucid. Bruce Delhomme had been a peddler of underage sex and drugs, and the senator had been an investor in his businesses. Of course, he'd been shocked to discover their true nature, or so he'd said. Repeatedly. Alex knew better.

She wondered if the senator worried about the FBI. If he considered the possibility that Bruce Delhomme would recover. If he did worry about such matters, the senator didn't show it. Today he'd seemed so vigorous. If it weren't for the cane and slight limp, she would never have known he'd been through any trauma. The white hair only added to his strange appeal. Alex shivered.

Danny would have some thoughts about it all—if she could pry them out of him. He preferred not to talk about the senator or those years after he lost Beth and Conor. She knew there had been a woman in that time period, someone who had lingered briefly and left him with another gaping wound. Alex wondered about Danny's taste in women. It was a worry.

That didn't mean she wouldn't try to extract some insights from him.

In any case, she liked his company. It was good to see her friend settled into something resembling a normal life, even if it was a bit secluded. She didn't blame him for hiding out, but he needed a shove into the world now and then. Otherwise he'd bury himself under stacks of books and disappear.

Her surgeon husband told her she was a nudge. So be it. She'd been called worse. Sam said Danny was still healing. He needed to stop punishing himself. Alex agreed. No matter how many guest columns he produced, Danny was still hiding. Eventually, he'd have to come back to the real world.

She pulled into the curved driveway, parked behind Danny's house, and gathered her shopping bags. She tried the back door, which was open, and walked in calling, "Yo, Ryan. It's me. Lunch lady."

Alex heard a chair roll above her and floorboards squeal as she stood looking around the kitchen. It wasn't huge, but it was large enough to eat in, and it had that wonderful fireplace with the bread oven. It also had a strangely large pantry that she would have remodeled, but Danny thought added charm. It would have been more charming if he actually used the damn thing.

She did like the kitchen's sage-green walls and the deep window seats with the burgundy pillows. It felt homey. It just needed a few little touches. Some flowers on the round copper-topped table. A few nice fat candles. A pot rack hanging over the island. Things a woman would notice.

Danny needed someone to take care of him. Left to himself, he'd stand over the sink and eat PB and Js or some junk he grabbed on the run. She didn't know how he managed to stay so slim. Most people called him boyish, but he never looked boyish to her.

He was like those beautiful, artsy guys who'd fascinated her in high school—the musicians and misfits who smoked too much dope and sported too many tattoos and piercings. Except Danny was one of the more conventional men she knew. He had no piercings and, as far as she knew, no tattoos. Of course, she'd never asked him to strip and bare all. Maybe she'd ask. She grinned.

"Yo, Burton."

He looked wired, jittery. His deep-blue eyes were practically sending out sparks, and she would have thought he was high, except she knew better. Danny only took pain meds for his rotten headaches. That look meant something else—he was on to something.

"What happened?"

"I don't know. Maybe nothing." He took a breath, and she watched him try to force himself to relax. He held out his phone to her. "It's stupid. Maybe a prank," he said. "But it wasn't a mis-dial. I've gotten a bunch."

She read the message. "You recognize the number?"

"Nope."

Alex rocked back on her heels. "That's weird."

"You think?" Danny gave her that half smile and tilted his head a little, kind of like a kid who'd made a super mud pie and was both pleased and sure he'd get in trouble. "I've been helping out this guy. Actually, I went to high school with him. He's been getting texts, too. It's a strange coincidence."

Alex nodded. It was more than strange. People didn't just send you messages like that. "I usually get, 'Go back to Africa, you tight-assed ho-bitch.' Did you tell Kevin?" At least Kevin was a cop.

"Kevin thinks I'm an idiot for having gotten involved in this whole thing."

"Well, yeah. So what's the plan here?"

"Well, I'm meeting this guy, Greg Moss, at two."

Alex sighed and thought about that lovely chicken she'd roasted just for Danny. She'd really been looking forward to this lunch, but no way was she letting him go alone. He had a weird knack for attracting trouble. "Okay. Forget lunch. I'm going with you."

"I'm not sure he's expecting two of us."

Alex glared at him. "Too bad. I brought you food, but it'll keep. I'm going to put it into your fridge, and I expect you to eat it. You know, real food?" She placed the roasted chicken and a salad in the refrigerator and turned to face him, hands on hips. "I made my special dressing for the salad. It's in that plastic container. Sam says it's liquid heaven."

"I'll bet he does. Since you probably make him beg for a meal."

"I do my best. You know, I work too." Alex sighed. "Maybe he's the one who sends me all that nasty mail."

Danny gave her one of those looks like maybe he suspected all wasn't well. She winked at him and smiled. He didn't need to know Sam hadn't come home again last night.

"Depends on how you keep him in shape." He grabbed his keys. "You can't be tight-assed and a ho-bitch. It's a contradiction, don't you think?"

"My correspondents aren't necessarily the brightest lights."

"Most of mine think I'm a gay fascist socialist."

"Also a contradiction."

"Alex? Thanks." His eyes had gone soft and sad. Sometimes Danny would get that look like he couldn't understand why anyone would want to take the time to do anything for him. It always made her chest tighten. *Oh, hell.*

Before she'd started at the *Sentinel*, Alex had heard about him. Dan Ryan, Pulitzer Prize winner, the columnist who won Keystones and everything else every year.

He'd been her mentor, and she'd needed one. Her big mouth and "bad attitude" had made her unpopular in Atlanta, where her editor had been more interested in her boobs than her byline. When she and Sam had arrived in Philly, she'd landed a floater's job on the metro desk, and the great Dan Ryan took a shine to a piece she'd written on child mortality in the North Philly combat zone. It had been buried on page nine.

"Alex Burton?" he'd said, sidling up to her desk. Of course, she'd recognized him, but she'd pretended she hadn't.

She'd expected an asshole. The soft-spoken, humble guy who'd introduced himself, congratulated her on the piece, and offered to take her to lunch had been a surprise. At first she'd thought he was hitting on her, until she'd realized he was married with a baby son. The ideal family, she'd believed at the time, but the guy who had everything turned out to be a good egg with a fucked-up life.

Somewhere along the way, they'd become friends. She'd been hurt when he shut her out after his wife and son had died and he fell into that black hole of despair. But Sam had said every man had to grieve in his own way, so she'd made Danny casseroles and baked him pies and waited for him to call. When he had, she'd let go of her hurt. He'd come back to the *Sentinel*, but he hadn't stayed. Nothing was the same anyway. After the paper was sold, many familiar faces had departed.

Danny never talked about the black-hole time, and Alex didn't ask. He knew she was around if he needed her to listen, and maybe that was enough. She knew he was damaged, but he was her friend. Nothing would change that.

He was still like those beautiful guys she'd crushed on in high school, but she could see he was as goofy and weird as she was. Since they now lived close to each other, they'd taken to dropping off stupid gifts for one another. He bought her a rhinestone tiara as a joke for her birthday. She got him a plastic ghoul for his.

Alex kissed him on the cheek. They were probably walking into a shitstorm.

The phone buzzed again.

6

As they motored across the Walt Whitman Bridge, Alex bopped in the seat to some tune on the radio that Danny didn't recognize.

"If I could twerk my booty on TV, I'd be making a lot more money," Alex said.

Danny glanced over at her, imagining. She was wearing a sleeveless blouse the color of fresh peaches, and a thick gold cuff gleamed on her slim wrist. Her honey-colored ponytail bounced and swayed with the music. Hot and cool. That was Alex.

"You're more likely to be stalking the mayor than twerking your booty," he said.

She sighed. "You know, your texter is probably like the Phantom Menace."

"The movie?"

"You don't remember? Karl Ratland, that committeeman from the northeast?"

"Oh, damn. The Phantom Menace."

"He did have an impressive lightsaber," she said.

"To make up for his other shortcomings."

They exchanged high fives.

Alex laughed. "The Phantom Menace. And that woman who thought she was Cleopatra? The one who stole a taxi?"

27

"Oh, yeah, but she thought she was Queen Latifah, not Cleopatra."

"You always got the colorful shit."

"Well, that's because I wrote a column. Don't worry, when you grow up you'll get a column of your own."

"Daniel, I'm not even going to dignify that. I'm just gonna work on my moves."

Danny smiled. He'd noticed her potential when she'd first started at the *Sentinel*. He'd also noticed the smoldering thousand-pound chip on her shoulder, but a reporter needed that spark. The moment chasing down stories became routine was the time to get out. For Alex, it was still a blood sport, and she was a lioness.

Once they passed over the bridge, she pointed and said, "We have to go straight on the Forty-Two. The Bellmawr exit's not far."

"Is that how you spend your off hours? Watching YouTube to perfect your skills?"

Alex gave him a sidewise glance. "Honey, you don't know what I do in my off time, besides looking after your ass."

"You don't have to look after my ass."

"If I don't, who will?" She folded her arms and nodded as if the argument was settled. In a weird way, it amused him to watch her try to run his life.

"I wonder if Greg Moss will be surprised to see you," she said.

"I was surprised to hear from him."

Danny wasn't sure what he was going to say to Greg when he saw him again. He didn't know much more about the guy than he had a week ago. The closer they got, the more bizarre this whole adventure seemed. Now he was getting these mysterious texts. It made no sense.

They reached Greg's street, a nice middle-class section of homes in a well-kept, quiet neighborhood in Bellmawr, which was part of Camden County but removed from the city's poverty and crime. Danny pulled up in front of a Cape Cod with blue shutters. A maple tree grew in the front yard and a neat row of alternating red and white begonias lined the path to the front stoop. It looked like a realtor's home. The azaleas lining the house were neatly trimmed, and the lawn glistened with the green perfection of a golf course. It could have fronted a postcard stamped "Buy Me Now."

Danny exchanged a look with Alex. "Maybe I should call and warn him there'll be two of us."

"No. I say better to ask forgiveness than permission." She hopped out of the car. "Come on, Comrade."

They walked to the front door, and he rang the bell. Silence.

"Greg?" Danny called and rang the bell again.

"I'm going to look around back," said Alex.

Danny peered through one of the glass panels on the side of the door. Everything seemed neat and still inside, and he wanted to kick himself. He double-checked his phone. They had agreed to meet today at two, which it was now just after. Where the hell was Greg? How hard was it to call and say, "I'm running late"?

Danny stepped down and eased behind the azaleas to look through the bay window into the living room. No one inside. Then he heard a cry.

"Danny!"

He ran to the back of the house. Alex had managed to clamber up onto the small balcony that ran along the second floor window by using a picnic table and three cushions to gain purchase. She stood with her hand pressed against her mouth.

"Are you all right?" he called.

"Oh, my God." She gripped the railing, white knuckled. "Danny, get up here."

He climbed onto the picnic table, grasped the edge of the post, and pulled himself up to the balcony, scraping the skin on his side when he pushed over the top of the railing.

Alex put her icy hands around his face and turned him toward the sliding glass bedroom door. Inside, on the bed, Greg Moss lay naked and spread-eagle. His mouth was a gaping hole, and the blood from the gunshot wound in his chest had already congealed into a deep-brown circle.

7

Blond, blue-eyed Detective Ted Eliot of the Camden County PD looked like a smaller, softer-faced version of Junior, if Junior had made it to his thirties. Danny leaned against the police car and tried to block out the memory of his brother lying on a slab in the morgue with a number two lead pencil protruding from his right temple. Junior had looked vaguely surprised, though maybe that was just the way Danny remembered him now. Time had a way of rearranging memories.

Detective Eliot's African American partner was interviewing Alex down by the crime scene van. If they thought sending the black cop to talk to Alex would make her more pliable, they were in for a surprise. Danny stuffed his hands into his pockets and balled them into fists.

A small group of neighbors had assembled across the street in the time it had taken the local cops to contact the county detectives. Danny kept his head down, glad for the sunglasses that shielded his eyes when he glimpsed the inevitable cell phones pointing his way. "Citizens with cell phones," his old editor used to say. Andy Cohen had believed that the news was the province of professionals, and the twenty-four-hour news cycle encouraged the nutballs and self-promoters to "crawl out from their slimeholes." Thinking about Andy still hurt.

"Mr. Ryan?" the detective said.

Has he been speaking the whole time? Danny blinked. "I'm sorry. I missed the question."

"You say you had a meeting with Mr. Moss."

Danny nodded. "Yeah. We arranged to meet a few days ago."

"And why were you getting together? Are you friends? Acquaintances? Are you a client?"

"I went to high school with Greg. He had asked me to look into something for him."

"I see." Detective Eliot gave him a brief smile and made a note. "And what were you looking into?"

"It was a personal matter."

"Mr. Moss is dead. It's not personal anymore."

Danny nodded. He knew he should just tell the cop what he wanted to know, and he would. He always fought that residual distrust. "He was getting texts. Strange texts. He asked me to look into it."

"Why you? Why not go to the police?"

"That's what I asked him. He said he wanted to keep it quiet. My brother's a Philly cop. We made some inquiries. I didn't think it was anything to worry about. Clearly, I was wrong."

"What kind of texts was he getting?"

Danny tried to pull up the quotes from the recesses of his mind. "One was about it being better to be at the house of mourning than feasting. The other was something about vowing and paying—I forget exactly, but it's in my notes."

"That seems pretty threatening to me. Did you figure climbing up on the balcony was part of your agreement as well?" The cop pursed his lips. He didn't have to say, "Are you stupid?" for Danny to understand what he was thinking. Danny almost nodded at the unasked question. This ranked low on the list of stupid things he had done in his life.

"I, uh, was worried."

"So you had a meeting. Then when he didn't seem to be home, you and your friend climbed up on the balcony for what purpose?" The cop looked at him through slightly narrowed eyes.

He was still friendly enough, but Danny could sense his growing skepticism. Hell, Danny himself didn't understand why they hadn't just turned around and gone home. He should have called Kevin. Except he hadn't driven to Jersey just to turn around.

"He was pretty definite about meeting today. I thought something might have happened." It sounded lamer each time he said it.

"I see." The cop's eyebrows rose slightly as he digested Danny's words with a vaguely bemused look on his face. "You and your friend will need to come down to the station to make statements."

"I don't know what else I can tell you."

Detective Eliot shrugged. "I'm sorry, but you appear to have been the last person to have heard from Mr. Moss. You discovered his body. You and your friend. We have a man who was killed and no apparent motive, and until we nail down time of death and get some more solid evidence, I'm afraid you're all we've got."

"Alex just came along for the ride," Danny said.

"That's her problem for now."

"Do we get to make phone calls?"

Detective Eliot gave him a toothy, fake smile. "Of course. It's just a formality. We just need to get your statements."

"Can we follow you?"

"That's your BMW?" The detective pointed to Danny's Z4. When Danny nodded, he said, "We'll have someone bring it along for you."

When he gave Danny a reassuring pat on the shoulder, Danny knew he was in for a long afternoon. He avoided looking at the neighbors who stood with cell phones at the ready as he slid into the detective's car.

*

Danny stretched out on the uncomfortable straight-backed chair in the interrogation room and prepared to wait. He wished he had come alone, though once she had gotten over the shock of finding Greg's body, Alex seemed to be holding up well. If nothing else, she was game. She'd given Danny a grim smile and thumbs up before she strolled off with the other cop to a second interrogation room.

Detective Eliot entered and set a cup of coffee in front of Danny. "I should have asked if you'd prefer a soda. Do you need milk or sugar?"

"No, thanks. This is fine." Danny straightened and put on his sincere face. There was nothing like shitty cop coffee. He pushed the red coffee stirrer around the black liquid. It gave him something to do with his hands.

"So you're a reporter, right?" The detective looked over his notes.

"I'm a freelance journalist, yeah."

"Is that like the guys who snap cell phone pictures and send them to the news?"

Danny was reasonably sure the detective had already done a background check on him, but he was willing to play along if it got him out of this room. "No. I was a columnist for the *Sentinel* until I quit a while back. Now I do freelance columns for papers like the *New York Times*."

"So this might be something you could write about?"

Danny shook his head. "I write about different issues. Last month I did a four-part series on human trafficking."

"Is that right?" The cop leaned closer. "For the *Sentinel*?"

"For the *Times*."

Maybe he should have told the detective that his very last piece was about the Shamrock, but he doubted that would have gained him many points. Detective Eliot didn't look like the type who hung in neighborhood tappies by choice. He dressed too well for a cop. His gray suit was custom, and he wore a red silk tie with a slim gold tie bar. Either the detective came from money or graft was profitable in the Camden area. Since Bellmawr was a working-class section of New Jersey and the detective worked homicide instead of vice, Danny opted for the former theory. For now.

The detective glanced at Danny's phone, then looked up at him, his face bland. "That's interesting background, Mr. Ryan. So tell me. Did you think this guy, Greg Moss, was involved with human trafficking?"

Danny almost dropped the cup of coffee. "What? No. I told you. I was doing a favor for him."

"Yeah, I understand that, but we have a little problem here."

Danny frowned at him. "What kind of problem?"

"Well, it's a funny thing. We didn't find Mr. Moss's cell phone in the house."

Danny processed what the detective was saying. He didn't like the way the detective seemed to be measuring him up, like maybe he had more than one reason to be at Greg's house. "I don't understand. You didn't find his cell phone?"

Eliot said nothing for a moment and then let out a slow sigh. He leaned a little closer, inviting Danny to do the same. "We didn't find his cell phone or computer. I have some of my people looking for them now. So I'm going to ask you again, do you have any idea why anyone would want to kill Mr. Moss?"

Danny folded his arms and didn't budge. "I don't understand why anyone would want to kill Greg. I haven't seen him since high school, but he seemed like a pretty normal guy. I don't understand why anyone would threaten him. It doesn't make sense."

"Okay. You went to high school together. You both stayed in the area. Maybe you have friends in common."

"I don't think so." The few people he had stayed in touch with from high school had no connection to Greg. Danny was sure of that. He saw no need to drag them into the investigation.

"Is there a possibility this has something to do with high school?"

"Anything's possible, but Greg and I weren't close friends. We knew each other in passing. We didn't hang out. He was a big-time jock, and I wasn't. He was in the very cool group, socially speaking."

"So you never hung out?"

"We existed in different universes. Greg was a social guy though. He was outgoing. Got along with most people. Like during senior week, he probably invited half the people in the class to stop by his shore house if they needed a place to crash."

"Including you."

"Sure."

"But you weren't friends."

"He invited a lot of people." Danny wasn't about to get into the whys of the invitation. "It was one of those 'if you need a place to crash, feel free' sort of invitations. That's the way he was."

Danny stared up at the detective, and he knew from the way Eliot's eyes narrowed that he shouldn't have mentioned senior week or the shore house or the party.

"Except you might have been his dealer."

That was a fast leap. Danny rocked back in his chair. So that was what Eliot had been doing when he ran to get coffee. It hadn't taken long for the cops to make the connection to the good old days. Why would it? He'd written about his adventures in drug dealing.

Danny'd been an idiot. He'd sold weed and pills in high school, though he'd never thought of himself as a dealer—more like a friendly supplier. His father hadn't seen it quite that way.

"I was never charged with dealing. I spent one night in a juvenile facility and was released."

"Because of your father."

"I was put in because of my father. Just because my father was a cop doesn't mean he ever went easy on me." That was the understatement of the year. Danny maintained eye contact with Eliot. This guy had done his research, but Danny wasn't about to give him family history.

"I think we both know your father got those charges dropped. Your sister, Theresa, was involved with Vic Ceriano, a known trafficker. You must have been aware of that. He did time for the distribution of marijuana and cocaine."

Danny almost smiled. He was more than aware of Vic Ceriano's reputation. Vic had been his supplier. He expected the detective already knew that. Danny said, "I understand marijuana's legal in a lot of states now."

"So it is. But marijuana and cocaine are still illegal in New Jersey. You've led an interesting life, Mr. Ryan."

Danny remained silent. What was coming next? A family history? A review of his marriage to Beth? A discussion of the accident that killed her and Conor? A snake of anger began to coil inside him, and he forced himself to breathe slowly.

"Can you account for your time between, say, Wednesday and this afternoon?" asked the detective.

"I spent Wednesday evening at my brother's house celebrating my nephew's birthday. Like I said, my brother's a Philly detective. His name is Kevin Ryan, but I'm sure you know that already." Danny kept his voice even and pleasant. He wasn't sure if he was a suspect or only a tiny thread for the detective to grasp. Maybe Eliot thought he'd break down and confess to a murder he hadn't committed. But this whole interrogation had grown tiresome. Danny leaned back in his chair and shoved his hands in his pockets. He was tired of playing.

Eliot nodded. "Okay, Mr. Ryan. We won't be much longer. Just a few more details to check out."

"Do I get to make a phone call?"

"Certainly. You aren't a suspect."

I feel like a suspect. Danny was glad he hadn't mentioned the anonymous texts he'd been receiving. Better to discuss those with Kevin.

"If you'll excuse me for a moment," Eliot said and left the room.

Danny put his feet up on the table as if he were relaxed. If the cops were watching, let them get a good look. He had nothing to hide. He could sit on this hard chair as long as it took. The Ryans were a stubborn bunch if nothing else. He closed his eyes and laced his fingers behind his head.

8

It was after eight before Eliot let them go. He'd agreed to release them after Danny had placed a discreet call to his brother.

"What the hell is wrong with you?" Kevin had said. "Jesus Christ. I really don't need this crap. I'm about to walk into a crime scene."

"I'm sorry, Kev. Your secretary didn't give me your schedule. I'd call my lawyer, but I thought that would look like I had something to hide. I'm here in Bellmawr with Alex, and I just want to get home."

"Alex Burton? Jesus. You all hate cops till ya need one."

"Okay. Just forget it. I'll call Sam Goldsmith. His firm has a branch in Jersey."

Kevin had given a pained sigh. He took his time, or maybe the Jersey cops took their time, but eventually Danny and Alex were driving home.

They'd switched from Top 40 to jazz on WRTI, and Alex leaned against the window as they headed back over the Walt Whitman Bridge, her brow wrinkled in a small frown. Twilight painted the city soft purple, and Danny could see South Philly stretching out before him. His old neighborhood didn't bring on any pangs of nostalgia.

"You get into some weird situations, Ryan," Alex said at last.

"I hope Sam won't be pissed at you."

"He's been getting home late all week. I think I'll skip telling him about this episode for as long as I can."

Danny nodded. Greg Moss had been dead about eighteen hours when they had arrived on the scene, according to the preliminary reports. That was as much additional information as the detective was willing to share. Danny had asked Kevin to find out what he could, but Kevin hadn't agreed to anything beyond the phone call.

Eliot said he considered Alex and Danny persons of interest, but he had no reason to suspect them of anything.

"It's just peculiar," Alex said. "Don't you think it's a little obvious? Greg gets Bible texts. Now you get weird texts. Who would do that? What's the connection?"

Danny gripped the wheel a little tighter. "Someone wanted my attention?"

"Or someone wants to tie you to Greg Moss?"

"Yes." He tapped on the steering wheel. "Maybe. Except that seems ridiculous. I spoke to him Wednesday—yesterday. We found him around two today. The ME got to him around four. The ME thinks he was killed Wednesday night. I had an alibi for last night."

"Not all of Wednesday night. You didn't spend the night at Kevin's."

"Okay. But the cops could check the videos on either the Ben Franklin or Walt Whitman Bridge. They could check my E-ZPass."

"If you'd really wanted to get Greg, you could have taken another bridge and not used your E-ZPass."

"But I have no motive."

She sighed and twisted her head back and forth as if trying to relax. "That is a problem."

"And what was the point of sending me those texts at all?"

"I don't know. It's weird." She looked out the window as they crossed into Philadelphia. "I don't know about Ted Eliot, but his partner gave me the creeps."

"All cops give you the creeps."

She shrugged. "Kevin doesn't. I mean I know he thinks I'm a bitch and all, but he's straightforward."

Danny concentrated on driving. The expressway was clear, and he headed down toward the I-95 bridge. "How was the cop weird?"

"A lot of it was about how well I know you. Were we involved? What were we doing before we came over today? Were we together last night? That kind of thing." She let her fingers brush against the lightsaber charm dangling from his rearview mirror. "I just have the feeling they found something in that house because that cop kept asking about Wednesday night."

"It isn't what they found. It's what they didn't find. Greg's cell phone is missing."

"Well, excuse me. Mr. Policeman didn't mention that to me."

"It doesn't matter. They were fishing because they don't have anything. You wouldn't have been there if I hadn't dragged you along. It's over. Can we put it behind us?"

"I guess we have to."

He hated the way she wouldn't look at him. He should have come alone today. He should have known something would go wrong. "Didn't you ever meet Officer Friendly when you were a kid?"

"Officer Friendly?"

"You know, Officer Friendly comes around to your school and tells you how cops are your friends and how you should be happy to see cops in your neighborhood."

"Officer Friendly shot my cousin Delroy." She scrunched down in the seat, arms folded, and he sighed. She looked like a kid trying to enclose herself in a shell.

"You don't have a cousin Delroy."

"I know."

He cut across two lanes of traffic and parked on the shoulder of 95 South. By now, the sky had gone dark purple and the city glowed pink and yellow. Planes rose from Philadelphia International, their red-and-white lights flickering.

"Hey." He put his hands on her shoulders, and he saw the gleam of tears she blinked back. "I'm sorry, Alex. I'm so sorry."

"No. It's okay. I'm fine now." She was trembling, and she let him pull her against him, the emergency brake uncomfortably between them. Cars zipped past, and the heavy, humid Philadelphia air weighed down on them. But he closed his eyes and blocked it all out. She smelled of coffee and jasmine, and he knew as sure as the sun rose in the east that Alex Burton wouldn't cry in front of anyone until he felt her body shaking against his.

"I'm sorry." Somehow he always managed to hurt the people he cared for the most.

"Can we just sit here a few minutes?" Her voice was muffled against his shoulder.

He stroked her hair and ignored the console digging into his ribs. "We can sit here all night," he said.

9

Danny couldn't sleep. Rain thundered onto the roof, trickling down the windows. Something, a tree branch or a loose shutter, banged against the side of the house. He'd done a great deal of work here, but the place always needed something. Maybe the "it" Mr. Rebus had left tucked away was a card reading, "Gotcha, Sucker!"

When they'd gotten back to his house, they had picked at the chicken and salad Alex had brought earlier, and then she'd gone home looking more than a little haggard. He'd gone online to revisit the article "Emergency Call Goes Wrong: Philly Surgeon and Wife Get Bad Medicine at Miami International."

It'd happened a few years ago. A guy had keeled over in the men's restroom in front of Sam, who'd tried to revive him. The cops thought Sam had attacked the cardiac victim after a citizen told them a black guy was mugging someone in the men's room. Sam had remained calm. Alex hadn't. At least they hadn't been shot, but she'd taken a public flogging for it. "Uppity" was the word used in a number of articles. The talk radio hosts had been less charitable.

Danny hadn't thought about the incident when he'd invited her to go with him today, because Alex never would discuss it, and anyone who brought it up received her patented ferocious glare. NPR had wanted to interview both Sam and her, but they had declined.

Danny hadn't been there for her. It had happened in the foggy time after Beth and Conor's accident, and he hadn't been able to see past his own pain. What a miserable specimen he'd been.

He'd stared at the photograph of Alex frozen in black and white—face defiant, her slender arms bent backward by a burly white cop—until points of light had begun to dance around in front of him.

Kevin always said, "We're not all like that."

Danny knew Kevin never would have burst into a men's room and assumed that the black man in a polo shirt and khakis administering CPR to an overweight white man lying prone on the floor was a mugger. He also knew his father had a shoot-first-and-regret-it-later policy when it came to "the goddamn apes."

When you dealt with urban crime, you saw a lot that made you doubt basic humanity. It tended to beat your compassion to a twitching pulp. Tommy Ryan's compassion for most people dried up the day he buried his wife and took up drinking as a competitive sport.

Danny swallowed a pill from a little foil packet. No more needles for the most part. Now he had little stacks of foil packets and a bottle of Valium to induce sleep when the migraines came. He reserved the heavy-duty painkillers for nights when pain sliced his head in two like a melon, and evil gremlins smashed at the pulpy insides with spiked clubs. He closed his eyes and tried to relax. Maybe he'd forget holding Alex on the side of the road. At the moment, it didn't seem likely.

Lightening cracked, followed by a great boom of thunder, and the house seemed to shudder. Danny almost thought he heard something near the front door. The mail slot protesting? Maybe it was a shutter creaking. He stood to look out his window in time to see a branch from one of the oak trees on the side of the house break free and crash to the pavement.

He wandered back to bed and picked up the long piece of polished jet sitting on his nightstand. Someone had given it to him a while back. It was supposed to protect against evil and bring comfort to the grieving. He didn't believe in magic stones but couldn't bring himself to throw it away. Lightening illuminated the room. Thunder shook the house.

On nights like this, he used to read to Conor, who would curl tightly against him, convinced that only the sound of Danny's voice would protect him from the monsters that waited in the closet and under the bed. He still kept Conor's favorites lined up on the bookshelf across from his bed: his *Star Wars* paperbacks, *The Wind in the Willows, Harry Potter*. Sometimes he'd run his hand over the books and could almost hear Conor begging for one more chapter.

"I miss you," he said aloud and pressed the stone against his palm. The rain continued to beat down.

*

Bright sunlight filtered through the windows, and Danny sat up, groggy. He hated the damn pills. They left him half a step out of sync with reality. Even after a shower, he walked into the wall on his way to the stairs.

Gripping the railing, he shuffled down the steps and stopped in the foyer. Someone had pushed a small package wrapped in white paper inside the front door through the mail slot. *What the hell?* Usually the mail was delivered to the box that sat on the curb. Danny walked over to it. *A prank?*

Across the back of the package there was a note written in red ink: *Had a great time yesterday.*

It had to be from Alex.

Danny picked up the package and shook it. He carried it to the kitchen and pulled off the paper. Inside was a small cardboard box. Danny weighed it in his hand for a moment before he lifted the lid.

"Jesus Christ."

He dropped it into the sink.

Inside, wrapped in plastic, was a human tongue.

10

Kevin Ryan almost dropped his mug of coffee when he answered his brother's phone call. He slammed the mug down on his gray metal desk and groped about for a pad of paper while Danny relayed the tale of his morning gift.

"Jesus Christ. What is it with you, Danny? Did you say a tongue? Are you shitting me?"

"No. Someone slipped it inside my mail slot."

"Give me an hour." Kevin slammed down the phone and waved at his partner, Jake Martinelli. "Yo! I've gotta run. Family emergency."

"Not Jean or the kids?" Jake's brows twitched. He'd lost the ability to frown about six months ago, just about the time his hair had gone a few shades lighter and his tan had become permanent.

Ever since his divorce, Jake had put himself through a self-improvement regimen. Kevin wouldn't have cared, but Jake insisted on leaving him helpful tips on dieting and workouts. It pissed him off. Everything pissed him off these days.

"Danny," Kevin said.

Jake nodded. "How long do you need?"

"I figure at least half a day. Can you cover?"

Jake grinned. His teeth were blinding white. "You got it. Though with your brother, you'd better take the whole day."

*

Kevin pulled up in front of Danny's place. Set back from the road, it was a simple stone house with a big weeping willow in the front and a twisting slate path leading to the red front door. Small compared to the giants that surrounded it, the house looked like something out of a storybook—a good place for Danny, whose head seemed in another world half the time.

Jean always said life had ground the sharp edges out of Danny. Kevin didn't believe that. Danny still had some edges left, but his need to give the finger to the world had lost its urgency. For the most part. He still had the same knack for getting himself in trouble.

Kevin noted the branch from one of the trees that lay across the front yard. It had barely missed taking out part of the roof. Kevin would have cut those bitches down before he moved in.

The front door opened before he got halfway up the path. Not too long ago he and Danny would have started the day hurling insults at each other, but this morning, his brother looked like a kid in his oversized black shirt and beat-up jeans. It didn't matter that silver was just beginning to thread through his too-long dark hair or that worry had cut groves between his eyes, Danny would be forever frozen at age ten. A big-eyed kid with a broken left arm, six cracked ribs, and a fractured skull, courtesy of their old man.

"Kevin, thanks for coming," Danny said.

"You need to cut back your trees."

Danny's eyes widened for a moment as if he was considering a smart-assed remark, but he smiled instead. "I'll get on it."

"Where is this gift?"

"In the sink." He ushered Kevin toward the house and held open the door.

"Jesus." Kevin sniffed the air. "You made coffee?"

"A nice dark blend reinforced with rocket fuel. You won't sleep for three nights, guaranteed."

"I mean, you're reasonably calm."

"Did you want me to stand and stare at it till you got here? Would that make me seem less suspicious?" Danny grinned at him.

"Don't be an asshole." Kevin followed the scent of coffee into the house, down the hall to the kitchen in back.

The tongue was lying in the sink, still encased in plastic.

Kevin leaned closer to examine it. "Jesus Christ," he said. "Does it belong to Greg Moss?"

"If I were betting, I'd say yes. Though Detective Eliot didn't mention that it was missing yesterday."

"Christ on a one-legged crutch," Kevin said at last. "Well, I'm calling your friend, Detective Eliot."

Danny's mouth tightened. "Can't you handle this?"

"I'll be here, but this case isn't my jurisdiction. You didn't do anything, so chill out. Ted Eliot seems like a decent enough guy."

"You weren't shut up in a room with him for six hours." Danny leaned back against the counter, trying to appear casual, but Kevin could see the tension in his posture, the way his eyes grew darker, and the way the muscle in his left cheek twitched. "He might have mentioned that Greg was missing part of his anatomy."

"He might have. He probably didn't want to see it turn up in the paper. If you'd called me before you went running off to Jersey, you wouldn't have been involved at all," Kevin said.

He waited for Danny to come back at him with some remark, but Danny just stared at the floor before saying, "What's going on here, Kevin? This is pretty weird, even by my standards."

"I don't know." There was no answer but the obvious: some nut-job was stalking Danny. Usually, stalkers fell under the annoying-but-mostly-harmless category. Danny would attract the weirder kind. "You weren't involved with Greg or his friends at all?"

"I sold Greg some weed back in the day. And then he asked me to look into whoever was texting him."

Kevin grimaced when Danny mentioned he sold weed. He preferred to forget that Danny had been the local dealer. Danny liked to play down those days, make it sound like a prank. Kevin knew better. Still, it was in the past, and Danny was never a major player. Kevin cleared his throat. "Well, someone's got you connected for some reason. Maybe you should get another dog, y'know?"

Danny's shoulders slumped, and Kevin could have bitten off his own tongue. *Stupid. Stupid.* Danny was never going to get over losing Beowulf. That dog had been like a second child.

"I, uh . . . no." Danny looked up and gave him a grim smile. "Whoever this is, he already has my home address and phone number. If someone's after me, I expect he'll find me."

Kevin took a breath and let it out. *Relax. Don't strangle him.* "All right, let's review here. No, let's not. You just tell me where you're going to be."

"Maybe taping some TV, because of that series on human trafficking that ran in the *Times*, but really not much. Do you think any of this is connected to my writing?"

"Not unless Greg Moss was into human trafficking." Kevin didn't think Greg's murder was connected to Danny's writing, though it was possible that the dead realtor was either a porn fancier or seller. Danny had written about sex clubs before, and he'd just finished a series on underage sex trafficking for the *New York Times*. It was possible he'd stumbled on a connection. You never knew. Since Greg Moss was an old high school friend, it was more likely something Danny was choosing to forget or, worse, didn't understand himself. In twenty-some years, memories grew hazy, and details became distorted. Assholes didn't change.

It was disturbing that three more of Danny's classmates were dead and that they had all been shot. Kevin had gotten reports on the classmates from those phone calls Danny had asked him to make. At least one other had gotten a Bible quote: "Woe unto them that call evil good, and good evil." Kevin remembered that one. It gave him the chills.

"You sell all of these dead guys weed?" Kevin asked.

Danny shrugged. "I sold to Greg, and he probably shared."

"And you said Greg was involved with some development group as well."

"Cromoca Partners. I have a feeling he hosted special parties for friends."

Kevin paused for a moment before he said, "And you think that because?"

"He sort of invited me to one."

"Jesus. If this is some kind of pervie sex thing, I'm gonna save myself the trouble and lock you up now."

"I don't know that Bible thumpers are big on kinky sex, but you never know."

"I'm gonna check in with Ted Eliot in Camden," Kevin said.

When Kevin had spoken to Eliot last night, the cop had implied the murder was somehow tied to Danny's days as a drug dealer. Kevin doubted it. He knew Danny had sold some pot and pills under the guidance of their sister, Theresa, and her scum suck of a husband, but Danny had never been much of an outlaw. Becoming a reporter was Danny's way of rebelling. Their old man never got over it.

"Little bastard," he'd mumble into his scotch when he'd reached the end of a long night at the Shamrock. "Going to work for that no good Jew cocksucker Andy Cohen. He's a fuckin' lap dog."

"Danny always wanted to write," Kevin would say.

"What the fuck do you know, you stupid son of a bitch?"

Tommy Ryan was a man with a bad word for everyone.

Kevin turned his attention back to his brother, who stood watching him with his head tilted slightly, like he could guess what Kevin was thinking. Kevin didn't know if Danny understood the potential for shit hitting the fan, but it pissed him off all the same. He didn't understand how Danny could be so freaking casual.

"Kev? I didn't have anything to do with Greg's death."

Kevin sighed. "I know. I'll get you through it. But first I've got to call Ted Eliot."

11

Danny watched Detective Eliot approach the tongue as if it were a piece of discarded gum. Maybe in his line of work that's all it was. If Eliot was surprised, he didn't show it. Instead he slipped on a pair of latex gloves and carefully inserted the tongue into a plastic evidence bag.

"You woke up and found this in a box in your foyer?" the detective asked.

"Yeah, I thought maybe Alex—my friend from yesterday— had left it. She doesn't live far." Danny cleared his throat.

The detective made a quick note, and Kevin said, "That tongue isn't terribly dehydrated. Someone took care to keep it . . . fresh. Maybe someone was making a statement."

Eliot nodded. "Could be."

"You knew this was missing yesterday," Danny said.

"It wasn't something you needed to know," Eliot replied. He looked at Kevin when he spoke, and Kevin gave the barest of nods as if to signify he agreed. "I didn't want this to show up in the paper. I still don't."

Danny didn't bother to protest. "So what happens next?" He looked from Eliot to Kevin. They both wore their cop faces, but the similarity ended there. Eliot wore another impeccable dark-gray suit with a white shirt and maroon tie while Kevin wore wrinkled khakis and a threadbare blue sports jacket. Kevin really needed to lose some weight, Danny observed. He was venturing into heart-attack land.

"We'll try to trace the blood and the prints," Eliot said, glancing at his watch. "In the meantime, I'd try to think about any connection you have to Greg Moss. Anything you can come up with will help us, and that will help you." Danny might have been tempted to give a smart answer, but he couldn't take his eyes off that watch. What kind of cop wore a Patek Philippe watch?

It wasn't a common timepiece. He had a nearly identical model sitting upstairs—a ninety-thousand-dollar anniversary gift from Beth, part of her efforts to remake him into a more socially acceptable model. It sat in a box in his bureau, a monument to everything that had gone wrong in their marriage.

He took a step back. Kevin stood there, in cop stance, his right hand tucked into his belt. He frowned, so Danny said nothing.

Kevin walked Eliot out to his car, and the two stood talking like old friends. They mirrored each other with their arms, right hands resting on their holsters, as they stood beside Kevin's Navigator.

What do cops discuss? Fingerprints? Blood spatter? Corpses? Danny knew cops liked telling stories, the grosser the better. They weren't that much different than reporters in that, except cops always had that look when noncops were around, like they were sizing you up, trying to figure out whether you were trustworthy or not, always suspicious. They saw people at their worst, so they tended to be a cynical lot. But Ted Eliot was a different kind of cop.

*

"Just stay the hell out of trouble," Kevin had said before he'd left. Danny tended to agree with his brother for once, though he wasn't sure he had control over the situation. He'd told Kevin about Eliot's watch, but Kevin had shrugged.

"Probably a knockoff," he'd said.

"If he wanted a knockoff, he'd probably get a Rolex. Everyone knows Rolex."

Danny didn't press it, especially since Kevin didn't seem to think it was important. He'd let it go for now. Investigating cops was something to be handled delicately. It was easier to start with his own skeletons.

"One last thing," Kevin had said. "Will you please keep your goddamn doors locked? Maybe use that fancy alarm system?"

"Oh, yeah. I lock my doors." He did at night, though he seldom bothered during the day. It didn't seem necessary. The worst thing that happened in this neighborhood was the occasional out-of-control teenage pool party. But Kevin always anticipated the worst.

12

Danny had been sure he was destined to spend the rest of the weekend picking body parts out of the trash, but so far it had been quiet. He'd dug his old high school yearbook out of one of the unpacked boxes in the attic.

He wasn't sure why he'd kept the yearbook, but he'd carried it with him every time he'd moved. Maybe it was a warning: don't forget where you came from. He generally didn't wax nostalgic about the good old days. He'd been glad to escape, though high school hadn't held any particular terror for him.

Neither a jock nor an outcast, Danny had been lucky. No one had picked on him because his brothers were Tom and Kevin Ryan, and thanks to his sister, Theresa, he could get his hands on decent weed, which made him semipopular. Theresa's significant other, Vic Ceriano, had been a South Philly legend. There wasn't a drug created that Vic Ceriano couldn't supply.

In a weird way, school had been a refuge for Danny, particularly after Ms. Taylor, his sophomore-year English teacher, decided he could write. She was the first person who told him he was good at anything, so he'd worked his ass off in her class and joined the student paper because she was the monitor. She'd submitted his essay about his romp in juvie to the *Sentinel*. After he'd gotten established, he'd written a column about her.

He flipped through the yearbook pages until he found Greg Moss, the quarterback with the symmetrical face and killer smile. He wrote "Greg Moss" on a notepad and circled it. Their only point of common ground was high school. The problem was they ran with different crowds. Greg's close friends were jocks—the Awesome Eleven, the starting offense for the football team. But they had all attended the same high school, so that was the first connection. Danny didn't personally know most of the other members of the Awesome Eleven, but he jotted down their names.

Since the text sent to him had read, "June 1992," Danny decided to eliminate the juniors and concentrate on the seniors for now. That left him with seven names. Four of the people they belonged to were dead. Danny looked up the last three.

There was fast-talking LeVon Winston, the team's All-State wide receiver. If Danny remembered correctly, LeVon had gone to play for Ole Miss and then had a stint with Oakland or Tampa Bay or maybe both before he'd torn his ACL. They used to call him "Smokes" because of his last name and because he'd liked to pretend to shoot off imaginary guns when he scored a TD. That had been the Smokes Winston victory dance: arms crossed, head slightly down while he gyrated his narrow hips. The girls had loved it.

Quintel Marshall had been the running back, a solid guy with good hands and a serious face. Danny thought Quintel Marshall might have enlisted in the army right before or after graduation. He made a note to check.

The last guy was Sherman Goode, the other wide receiver. Sherman had been sort of the class showboat, a kid who loved being onstage. He'd been a rapper and had a minor local hit called "Get Me Booty" or something like that. He'd been fast, but not a supernova, and had planned on heading for LA, though Danny had no idea what had happened to him.

Danny found it interesting that the three black players hadn't been targeted. At least not yet. Was this really about the football team? If so, why include him? Danny hadn't been part of the Awesome Eleven.

Danny flipped back to the pages of the senior class and looked at the pictures at random, trying to dredge up memories to go with the faces. There was Ray Gretske, looking small and dazed, his blond hair sweeping his shoulders, his pale eyes and happy smile giving him an otherworldly look. He had a nickname. The Alien? The Phantom? No, that wasn't right. It was something unearthly. Danny couldn't remember. Not a football player, Ray spent most of his time on the streets, trying not to go home to his mother and her boyfriend of the week. Danny used to buy him a slice of pizza or a soft pretzel when he'd see him hanging around after school. After all, Ray was one of his best customers. He'd done at least six months in juvie for drugs.

Poor Ray. They might have gotten caught together in a dope transaction, but Ray never seemed to hold it against him. In all probability, he was dead.

Just above Ray, Frank "the Ferret" Greer stared up from the page with his intense, close-set eyes. He was the kind of guy who liked dissection, not because he wanted to study biology, but because he liked killing frogs and other small creatures. He probably killed for a living now. Maybe he was the guy behind these murders.

A little down from the Ferret was poor, chubby Jenna Jeffords, who read too many romance novels and tried to dress like the skinny girls. She used to tell Danny he looked like Johnny Depp and would blink at him and smile.

"No, I don't," he would say.

"Yes, you do. Same cheekbones and eyes and voice and hair, and you're just like him. He's my favorite actor in the world."

"I have blue eyes and look like my Great Uncle Francis, the priest," he'd say, though Great Uncle Francis was six inches taller, had a lumpy face with a broken nose, and hadn't seen the inside of a church in a decade. "I might have a vocation."

"Yes. You're going to be a writer. Like on the bestseller lists." Jenna had smiled, looking like a placid cow, and he'd wanted to shout at her to shut up. It probably wouldn't have annoyed him if one of the cute girls had gushed over him.

Frank Greer was the guy who'd started calling him Danny Depp after he'd overheard Jenna. Danny had hated her for that, though he'd tried not to show it.

Danny looked at Jenna Jeffords's round face and heavy-lidded eyes. She'd had a small black mole high on her left cheekbone. She'd called it a beauty mark. The guys used to call her Jumbo Jen—JJ for short. Danny heard she died not long after graduation, or maybe it was a rumor. She'd been easy to forget.

He flipped the page to Ollie Deacon, the goofy, wide-eyed kid who was the general target of Frank Greer and every bully in the class. He had taken Jenna to the prom, and Danny still remembered the unsubtle sneers and laughter over Jenna's tight red dress and Ollie's white tux.

"Together they make a beach ball," one of the girls had said.

Danny didn't know whether Jenna and Ollie heard the snickers or not. At the time, he'd figured they deserved one night of fun. Now he wished he'd stood up and told the bullies to shut up. He'd spent twenty-some years atoning in print for the times he hadn't spoken, and it still gave him a twinge of guilt to see Ollie's earnest round face peering up at him.

He remembered Ollie telling him how much he wanted to be a cop.

"To serve and protect, y'know?" He'd nodded, hands clenched together. "Maybe I could talk to your Dad?"

"My dad isn't the best . . ."

"He probably hates talking about the job, right? Doesn't want to freak you out?"

"Yeah, something like that." How did you tell someone like Ollie that catching the old man sober would involve walking to the Shamrock and waiting at the front door? And getting between the old man and his scotch, especially after a bad shift, was always a perilous idea.

Danny had learned to survive by becoming invisible, and it was an arrangement that seemed to work for both his father and him. He wasn't about to risk his front teeth so Ollie could get a few vicarious thrills, though maybe he should have let Ollie meet the old man. He might have changed his mind about becoming a cop. He might still be alive.

He turned the pages. There was Frank's sidekick, a goof named Stan "the Skunk" Riordan, a gangly kid with jug ears and small teeth. His main role in life was to suck up to Frank and annoy the shit out of everyone else. Stan was the water boy for the football team and thought he was one of the guys. Greg had always treated him like a slightly backward puppy.

But Frank could always talk Stan into doing his bidding: petty theft, vandalism, anything small and mean. Stan would always go along because he thought Frank was his ticket into the inner circle.

Danny flipped the pages to Michelle Perry, his senior year girlfriend. He'd loved her golden-brown hair and deep-hazel eyes. Her mother hadn't liked him because she knew about his family and believed he'd become abusive. Maybe that was why Michelle dated him. Underneath her National Merit exterior beat the heart of a bad girl. They'd spent a wild spring rocking the springs in his narrow, single bed.

She'd gotten into NYU and never looked back.

Nate Pulaski was a few photos down from Michelle. He barely remembered Nate. Small bullet head, massive shoulders—he was a mountain.

Danny closed the yearbook. What good did remembering do? Whoever killed Greg Moss might have been a member of their class or might have been connected some other way. It was possible, however unlikely, that Greg had a connection to a story Danny'd written. Still, he had a list of names, a starting place.

Maybe the Jersey cops would find something to tie everything together. Danny doubted the cops would call to tell him their findings, but maybe they'd call Kevin.

Or maybe not.

Something was peculiar about Ted Eliot. That watch still bothered Danny. If you were going to get a knockoff watch, you'd go for a Rolex. It would be easier—the knockoffs abounded. No, Ted Eliot had bucks.

Why would a guy with that kind of cash become a cop? He made a note to do a search.

Danny looked at his list of names. Not very promising. He erased Jenna Jeffords and replaced her with Barbara "Babs" Capozzi, Greg's old girlfriend and the class dream girl. What Babs lacked for in intellect she made up for in street smarts, though Danny wasn't sure if that made her a potential suspect or victim.

He'd have to go through the book again more carefully. Greg had a large circle of friends. It would take time to remember them all. He needed to write down all of the names of the Awesome Eleven.

"Yo, Daniel."

He started at Alex's voice. She bounced up the stairs a moment later and poked her head in his office door. "It's a beautiful evening. What're you up to?"

"Research."

"Looks more like a trip down memory lane."

"Same thing."

"Put it aside for tonight. I'm inviting you to the official opening of our pool. Sam's in a snit. He wanted a quiet evening, and now we're having company. God forbid. He'll get happy if you come."

"Don't you ever cut that poor man any slack?"

She sashayed into the room and sat on the arm of the sofa. "I cut him all kinds of slack last night."

Danny leaned back in his seat and assessed her bright-yellow dress. It clung to every curve. He was sure Sam had no complaints. Alex brought zest and passion to his life. He brought soothing tranquility to hers. Twelve years of marriage hadn't broken them. Yet.

"If you come, he'll make an effort to be social."

"Maybe he's tired."

Her face hardened a little. "Yeah, he's a saint with a bitch for a wife."

"I never said that."

"I should be more like my sister, Thea. The dermatologist. She's a perfect lady, you know. She has a perfect cardiologist husband and two perfect children—a boy and a girl who go to the perfect private school where they get perfect grades. And did I mention that they have a perfect Golden Retriever? It even wears a red bandana. They live in New York."

"I'm sure she's not as interesting as you."

She waved him off, but she gave him a little smirk. "Listen. I talked to Paul Gargan, who covers business and economic development for the *Camden Journal*. Something's very funky about old Greg."

"No shit. Someone mailed me Greg's tongue."

She jumped up. "Oh, no, babe! Are you kidding me? Why didn't you call?"

"I figured you didn't want to be part of this after the last Greg experience."

Alex said nothing for a moment, just tapped her foot. "I shouldn't have freaked out. Okay?" When he started to protest, she held up her hand. "Just shut up, Ryan. It's on me. I'm not pissed at you, so don't go all white knight on me."

"You're tough, is that it?"

"You know I am." She jerked her head up, looking like she was ready to devour him. The lioness was back, and he was glad he was sitting. The electricity shooting out from her was tangible. It zapped over his skin, hot and powerful enough to bring him to his knees.

"Good." She gave him a small, triumphant smile. "And I have news. Greg Moss was more than a realtor. He had a lot of high-powered political ties. The rumor is he was tight, as in close personal friends, with Congressman George Crossman and possibly—though I don't have this confirmed—Robert Harlan."

Bile began to work its way up toward Danny's throat. It was a familiar thing, and it followed a well-worn path. The poisoned undercurrent of political sludge, creeping up his sunny lawn, sliding in through the cracks in the foundation to hover just out of sight; it lingered, waiting to pull him back into the shadows.

Danny ran his hand over the pebbled black vinyl cover of the yearbook and stared at the gold embossing. It was a cosmic oddity: the curious coincidence of graduating from the same high school in the same year. Maybe it was more of a karmic fuck-you.

Everything happens for a reason.

Somehow that didn't make him feel better.

Alex came over to him, sliding a hand around his shoulder. He forced himself to look up at her. Golden. Alex was golden. Gold-brown hair. Tawny skin. Amber eyes. Funny how he'd never thought about it before. She'd probably been popular in high school.

"Danny?" She spoke softly, as if he were a child, and he wondered at the slip-slide of their positions. Comforter one day, wreck the next.

"Does Gargan have proof?" he said with some effort.

"Nothing solid. Just innuendo at this point. Greg had a lot of high-powered clients. Of course, he was a top real estate guy. He did seem to have been friends with Crossman. He did recently close a sale on a huge property in Avalon for Senator Harlan."

"Residential property?" Danny couldn't recall the senator owning any private property on the Jersey shore. He had preferred the privacy and exclusivity of his Maine retreat.

"It was commercial property, and it went for a ton of money."

"I wonder if Pulaski, Soldano, or Farnasi was involved with any property development."

"I don't know, but I believe Greg went to their funerals."

"Pulaski." Danny flipped back through the yearbook. Nate Pulaski was the huge kid with the smooth bullet-shaped head, turned-up nose, and close-set eyes. He was a bull of a guy. Danny couldn't imagine someone overpowering him.

"When did he die?" Alex asked.

"According to Kevin, around December, two years ago. He was living in Austin, Texas, at the time. Some folks found him outside his apartment."

"When did Farnasi buy it?"

"Last September. In Boston, or maybe it was Cambridge. He was shot, supposedly while being mugged. Nine millimeter."

"How about Soldano?"

"Same thing. Mugged in New York. He died six months ago."

Alex frowned. "That's kind of a nasty pattern, don't you think?"

"Yeah, it is. And how did Gargan find out about the development stuff?"

"He talked to one Barbara Capozzi." She sat back down on the arm of the sofa. "Do you know her?"

Greg's old girlfriend, the queen of the social pyramid. "Everyone knew Babs," he said.

"Then she's the person to start with."

13

In the back booth, Kevin hunched over his Yuengling and watched the top of the Phillies batting order go down. One. Two. Three. He squeezed the bridge of his nose and tried to shut out the voices that buzzed around him in increasing volume as the bar began to fill. An Old City sports bar, it faced I-95 and the Delaware River beyond and hosted a younger crowd of twenty-somethings who sported tattoos and spent every cent on fancy cell phones, computers, and booze.

The padded green vinyl seats and dark paneling were almost enough to make him nostalgic for the Shamrock, but that hole had been a second home to the biggest rat bastard who ever walked the earth. Kevin finished his beer and held up his bottle.

Fuck you, Dad.

The cute dark-haired waitress with a nametag that read "Amy" approached his table smiling. "Another beer, sir?" God, he was so old, young women called him "sir." Not like the old days when the girls would drape over him and feel his bulging arm muscles.

"Just one more, thanks. And you don't have to call me 'sir.'"

She tilted her head toward him. "Okay. Do you have a name?"

"Just Kevin."

Her smile broadened. "Okay, 'Just Kevin.' I'll be right back."

He knew she was trawling for tips, but his mood lightened a tiny bit. Nothing like having a cute girl smile and tease you.

"Hey, man. Sorry I'm late. I had to drop the kids." Jake appeared at his right and sat down at the table. "If I'm ten minutes late, Cindy calls her lawyer, then I don't see 'em for a month."

"That's rough."

"I was a shitty husband." Jake slouched in the seat, leaned his head back, and closed his eyes. "I miss the boys though. Twice a month sucks. I'm afraid they'll get used to Uncle Daddy."

"The boys love you," Kevin said. Jake may have been a shitty husband, but he'd always been available for his boys. Every game, every school event. If only he'd learned to keep his fly shut, but Kevin didn't judge. The job was hard enough. Stress wore you down in so many ways, like water running down a rock. Some guys dove into a bottle. Some slept around. Everyone got a little harder.

The waitress arrived with Kevin's beer. "Hey, Jake. Long time," she said. "The usual?"

He waved and gave her a wan smile. "Thanks, yeah."

"She's cute," Kevin said.

"And young. Some days, man." Jake grimaced when he shifted. "I pulled a muscle at the gym a couple days ago. It still hurts."

"Well, you can do some research then," Kevin said. "I need some background on a cop, but it has to be done quiet-like."

"Someone I know?" Jake leaned forward, his eyes alert.

"Camden County cop named Ted Eliot. Ring a bell?"

"This the cop that dealt with your brother?"

"Yeah."

"So what's up?"

"How many detectives you know wear custom suits?"

Jake chewed on his lip. "Well, Dez Hinton dresses sharp. I always wondered where he gets his threads. I mean, he must spend his whole paycheck on clothes."

"Like four-grand sharp? I don't think Dez is dropping four grand on suits, man."

"Not four grand."

"And this guy wears a . . . wait a minute." Kevin dug in his pocket and pulled out his notebook. "A Patek Philippe watch. Ever hear of them?"

Jake shook his head. "I thought rich guys wore Rolex watches."

Kevin nodded. "Nobody owns these except really rich guys. Twenty thousand is low end. Okay?"

A cheer went up at the bar, and Kevin glanced over. The Phillies had scored a run. Now they were only behind by two. Three guys in sidewise baseball caps were dancing, and Kevin looked away. The old man would have clubbed him for wearing a hat inside.

"So you're thinking this guy's a dirty cop? Or maybe he's a dumb cop because he's wearing that bling to work? Or maybe he's working undercover. Is this relevant to anything?" Jake asked.

"I don't know. I just need more information, but I don't want him to know I'm looking into him."

"It's pretty weird. A cop wearin' suits that expensive. And a watch like that? Shit. I'd be afraid it'd get smashed up or caught on something."

"Well, he's not on patrol, but yeah, you're right."

"So what brought this on?"

Kevin could have told Jake that Danny was suspicious of Ted Eliot, and he would have looked into him just the same. They'd been partners for too long. He didn't say anything, and he wasn't sure why. He trusted Danny's instincts, and he trusted Jake with his life. But Jake didn't need to know the source of his distrust, just like Danny didn't need to know he was checking out Ted Eliot.

"Could you just do it?"

Jake nodded. "Okay. Give me a day or two. My cousin's in the Camden County PD. He's cool. It won't come back to you."

"Thanks. You're okay."

Jake grinned. "Aw hell, Kevin. You'll make me blush." He watched the waitress approach with his Sam Adams. He nudged Kevin. "Now if you really want to be a pal, you could head on back to your adoring wife and let me entertain a certain waitress."

"I thought you said she was too young."

"No. I said she was young." Jake winked. "But I'm up for it."

Kevin sighed. He owed fourteen for his beers and dug out a twenty. Jake could pay for his own drink.

"Hey. You're not leaving yet, are you, Just Kevin?" Amy said as she set down Jake's beer.

"I'm afraid so," he said. "Family commitments." He handed her the twenty. "Keep the change."

14

Even on a bright spring evening, coming back to Northern Liberties, a gentrifying section of lower Northeast Philly, still raised specters of memories best forgotten. Danny drove around the neighborhood, past the street where the Sandman Case had started, past the rebuilt warehouses where young girls had been held captive waiting to be sent to slavery or death, past the deserted club that had once held a chamber of torture. His ghosts drifted along, almost transparent, but always present.

It hadn't been hard to find Babs Capozzi. She ran a catering business called DelecTable, located on the edge of Northern Liberties, down the street from the new tapas restaurant on Second Street where she agreed to meet Danny for dinner.

Babs had been the fantasy girl for many of the guys. She had always been the kind of girl who made you dream of breathless nights with your mouth on her perfect breasts, her long toned legs wrapped around you. She walked with the sleek assurance of a queen, and tonight when she'd entered the restaurant, she'd paused in the doorway, adjusted her low-cut aqua dress, and sauntered toward him. Her short red hair was slightly more blonde now, and her face was a little harder, but she was still Babs, and her full red mouth with its perfect teeth opened in a knowing smile when he stood to greet her.

"Dan Ryan," she said and leaned in to kiss him. "You haven't changed a bit." She'd never noticed him in high school, but now she seemed happy to see him.

"Babs, you look beautiful as always."

"What have you been up to these days? I heard you left the *Sentinel*."

"I still do the occasional guest column. Now I freelance."

She looked him over, and he watched her calculate the cost of his wardrobe. "It must be lucrative."

"I get by. What about you?"

"I have my business. It took a few years, but I'm finally making a profit."

"Good for you."

The waitress came, and Babs ordered a pinot noir. "You don't drink?"

"Not much." He pointed to his head. "Migraines."

"That's a bitch. I heard about your family. I'm sorry." She made a face. "Our class has had its share of bad luck, hasn't it?"

"Yeah, it has. Like Greg Moss."

Understanding dawned on her face. "So I'm assuming we're not getting together to reminisce because you've been pining for me." She laughed a little. "Not that I'd mind."

"I was the one who found Greg's body." He figured he might as well come out and tell her what had happened. It might establish some level of trust between them. "I was supposed to meet him that day."

She blinked. "You were meeting Greg?"

"He was getting some pretty strange text messages. He asked me to look into it."

"Jesus Christ."

The waitress brought her wine, and she took a swallow. Some kind of Spanish guitar music began to play, but Babs sat staring into the ruby liquid.

"You stayed in contact with him. Was he worried about anything? Having trouble with anyone?" Danny asked.

Babs shrugged. "Of course, he didn't tell me everything, but I guess he would have mentioned if he was being threatened. Why?"

"I'm trying to figure out why someone would send him Bible quotes."

"That's pretty strange."

"He never said anything to you?"

Babs sucked in her breath, and Danny watched the way she avoided his eyes as she considered her answer. Babs was a cool one. She always had been.

"Greg wouldn't have wanted to worry me."

"But you talked."

"Poor Greg. He was a good guy, y'know?" Babs said at last. "We kept in touch. He was that way. If he knew you, he knew you. Like you could have called him up out of the blue, and he would have been glad to hear from you. That's why he was so good at his job. I know he lived in that little house, but he did quite well, all things considered."

"So you don't know anyone who'd want to kill him? A deal gone bad? Pissed-off girlfriend?"

"Honest to God, no. Greg was just a happy guy." She picked up the menu and pretended to study it. Danny glanced at his own menu, giving her time to work out what she was going to tell him. He'd have to sift through the information and decide how much of it was true. When the waitress returned, he ordered a bottle of pinot noir. It would be worth the migraine if it pried loose her tongue.

"So Greg wasn't worried about anything?" he said.

"Well, okay. He did mention he'd gotten some messages. He didn't tell me what they said."

"So he never showed them to you?"

"No, but I think the others were getting them, too."

"The others?"

Her eyes opened wide for a moment. "Yeah. The others. Greg kept in touch with Ricky, Chris, and Nate. Ricky was kind of an asshole, and I don't remember Chris that well, but I liked Nate. The guys used to call him Penis Head because he had that shaved head sticking out of those massive shoulders." She laughed a little. "You ever see Nate Pulaski in a bathing suit? It was scary."

Danny recalled Nate from the photographs in his yearbook. He was a fragment in the primordial soup of his memory. Babs was smiling at him, avoiding his eyes. She was playing games with him, pretending to know less than she did.

"It just seems weird that Nate died, and Chris and Ricky as well. Now Greg," Danny said.

"Sure. But probably they aren't the only ones from our class. I mean, people do die."

"They were all shot with the same caliber gun."

Babs's smile faltered for a second, and something in her eyes flickered. "Oh, but what's her name died, too, and she wasn't shot, though that was years ago."

"Who?"

"You remember. The fat girl. She had a crush on you."

"Jenna Jeffords?"

"That's the one. She was pretty pathetic, old Jenna was. She died in a house fire."

"I'd heard she'd died."

"It was bad. Her mom identified her."

"That must have been rough."

"Yeah, well, it wasn't like Jenna was going places." Babs finished her wine and set down the glass. She looked at Danny like she wanted to say more and then decided against it. "Yeah, I know, it sounds cold, but it's true. Don't you remember that awful romance she wrote?" She put her hand against her heart and said in a breathy voice, "'And as their lips met, her being filled with the molten lava of sensation.' Give me a break."

Danny sighed, trying to think of something that didn't sound quite as harsh. "She wasn't really a literary writer."

"That's one way to put it." Babs laughed while the waitress brought their bottle of wine. Babs watched him, her eyes glittering with a sort of predatory calculation as he went through the motions of tasting the wine he had no intention of drinking.

Babs said, "I always thought you were a nice guy. I never thought you'd become a reporter though. Always figured you'd write some big literary novel."

"Sorry to disappoint."

"Like a Pulitzer isn't big deal. Jenna J. was in love with you because you were nice to her." She chuckled and touched his hand. "And you never were hard on the eyes."

"I wasn't that nice." He decided to ignore the compliment.

Babs pulled out her phone. When the waitress came back to take their dinner order, Babs asked her to take a picture of the two of them. "Here's to us. Survivors. We can be Facebook friends. Isn't that what people do now?"

"I guess so."

After they had ordered, Babs settled back into her seat, relaxed and smiling. Once again the queen. "I never asked if you like tapas. I like all the dishes. So many little delights."

"Not too much of any one thing?"

"Enough variety to satisfy." She moistened her lips with the tip of her tongue and slid a finger up the stem of her glass.

He blinked. Babs may have gotten older, but she hadn't lost much of her appeal. Weird to have her turn it on him. It worked, too. Almost. Did it matter if the chemistry felt slightly off?

"Have you ever gone to a reunion?" Danny asked, and Babs shook her head.

"A reunion? Are you kidding? I don't want to remember high school. Most of those people were losers. Do you go back? How much time do you spend in South Philly?" Babs sipped more wine. "Don't answer. I'll tell you. Not much. You got out as fast as you could. Sure, you became a columnist and all that, but you weren't living in the city. I read all about you." She fired off her points like so many bullets. She was right, too. He'd run away from his past as fast as he could. Funny how he couldn't quite seem to escape it. "Hey, I don't blame you. I couldn't wait to graduate either. I didn't get out of the city, but I've done okay."

"You have your own business."

Babs finished her wine and he poured her another glass. "Yeah. Turns out I'm good at planning shit. You know, special events, parties. Greg told me to get my real estate license, so I've been studying for that. I used to think about calling you for catering work."

"Why didn't you?"

"I don't know. Your wife seemed like she probably had her own list of caterers. Some of the people I called enjoyed slamming the phone in my ear."

He nodded. It would have been tough trying to appeal to the generosity of her fellow classmates. There was nothing like a little schadenfreude to make the world go round. "But you and Greg remained friends."

"Yeah. Greg was a good guy. He threw me work, and I'm real sorry for what happened to him. Hell." Her eyes filled, and she used her napkin to dab her eyes. "Damn it. I don't know who killed Greg. But I hope he rots in hell." She stared at the table, and Danny gave her a moment to compose herself.

"Are you sure you didn't get any weird texts?"

She continued to stare at the table, and he watched the pulse in her throat jump as she crumpled her napkin. At last she nodded. "I got a text before Greg died."

"Just one?"

"Just one." She looked up, her face carefully composed. If she was lying, he couldn't tell for sure, and he gave her grudging points.

"Do you remember what it said?"

"I remember it was Ecclesiastes 7:26 and kind of nasty."

Danny looked it up. "'And I find more bitter than death the woman, whose heart is snares and nets.'"

"That's the one."

"And you have no idea who might send something like that?"

"If I did, I'd have the police on his ass. Look. If you're looking for a football connection, you might try reaching out to Smokes Winston. He and Greg stayed in touch. Smokes is living in DC. He owns a bunch of apartments. Maybe he knows something. I think he bought some property in Jersey through Greg. You could also try Quintel Marshall, though I'm not even sure he's in the US. He's some big something with the army."

Danny nodded. "One last thing. This is going to seem really odd, but do you think this had anything to do with our senior year? I didn't really come across Greg's radar until then. He invited me to his shore house. I don't remember anything happening, but it was a long time ago."

Babs held out her empty glass. "You were there. Nothing happened."

Danny filled the glass. "I wasn't really there. I might have spent the night on the porch."

"With Michelle Perry. Miss National Merit Perfect. You still in touch?"

"Not since we graduated." It was a night for memories, but Danny didn't care to indulge. He pushed Michelle aside. "Do you remember anything? Anyone stand out?"

Babs looked at him as she raised her glass to her lips. Something passed in her eyes—that glimmer of unease—but she smiled and leaned close, sliding her hand over his. "Nothing."

"You're sure, Babs?"

"I think we should do this again," she said.

He gazed at her for a moment. Babs Capozzi wasn't the woman he'd dreamed of spending his life with, but it wouldn't hurt to keep in touch. Dinner had been more interesting than he'd expected. Maybe she'd turn out to be a little delight.

"By the way, no one calls me Babs these days," she said. "Just Barb. It's old-fashioned, but I kind of like it, and it's more professional."

"You should have said something."

"I don't mind when you do it." She squeezed his hand. "Will you call me? It would be nice to get together and not talk about Greg."

"I'd—yes. I'll call you after I get back from DC."

She smiled. "Wonderful. Next time, you can come to my place. I cook, you know. I'm a great cook."

"That is most certainly a date."

*

After walking Barb to her car, Danny headed up North Second Street toward Germantown Avenue. Cheery voices surrounded him, and he could smell the faint scent of barbeque and citronella in the warm air. People were still sitting outside drinking, and Spanish guitar music was playing. Maybe he should have taken some initiative with Barb and invited himself back to her place, but it didn't feel quite right. It was still too soon.

Kate still lingered in the shadows. A ghost he reached for at night, a ghost who slipped away from his grasping fingers. His grandmother used to say you only learned how strong you were when your heart was crushed. After Beth and Conor, he was just strong enough to put himself back together, only to find Kate, and he had lost her as well. He wasn't sure he could risk his heart again.

On the other hand, Barb Capozzi didn't seem on the prowl for a long-term commitment. He smiled.

Barb had given him a number for Smokes Winston, and he'd make a call in the morning. They needed to get reacquainted. Relive old times. Danny had never been particularly friendly with Smokes, but he hoped that, for Greg's sake, the former wide receiver would talk to him.

Smokes and Greg had been close. Maybe he knew something. It was, at the very least, a place to start. He'd try to find out about Quintel Marshall on his own.

"Sorry," he said when he bumped into a person coming from a side street.

"No problem, man."

Danny glanced at the speaker, who was illuminated by the streetlight. A young guy. Dark haired with bright-blue eyes. He looked familiar, and Danny was about to ask if they'd met before when the kid took off down the street. He automatically felt for his wallet, but it was still there.

Danny was tempted to pursue. He didn't. There was no reason to chase a random stranger, and yet . . . He'd seen that face before. He knew it. Didn't he?

A shudder passed through him, and he turned back to his car.

15

The drive to DC was tedious. Alex had wanted to come along, but she had a book signing to attend. Danny headed down I-95 on his way to meet Smokes Winston, who owned a new luxury apartment building in northeast DC. The neighborhood was a gentrifying section of mixed row homes and new luxury apartments. Four blocks to the left and you were in the ghetto. Eight blocks south and you were at the National Mall.

Danny found a spot on the street, fed the meter, and headed toward the lobby. The soppy heat crashed over him, and he could already feel the sweat trickling down his back. He'd forgotten how much he hated the swamp that was the Capital, especially in the summer. After giving his name to the smiling receptionist, Danny sat on a black leather bench and stared at the artificial fire burning away in the visitors' lounge. The fire burst forth as if by magic from coral rocks behind a floor-to-ceiling glass wall. It was mesmerizing but fake. It was DC.

He'd always loved the cooler climate of Maine. The Harlan summer house had been a grand retreat, even if he and Beth had to share it with her parents. It had overlooked the rocky beach in Northeast Harbor, and he'd enjoyed the quiet days, the misty evenings with the lonely fog horns calling out, the restless surf pounding against the shore. He'd done some of his best writing in Maine. Here, he'd have to enclose himself in a sealed room.

"Danny Ryan. Damn, I'd know you anywhere."

Danny turned around. He recognized that distinct Philly drawl. Smokes still looked trim and athletic, but he walked with the deliberate care of a man in pain.

"LeVon Winston," Danny said.

"Shit, man. Jus' call me 'Smokes' like everyone else. Can' seem to shake the name." Smokes Winston held out his hand and gripped Danny's. His pupils were pinpoints, and Danny wondered what the hell he was on. He didn't have the junkie lean, but he had heroin eyes. Is that what you took when pain killers stopped working?

"Movin' a little slow today. Goddamn knee." Smokes led Danny to an elevator.

"Looks painful."

"Yeah. My glory days. Too bad I didn' play today, right? At least I'd be a multi-multimillionaire. Still. I had a decent manager. Invested my money good."

"I'm glad to hear it," Danny said, and he was. His high school acquaintances were beginning to take on a maudlin cast, if not a macabre one. Greg Moss, Rick Farnasi, Nate Pulaski, and Christopher Soldano were all dead. Who else? Jenna Jeffords and Ollie Deacon. Danny wasn't sure whether they counted in the lineup or not.

They reached an apartment on the top floor. It was spacious, and Danny could see the Capitol Dome in the distance through the French doors in the living room that opened onto a roomy deck. There was a modern kitchen with black granite counters and black cabinets, and the living room featured black leather sofas with red throw pillows and a huge flatscreen. Photos of Smokes in action hung on the walls. He'd been one hell of an athlete. Photographs of a young boy and girl sat on a red lacquered table behind a sofa.

"My kids. Keshawn and Kenya," Smokes said. "They're living with their Mama in California right now. She got the mansion.

That hurt. I see them every other month. Some holidays. You wanna drink?"

"Just water."

"You ain't changed much." Smokes pulled out a bottle of Pellegrino from the refrigerator and poured a glass. He fetched himself a double shot of vodka from a bottle of Stoli in the freezer.

On the left, a dining room stretched into a second, more formal, sitting room. On the right, Danny glimpsed an office. The door to the second room stood closed. A bedroom, Danny assumed. Smokes lowered himself onto one of the leather sofas, and Danny sat opposite him.

"So how have you been?" Danny said.

"Hanging in there. I got good days and bad days like everyone. Once I get my new knee, I'll be fine. Just bought a few acres up your way, in fact. Gonna build some luxury apartments. Greg helped me get the property."

"Greg Moss?"

Smokes grinned. "That's why you're here, right? Poor old Greg got himself killed."

"Can you think of anyone who'd want to kill him?"

"Honestly? No. Greg, he was a good guy, you know what I mean? Like if you got into town and needed a place to crash, you could always call Greg. When my knee got busted up, he called me. Can you believe it? Asked if I needed anything." Smokes shook his head and leaned back into the sofa. Danny could see the deep lines pain had etched around his mouth, between his eyes. "Sometimes I think Greg was my only real friend. All them others. The hangers-on, the chicks, the power guys—they all like you when you's a player. Once it's done, it's done. Ain't like I was Jerry Rice, you know?"

"Yeah, it's brutal. My brother played. He never made it to college ball."

"Your brother Kevin?"

Danny nodded. Kevin had been a starting tackle when Smokes was a freshman. He'd forgotten that.

"Kevin Ryan. He was a big mother. What the hell happened to you?" Smokes asked.

"Runt of the litter?"

Smokes chuckled. "I guess. Your brother was something else. Man. He shoulda played. He was All-State for three years. Why didn't he? He didn't get hurt."

"He became a cop."

Kevin hadn't been given a choice. When the old man told him to forget Penn State, Kevin had just bowed his head and acquiesced. What would his life have been like if Kevin had told the old man to fuck off and gone for it? Maybe he would have failed and still ended up in the Philly PD, but at least he would have taken a chance at getting what he wanted.

"A cop?" Smokes voice was softer now, just slightly slurred. "He lookin' into who killed Greg?"

"No, it happened in Jersey. Not his jurisdiction. You can't think of anyone who had a beef with Greg?"

Smokes opened his eyes. "Greg was the most solid guy I ever knew."

"No shit?"

"No shit."

"Not even anyone from high school?"

"You knew Greg in high school."

"Only senior year, and not that well."

"Well, I can't think of anyone. Unless, maybe—who was that guy? Short, real mean-lookin' dude. Had a face kinda like a rat. Real asshole?"

"Frank Greer?"

"Yeah. That's the one. He was always hanging around. Real fuckhead."

"You think Greg kept in touch with him?"

"Yeah. Probably." Smokes shook himself and pushed up on the sofa. He squinted at Danny and rubbed his hands against his thighs. "You know, I'm wonderin' why you want to know. You writin' the story of Greg's life? You workin' with the cops? Why the fuck you asking me all these questions?"

"I'm a reporter."

"So you want to turn Greg's death into some big story." Smokes's face turned hard, angry, and Danny didn't understand. Why wouldn't Smokes want to know who killed his friend? But the hostility slammed down like a barricade. "Like maybe win yourself some writing prize?"

"No, you don't understand. I found Greg's body. I think whoever killed him wanted me to find it, and I don't know why."

"That's fucked up."

"I know. It could be something tied to high school, but I don't know what. I didn't know Greg that well. You did."

"Greg was a regular guy. He wasn't no saint, but he wasn't an asshole. He was the kind of guy the girls liked 'cause he looked good and dressed fine and treated people like people." Smokes paused, his eyes drifting out of focus for a moment. He sniffed and rubbed his nose. He was buying time. Something about Greg Moss made the people who knew him best try to cover for him. So maybe Greg wasn't so upright, but then again, who was Danny to judge?

"I talked to Barb Capozzi," Danny said.

"Babs. Yeah. What did she tell you?"

"Not much."

"I'll bet. Babs is okay though. Loyal."

"How so?"

Smokes swallowed his vodka and swiped his mouth. His eyes didn't burn with anger any longer, but they regarded him with caution. "Are we off the record? 'Cause I'm not talkin' if we aren't off the record."

Danny sighed and closed his notebook. "If you want."

"I do. Because this is a big deal, and it might or might not be important." Smokes leaned forward even more until he swayed slightly over the table. "Greg? You know? Greg? He, uh, had a sideline. Greg, y'know?"

"Greg had a sideline?"

"He used to set up these parties for clients, y'know?"

"What kind of parties?"

"I mean they was for his high-roller clients. 'Cause you know he did a lot of major deals. I mean his clients were real players."

"Like you?"

"Oh, hell no, man. I was just small shit. He was sellin' to some big, big money dudes. He had connections, 'cause his clients were the kind that keep their money offshore, dig? His parties was like a side business. A way for folks to make connections. Greg was big on connections. He'd get actresses to come in and shit. He took me to one 'cause this one client was an Oakland freak, you dig? Like batshit crazy for the Raiders. Man, this guy wanted to jack me off in the pool. He was willin' to pay me twenty grand. Can you believe it? It was insane. I told Greg thanks but no thanks to that shit."

Danny tried to put this information together with the image of Greg the Saint. "So maybe something happened at a party?"

"I don't know. Yeah. It could've, but I don't know. I think I would've got wind. Anyway, Greg wasn't a bad guy. Yeah, he arranged parties, but it was all consenting adults. Them women? They weren't those drugged-out sex hos you read about, y'know? None of that underage shit."

"But they might have been escorts?"

Smokes's head drooped down for a second, and Danny wondered if he had nodded off. But he rubbed his hands together. "Yeah, no doubt. Escorts. A lot of them actresses was doing porn. I mean it's Philly, not LA, right? But that don't mean you can't find some high-quality hookers."

Danny figured the same kinds of groups got together in LA. Special parties for special clients. High-class escorts, dubious actresses. Anything to please a client who paid. He said, "Escorts and drugs?"

"Yeah. No doubt, but that wasn't my scene."

"Did you ever get a text with Bible quotes?"

"Hell no. But some of them others did." Smokes held up his hands as if he were warding off evil spirits. Of course he knew about the texts. It made sense. Greg would have talked to him. "I never got a text. Swear to God. But Babs did. It worried Greg.

He was afraid they was bein' targeted, but then he found out that other folks was gettin' them, too."

"Targeted by whom?"

"Don't know. Greg never did say."

Smokes leaned forward, staring into Danny's eyes, and for that moment, he seemed more alert than he had the entire visit. "Greg threw kinky parties, but they were for clients, and it was business."

Greg was providing a service for clients who could pay. Jesus. Why did that sound familiar? Except these appeared to be consenting adults. Greg was in the vice business, but his clients could afford it. Unless the women were being forced to have sex, where were the victims? Except these parties were happening in New Jersey, not Nevada, and who knew for sure whether the women were consenting or not.

"You're sure about the women?" Danny asked.

"I'm sure they weren't being forced. They were getting paid good, and I'll let you in on a little secret. Some of them weren't even shes, but that was okay, too."

Greg apparently catered to a wide range of tastes. "No kids?"

"Hell no."

"Drugs?"

"Mos def."

"Greg never hosted a reunion, did he?"

Smokes shook his head. "Sometimes informal shit. Like he an' Rick and Nate and some others. I was playin' back then. I don't think he had anything more recent. I'd have heard. Someone would've posted it somewhere."

Smokes was right. Someone would have posted photos. There were none on Greg's Facebook page, none on Barb's. Maybe this had less to do with high school and more to do with one of Greg's parties, but if that was true, why the hell was Danny getting texts?

"Hey, Smokes? Were you at Greg's house for senior week?"

Smokes laughed. "No way, man. I had to be in Mississippi for a special get-to-know-you program. My life was football."

"You were a talented guy," Danny said. He meant to add, "and lucky." He wasn't sure Smokes would agree with that, but not going to the party might explain why no one was texting him. "Was Quintel Marshall there?"

"No. He enlisted right after school, and I mean right after."

"So of the Awesome Eleven, who'd have been at the senior week party?"

"Just Ricky, Chris, and Nate. Oh, and the water boy. That goofy motherfucker. Stan. The juniors wouldn't have been invited."

"How about Sherman Goode? He was one of the Awesome Eleven and a senior."

"Yeah, but he was a squirrel. He lit out for LA, man. Said he was gonna be a star. Who the fuck knows what happened to him? He probably got shot along the way." Smokes rubbed his head as if he were trying to extract memories from some deeply buried vault. "Y'know, it's weird. If it's got to do with high school, why's it happening now? Don't make sense."

"Maybe whoever's doing it was away."

Smokes sat up straight and shook his head. "Hell, yeah. I shoulda thought of that. You oughta look at Frank Greer, man. Greg told me. He did something like seven or eight years in the slam. Hard time for drugs, I think. He got out something like five years ago."

Danny nodded. "That would explain some of the time, but what was he doing before he went away? The timeline doesn't quite match up."

Smokes finished his Stoli and shrugged. "Man, who says he's workin' alone?"

16

Barb Capozzi's staff had arrived at the Academy of Natural Sciences, and they were setting up for the book signing when she entered. She liked the purple-and-blue-tinged ambiance of Dinosaur Hall, with the huge Tyrannosaurus Rex dominating the room. She'd chosen purple linen tablecloths for the occasion—an excellent decision. It was the small touches that made a difference.

These creative types always wanted to have fancy receptions and seldom had the bucks to do it right. Barb liked arranging corporate events where the budgets were big and the venues were first class. She got plenty of nice perks out of those gigs, even if CEO Clarence or Executive Edward grabbed her ass. So what? It was all part of the job. Those fools tipped well, and all those big tips went right into her portfolio.

Now that Greg was gone, she couldn't count on making that lucrative side money unless she heard from his partner, and so far, she hadn't. She expected he'd already hooked up with a new front man, which was a shame, but Barb could handle it. Her business was good, better than good, and she'd taken Greg's advice: don't live large, hide your money offshore, and be patient.

Greg was right about the real estate license, too. It was important. Her mother couldn't carry on forever, and soon Barb would get her share of the family business. More than her share, if she played it right.

Barb still lived in South Philly, but not for long. In a year, two at the most, she'd be completely secure. Her business was humming, and she could hire another assistant. Then she'd have some time to take off. She had a killer bod that she maintained with religious fervor. Maybe she'd travel a little. She'd definitely buy herself a new place to live. Greg always warned her about showing too much wealth, but she had her heart set on a sweet little house off Rittenhouse Square. She'd earned it.

"You look like a twenty-something," everyone always told her.

Barb knew that wasn't true. She'd lost that fresh bloom of youth, but she was a hell of a lot smarter than when she was twenty.

"Hey!" She waved at a woman in a frumpy blue suit. "Nancy. Where are you setting up the bars? I told you we need one on each side."

Nancy Aikens, the liaison from the museum, paused. "Oh, Barb. You're here." She clutched her clipboard. "Mr. Geiger wanted to set up closer to the door."

"Well, he's not in charge," Barb said. "I am. He's just the writer. I've got the floor plan. If we set it up his way, we'll have a huge line of people trying to get to get to the books and then the line for him to sign the damn things. I've brought in extra people to help your staff."

"But we don't—"

"It's all right, Nancy. The museum will get be compensated as agreed. But if we have a table in the lobby, your gift shop won't be swamped—plus less opportunity for theft and breakage, right? Don't worry, I already cleared it with your boss."

Barb produced the appropriate paper and smiled, enjoying the look of confused annoyance on the older woman's face. It was good to establish dominance early. She placed her slim black leather bag against the wall behind the bar where it wouldn't be noticed.

"Let's get moving, shall we?" Barb said.

*

Barb paced the floor, Diet Coke in hand, and watched the crowd. So far everything was flowing. Ron Geiger had arrived on time and meandered through the guests, chatting and shaking hands. A slightly built guy with a full head of silver hair, he'd been a Philadelphia political reporter. Barb supposed that's what his book was about. She didn't care about politics. It was all the same blather.

But she recognized some of the people in attendance. There were a couple of style reporters she'd seen at some of the corporate bashes she'd organized. There was an attractive black woman with her husband. She looked familiar, and Barb would have killed for her gorgeous honey-colored skin. The husband looked like an athlete: tall, slim, and muscular with close-cropped hair and intelligent eyes.

Barb clutched her glass. She'd thought Danny Ryan might be here. It was odd that he'd popped back into her life again. Well, not so weird, all things considered. She wished now that she'd told him she'd gotten more than one text. She would. It would be a good reason to call him.

He'd aged nicely. Hadn't packed on the pounds or lost his hair. He dressed well. At dinner he'd worn a white button-down with black jeans and a blazer, but Barb knew designer when she saw it. Danny Ryan always had been a little too much of a smart-ass for her in high school, but Barb didn't hold grudges—not against attractive men, especially if they had money.

Maybe it was just as well he hadn't come. Barb didn't like to mix with the clients. Not very professional. Her job was to make sure everything ran smoothly. She tapped her bright-red nails on the empty glass. She hated these book signings. The food was usually on the lower end of the scale, but she'd thrown in some extra tonight because Mrs. Geiger had been so pleasant and easy. Plus, reporters were friends with other reporters. Barb figured someone from the style section might show up. Maybe she'd give the business a promo.

"Another Diet Coke?"

Barb handed off her glass to the waiter and took the second drink. She gulped the soda and shuddered. A lime floated in the liquid. She hated limes. Why did bartenders throw random pieces of fruit into drinks? She always insisted that her waiters ask before foisting fruit on the unsuspecting consumers of diet soda. This waiter should have known that, and she turned to go after him.

"This is going very well, don't you think?" Nancy Aikens appeared at her elbow, her plain, pinched face contorted in a smile.

"It's going very well," Barb said.

"The spread is lovely. That style reporter took one of your brochures."

"Did she?" Barb smiled as if she expected no less, but she wanted to jump up and down. Maybe she'd casually wander over toward the reporters. "I think we have a few more people than we anticipated."

"It is very lively." Two red spots appeared on Nancy's cheeks. "I had to chase a couple out from our North American exhibit. Can you imagine? I don't know how they got in."

Barb started to laugh. *A little sex on the prairie.* A cough welled up in her chest, and she couldn't get the words out. She couldn't get anything out. Or in. She stumbled toward the lobby where the bright lights burned her eyeballs.

"Barbara!"

The glass slipped from her hand and shattered as she clawed at her chest and tore at her throat. Air. She couldn't breathe. God almighty. She fell to her knees. A great polar bear stared down at her. Voices swirled around.

"We need a doctor!"

"Somebody call nine-one-one!"

"Help us, she's turning blue! She can't breathe."

"Does anyone have an EpiPen? Please!"

Don't let me die. Don't let me die. Don't—

17

The nightmare of Barb Capozzi ran like a horror film on an endless loop in Alex's mind.

She'd watched Sam push through the crowd and call out for an EpiPen. Someone had offered him one, but Barb was in such horrible shape, he'd been forced to perform an emergency tracheotomy to open her airway. By the time the EMTs had arrived they were able to hook her up to oxygen, but Barb was barely breathing.

"Severe anaphylaxis," Sam had said. "She must have consumed something that triggered the reaction."

The EMTs had started an IV and wheeled her out.

The police had collected the shards of Barb's broken drinking glass and conducted brief interviews, but for now, her anaphylaxis was being treated as an accident.

Alex watched them rush her out. Barb wasn't dead, but it didn't look good. It was a weird coincidence that she had dated Greg Moss back in the day, but all the cops could do was wait for the toxicology reports, gather the security footage, and hope that Barb's brain wasn't fried.

Sam shook his head at that. "I trached her," he said as they waited for the police to finish up. "But she was cyanotic, already in respiratory failure. By the time the EMTs arrived, she barely had a pulse. Under those conditions . . ." His voice trailed off.

Sam was a damn good trauma surgeon. He knew his percentages. If he believed Barb was doomed, her odds of survival just shrank from bad to negligible. Still, Barb seemed like a fighter. Alex wanted to believe that she had a chance.

Danny had said she'd been one of the popular girls in high school. Greg's girl. They'd been a golden couple. This afternoon, she'd seemed quietly competent; not trying to interfere with the guests, just overseeing the flow.

"Did she say anything?" Alex asked Sam.

"She couldn't breathe, Alex. I was able to get her airway open, and I asked them to take her to Penn. I'll follow up with them." He watched her for a moment and sighed. "Okay. I see where this is headed. Drop me off at the ER. I'll take the train home tomorrow."

Alex hugged him. "You know I love you."

"Because I don't say no to you."

"That is part of your charm." She hugged him again. "You come around tomorrow night, and I'll show you how much I love you."

"Oh, Alex. Tomorrow, there'll be something else." He shook his head before going over to talk to yet another police officer, and she absorbed the sting for a moment. It wasn't bad, just a little one.

Alex scanned the room. People were still milling around as the police tried to get a sense of what happened. Alex walked over to the bar. A guy who looked like he'd escaped from a Latin boy band blinked his sad dark eyes at her. A waiter or server of some kind.

"Hey," Alex said. "Weird night, huh?"

"I don't know what happened. One minute she was talking and then she hit the floor."

"Did you make her a drink?"

"Miss Barb never drank liquor when she worked. She only ever had Diet Coke."

"Did you give her a Diet Coke?"

"When we first got here, yeah." His eyes filled with tears. "But she had a fresh one. I didn't pour it for her. At least, she didn't ask me for one. The bars were crowded."

"You mean she didn't come to the bar for a drink."

"No, but when she . . . when she passed out, her glass was at least half full. I heard the museum lady say she had a drink."

"And you didn't give it to her."

"No."

"Maybe she ate something."

He gave a little bark of laughter. "Miss Barb doesn't eat. Especially not at these parties. She calls them cheezers."

"Cheezers?"

"Yeah, she says they're cheesy and cheap, and the clients are usually slow payers. But if the client is nice or extra easy, Miss Barb throws in extra. Like she threw in extra fruit tonight and some fancier hors d'oeuvres 'cause the client and his wife were real nice, plus they paid everything up front."

Alex nodded. Barb Capozzi appeared to run an organized and efficient business.

"Miss Barb wouldn't eat anyway. Not on a client's dime," he added.

"She's particular, huh?"

"She always keeps watch at parties. That's why she doesn't eat. She really watches the staff, makes sure no one makes off with the shrimp or anything, 'cause the client paid for the food. But she's really good about tipping. Like she's strict, but it's okay 'cause we get paid good."

"So she's a good boss. No one has a beef with her."

"No. Most of us been with her for a while."

"Thanks. What's your name?" The waiter hesitated, so Alex brightened her smile. "Come on, I don't bite. I'll give you my card. Call me if you think of something."

"Carlos."

"Just Carlos?"

"For now."

"Okay." Alex handed him her card. "If you think of anything, give me a call, Carlos. Your boss seems like an okay lady. It's a real shame this happened."

"She's a good person. She has to be tough, but she's a nice person underneath. She says she has a lot to make up for."

"What do you think she means by that?"

"I don't know, but she's a good lady. We all like her."

Alex nodded. She looked around. The police were talking to other members of the staff. "Did you pour a Diet Coke for anyone else?"

"All night. Like I wasn't the main bartender. I was mostly pouring soda. There were two bars and two bartenders for each bar, you know."

"I know. But she was standing closest to yours. Did you pour any Diet Cokes near the time she passed out?"

"I don't remember. I don't think so."

He was fidgeting. If he had poured one, he wasn't going to tell her. Not now. The cops had one of the other bartenders and were questioning him. She wanted to get closer, but every reporter in the room was trying to get in on that conversation. The cops eventually walked the bartender from the room into an office. A second set of officers came to claim Carlos and lead him to the gift shop.

When he moved out from behind the bar, she noticed a woman's black bag with the initials BC stamped in gold sitting on the floor. Alex glanced around before she sauntered behind the bar and picked it up. She could see a cop talking to Sam and wondered whether she had time to run to the ladies' room to examine the bag when Sam shook hands with the cop and came toward her.

"Are you ready, Alex?"

"Sure thing."

She slipped her arm through his. Were the cops going to notice? Nobody stopped them as they walked through the doors. It was still sunny and warm out, though purple clouds were starting to fill the sky. Alex walked down the steps, her heart throbbing. She opened the purse and pulled out the wallet inside to examine the ID—just to be sure.

"Sam, we need to go to the hospital," she said once they had reached the car.

"Are you all right?"

She held up the rectangular black leather purse. Its gold handles glinted in the setting sun. "Barb's bag."

"Oh, Alex. You stole her bag? What were you thinking? We need to return it at once."

"She left it tucked against the wall. I think we should take it to her." Alex opened it and began to go through the contents. "Sam, it's important." She held out a small medic alert card in Barb Capozzi's wallet. "She's allergic to naproxen. You have to find out what was in that Coke."

18

An accident just outside Baltimore shut down I-95 to all but one lane, and it took over an hour of creeping bumper to bumper before traffic cleared out. It was almost midnight before Danny reached home. When he pulled into his driveway, he saw Alex sitting on his back steps, legs stretched out, smoking a joint.

"Don't say a word, Ryan. It's been a shitty night."

He sat next to her. "You tell me about your shitty night, and I'll tell you about my weird afternoon."

"Barb Capozzi is in the ICU at Penn."

He closed his eyes for a moment. "How?"

"Severe anaphylaxis. Something—we think naproxen—was put in her Diet Coke tonight."

"Excuse me?"

"I was at a book signing that she was catering. She drank a Diet Coke with naproxen in it. Barb is allergic to naproxen." Alex spoke very slowly as if he were a child.

Danny let her words sink in, felt them settle into his gut. Had he caused her to be poisoned? He thought of the young guy on Second Street, and a chill passed through him. Something about those eyes. Had someone hurt Barb because of him? When

Danny opened his eyes, Alex was watching him through a thin thread of smoke.

Danny took the joint from Alex's fingers and took a hit. Despite his high school occupation, he'd never been much of a smoker. He'd sold dope because it was a way to make money, and money bought freedom from the old man. Using was for people like his sister. When he exhaled, he closed his eyes and leaned back on one elbow.

"Jesus Christ, Ryan. You're getting high."

"Barb Capozzi is in the ICU. Greg Moss ran sex parties. So yeah, I think I'm getting high." He took another hit and handed her back the joint.

"Sam is staying downtown tonight. He's going to let me know what's the deal with Barb." She took a hit. "Whoa. I must be high. Did you say Greg Moss held sex parties?"

He nodded. "According to Smokes, they were pretty intense, but they were also consenting adults. So unless someone was killed or raped at one of said parties, they don't count at the moment."

"Were you ever invited to one?"

"No."

"Then why are you getting texts?"

"Good question."

"So this still probably goes back to your high school adventures."

They sat in silence. Danny never gave much thought to high school beyond the famous arrest incident. He got caught selling dope to Ray Gretske, and his father allowed him to sit in an overcrowded juvenile detention center rather than bail him out. It was a life lesson, the old man had said. Danny had written an essay about it that got published in the *Sentinel*. So he'd won in the end. Or maybe he'd just been fooling himself.

In his father's world there was only one way to live: you obeyed your parents, grew up, became a cop, got married, had kids, and started the cycle all over again. It didn't matter that his father had failed miserably at the parenting part. Tommy Ryan had expectations. You met them or you got out. Danny had gotten out, but he'd been so busy escaping that he'd forgotten something important. Something he needed to remember.

He didn't want to think about Barb gasping for air on the floor, because everyone he got close to seemed to end up grasping for the last strings of life. Maybe he was some kind of fucking banshee. "Naproxen?" he said with effort. "You can get that over the counter. So someone slipped it into her whatever?"

"Her Diet Coke." Alex handed him the joint. "The cops are looking at the security footage, though who knows what they'll find. Greg Moss threw sex parties. Jesus Christ." She tucked herself under Danny's arm and leaned against his shoulder. "You knew some strange people, Ryan."

"That's the thing. I didn't know them all that well."

He was never part of Greg's world. But because Greg spoke to him, even Barb and her pals smiled in his direction. Barb. He'd liked her. She didn't deserve to end up choking on the floor.

What was this really about? Sex parties? Real estate? Or was it all about high school? The cool kids versus whom?

Danny couldn't remember picking on anyone, though he'd been a smartass back then. He'd come from a weird home. His father had been a drunk who also happened to be one of the top detectives in the Philly PD. His two older brothers were tough. It tended to keep the bullies away because nobody wanted to mess with the Ryans.

By the time Danny was in high school though, he'd been able to elude the old man for the most part. He'd stayed out at night and hung with average guys. He'd scraped together money with a bunch of other guys to rent a deathtrap in Wildwood. Danny barely remembered the house. He was dating Michelle Perry and stayed with her the whole time, though they had ended up at Greg's place that one night. No, they had been on the porch. He tried to pull the memory forward.

He could almost grasp it. The salt air, the song on the stereo with a driving beat, the girl in his arms. A lot of whooping from inside. He couldn't remember now. That wasn't good enough. He had to do a better job. Something about Greg's house nagged at him. It glittered just below the surface.

He handed Alex the joint. She took a last hit and carefully crushed it out. "Goodnight, baby. I'm saving you for later." She looked up at Danny with drowsy eyes. "I believe this is a first. Daniel Ryan got high."

"You're a bad influence."

"Oh, no. I'm a good influence. I am very, very good. I want you to loosen up. You've got all this garbage floating around in your head. You need to let go of it."

"Stop wearing black, you mean."

"I mean the whole Greg Moss experience. Just let it flow. Maybe something happened that you forgot? So you need to look inside."

"I've been trying to look inside and there's nothing. Just trying to remember. It doesn't make sense. Maybe Barb got hurt because of me."

"You don't know what it's about yet, baby. More likely Barb got hurt because of Greg."

Danny gazed up at the sky and tried to remember the constellations. Only a few years ago, he would have been sitting in the grass at the old house with Conor. He would be pointing out the Pleiades and Orion's Belt and telling Conor all the myths he could remember. Conor would ask if that was before or after *Star Wars*, and Danny would say he thought it was a different kind of time.

Moonlight filtered through the leaves, making silver patterns on the grass. Fireflies twinkled. He breathed in the warm air. Conor used to chase the fireflies. He'd catch them and cup them in his hands because he liked the way they made his skin glow pink. The force was with him, he'd say.

The expected pain dug into Danny, a second delayed but no less sharp. His child danced just out of reach, a luminous spirit, forever chasing fireflies while he kept struggling to rebuild his life.

Danny sighed. He had no right to wallow in his own misery. As someone he'd loved once told him, he was still young. He needed to get on with the business of living.

Alex squeezed his knee. "You okay?"

He nodded. "In another galaxy, far, far away."

"I don't know if that's good or not. You're the tensest man in the world."

"Not tonight. Tonight I am definitely not tense."

She touched his cheek and pressed against him. She smelled of jasmine, and her mouth was so close he could taste the pot on her breath, even as he felt her heart bumping against his. He watched her eyes darken as he let his hand slide down her back over the curve of her hip to where the edge of her dress met the smooth flesh of her thigh. Her skin was a warm feast, and he was a starving man.

If he kissed her, he'd be lost. He didn't care. Her mouth was warm and yielding, and she molded against him as she pulled his shirt free and ran her hands up his back.

Suddenly, something smashed against the house, followed by thrashing in the bushes near the edge of the yard. An owl protested and fluttered in the high branches of the red oak.

Danny startled and jerked away. "What the hell was that?" He thought he heard footsteps pounding down the street, but maybe it was just his heart.

"I don't know. Was someone there? I thought someone was there." Alex pushed herself up, slightly unsteady on her feet. Her hair was a tangled mane around her face, and her eyes were wide and filled with something akin to remorse. She tugged at the straps of her dress. "Oh, shit. It's late. I've got to get home."

"I'll walk you."

She shook her head, as if trying to clear it. "No. I think I better—I need to think." She squeezed his shoulder and took off down the driveway. "Night, Ryan," she called over her shoulder.

"Alex." He watched her hurry away. *Damnit.* He slumped down on the steps and pressed his fingers against his forehead.

What an idiot he'd been. He'd felt the chemistry. It had always been there, but he'd figured it had distilled into friendship. No, he'd been lying to himself. He knew something stronger existed between them. It had flared up that night by the airport. What next? Right now he couldn't think straight.

He stood and walked into the backyard. Using the small flashlight on his keychain, he looked at the back wall of the house. A baseball-sized rock lay on the ground. It had been hurled with enough force that it left a white mark on the gray stone. A little farther to the right and it would have gone through the kitchen window.

Danny walked to the far corner of the yard, by the tall boxwoods. Several branches had been broken, like someone had pushed through them. He couldn't see footprints, but someone could have stood here watching tonight. Whether it was a neighborhood kid or someone worse was yet to be determined. Should he call the police? He gazed back toward the driveway. If he called the police, he'd have to get Alex involved, and he didn't want to do that. It was possible that it could have been an animal. A raccoon or even a deer. A rock-throwing animal.

Not likely.

He returned to the back door. One of Alex's gold hoops glittered in the moonlight, and he picked it up before he unlocked the door.

"Christ, you really fucked up this time, Ryan," he said and dropped the earring on the counter.

*

Two blocks down the street, the watcher rested against a thick maple and considered the couple on the steps. Would they have done it right there? Out in the open? That would have been interesting. He shouldn't have lost his temper. He should have taken pictures. Or better yet, filmed them.

They weren't being very subtle, though the position of the house and the well-placed shrubbery hid them from view of the neighbors. A pair of would-be adulterers. They deserved whatever bad thing happened to them.

And something would.

It was just a matter of time.

"The eyes of the wicked shall fail, and they shall not escape, and their hope shall be as the giving up of the ghost," he said and sauntered back toward Ryan's yard. He slipped in through the hedges and melted into the shadows.

19

Kevin Ryan shifted in the leather lounger in the basement rec room. Out front, the twins were playing soccer in the cul-de-sac with the neighborhood kids. He could hear the shouts as someone made a goal. As a playing field, it wasn't the best of spots. Cars stood in driveways or rimmed the edges of properties, but it was safe. Kevin believed in safe.

Sean and Mike stood at close to six feet already, though they had just turned twelve, and he figured they'd head well north of that number. They took after him. Big and blond, goofy, like oversized pups, the way kids should be. In a normal home, he might have been that way himself. Kelly and TJ were slim and dark with those wide, deep-blue eyes that reminded him too much of Ma and Danny.

"June 1992."

Kevin jumped at the sound of his brother's voice. He hadn't heard Danny come down the stairs. Danny always had a way of slipping in and out. It came from years of trying to become invisible. Now he perched on a barstool and watched Kevin, his head tilted slightly and his mouth drawn in a half smile.

Once Kevin had asked him why he tilted his head that way, and Danny had told him it was a less intimidating position to the people he interviewed. "You want people to talk to you, and you want their stories, so you do everything you can to make them feel comfortable. If you lean in too hard and stare them down, it scares them. You don't lean in until they trust you."

Danny was a great bullshitter, but people liked talking to him, including Kevin's own family. All that crap about body language though. Kevin wasn't sure if it was true or not, but he knew from years of interrogations when to be aggressive and when to hold back.

"What about June 1992?" Kevin asked. Then he remembered that Danny had graduated in June of 1992.

"I've been trying to figure out what connects me to Greg Moss other than high school and the occasional bag of weed. The only other time we crossed paths tangentially was senior week, June 1992. He had a party at his house, and I spent the night on the porch. Everyone who died was there."

Of course. Danny would have to come here to ruin a perfectly good Memorial Day afternoon with this goddamn murder investigation. Kevin knew, he just knew, life was going to get shitty.

"So what happened that night?"

"That's just it. I don't know. But something happened. Barb Capozzi was Greg Moss's girlfriend, and she went into anaphylactic shock at a book signing last night under mysterious circumstances. Alex was there. If her husband hadn't been, Barb would have probably died."

Kevin sat up. *Wonderful.* Danny was going to drop this goddamn revelation in his lap and expect him to do something with it. Kevin chewed his lip and considered.

"You think something happened where?"

"Greg had a house down in Wildwood. Every night was a party down there. I was there with Michelle—you remember Michelle Perry—but half the senior class probably showed up at some point or another. Even Jenna Jeffords was there, for Christ's sake."

"Wait, wait." Kevin put up his hand. "Greg had a shore house in Wildwood that you visited, but you don't remember anything happening. Yet you suspect something *might* have happened.

That's not helpful. It may be a pain in the ass, but you know the way us cops are. We like evidence."

Danny shrugged. "Yeah, I know. But just because I can't remember doesn't mean something didn't happen. It's either that or it's something connected to the client parties Greg ran. But I never went to a client party, and I'm pretty sure Nate Pulaski didn't either. He hadn't lived in Philly for ten years. Neither did Rick Farnasi or Chris Soldano."

"That doesn't mean they didn't visit."

If Greg Moss's death was connected to some dubious client party, Kevin could relax a little. That would involve a familiar line of investigation. This whole revenge killing idea was a whole different beast. How did you investigate past bad behavior—especially when people had moved on and settled into their real lives?

Still, he expected Danny was right. Danny had never been a lover of the kinky. He wouldn't have been a participant in any weird sex party, but it was more than possible he was a bystander at a teenage party that zoomed out of control. It didn't take much booze and dope plus teenage hormones to combine into a toxic mix. "Do you remember who was at the shore?"

"Some football guys and their girlfriends, but others showed up. Greg was pretty relaxed about people coming and staying. I expect he had no idea who was hanging out. I guess we need to find some of the people who might have been there." He hesitated. "I spoke to some former classmates already."

"And you have a list."

"I have a list of possibilities. Like I said, I don't remember for sure everyone who showed up. I wasn't paying close attention."

Kevin sighed. "Okay." It wasn't much, but it was a place to start. Kevin could at least see what he could find out about the people Danny could remember. He could check to see if anyone else on the list had a record. "Though if these deaths are connected, why didn't you get a Bible text?"

He could see from the way Danny wouldn't look at him that it bothered him as well. "I don't know. I need to get a list of my class and see if anyone else is dead."

"That would be nice," Kevin said. "Unfortunately life ain't so easy. Most people don't send obituaries to high schools, and we don't collect them. So you'll have to do an obit search for every person you think might be connected to you or Greg Moss in some way."

"Lucky for me, there's the Google," Danny said with just the right touch of sass. It pushed Kevin's blood pressure up a notch, but he told himself it wasn't worth getting into it with his brother. Kevin struggled with the complexities of social media. To him, it was a gross invasion of privacy. Computers were necessary for gathering and compiling data. Smart phones were a little too smart.

Kevin knew about the Internet, but not the fun parts. He knew about the dark web where children were used and abused by sick old bastards that he would gladly throw in a dark pit, if he only had the resources to catch them.

It annoyed him that Danny knew about all the fun stuff—the things that his kids seemed to find important. Maybe he was jealous. He loved his brother, but they always seemed to scrape against each other. That was his burden and his penance.

Kevin was about to stand when the back door banged open and Kelly bopped into the room. She yanked her earbuds out at the sight of Danny and dropped her shopping bags, her face lighting up as she ran to hug him.

Danny was her godfather—something Jean had insisted on—though how she could have known that their eldest would bond with his brother was a mystery. It was a perfect match. Kelly was born questioning authority.

Kevin didn't know if Danny had done them a favor by paying her tuition to Penn Charter, the Quaker prep school down the road. They could just have afforded sending her to Hallahan, the Catholic high school in town, but Jean had been adamant. Kelly needed to be pushed, and Penn Charter was closer, just a couple of miles from home. Kelly loved it.

Danny had paid her tuition. He'd donated to the school's annual fund. People recognized him at events and milled around him. It wasn't that he tried to stand out; it was just his kind of crowd. Jean said it was because they actually read newspapers and cared about the world, and in some ways, Kevin was grateful. It relieved him of some of the burden of having to make awkward conversation. Not that anyone was ever unpleasant; he just never seemed to get his footing.

When Danny set up education funds for all the kids, Kevin was left struggling for a way to cope with his guilt. He needed the money but hated owing his brother. Danny had only shrugged and said, "Kevin, I have more money than I need. I don't have any kids. Why not set up funds for yours? I owe *you*."

Kevin didn't understand Danny's sense of obligation. He did understand that the money took a huge burden off Jean and him. In the last year, his wife had lost some of that anxious, tight look that always seemed to constrict her mouth into a permanent frown. They'd been able to take a family vacation for the first time in years. Danny of the Open Wallet was a popular guy in his family, especially with Kevin's daughter.

"Uncle Dan!" Kelly was saying. "Are you staying for dinner?"

"If your dad says it's okay," Danny said.

She looked at Kevin. "He is staying, right?"

"Sure."

"Did Mom tell you I'm going to Costa Rica at the end of June?"

Danny shook his head. "No she didn't. That's pretty great though."

"It's a school trip for my Spanish class. Dad doesn't want me to go. He thinks I'll be stripping and posting the pictures on 'The Google.'" She held up her fingers to make quotation marks.

To his credit, Danny said nothing, though the corners of his mouth twitched. Kevin shook his head.

There was no real discussion to be had. Jean already wanted Kelly to go on this trip, so she was going. Danny would slip her extra cash, and everyone but Kevin would be happy. Worse, he'd be the bad guy because he worried about his daughter's safety. Bad shit happened out there. He saw it every day. Kelly was smart, but even smart girls got in trouble.

Somehow he always ended up being the asshole these days. Danny should also realize how easy it was to die, but knowing and believing were two different things.

*

Kelly Ryan glanced around at the pink-and-white checked wallpaper and the flouncy white bedspread and sighed. Her stuffies still collected dust on the shelf above her bed. She should gather them up and toss them. After all, she was too old for that nonsense, and yet she couldn't quite force herself to toss the furry collection, especially Boo Bear. She kept Boo stashed under her pillow so no one would see him.

What is wrong with me?

She dumped her shopping bags on the bed and surveyed the tiny orange bikini she planned to wear to the end-of-class pool party. It would drive her dad up the wall if he saw it. Maybe she could talk Uncle Dan into taking her. He'd fit in so much better with the collective parents. Kelly loved her dad, but he always looked like he was sizing everyone up.

Guys talked to her all the time, and she'd even had a sort of boyfriend. For a while. Until he'd met her dad.

Of course, everyone was afraid of her dad. She loved him, but she wished he was a little more like Uncle Dan.

20

"Do you remember Barb Capozzi?" Danny said to Jean. The kids had scattered, and he sat with Jean and Kevin at the dining room table after dinner. He could always count on Jean to feed him some comforting family dinner. Grilled steaks, roasted potatoes with plenty of dill, green beans, salad, and homemade blueberry pie for dessert. It wasn't fancy. It was homey, and with four kids under her roof plus Kevin, that was her specialty.

Jean had settled into middle age well. She'd never been glamorous. She wore her light brown hair short and never worried about the latest fashions. But her smile was warm and her eyes intelligent. Danny liked the way she'd rest her hand on Kevin's arm and he'd place his big hand over hers. It was always a brief intimacy, but it made Danny's chest tighten.

Jean seemed more relaxed these days. Danny knew it came partially from not having to worry about how to pay for the kids' schooling, and it pleased him that he could help out with that. Setting up education accounts for Kevin and Jean's kids had been one his brighter ideas.

He owed Kevin.

Danny knew Kevin couldn't get that fact through his head, but Danny didn't care. Their relationship had never been quite normal, but it was getting better.

"Barb Capozzi?" Jean frowned and took a sip of her coffee. "Barb Capozzi. Oh, wait. I remember. Cheerleader, right? The tall redhead? She'd have been a year behind me. We didn't exactly hang in the same circles." She laughed a little. "I wasn't very glam."

"She's not hanging in any circles now," Danny said. "She's in the ICU. Anaphylactic shock."

"How horrible."

"Do you remember anything about her?"

Jean thought for a moment. "It was so long ago, and she wasn't in my year. I just remember she was a cheerleader, and she dated the quarterback." She looked at Kevin. "You must remember her."

"I remember the red hair," Kevin said. "She dated Greg Moss. It was my senior year, and he mostly rode the bench."

Jean smiled and patted Kevin's hand. "You were a star, darling."

Danny watched Kevin's fingers curl into a fist and knew he was remembering the old man's taunts: "Ya big dumb ox. They're gonna give you a scholarship? You're too stupid to get through school."

The old man wouldn't give Kevin any shred of self-respect because Junior had never been scouted. Junior had been a quarterback and a good one, just not a great one. He never did break through the thousands of kids slaving and sweating for a spot. Kevin, a lowly offensive tackle, had happily lifted weights and run. He'd done agility training and strength training and worked for hours mastering the playbook. Kevin had been a beast.

Kevin wasn't a dumb ox, either. He'd been fine at subjects like science and math, passable at Spanish, but lost at history and English. Though he was three years younger, Danny would correct his homework and rewrite his papers because he'd already read most of Kevin's assigned reading. They had come to a silent agreement when Kevin turned sixteen. By then Junior had moved out, and the old man had started coming home so late from the Shamrock that he'd pass out on the sofa in the living room.

"Don't make it too smart," Kevin would say. "I just need a *C* average to stay on the team."

Now Danny looked at Kevin, who seemed more tired than he had in years, like Atlas bearing the weight of the world on his shoulders. The past left scars that faded but never disappeared. They seared your soul, and you felt them bumping against you when you were at your most vulnerable. Danny sighed. His brother's scars, like his own, ran deep and ugly. They were just harder to see.

"Kevin was awesome," he said. "Still is."

Jean smiled. "I fell in love with him in high school. He was so handsome in his uniform. He just never noticed me."

"That's not true. I figured you wouldn't be interested in a dumb jock like me."

Danny smiled. Kevin and Jean had already had this conversation or a variation on it many times. It was as close to a real love story as he'd ever seen, and he figured Kevin deserved it.

"You were a great player," Danny said.

"It was a long time ago," Kevin said. "Today those defensive guys would run right over me."

Danny knew that wasn't true, but he said nothing. He just looked at Jean, who shook her head.

Later, Danny walked with Kevin out to his car. The night was warm, and he was full and content. But he still had questions.

"I wish I could remember Greg Moss, but I really don't," Kevin said. "The QB when I was there was a guy named Termaine Olander. Projects kid. He had talent but got arrested senior year on an armed robbery rap. Ended up doing ten years."

"Termaine Olander?"

"Don't bother trying to look him up. He got killed a few years back tryin' to pull another armed robbery at a Vietnamese joint near the Italian Market. Owner put two shotgun slugs into Termaine." Kevin shook his head remembering. "He had a hell of an arm. We had a great offense that year. No goddamn defense but one hell of an offense."

"Why didn't you tell the old man to fuck off and just go to Penn State or wherever?"

Kevin didn't reply for a moment. He stared up at the sky as if the moon would give him an answer. "I'd never have made it in college. Division A? Not with practice and all that. I wasn't like you. I just never got into books and all that."

"You could have made it. You'd have been fine. I could have visited you on weekends and—"

"And what? Sold dope?"

Danny's breath caught at the bite of Kevin's words. He'd never considered how deep Kevin's well of bitterness ran. The Ryan Legacy was the poison the old man had sowed in their hearts.

Kevin sighed and rubbed his mouth, a gesture reminiscent of their father. "What difference does it make now? There's no good looking back and saying I should've done this or that because you can't go back and change things. There's no magic doorway, and even if there was, who knows if things wouldn't be worse?"

"I'm sorry, Kev."

"Not your fault." Kevin folded his arms.

"I stopped into the Shamrock the other week."

"Yeah. I saw your piece. Eddie Doc called me. He was in tears. 'Last Call at the Shamrock.' He wants to give you Tommy Ryan's official barstool."

"Jesus Christ. I don't want it."

Kevin shrugged. "Then you shouldn't have waxed poetic about the loss of that great neighborhood institution." He pulled out his phone and punched a few buttons. "'These nebulous strings of circumstance tie us together long after the music has faded and we've shared that final pint.'" He slid the phone back into his pocket. "What does that even mean? It was just a fucking tappie our father used to drink himself blind in. Then he'd come home and beat the living shit out of you."

Danny shrugged. "I know that."

"Do you? Why do you have to always look at things like they reflect the Virgin Mary's arse? The way you write . . . like the Shamrock—the fucking Shamrock—was some holy place. It wasn't. It was a bar. Eddie Doc sold it to a developer, so he wasn't so sentimental about it in the end. You see things the way you want to see them."

Is that what he did? Danny wasn't sure what he had been looking for at the Shamrock. Maybe some tiny key to the puzzle that was his father. He hadn't found it, of course. All he had found were war stories, and he had fallen in like, if not love, with the ghosts who dwelled at the bar. It had once been a South Philly institution. Now Danny wasn't sure how he would even begin to describe South Philly. Even the Italian Market was no longer particularly Italian.

Or maybe he was looking for absolution. The old man used to say, "Once you've killed a man, you're scarred forever. Don't matter if he's a bad man or a good man. It changes you. Leaves a black mark on your soul." If that was true, the old man's soul was rotted through, but Danny could feel the blackness in his own soul.

Murder changed a man. Maybe that was part of the Ryan legacy, too.

In the dim light, shadows played over Kevin's face, casting darkness over his eyes. His lips compressed into a tight frown.

"Why are you so angry?" Danny asked at last.

"Just . . . you gotta look at things rational-like, y'know? Don't go spinning tales in your head. Some psycho out there maybe has you lumped in with Greg Moss, and whoever he is, he wants you to know it."

"Did you hear anything more from Ted Eliot? That tongue . . ."

"Cut out postmortem, according to the ME. Looks like the killer was trying to send a message."

"Don't talk to reporters?"

Kevin shrugged. "I don't know."

"Poor Greg. He asked me to help."

Danny wanted to tell Kevin about the watcher in his backyard, but he couldn't. If he mentioned what occurred between Alex and him, Kevin just wouldn't understand. So instead he said, "I had dinner with Barb before the book signing. Do you think that had anything to do with what happened?"

"I don't know. It's not my investigation, but I'd say her swallowing that glass of tainted soda probably had more to do with Greg Moss than you. All the same, you better watch yourself."

"Everything happens for a reason?"

Kevin shrugged. "Probably not in the way you're thinking, but yeah. Things happen for a reason." Kevin stared up at the sky for a moment. He didn't look at Danny when he said, "That shouldn't make you feel better. Do you understand?"

"I think so."

"Good. Then you'll be careful."

21

D anny walked into the air-conditioned lobby of the University of Pennsylvania Hospital emergency room and looked around. The vast waiting room appeared relatively empty, and Danny collected himself as he approached the front desk to ask for Sam Burton.

The trim, gray-haired nurse glanced up from her computer, her dark eyes assessing him from behind neat rectangular glasses. She looked familiar. Danny watched her lips compress slightly before she stretched them into a tight smile, and he glanced at her name tag. Rita Perry. His high school girlfriend Michelle's mother. How was that for nebulous strings of circumstance?

"Daniel Ryan," she said in a neutral voice.

"Mrs. Perry. How are you? Last time I saw you, you were working at Methodist," he said.

His father had favored Methodist Hospital because it was in South Philly. Mrs. Perry was on duty in the emergency room at least three times when he'd been brought in. No wonder she hadn't wanted Michelle anywhere near him.

"Yes. Well, this is a better position. How are you, Daniel? I read about your family. I'm very sorry." If her voice got any chillier, it would have brought down the room temperature. Danny didn't understand it. He hadn't seen Michelle in years. Why hold a grudge?

"I'm getting by," he said. "How's Michelle?"

Rita stood and folded her arms. "Michelle is very happily married with a wonderful husband and three lovely children. She doesn't need you bothering her. Do you understand?"

Danny took a step back. "I haven't been in touch with Michelle in over twenty years. She made it pretty clear that she didn't want to hear from me again." She'd left for New York not long after senior week, and he'd never heard from her again. He'd written one letter after another, but he'd never gotten a reply.

"I don't believe you." Her cheeks reddened, and her eyes flitted over the desk as if she was looking for something—a pen, a pencil, something sharp—to hurl at him.

"For God's sake, I had a wife and son. A life." *I won a goddamn Pulitzer Prize.* Danny took a breath when the memories choked him. He shoved his hands into his pockets and waited until his breath slowed. "Look, I have an appointment with Dr. Sam Burton. If you page him, I'll get out of your way. I had no idea you worked here. Why would you think I was trying to get in touch with Michelle?"

"Dr. Burton?" She blinked a couple of times. "He's the head of emergency medicine."

"Yes, I know. I'm here to see him."

Rita stared at him a moment longer then slumped down in her chair, her face taking on a gray hue. "I'm sorry. It's just . . . Michelle's been getting text messages. Odd messages. I just assumed."

"You assumed I was sending her messages after twenty years?"

She shrugged. "Your wife was killed. I don't know. Seeing you again. I—It brought back memories. I'm sorry."

Danny nodded. She didn't want him around her daughter, but she'd been kind to him. Rita had been the day nurse when he was fighting his way back from the skull fracture. She'd brought him orange Jell-O because he didn't like green and a lined notebook when he told her liked to write.

"I hope you're right handed," she'd said. "Your left arm'll be in a cast for a while."

"I'm right handed."

"Are you sure you got hurt playing with your brothers?" She'd sat on the edge of the bed and leaned toward him, her head tilted a little to the right, and he understood without knowing how that she was trying to show him that she wasn't a threat. But Danny had learned early that grown-ups spoke in sweet, soft voices when they wanted something from you. Most important, he knew if he told the truth, he'd be lost in the system. He hadn't been quite sure what that meant, but his brothers had assured him many times that the system was far worse than any punishment the old man ever dished out.

Now he tilted his head slightly to the right and leaned a little closer. He nodded and gave Rita a sad smile. Of course he understood. He wanted her to talk.

"She's getting messages. What kind of messages?" he asked.

"I don't know. She wasn't very clear. Bible quotes mostly."

Danny swallowed his anger. "Did she call the police?"

"I don't know. She thought it was silly. A prank, but they haven't stopped."

"Tell her to call the police," Danny said. "I don't think it's a prank. Other members of our class have gotten messages. That's why I'm here today."

"Oh, my God." Rita clasped her hands together.

"If she doesn't want to call the police, do you think Michelle would talk to me? We don't have to meet. We can talk over the phone."

Rita hugged her arms against her chest, considering.

"I'll give you my number," Danny said. "You think about it and let me know. You may not think much of me, Mrs. Perry, but Dr. Burton will vouch for me. I'm not sending messages to your daughter."

He set his card on the counter, and after staring at it for a moment, Rita took it. After she called Sam's office to announce him, she said, "I'm worried sick."

"How long has she been getting these texts?"

Rita's eyes filled. "I'm not sure."

"You said Bible quotes?"

She nodded.

Danny saw Sam approaching him and waved, but he looked at Rita. "Tell her it isn't a prank. I've gotten texts. Other people have, too, and now some of them are dead."

*

Sam's office was painted a soothing shade of green, and photographs of the ocean from various vantage points covered the walls. Sunsets, a tranquil harbor, a lighthouse—all were designed to set the visitor at ease, because visitors to Sam's office were seldom there to hear good news. Trauma surgery tended to leave deep and lasting scars behind even if the outcome was successful.

Now Danny faced a man who had hosted him for dinner more nights than he could count and with whom he'd shared plenty of enjoyable conversations. He leaned back and put on a neutral face. Good old Danny Ryan, the would-be adulterer. How was that for Catholic guilt? He told himself that Alex and he hadn't done anything. Much. They had smoked some dope and what? He still hadn't figured that out. Maybe it was just the dope. They were both having a bad day. That's what he was going to tell himself for now. Even if it wasn't quite true.

"So what can you tell me about Barb Capozzi?" Danny asked.

"Officially, nothing," Sam said. "Except she's very lucky, and she's doing better than expected. She might pull through this with nothing to show but a minimal tracheotomy scar."

"So I can visit her?"

"I believe they moved her from the ICU last night. She was breathing on her own."

"I'm not writing a story about this, Sam. She might be here because of me."

Sam sighed. "She's here because she's highly allergic to naproxen. We found traces of it in her blood, and Alex found a

113

medic alert card in her purse. She's apparently allergic to kiwis and naproxen. An interesting combination."

"There's no way this could have been an accident?"

"It's highly doubtful. I suppose it's possible a bartender could have taken naproxen before he handled the lime or ice in her glass. Ms. Capozzi is so allergic that just skin-to-skin contact would set off a reaction, and the amount of naproxen in her system wouldn't have set off alarms in a toxicology test. It wouldn't have been notable if we hadn't found that card. If it was intentional, whoever gave it to her must have known she was highly allergic."

Danny shifted in his seat. How would someone know Barb was allergic to naproxen? Presumably her staff had worked with her for a long time and knew. He said, "Her staff would probably know about her allergy."

"It seems likely. She worked with food. The police were interviewing her staff."

"So someone slipped it into her drink, and she had a reaction."

"It seems so, yes. With allergic reactions, successive exposures generally increase their severity. She was lucky someone had an EpiPen. It slowed the swelling."

"She was lucky you were there."

Sam waved his hand and smiled. "She was lucky that my wife is an incurable snoop. It was interesting explaining to the police how I came into possession of her purse. They were somewhat less than pleased." The smile wavered, and Sam leaned forward, placing his hands flat on the desk. He had large hands with long fingers. Danny could see him slicing open Barb's throat in a desperate effort to open her windpipe. He then imagined Sam wrapping those large hands around his own throat and throttling him for attempting to sleep with his wife.

Sam said, "Tell me the truth. Alex isn't in any danger, is she?"

Danny shook his head. "Whatever this is, it has nothing to do with Alex. But tell her to keep her distance if it makes you feel better."

"As if she'd listen. She doesn't listen to much these days. Or talk much." Sam cleared his throat. "I know you're close. Perhaps she's said something to you?"

Danny managed to open his eyes wide. "Said something to me about . . ."

"She doesn't seem very happy."

"Honest to God, Sam. She hasn't said anything to me." That much was mostly true. "We generally talk about work."

"You seem so close."

Danny clenched his hands together. "We are, but in a weird way. It's personal, but not." Danny no longer knew what they had become. Alex and he had tangled together, and this morning he realized just how complex life could be.

"We've talked about children, but she—well, she doesn't seem interested in children right now."

Danny stared down at his hands, unsure how to respond. He and Sam usually discussed books and politics and sports in passing. Danny had read up on medical practices so he could hold a reasonably coherent conversation about the state of the modern emergency room and medicine around the world in general. They had an affable relationship, not a deep one.

"I've made you uncomfortable," Sam said.

"No, I just never discussed that with Alex. She talks about work and you and that's about it." Danny thought he might burst into flames—the Irish guilt was working overtime—but he managed a wan smile. "The only thing she's said is she wants a column. My old one. She has ambitions." That much was true.

"I understand." Sam sighed. "I can't say that's what I wanted to hear, but thank you." He picked up the phone. "Let's see if I can't get you in to see Ms. Capozzi."

22

Barb was corpse-gray, and she lay so still, Danny would have believed she was dead if it weren't for the persistent beeping of the heart monitor, the gentle suck of the blood pressure cuff, and the slight gurgling of the oxygen humidifier. Her bright hair flamed around her head. She looked fragile lying in the bed in her pale-blue hospital gown. The sharp odor of antiseptic and alcohol mingled with the more basic aroma of blood and sweat. Danny could almost see her body fighting to survive.

"Hey there," Danny said. He walked over to her and took one of her icy hands.

Her eyes rolled open, and she swallowed. Her neck had been bandaged, and she sucked oxygen through the nasal canola. When she looked up at him, tears filled her eyes and spilled down her cheeks.

"No, don't cry," he said and touched her cheek. "You're going to be okay. Swear to God." He'd wanted to question her but knew it would have to wait. "I would have brought flowers, but I wasn't sure if you were out of the ICU."

The corners of her mouth lifted for an instant and her fingers tightened against his. She licked her lips and made a gurgling sound.

"Bad drink," she mouthed.

"Just try to rest," he said.

"Dinner?" she whispered.

He smiled. "That's a date."

Barb closed her eyes for a moment before she motioned with her hand. "Paper?"

He handed her his notepad and a pen. She labored to write a few words in the pad, hands shaking with the effort, and Danny watched in silent admiration. Barb was a fighter.

She handed the notebook and pen back to him.

"You need to sleep. I'll come back to see you soon. Okay?" He leaned close and kissed her cheek.

Her head was drooping to the side. When he paused in the doorway, he could see she had already drifted back to sleep. Outside, Danny opened the notepad to see what she had written. It was a single name: Frank Greer.

*

Frank Greer wasn't on Facebook. Either his phone was unlisted or he had moved out of Philadelphia. But there had to be a reason Barb had given Danny his name.

Danny sat at a small café on Rittenhouse Square, drinking coffee and watching people meander through the square with their dogs. It was a curious mix of business people, upscale residents of the surrounding luxury apartments, and the odd homeless person huddling on the edge of a park bench looking like someone in the old Sesame Street song Conor used to sing: "One of these things is not like the others."

He turned back to his computer. Why wouldn't Frank be online? He could be dead, and Barb might not have heard. He could have turned into a recluse. He could have changed his name. More likely he was back in prison. Danny could find that out easily enough, and he didn't have to bother Kevin. At least not yet.

An hour later, he'd located Frank and his place of business— G and R Scrap, up on East Tioga Street in Port Richmond, the industrial section of the city that ran northeast along the river.

The company was owned by Francis Greer and Stan Riordan. Frank and Stan must be working together because Frank always needed an ass to kick, and Stan . . . God only knew what Stan got out of that relationship. G and R appeared to have a third partner who had gotten involved five years ago: Cromoca Partners LLP.

Cromoca. That was the development company working with Greg Moss, the company that had bought out the Shamrock.

When he ran a quick check, Danny found that Cromoca owned a lot of riverfront properties in New Jersey and had been buying land on the Philadelphia side as well. It might or might not be significant, but Danny had a feeling tracking down the partners would be as difficult as catching smoke.

*

Danny headed north on Delaware Avenue, passing under the Ben Franklin Bridge. He could have taken I-95, but he preferred the slower route. It gave him a better feel for the area. Hotels quickly turned to industrial facilities as he drove north, and he remembered that Philadelphia had at one time been a thriving industrial city. Manufacturing was all but dead now, and Philadelphia was trying to reinvent itself. Danny wasn't sure the city would ever quite figure out what that identity was. Trapped like the awkward sister between New York and DC, Philadelphia lingered in the shadows, self-deprecating yet filled with what the neighborhood folks called "attytood."

Danny made a left onto Tioga Street and took a deep breath. He was about to get smacked in the face with some "attytood." Frank Greer had never been shy about expressing himself, especially when he had a cheering section.

He turned into G and R Scrap. Life was about to get unpleasant.

Danny pulled up the driveway. It forked left toward the scale and right toward a parking lot and a low-slung, beige, prefabricated office building. Slightly beyond the office sat a beat-up, gray metal trailer from which a video camera protruded. He swung right, passing an idling dump truck, to slide into a space in the small lot near the side of the building and took a moment to observe the activity in the scrapyard.

Dump trucks rumbled into the yard, filled with everything from copper pipe to old refrigerators to aluminum siding, while smaller cars and people with shopping carts maneuvered with their own treasures. Peddlers. Some of them were addicts looking for enough cash to score a fix; some were people looking to get by cleaning out homes or scavenging from construction sites, ripping off whatever they could find. They all waited in line to weigh their goods on the scale in front of the trailer about two hundred yards inside as exhaust choked the hot, grimy air. In the very back of the yard, a metal shredder growled as workers fed its conveyor belt hunks of scrap that would be shredded, sold, and shipped out of the country.

It was a living.

Danny walked to the administrative offices and hoped the red Caddy in the reserved space with the SCRAP U license plate belonged to Frank. When he opened the door, a rush of stale, frigid air greeted him, and he found himself in a long corridor that branched off in the middle like a cross. The floor was covered in beige linoleum.

A skeletal receptionist with spiked black hair and a pierced nose glanced at Danny with disinterest. Her desk was piled high with manila folders and knickknacks—troll dolls with orange-and-purple hair and a large bowl of silver-wrapped Hershey kisses that sat by her keyboard. She pulled her red fleece jacket tighter. "Who're you?" she asked.

"I'm Dan Ryan. I'm writing a piece on the scrap industry," Danny said, holding up his ID. It was a temporary one, given to him when he'd helped out with the elections last November, but it was authentic enough. "How small scrapyards are keeping alive. How they compete against large operations. That kind of thing. I was wondering if I could talk to your boss."

"You got an appointment?"

"I sure hope so. My secretary was supposed to set one up. She's on vacation this week, and I'm using a temp. I hope she gave me the right day." He gave her an innocent smile.

"Yeah, right."

"I know Frank. I went to school with him."

She pulled her jacket zipper up and down a couple of times. "Okay. Let me buzz him. What's your name again?"

"Dan Ryan."

She pushed a button. "Frank. Some guy named Ryan is here. He wants to write about the business. You want to see him?" She listened for a few moments before she hung up the phone and pointed. "Make a right and go straight down the hall."

"Thanks."

She shrugged. "You got lucky. Frank's in a good mood."

"I'm a lucky guy."

23

Frank Greer's office was an oasis in the great beige desert that was G and R Scrap. It was almost luxurious—spacious, with a bright-blue carpet and light wood paneling on walls covered with large photographs. They were of scrap, but someone with some proficiency with a camera had taken the photos. Danny liked the wide shot of three bright-orange valves lying against a mountain of silver-gray rubble.

The usual pictures of VIPs lined the wall behind the desk. Danny recognized the mayor and a couple of city council members. There was a photograph of Frank, in a shiny green suit, standing with a tall, distinguished, and oddly familiar blond man. A politician? On Frank's other side hunched a wizened fellow in a blue hoodie and spotted jeans. Danny started to look away, but the photo drew him back. The little guy in the hoodie had Stan Riordan's small teeth and jug ears. He must have been Riordan Sr.

Then it hit Danny. The blond guy was Congressman George Crossman from New Jersey, the House majority whip. Danny was sure of it. What the hell was the congressman doing in a Philadelphia scrapyard?

Frank sat behind a wide oak desk in a black leather chair. His desk was covered by a large desk calendar on which laid an assortment of odd bits of scrap—some railroad spikes and oversized bolts, a large iron key, and a smooth black marble paperweight shaped like an egg. Frank didn't stand but gestured to one of the leather chairs in front of the desk. He looked the same, yet harder, with bluish bags under his dark-blue eyes and deep lines around his downcast mouth. His hair was a little thinner, and he now sported a moustache, but he was still Frank the Ferret, shifty eyed and sneering. Danny noticed the prison tat of the ace of spades on his left hand.

"Danny Ryan." Frank spoke his name like it evoked a particularly bad memory. "What are you doing here?"

"I'm doing a piece on new enterprises in Philly. How manufacturing is holding on."

"Yeah? I thought you only wrote about sex these days." Frank leered at him. "You not getting enough so it pisses you off or what?"

"I'm a reporter. I report."

"You don't report for the *Sentinel* no more."

Danny shrugged. Frank was going to make this as difficult as possible. The only thing he could do was take one breath after another. Stay calm. Remember why he had come. "I work freelance now. I just finished a series for the *New York Times*." He looked around the office. "You seem to have done very well for yourself. Tell me about the scrap business."

Frank blinked. "You're fucking serious."

Danny pulled out his pad. "I'm serious." If he came right out and started grilling him, Frank would close up, and he'd get nothing. The longer Frank talked, the looser he'd get. In any case, maybe Danny would get some kind of story.

"What the hell, it's a slow day."

Danny pointed to the photograph. "I see you're keeping company with Congressman Crossman these days."

"We bought a small feeder yard in Camden a few years back—part of our expansion plans. The congressman is trying to get businesses to relocate into Camden."

"Helping you get tax breaks and that sort of thing?"

"Yeah. Making it easier for small business to do business in Camden. He's big on that."

"How so?"

Frank described the incentives Congressman Crossman was offering in New Jersey, most of which amounted to tax breaks, but one involved reasonably priced land options. Frank was vague on the details, and Danny made a note to check into the program. Danny let Frank ramble about the operations before they wandered out to the yard to watch the trucks pull onto the scale. Afterward, their cargo would be separated into ferrous and nonferrous metal and the driver would be given bar-coded receipts.

"You can take 'em to an ATM and cash 'em in," Frank said. "Easy."

"How did you get into this?"

"Well, when I got out—you know I was in the slam—I couldn't get work nowhere. But Stan—you remember Stan Riordan, right? Stan's old man had this scrapyard in South Philly. You must've seen it down near the I-95 bridge, y'know? So he hires me. It turns out I got a good head for all this, and old man Riordan and I got on good. So when he keeled over, I find out he's left the business to me with the condition I look out for Stan."

"So you're his guardian?"

"Kind of." Frank shrugged. "Stan's not completely simple. Not really. He's just strange. Like he don't exactly know the arrangement. Stan couldn't run a one-car funeral, but he thinks he's a big shot. So I don't tell him the old man left the yard to me and money in trust for him. He just knows he gets money every month, and he's the chief scale man at the South Philly yard. I told him it was the most important job there."

"Chief scale man?"

"It's an important job." Frank scowled. "And you don't need to enlighten him about the details, either. You got me?"

Danny looked up from his notes and smiled. "Sure, Frank. You always did watch out for him." He didn't miss the flicker in Frank's eyes. Something between contempt and relief. If he were writing a real story, Danny would have jumped all over him, but he already knew who owned what at G and R.

"Yeah, well. We grew up together, and like I said, he ain't completely right in the head. But his old man was a stand-up guy."

"You have a third partner. Cromoca Partners? Who is that?"

"Cromoca is just an investor. We're taking G and R across the river into Jersey, and they fronted us the money. We got a feeder yard. We're looking for a bigger property to build another shredder."

"So this was part of the congressman's investment incentive?"

"Well, yeah." Frank hesitated. "Greg Moss was involved. You remember him, right? He helped us hook up with Cromoca."

"Greg Moss? Is he tied in with Cromoca?"

"They're clients, I guess."

"Have you found property?"

Frank hesitated, and his mouth tightened. "Well, the scrap market ain't as booming as it was four years ago. It's gonna rebound, but for now, it's in kind of a slump. We bought a small parcel, but we're holding off expanding."

"That seems smart." Danny didn't ask if Cromoca Partners was putting pressure on Frank to expand or pay back their investment. It didn't seem wise, though he was curious. A thick haze of dust filled the yard, and Danny wondered how to phrase the next question. There probably wasn't an easy way to phrase it. "Then I guess you know about Greg."

Frank stared past Danny to the cars zooming down I-95. His eyes narrowed slightly. "I heard he's dead. Why do you care?"

Danny shrugged. "Greg was a realtor. I wondered if he was helping you find Jersey land. Wouldn't that be kind of a setback?"

"Umm, I talked to Greg, but like I said, we were in a holding pattern. He knew a lot of people."

That was bullshit. Greg Moss had more than a casual relationship with Cromoca Partners somehow. Maybe he was putting pressure on Frank. Maybe not.

"It's weird to find out someone from your high school class is dead. It makes you feel old," Danny said. He needed to ease back, not push. Maybe Greg's death had nothing to do with high school and everything to do with land development. Maybe he didn't want Greg's death to have anything to do with high school.

Frank squinted at him, and Danny knew he was looking to see if it was a bullshit line. It was, but it was also true. Greg's death had made him remember and rethink his own choices. The opened and shut doors in his life. There were so many.

"Greg was okay," Frank said at last. "You know he visited me in prison? Him and Stan."

"That was nice. You stayed in touch?"

"No. That's the thing. Stan called him for a lift one day because his car broke down, and Greg gave him a ride. He couldn't even come in to see me that day. Had to fill out special paperwork and all, y'know? But he gave Stan a ride up and back, and he filled out the goddamn paperwork. Greg was okay."

"What were you in for?" Danny asked, though he already knew the answer.

"Possession with intent to distribute a controlled substance. Heroin." Frank laughed bitterly. "I did seven years. Guess I shoulda had your lawyer, huh?"

"You mean my father."

"Your old man was one scary dude."

"He's one dead dude." It was getting frustrating. Frank wasn't going to give him any information. He was too careful. The only thing he'd learned was that Greg was a better guy than he'd seemed at the beginning of the day. That wasn't helpful.

"Is it true Greg was whacked?" Frank asked.

"Yeah."

"Anyone got any theories?"

Danny shook his head and considered how much to tell. Maybe a slightly altered version of the truth. "I got this text message."

Frank swiveled around, and he leaned in close, the muscles in his face twitching in anticipation. "What kind of text message?"

"'Do you remember me?'"

"What the fuck kind of message is that?" The color slowly drained from Frank's face, and he stood completely still for one moment, hands clenched, a bead of sweat running down his left cheek. The old hatred filled his dark-blue eyes, and he said, "I don't have any more time for this shit. I have work to do. You need to leave now."

He almost ran back to the office.

Danny watched him disappear through the door and headed for his car.

24

Alex shifted in her seat at the mayor's press conference. He stood with the head of the service workers union and announced that they had reached a contract agreement. Alex dutifully wrote down the terms. It seemed like it was based on the most fragile of assumptions: the city would get more money from Harrisburg and the city's own cost-cutting measures would actually be effective.

She raised her hand and asked, "What if Harrisburg cuts the city's funding?"

The mayor chuckled and said they already had assurances that wouldn't happen. She wanted to follow up, but someone else shouted a question that led in another direction. She let it go.

In truth, she knew she wasn't pushing herself today. She was just taking up space. Her mind kept traveling back to Sunday night and whatever had possessed her to slither all over Ryan like a snake. It had been catching.

Maybe she'd needed to know if he'd felt anything for her, but now that she did, what was she supposed to do with the information? Once sex entered into the equation, it inevitably messed up friendship, and they had a fine friendship. Some days she could just kick herself.

When the press conference ended, her photographer said, "You okay? You hardly said anything."

"I'm fine, Santos." She patted his arm. "Just got a lot on my mind."

"I guess. You went real easy today."

"Does it matter?" She headed back to the paper.

Fifteen years ago, the *Sentinel* had moved its printing operation to the suburbs, and the rumors constantly circulated that any day now, their flagship building on Broad Street would be sold to help prop up sagging revenues. Danny used to talk about the low rumble of the presses as they started, the feeling that his words were rolling off the big machines onto paper that would be cut and stacked and piled into trucks to be consumed, discussed, and debated. Those vibrating presses would have added a fiercer sense of urgency to the newsroom—the height of the glory days, when Andy Cohen was in charge and Sam Westfield was the city editor.

Excellence. Honor. Integrity. The words were engraved in gold on the black marble wall in the front lobby, where plaques displayed the *Sentinel*'s Pulitzer recipients by year. Photographs of the winners adorned the walls.

Danny's picture always made her smile. He looked like a teenage heartthrob, with floppy dark hair and a smile somewhere between shy and cocky. Damn if he didn't have movie-star cheekbones. Alex stepped into the elevator. She wanted her picture on that wall. She wanted her own column. It was looking less and less likely to happen in Philadelphia. The elevator reached her floor, and she stepped off.

Alex made her way through the maze of cubicles that was the newsroom. A few people were busy typing, and phones were ringing. In an hour or so, as the deadline grew closer, the cubicles would fill. Along the far wall ran a series of glass-enclosed offices housing the various editors. She ignored them and slipped into her cubicle. She was lucky. At least she sat by a window.

Alex filed her story on the union and then started pulling up everything she could on Jenna Jeffords. Jenna didn't pertain to the city or politics, but Alex was involved now. This whole story was beginning to feel a little too personal. Besides, she was helping a friend—who might be something more than a friend. Alex shoved the thought aside.

Jenna had died in 1992. Her death didn't seem related to any of these texts, but Alex figured it was worth spending a few hours researching. Jenna had been at Greg Moss's house that night in June. Maybe she had seen something. She could have been the first in a string of murders, however unlikely.

The fire that had killed Jenna seemed straightforward enough. The investigators had ruled out arson, though Alex knew arson was difficult to prove. There was a leak in the gas main, and a terrible explosion destroyed three homes and damaged six more. Jenna was so badly burned, her mother had identified her by a necklace she wore and a few scraps of her clothing that remained intact. Afterward, Rachel Jeffords had moved out of South Philadelphia to live near Lancaster.

All Alex knew about Lancaster was that it was west of Philly, surrounded by a bunch of outlet stores that had sprung up along Route 30, and that it was Amish country. She'd always thought the juxtaposition of retail paradise and reclusive Amish made for an interesting culture clash. Even the souvenir shops hawked model horse and buggy sets. If the Amish objected, nobody seemed to care.

Rachel Jeffords had received an insurance settlement as well as an undisclosed seven-figure settlement on Jenna from the gas works and the city. That was to be expected. Rachel had agreed not to disclose the terms of the agreement, which was interesting but not unusual.

Rachel had moved west of Lancaster, where she had bought a small farm. Alex wondered if it was worth giving her a call. Maybe it would be better to drive out to talk to her in person, though she wasn't quite sure what she'd ask her. Maybe she'd just take all the information and show Danny, though Jenna didn't seem to fit in with the other victims, even if she was connected, however vaguely, to them.

Alex went through her notes. Everything seemed straight-forward, but she was sure she was overlooking something. She needed to look at the autopsy, but she really wanted to talk to Rachel Jeffords.

Alex stared down at the information. How awful would it be to relive all this? Would it be worse or better not to know the truth, if there was a different truth? Alex hesitated another five seconds before she picked up the phone and dialed.

25

Stan Riordan had morphed from a skinny kid with jug ears and small teeth into a mountain of flab with a bald head and triple chins. He still had that high-pitched voice and the uncomfortable habit of standing too close. Danny edged away from him to no avail. Stan continued to fill the space between them.

"Danny," he said, prolonging the *y* into a grating squeal. "What are you doing here? Do you have scrap? That's my business. Scrap. Me and Frank. It's really mine, but I let him manage it. I own it." When he grinned and leaned closer, Danny could smell garlic and onions and the faint aroma of alcohol on his breath. Did Frank know Stan was drinking on the job?

"I hear business is good," Danny said.

"Business is great. I'm the chief scale man here. Well, I really own the place, but Frank says he can't find anyone who can do the scale like me. So he hired a guy to do the day-to-day stuff. I like being outside."

Stan had no clue that he'd been cut out of the business. Or rather maneuvered out. With Frank running things, it was hard to tell. He had possibly manipulated Stan's father into signing away his business. Even if Stan's father had made an arrangement for Stan, Frank was capable of taking over in Stan's "best interests."

"It's nice that you and Frank stayed friends," Danny said. "Did he tell you I'm writing a piece on your business?"

"You are? He didn't tell me." Stan's face fell and for a moment his eyes narrowed.

"I just spoke to him today. Maybe he was going to tell you later."

Stan nodded. "That must be it."

A man emerged from the office—tall, wiry, with lanky black hair and close-set dark eyes. He yelled, "Hey, Stan. Who you talking to? We got trucks unloading."

"Is that your boss?" Danny asked. "I don't want to get you in trouble."

"I don't have a boss. I'm an owner." Stan frowned and turned to the intruder. "I'm on break, Len. This is a friend."

The man hesitated, eyeing Danny, before he walked over. "Len Piscone, the manager. You're a friend of Stan's?"

Danny nodded. This guy also had a tattoo. It was the king of spades, but it was a professional job on his right bicep and in color. Interesting coincidence or a connection to Frank? He was sure Frank had called and told Piscone to watch out for the asshole reporter.

"Dan Ryan," he said. "I'm writing a piece on Philadelphia industries."

"Frank said he already talked to you about the company."

Danny appreciated predictability. "He did, but he mentioned there was a second yard. When he said Stan here was his partner, I thought I'd stop by to say hello. After all, we went to school together."

Piscone's brows drew together as he looked from Danny to Stan. "You and Stan?"

"That's right," Stan said. "Me and Frank and Danny was all in the same class."

"You got ten minutes," Piscone said.

Stan's eyes darkened, and his hands curled into fists. "I'm an owner."

"It's okay, Stan. I know you're busy," Danny said. "I really just wanted to see how you were."

Piscone gave them one last scowl and headed back toward the office.

"He gets kinda grouchy some days," Stan said.

"Well, he is the manager."

"I'm the owner."

Danny figured Piscone was calling Frank right now. He didn't have time to be subtle. Stan wouldn't get subtle, in any case. "Look, Stan, I have to ask you something important." Stan's eyes widened a little, like no one ever asked him anything important. "Have you gotten any weird texts lately? Has Frank?"

"What kind of texts?" Stan rubbed the back of his neck. "Like something scary?"

"Well, maybe a little peculiar. Like from someone you might have known a while back. Like a 'remember me' kind of thing. Or maybe Bible verses?"

Understanding lit Stan's face. "Oh, that kind of text. We got a bunch of Bible verses."

"Do you remember when?"

"Me and Frank did." Stan smiled and nodded.

"When, Stan?"

"You'll never guess who sent those texts."

"No. I probably won't."

"Come on, try to guess."

Danny fought the urge to grab Stan by his ears and scream, "Give me the goddamn name!"

The office door opened, and Len Piscone stormed out. His face was bright red, like he'd just taken a verbal ass kicking, and he raised his hands in the air.

"Who was it, Stan? Tell me." Danny grabbed Stan's arm hard enough that Stan's goofy grin dissolved into a slack-jawed gape of surprise.

Stan blinked. "It was Greg Moss. He's been sending them for a while," he said, jumping when the red Caddy swerved into the yard, sending up a spray of gravel. It jerked to a halt, and Frank Greer emerged, hands balled into fists, looking angry enough to kill.

"You fucking asshole!" He shook off Len, stomped over, and before Danny could react, leveled him with a punch to the left side of his face.

26

"Mrs. Jeffords?" Alex grabbed her purple pen when a high-pitched woman's voice answered the phone. She explained who she was and why she was calling as quickly as she could. She hoped Rachel Jeffords was willing to talk.

"Why do you want to know about Jenna?" Rachel asked. Her voice had grown tight with suspicion and something else that Alex couldn't quite place. It wasn't exactly anger. Fear? Was that possible?

"I'm working on a piece on development in Philadelphia," Alex said. "I had questions about Jenna. Whether she knew someone named Greg Moss."

Silence.

"Mrs. Jeffords? I'm not trying to damage Jenna's memory." Alex knew she had to say something soothing to fill the void. "It's just that I think her death might be connected to something."

"I don't have anything to say about that." Her voice was hard and flat now.

"What if I were to come out to talk to you in person? Do you think maybe you could just talk to me?"

"Jenna's dead. Why can't you let her rest in peace?"

"I'm not sure she's resting in peace," Alex said. It was a gamble. Either Rachel would hang up or she'd open the door.

"I don't want to talk about Jenna right now."

"Later?"

"I can't talk about the settlement."

"I know. I wanted to talk about high school."

"What? I don't understand. I can't talk now."

Alex knew when to stop pushing. She gave Rachel her phone number. "Call me if you change your mind," she said. She wasn't done with Rachel Jeffords, but first, she wanted to look at Jenna's autopsy. Jenna's mother didn't want to talk to her for some reason, and Alex was going to figure out what that reason was.

She sat tapping her pen for a moment and staring out the grimy window at North Broad Street before she decided to make a quick call to the medical examiner's office. Jenna's file should still be there in some form. It was an official death that had been investigated and recorded by the city. She was reasonably sure someone would give her access.

Her phone rang, and she grabbed it, hoping that Rachel had changed her mind.

"Alex Burton," she said.

"Ms. Burton, it's Carlos."

She paused, trying to remember who the hell Carlos was. Then the sad, dark eyes of the bartender came back to her. Latin boy band Carlos, from the book signing. "Carlos, I'm glad you called."

"You said I could. Is Miss Barb okay?"

"She's in intensive care, but she's hanging in there for the moment." Alex didn't want to give too much away, so she added, "It's early. The doctors will know more tomorrow."

"I called, but no one would tell me anything."

"The hospital is just being cautious. Is that all you called about?"

"You asked me if I remembered anything, and at the time I didn't think it was anything important."

Alex grabbed her notebook. "Go on."

"It was a little before Miss Barb got sick. Not long before. A guy came up to the bar. He ordered a Diet Coke and squeezed lime into it. Then he dropped the lime in the glass."

"That's not so unusual, Carlos."

"I know, but it was the way he was dressed. We all wear black jackets and white shirts with black pants. It's a uniform. He was dressed that way, but he didn't work for us."

"That's also not so unusual."

"We also wear red roses in our lapels. He was wearing a red rose."

"Okay, maybe that was something." Alex noted it down. "He was trying to blend in."

Carlos said nothing for a few seconds. "I saw him give the glass to Miss Barb."

"Wait. Are you sure about that, Carlos?"

"I'm positive."

She took a moment to speak because she didn't want to jump all over him. When she finally asked the question, she tried to keep her voice gentle, not accusing. "Why didn't you say something on Sunday?"

"I was scared."

"Did you mention this to the cops?"

"I don't trust cops."

"Jesus, Carlos. Do you know how that makes you sound? Did you tell anyone about this guy?"

"I'm telling you. I didn't think anyone else would believe me. I didn't get a good look at his face, and he just disappeared. He had dark hair and wore glasses, but he kept his head down. He was young. I'm pretty sure. Medium-tall and thin."

"Well, I don't know if the police were able to pull any prints off the glass. Barb dropped it when she fell and it shattered. I don't even know if he's the person who gave her the glass, but we can see if he showed up on the security tapes. Do you think you could identify him?"

"I don't know." Carlos's voice wavered, whether from fear of the killer or the police or INS. Maybe all three. "I didn't see his face good. I have to go."

"Carlos, wait."

But he had already hung up. She made a quick call to her friend Eric, the paper's tech reporter. "I wonder if we could back-trace a number," she said. "I had a possible source call me, but he's squirrelly."

"Sure," he said. "We probably can."

"Fine."

Carlos's number turned out to be untraceable. Eric told her that he must have used a pay-as-you-go phone. "You can't trace 'em because they don't have a plan. You pay your minutes up front. Popular with our local druggies, or they used to be."

But that was okay, for now. At least she had an idea who to look for on the security tape. Now all she had to do was find out what detectives were handling the case. Then she could go back and see if he looked like anyone from Danny's yearbook.

She handled politics not police, so her list of Philly PD contacts was not extensive. She picked up the phone and dialed Kevin Ryan's number.

27

anny leaned against his car and rubbed his cheekbone as Frank paced up and down. Stan shifted from one foot to another. Danny could see he wanted to speak but had the sense to remain silent. The other asshole, Piscone, stared at the dirt.

"I oughta smash in your head, shove you in the trunk of that goddamn car, and send you to the shredder," Frank said at last. "Add a couple of propane tanks, and you'd be a memory."

"And we were having such a nice reunion," Danny said. He didn't think Frank would carry through with the threat. Frank wasn't the type to warn you. He'd just sneak up on you and slit your throat—or better, get Stan to do it. Frank didn't operate in the open. He liked to corner his prey—in the locker room, under the stairs, in an alleyway. In high school, plenty of kids bore scars dealt by Frank, like badges of dishonor. "What's the big deal about getting texts? You aren't the only one."

"You're an asshole, Ryan," Frank said, but his eyes no longer burned with that insane fury. He glanced at Piscone and Stan and gave an irritated jerk of his shoulder. Piscone headed back to the office, and when Stan hesitated, Frank said, "Get back to work, Stan. I'll talk to you later."

Stan didn't object, though his mouth turned down. His shoulders slumped, and he nodded to Danny before he shuffled off, kicking up dust and pebbles as he walked.

Frank turned to Danny and scowled as if he were a particularly annoying insect. "I thought I'd seen the last of you twenty-some years ago."

"Yeah, well. Life's a bitch that way. Tell me, Frank. What happened at Greg Moss's beach house?"

"What're you talkin' about?"

"I have this theory that all this is connected to senior week at Greg's house."

Frank turned angry again for a moment, his whole body tensing. Then he laughed. "Shit, Ryan. You were there when whatever this big something supposedly happened. You see anything?"

"I was on the porch."

"Bangin' Michelle Perry. Yeah, yeah. I remember that stuck-up bitch. You were perfect for each other. Point is, you would've heard something, don't you think?"

Would I have remembered? It was so long ago. The whoops and shouts. Music playing. If he could only remember the song, but it played at the edge of his mind, almost there, yet not. Why did that seem important? He and Michelle making out on the porch.

"It was a long time ago," Danny said.

"Yeah, it was. It was a party. Everyone was drunk or high, and how the fuck do you remember everything that happened? I don't remember. We smoked some pretty good weed that night. Excellent weed, in fact." Frank smirked, and Danny recognized the subtext. They smoked some pretty good weed that Danny had supplied. Yeah, he got it. Maybe Frank should have gotten "Danny Ryan was my dealer" tattooed on his hand. "Now I'm getting these goddamn texts."

"That's the problem, Frank. Nobody I talk to remembers, but something must have happened just the same. It's the only time we were all together."

The muscle under Frank's left eye was twitching, but otherwise his face was expressionless. "Look, I didn't say anything about the texts 'cause of this." He held out his hand, the one with the prison tat. "I'm an ex-con, dumbass. Last thing I need is people looking into my connections." Frank rubbed his mouth, looking around, and Danny could sense his unease and something else—a bright thread of fear running under the bravado and anger. When Danny didn't answer, Frank said, "Why did something have to happen?"

"I don't know," Danny said. "But I think something did, and it pissed off someone enough to kill. So you'd better put on your thinking cap, Frank, and try to come up with what that something could be."

"No one's coming after me."

"You want to bet on that? You willing to put money on that?"

"You gonna bet your fortune, Ryan?"

"No. I know someone's out there."

Frank glanced toward the road, squinting his eyes. He looked apprehensive for a moment and then smiled. "Let him come. I'm not afraid. I'm not like Greg."

Danny shrugged. Frank the Ferret was back. Maybe he would be able to handle whoever was out there. Danny was sure he'd put up a fight. "Good luck. You'll need it."

*

Frank watched Ryan take off in his slick BMW. He lit a cigarette and stared after the trail of dust. *Fucking Danny Ryan. After all these years.* And here he was, all concerned about Greg Moss. Not that some whack job didn't kill old Greg off for that beach party bullshit, but Greg was up to his ass in dirt with his land deals and parties and other schemes.

"Hey, Frank, everything okay?" Stan came shuffling up to stand beside him.

"Yeah. Everything's just great," Frank said. "What'd I tell you about talkin' to people you don't know?"

"But I do know Danny. We went to school together." Stan gave him that stupid grin, and Frank wanted to backhand him or worse. He still might do it, but not yet.

When the first text came, Frank hadn't told anyone. Then he'd heard about Nate Pulaski. Okay, small loss there. Old Penis Head got whacked. Big deal. But then he got another text. It spooked him, enough to get in touch with Greg, and Greg told him about Soldano and Farnasi.

He'd been kind of relieved to find out Greg had gotten texted as well. They weren't alone. Then Stan had come blundering in, flapping his gums about the goddamn texts. Frank had told him it was a stupid prank, and Stan had grinned like it was a great joke. Frank hadn't told him about what had happened to Pulaski and the others, but he'd never expected Ryan to show up asking questions.

Why Ryan?

He stared into Stan's smiling face. He'd always figured Stan was nine cents short of a dime, but maybe he was wrong. Maybe there was something going on inside that idiot head.

Stan patted him on the shoulder. "I got work to do," he said.

"Yeah." Frank watched him amble away. "Sorry I lost it earlier, Stan. That wasn't right."

Stan didn't turn around, but he gave him the thumbs up.

Frank headed back to his Caddy. These texts were making him crazy, and he needed to figure out who was sending them before Danny Ryan or the goddamn police beat him to it. His stomach gave a sour lurch. The worst part was that the texts weren't the beginning. This shit started long before Nate Pulaski, and it was going to get worse.

But no one was going to catch him sleeping. "Good luck," Ryan had said. Fuck him. It would take survival skills, and Frank had plenty of those.

Goddamn Greg Moss.

28

The Philadelphia Morgue was located in the same place as the medical examiner's office, an unassuming brick building behind the University of Pennsylvania and across from the VA Hospital. Alex normally didn't spend her time there, and she hoped to avoid it in the future. She still smelled the faint aroma of formalin and death, but she'd gone there to satisfy her curiosity.

The police weren't ready to let her look at the security video, probably because she hadn't done a very good job of selling herself as a potential witness. Kevin had listened to her stumble through her story about remembering a dark-haired man hanging around Barb Capozzi, and he'd only said, "You're just remembering this now?"

"Well, I . . . it was a pretty crazy night." She should have told Kevin she was making out with his brother. He probably would have exploded.

"I wasn't there that night, and the detectives who were are on another call."

"Well, maybe I could come in and just take a quick peek at the video."

She'd understood from his long silence that she'd said the wrong thing.

"You mean like an advance screening? This isn't a movie, Ms. Burton. A woman almost died on that tape. We're not giving special viewings to reporters, even reporters who are friends of my brother. You can tell him that."

"Danny didn't—I'm not looking for an advance screening." She'd been surprised that he thought so little of her.

"Is there anything else?"

She'd hung up, pissed off. Of course, he would believe she wanted to see the tape to get some kind of awful scoop. *Fuck him.* She didn't need the tape. She'd been there. In fact, she'd kicked the story over to Eddie Overstreet, the stringer the paper had sent to cover the event. Kevin Ryan had assumed the worst. Asshole.

To mollify herself, she'd left a blistering voicemail for Danny, and then she went to the medical examiner's office because Jenna Jeffords was nagging her. She'd seemed like a misfit. A sad kid who never fit in. She'd been at the shore house, though Alex couldn't quite force the picture into her head. Had she come alone? Had someone invited her? It didn't make sense. She had died long before any of this had started. And yet Alex couldn't get the picture of the sleepy-eyed girl from Danny's yearbook out of her head.

A girl with dark hair and a round face, she'd been unexceptional in appearance. Alex imagined Jenna had gone through high school under a veil of invisibility if she wasn't outright tormented—a heavy girl, uncool, unstylish, just there. Had Jenna hoped that one day she'd turn into a swan?

High school must have been a special brand of hell for Jenna.

Adults always told kids high school was the best time of their lives, but it was a lie. High school was filled with traps and pitfalls for the innocent, the socially awkward, the different. Jenna seemed to have been all those things.

Alex figured she would just stop in, discuss the autopsy with the ME, and take it to Danny. Then they'd both have a laugh at her inability to stop picking at stupid details and his need to beat a story to death. She'd invite him over for dinner because Sam would be late as usual, and when he did get home, he'd shake his head at them, puzzling over their mutual obsessions.

Sam always said if she'd been a dog, she'd have been a bloodhound. Relentless and single-minded when she caught the scent of a story. She told him he'd be a poodle, a big old standard poodle. Smart and handsome but a little prissy. Besides, Alex had always been a cat person. Danny called her a lioness, and she liked that. It went with her astrological sign. Sam didn't believe in astrology.

Maybe it would be easier to avoid going home.

The sun was starting to set by the time Alex headed out of the medical examiner's office to the parking lot. She slid the copy of Jenna Jeffords's autopsy report into her overlarge bag along with every article the paper had run about the fire. Cars whizzed past, and the gritty exhaust seemed to hang in the humid air, but Alex stood for a moment in the parking lot, just breathing. She could see the hospital down the road, and she almost wanted to walk down to wait in Sam's serene office at HUP and stare at his ocean photographs.

She wouldn't. Sam didn't appreciate her just appearing. He had meetings and patients. He preferred that she schedule her visits. It was neater that way. Sam liked his personal life orderly, in contrast to the chaos of the emergency room. They were in so many ways ill-matched.

Alex walked to her car, thinking about Jenna's autopsy. Poor Jenna had been burned almost beyond recognition, and the photos had been gruesome. She had shrunk up against herself, her arms drawn up against her chest in a fighter's stance, except there was very little body left to protect, mostly black and twisted bones and some patches of her clothes. There wasn't much left of Jenna, and nobody had demanded any extensive testing. Dead was dead.

Apparently there had been some question of arson, however. The gas main had erupted, and three homes had been destroyed. The firefighters on the scene had noted that the fire had burned unusually hot, but there had been no hard evidence of accelerant.

In any case, the report had not been extensive, whether because the city wanted to get the case resolved or simply because arson was notoriously difficult to prove.

Rachel Jeffords had identified Jenna by a blue necklace that had partially melted into her bones and those scraps of clothes. Indeed, in the autopsy photo, Jenna's breastbone appeared to have been lacquered with blackened turquoise paint. Rachel had a very good eye for detail if she could identify that as a necklace.

Alex shivered despite the late afternoon heat. It had been an unusually warm spring, even for her, but goose bumps rose on her arms. She should put all this aside for one evening. She'd already gotten too close to Danny for her own good. One of them was bound to get burned.

Besides, his brother had pissed her off. Alex stood for a moment longer. She didn't like this case, but she couldn't let it go. Something about it was uglier than the politics she usually covered. On the surface this seemed to be about murder, but it ran much deeper. It was about deep cuts inflicted on vulnerable souls. She understood something about those deep cuts, and she knew Danny did as well. Looking back was dark and dangerous. Soul crushing.

Alex opened her car door and slid in. Who was Jenna Jeffords anyway? Why did it seem to matter? She had to look at everything together.

She started the ignition. She'd show all this to Danny. Maybe it would make more sense to him. After all, he knew Jenna to some degree. Alex cast a look over at the hospital and sighed. Sam might or might not come home tonight, but she needed to hustle.

For a moment, Alex rested her head against the steering wheel. She'd spent all day running around trying to put Sunday night out of her head, but it hit her now. She'd been waiting for Danny to notice her as a woman for a long time, and now that he had, she didn't know what to do about it.

29

Danny sped down Kelly Drive, a packet of autopsy photographs courtesy of Kevin on the passenger's seat. Normally he would have driven with the top down, but the heat had grown too oppressive. Summer, in its humid glory, had arrived in Philadelphia, and it wasn't even June.

He'd stopped in to visit Kevin, who hadn't been overjoyed to pull everything he had on the South Philly fire that killed Jenna Jeffords. Kevin had done it, but he'd bitched and moaned about Alex wanting to see the security footage from the book signing. Danny was still smarting from Alex's succinct, but to the point, voicemail: "Fuck you and your sonofabitch brother. Teach him some goddamn manners, or take this case and shove it up your ass." It had taken him half an hour to soothe her before she informed him she was heading off to fetch Jenna's autopsy.

"It's my fault," Danny had said to his brother. "Don't blame her. I thought if she saw the footage, she might recognize someone."

Kevin had harrumphed a little longer before he took Danny to see the tape. Danny had recognized Alex and Sam, other reporters, and Barb. The figure who sauntered up to Barb with the drink had his back to the camera, and yet something about him was familiar. Danny tried to trace him through the crowd, but he must have been aware of the cameras. He faded back into a dead space and disappeared. He reminded Danny of the kid he'd bumped into in Northern Liberties. The kid at the Shamrock. Was it possible? Danny couldn't swear to it.

"Whoever he was, he slipped out before the police came," Kevin had said. "We're trying to get a shot of his face, but he was smart. He knew where the cameras were."

Kevin had managed to get a rundown on Frank Greer and Len Piscone. Frank had stayed clean since he'd gotten out of jail; Piscone had never done time, but his brother Mark had. He'd been in Graterford with Frank doing time for the sale of narcotics. Small world. Now Mark Piscone worked in the Tioga scrapyard doing maintenance. But there was no evidence that anyone was doing anything illegal over there.

Danny stopped at the light at the Falls Bridge and half-listened to the traffic report on the radio. So far, traffic westbound on the Schuylkill wasn't horrific. He might beat Alex home. She'd bitch about coming to his house for a while, but he knew she'd secretly be relieved. It was easier for her to relax while away from Sam's watchful eye. Sam liked having Alex's undivided attention when he was home. She seemed less inclined to give it to him these days.

The light changed, and Danny wrenched his thoughts back to Frank Greer and Greg Moss. The only connection between Frank and Greg beside high school was Cromoca Partners, the land development company that owned a stake in Frank's scrap business.

Cromoca had acquired a lot of prime real estate in Philadelphia and South Jersey over the years, and Greg had been the real estate agent who brokered the deals. Greg was tied to the senior week party, and he was also tied to Cromoca. Now he was dead, and both of those factors involved Frank Greer.

Danny was still trying to piece together what he had learned from Frank and Stan. It wasn't much, but they'd both gotten texts. Danny was sure that something had gone on at Greg's shore house all those years ago. Frank had been too defensive about it.

His phone buzzed. Danny didn't recognize the number. "Ryan," he said after he picked up.

"Danny? It's been so long." He didn't recognize the tentative voice on the phone, but he let her go on. "Mom called me today. She said she spoke to you."

He almost drove into oncoming traffic. "Michelle? Michelle Perry?"

"It's Michelle Martin now."

"Jesus, Michelle. I didn't really expect to hear from you." That was an understatement. He would have put the likelihood of connecting with Michelle between zilch and nil. She must be beyond frightened.

"I know. I'm sorry. I don't mean to bother you. Listen, I can't really talk right now, but I'm coming down to Philly tomorrow to see my mom. Maybe we could meet? I'd really like to talk to you."

"I—yes. Of course. Wherever you'd like."

"Maybe at the Ritz Carlton? At ten? I'm picking up Mom at one, so it would give us time to talk and catch up."

"That would be fine. I'll—"

"It's a date then. I have to go. Good-bye."

She hung up before he could say anything else, and if he'd been home, he might have gone in search of his small cache of memorabilia. It was a silly thing to still feel a pang at the sound of her voice, or maybe you really never did forget the first person who broke your heart.

Somewhere, buried in the recesses of his boxes of junk, was a picture of Michelle looking like an angel in her sparkling white prom dress. Looking much too good for the likes of him.

There was no use trying to go back. Whatever small flame burned between Michelle and him had died within weeks of high school graduation. She'd moved to New York; he'd stayed in Philly. The door had closed. He knew well enough that those were the doors best left closed.

On KYW, the five-day forecast was calling for record-breaking highs of over one hundred for tomorrow. Danny glanced out the window at the other hermetically sealed commuters on the expressway as traffic slowed toward the Conshohocken Curve and the top headlines began to replay. Funny how news had always been the only constant in his life. Right now, he wished he could talk to Andy Cohen about this mess of a story.

Andy would tell him to look for the why. "You find the why and everything else will come together," he'd always say.

He hoped that wherever Andy was, there was an unending supply of Glenfiddich.

Traffic lurched forward, and Danny tried to put his thoughts in some kind of order. He was meeting Alex in a half hour. There was a story they needed to get. They had autopsy photos to review, notes to check, and he still hadn't figured out a way to traverse the land mines that now lay between them.

*

Danny watched Alex spread copies of photos, reports, and news articles across his kitchen table as he tapped the manila folder in his hand and tried to come up with a way to bring up the previous night's folly. Except it hadn't felt like a folly. Everything had seemed to click into place like a Chinese puzzle box just before it snapped open. Or maybe everything had snapped shut. She was doing her best to pretend everything was normal.

They stepped around each other with extreme deliberation, taking care not to get too close. She crackled with a shivering energy that made his heart thump against his chest and his muscles ache with tension. Dangerous energy.

"Okay, here's everything I could dig up about the fire plus Jenna's autopsy," she said without looking at him. "Do you have anything alcoholic in this house? Why are we here instead of my house where there's food?"

Danny pointed to the refrigerator. "Beer and wine in the fridge. Booze in the wet bar. And we're here because I beat you home. Plus, I have police reports on the fire."

"Not really fair. You had your asshole brother get them for you."

"He regrets his temper tantrum," Danny said. "He was having a shitty afternoon."

"Yeah. My heart bleeds." She leaned into his open refrigerator. "Jesus God, Daniel. What do you eat?"

He blinked. He never thought about it. If there was nothing in the house, he ordered out. Sometimes he went to the store and bought food, but it didn't occupy his thoughts. He'd let go of so many things after Beth and Conor died.

She turned on him, hands on hips. "And what the hell is that mournful man singing?"

"Whoa, that's Clapton. 'River of Tears.'"

"Well, of course it is. Don't you have some Beyoncé? I worry about you, Daniel. Once a week, you and I are going food shopping. Normal people don't live this way." Alex shut the refrigerator. "Jeez. 'River of Tears.' No food. I'm ready to cry." She opened cupboards until she found a bag of pretzels.

"See, pretzels and beer," he said. "There's stuff in the pantry."

She gave him a baleful look and stalked into the pantry. "What the hell do you use this space for?" she said, and he laughed. Alex's way of coping with tension was getting angry. That was fine. Angry he could handle.

"I don't need the space. It was just there."

"When you renovated, did you put the wet bar in here?"

"No. The wet bar was always in there," Danny said, half-listening.

He heard her rooting around inside the pantry. "Damn. Is this like a butler's pantry? You could have a conference in here. The walls are decorated too. So what's with the writing on the wall? What is this? *S T* in *E P*? I don't—Oh, wait, I get it. Instep. It's a—what do they call them? Rebus puzzle? They're all over. Look, the word 'Push' slants up. Push up. An exploding pie in oven? What the hell? I don't get that one. Oh, hell, you probably didn't even notice. Hey, I found chips and salsa."

"Oh, the decorations? Yeah. They're rebus puzzles. The owner's name was Rebus. Get it? I guess he was being sly. I sat in there and solved most of them one afternoon. I didn't get the pie either. Except I think it's a mushroom." He still half-believed Mr. Rebus had hidden something in this house. Danny returned

151

to the articles. "You know, I used to write obits when I was in college."

Alex stuck her head out. "What?"

"I used to write obits."

"I guess we can order out." Alex set the chips and salsa down on the table with the pretzels. "Jenna wouldn't have been your standard obit. She was front page. Rebus puzzles. Damn. Why would he leave all those puzzles in there? That's weird."

"I used to think they spelled out a clue of some kind, but they don't." Danny studied the photograph of Rachel Jeffords. "The originals of these photos are still down at the paper, right? Who took them?" He squinted at the photo credit. "Al Frederick. I remember Al Frederick. He retired in 2006."

Alex peered over his shoulder. "He'd be shooting film in 1992, right? What kind of clue?"

"Oh, yeah, he'd be using film."

"Why do you want to see the originals?" Alex asked.

"Of the photos? I'd like to get a clearer look at the shot."

"Obviously, but why?"

"Because there's a crowd. If it was arson, Al might have caught a face in the crowd. Arsonists like to watch their work. If we can get the original, maybe someone will stand out."

"Poor Jenna. It's kind of sad really."

"She wanted to be a writer."

Alex's eyes widened. "Really? Like a reporter?"

"Like a romance writer. She wrote a novel senior year. *Jenny's First Love.* It was pretty awful."

"Are you being a snobby literary person?"

He shook his head, remembering. "No. I felt sorry for her. She gave me a copy."

"I hope you were kind." Alex sighed. "Poor Jenna. I can see her giving her precious manuscript to the one boy in the class who could write, the one boy she hoped wouldn't laugh at her."

Danny winced slightly. "It was awkward."

Alex crossed her arms and gave him a knowing look. "Oh. You weren't kind. I can tell."

"I tried to be nice to Jenna, but do you know how bizarre it is to discover you're some deluded girl's fantasy? She wrote the book about the two of us. It was beyond creepy. They don't teach you how to handle that when you're seventeen."

Alex stared at him for a moment and nodded, and he realized she was conceding the point. He wasn't about to admit that he'd spent years trying to forget Jenna and her awful literary effort.

"What was Jenna doing at Greg Moss's party? She didn't seem like a party type of girl." Alex picked up a photograph and frowned as she examined it. "Certainly not with the football crowd."

Danny shrugged. "I don't know. Maybe someone invited her. She could have come with Ollie Deacon."

"So she had a boyfriend?"

"I guess. She and Ollie went to prom together." He thought of Ollie's wide-eyed face in the yearbook, in the photograph hanging over the bar at the Shamrock. "Jesus Christ."

"What is it?"

"Ollie Deacon." He paced the room, trying to pull the strings of the story together in his mind. "He became a cop and got killed in the first year out of the academy."

"And this means?" Alex watched him, her face expressionless, but her eyes filled with questions.

"Ollie was shot in the chest. I don't think they ever caught the perp."

Alex's eyes widened a little, and she blew out a breath.

Danny paced to the refrigerator and back. "I'd like to know if he was shot in the heart." He walked into the pantry and turned back to Alex. "I'd like to find out if the ballistics match on the gun that killed Greg and the others. Then we can see if there's a match to the gun that killed Ollie." Danny stopped pacing and watched Alex latch onto his idea.

"You think he's the first victim."

"Weird, right?"

"No. Not necessarily." Alex set down the photograph of Jenna. She was trying to make the pieces fit just like he was. "So connection? No connection?"

"I think everything's connected, but I'm not sure how," Danny said. "First thing I have to find out about is Ollie. The next thing is to find out about this Cromoca Partners and if it fits in. Something is off there."

"You find out about Ollie Deacon, and I'll hit the *Sentinel* morgue in the morning. They'll have Al's shot. It made the front page. If not, I'll see if I can track him down." She frowned. "Crap. I have to do a city council meeting and turn in a piece."

"Resurrecting Al's photo from the dead files? Fitting, but unnecessary. I have his address. I'll check him out. He knows me. I have to be in town tomorrow anyway."

Danny knew Al well. A double Pulitzer winner, Al was nicknamed the Spook because of his ability to slip into any situation and emerge with a perfect shot. He'd provided the pictures for some of Danny's best stories.

"You aren't trying to cut me out, are you?"

"We're in this together. You know that." He wasn't ready to tell her about meeting Michelle, but in everything else, they were partners.

"I guess I can try to dig up something on Cromoca." Alex stood watching him while she played with a loose strand of hair. Buying time. "Danny, I, about last night . . ." She looked away, and he knew she was going to tell him that it couldn't happen again. It wasn't a huge surprise. What had caught him off guard was the depth of his feelings for her. He'd always liked her and respected her as a journalist. It never had occurred to him that something more lay buried there. Dope brought strange things to the surface. As long as he didn't indulge, he'd be fine. He wasn't going to be the asshole who broke up her marriage.

"I know, Alex."

"And we're okay? I mean, we're friends. Still friends."

He caught her hand and squeezed it. "We'll always be friends. Is that good enough?" He heard her soft intake of breath even as he fought to ignore the quick flood of warmth that spread from her fingers to his. This was going to be a whole lot harder than he anticipated.

She nodded without speaking and withdrew her hand from his swiftly. "What happened to your face?"

"I walked into a fist."

She started to touch the bruise on his cheekbone but pulled her hand away. "You need ice," she said.

"I'm fine. I've had worse." Frank Greer was a relative weakling compared to Tommy Ryan.

"You're an idiot. You should have waited for me."

"No. Frank Greer is a guy you definitely didn't need to meet."

They stood for a moment in silence until she said, "Maybe we should look at these files. I know you're thinking Ollie Deacon was the first victim, but what if it all started with Jenna Jeffords?"

He could still feel the warmth where her hand had been. "I guess it's possible, though she's the one person who died in an accident."

"I know, but anomalies bother me." She put space between them, and he smiled. Tonight she was dressed in her version of conservative: a black sleeveless turtleneck and white jeans, big white-and-black button earrings. It did nothing to make her look conservative.

"I have your earring," he said. "Your hoop." He went over to the counter. Where had he put the damn thing? "I thought I put it on the counter."

"Don't worry about it. It'll turn up. Let's order pizza."

"Fine."

She went to the refrigerator, pulled out two beers, and handed him one. He took it and clinked his bottle against hers. Being a little numb could be a good thing.

"You and your old 'River of Tears.' You need to lighten up, Ryan, but for now, I guess it's appropriate to the subject at hand."

"Let's get to it," he said.

*

From his special place, the watcher had a clear and unobstructed view into the kitchen. Ryan sat with the woman—Alex

Burton—at the neat round table, their heads close together while they looked at files, as if files would tell a proper story.

Ryan should know that every story has many facets.

He should know it, but he wouldn't accept it. For a man who loved to dig beneath the surface of life, Ryan was born with a huge blind spot about his own. It was funny, really. Ryan was a horror story steeped in romance and wrapped in tragedy. That was his fortune and misfortune. That was his story.

The eye also of the adulterer waiteth for the twilight, saying, No eye shall see me.

He repeated the words to himself. Maybe he'd send the words in a text to Ryan, but it was too soon. Everything in proper order.

This silly reporter woman was a problem. She had to go.

And the dogs shall eat Jezebel.

Ryan had experience with that as well. At least that's what he'd heard. Once the reporter woman was gone, everything could proceed.

The players were in motion now, and it would be fun to watch the drama play out. He slipped the gold hoop into his pocket. Pieces of Alex.

They found no more of her than the skull, the feet and the palms of the hands.

30

George Crossman left his office in the Rayburn Congressional Office Building and set off down Independence Avenue toward the Ulysses S. Grant Memorial. It was a pleasant enough place to meet. The memorial faced west, overlooking the Capitol Reflecting Pool. Today had been another DC scorcher, with the temperature hovering in the high nineties and the humidity set to jungle levels, and the congressman would have preferred the air-conditioned comfort of his office. But when Senator Robert Harlan demanded a meeting, one didn't question the time or place.

Only a few tourists milled about the memorial, and he walked to the front where the tall, white-haired senator stood between the two bronze lions on their marble pedestals flanking the memorial. He wore a dark suit with a crisp white shirt and red tie. Mirrored sunglasses shielded his eyes.

"George, how are you?" Robert Harlan held out his hand, and the congressman wondered if he was expected to kiss it. He resisted the urge and shook it instead.

"I guess you're wondering why I wanted to meet out here instead of in your office."

"I was a little curious." *More than a little curious.*

"You're wondering what this is about."

Sweat was pooling at the back of the congressman's neck, and he shifted. "A little. I was under the impression that you wanted to avoid public scrutiny."

"Come now. There's no reason at all that two colleagues shouldn't be seen in public together taking in the glories of a Washington afternoon."

"We might have met at a club. It'd have been a damn sight more convenient."

"And a bit too conspicuous. We need to discuss this Greg Moss situation."

"I hardly think—"

"That is the problem, George. You hardly think."

The congressman swallowed several times. He wished he could see the eyes behind those glasses, but the low, monotone voice chilled him. He made one last attempt to clarify the situation. "Greg's death is under investigation. It's being handled. It's just that there's a reporter involved."

"A local reporter?"

"Yes, local. Dan Ryan. He's not important."

Robert Harlan's mouth thinned to a tight line. "Did they remove part of your mind when they rearranged your face? Daniel Ryan was my son-in-law. What does he think about Greg's death?"

"I don't know." The congressman felt the blood draining from his face. "He and Greg went to school together. Greg spoke to him before he died."

"Is there something about Greg's death I should know about?"

"I don't know why Greg was killed. He was getting threatening text messages. It was insane."

"Text messages?"

"Bible quotes. Weird stuff. It might be related to some other murders of his former classmates. That's all I could find out."

"We can't afford to have people looking too deeply into Greg's business dealings, George. It could become ugly."

"You mean Cromoca."

Robert Harlan waved his hand in disgust. "If it was just that, we could cut our losses and get out. It's a thread. You pull the thread hard enough and who knows what you unwind?"

"Ryan's not looking into Cromoca."

"Not yet. But he will. He's crossed me twice." He looked at Crossman for a long moment. "He doesn't get to do it a third time. Do you understand, George? Not a third time. He needs to be dealt with."

Crossman sighed. He wasn't about to stand here and argue with Bob Harlan about the fate of one journalist. Accidents could be arranged if it came to it, but he preferred that things not come to that. Accidents caused undue scrutiny. They had nothing to worry about. Greg Moss was most likely the unfortunate victim of a random serial killer. It was inconvenient, but it could be managed.

For now, Crossman was willing to let things drift along, but he nodded and said in his most placating voice, "Of course, Bob. If necessary. Trust me."

Crossman turned his head to look out over the reflecting pool. To the west, the Washington Memorial rose up, a white finger pointing to the evening sky. In the distance, he could hear evening traffic, the chatter of tourists, the twitter of birds. His heart beat against his throat.

"Don't worry, Bob. We'll deal with the journalist if and when we have to."

"Don't screw it up."

31

The lobby of the Ritz Carlton was pleasantly cool. Housed in the old Girard Bank Building, the hotel sat on the corner of Chestnut and Broad across from City Hall and featured an impressive domed lobby complete with marble columns. For a moment Danny stood, getting his bearings and listening to the clicking of women's stilettos on the shiny marble floors before he headed for the Lobby Lounge to wait for Michelle. He still wasn't sure how he felt about seeing her again. Once she'd occupied his thoughts to a ridiculous degree, but the memories had grown fuzzy after twenty-odd years.

He supposed she'd always be his golden girl. At the very least, she was his first serious girlfriend.

Danny walked into the lounge, crossing the soft brown rug with its pink-and-gold design. It matched the booths and complemented the rich mahogany bar. He gave a cursory glance to the occupants spread out among the tables. A couple huddled close together at a table near the bar while an older man with a *Wall Street Journal* was ensconced in a booth; a hipster with a man-bun, sporting tight red skinny jeans, lounged at the bar, and a slim blonde clad in white and pink sat tucked away in a booth toward the back. Danny was about to order coffee when the blonde stood and gave him a jerky little wave.

"Daniel? Danny Ryan?"

He recognized her, sort of. She still had that glow, the well-bronzed look that came from spending a lot of time on the tennis courts; her mother had spent a small fortune on lessons. He recognized the wide hazel eyes, though her nose looked different—narrower, less Roman. She'd lightened her hair to a frosted blonde and cut it chin length to emphasize her long neck. When she held out her hands, he saw that her wedding ring was an eye grabber—maybe three carats. It looked only slightly smaller than Beth's, but it was hard to judge. She had such fine, small hands.

One thing was clear: Michelle had married up, just like her mother wanted.

"My God, you haven't changed at all," she said in a too-bright voice. She looked at him with a wide smile, as if waiting for approval.

"And you're still beautiful," he said. "Coffee?"

"Oh, no. I limit myself to three cups a day. I've already had my first."

"Shall we sit?" He took her arm, and they walked back to her secluded booth. He found himself searching for the girl who taught him to curse in French and who liked sneaking up to his bedroom to rock the bedsprings while his old man lay passed out on the sofa. This version of Michelle seemed almost alien to him. Brittle and somehow false.

"You keep looking at me so strangely," she said. "Do I look that bad?"

"No, not at all. I think . . . I was just remembering. It was a long time ago."

"I'm a very different person now. Aren't you?"

He shrugged. *Am I?* Older, certainly. A little wiser, perhaps. "Everyone changes." If he had changed so much, why did he keep making the same mistakes? Did that make him stupid or insane?

"That's right. I have this very normal life now," she said. "A husband, three kids, and a dog. I just don't understand why anyone would send me these texts. Look." She whipped out an iPhone in a gold case and scrolled through pictures. Three handsome boys in their early teens, one tall blond husband in a pink polo shirt, hugging said kids, and a huge Bernese Mountain Dog. She was right. An all-American family—just like he used to have. He swallowed the bile that rose in his throat.

"You have a nice family," he said. It sounded so lame.

"Mom told me about—"

"Yeah." He held up his hand. "It's fine. I'm working. I've gotten through the worst of it."

"Danny, I'm so sorry. Your little boy."

He wanted her to stop talking so he could cough free the shards of glass that had lodged in his chest. They were always there. Some days he felt them more keenly than others. He had gotten to a point where he could go for weeks without noticing them, but this morning, the pain was fresh and sharp.

"I am sorry," she said. "For so many things." When she reached up and touched his cheekbone, he almost flinched. "Who gave you this?"

"An old friend. It doesn't matter."

"Danny, I didn't know you'd written to me until yesterday. Mom never gave me your letters. She destroyed them. I wrote to you, and she was supposed to forward my letters, but she never did."

"Please don't. You don't have to apologize for anything," he said. "I'm not . . . I just want you to be happy."

Michelle shook her head. "No, you don't understand. I should have called, but I was afraid of your dad. So I just waited. I guess I always hoped you'd come to New York."

He took her hand and squeezed it. "It wasn't meant to be. You have a good life. Better than I could have given you, I'm sure. Things worked out. I'm glad."

She was looking for forgiveness, and he gave it to her. Maybe she had even missed him for a week or two, but she hadn't mourned for long. In late July that summer, he had gone to New York to find her, only to find that he was too intimidated to knock on her aunt's door. He'd ended up following her from her aunt's house in Brooklyn to Midtown where she'd met up with friends dressed in clothes he couldn't afford and headed for a club where there was a rope line he could never pass through. He'd told himself she'd become a snob, but he'd never given her the chance to reject him outright.

He'd walked back to Pennsylvania Station and come home, crashing for the weekend with his sister, Theresa. He'd never said a word to anyone about his ill-fated trip, just filed it away under lessons learned. He'd never to written Michelle again, though he'd filled quite a few notebooks with heartsick garbage.

Her eyes filled, and she fumbled in her purse for a tissue. "Damn it. I have this wonderful life. A beautiful family, great husband, and some days I sit in car pool, and I just don't know what I'm doing in Connecticut. I didn't think it would hurt so much to see you again."

What did he say to that? It did hurt, because looking back was futile. Once you'd passed through a door, you couldn't undo what was done. You could only keep going. It wasn't profound. It was real and harsh, but life was harsh.

"I guess it's what might have been," he said at last, "and that's what breaks your heart."

"No, we had something. That's what breaks my heart."

Regret did neither of them any good. What difference did it make now?

She blinked and wiped her cheeks with the tissue. Then she took a breath. "I—these texts. I keep getting them. I haven't told Paul. I'm afraid he'd get upset."

"When did you start getting them?"

"A while ago. I don't know how this person got my cell number. I've tried blocking him, but it doesn't matter. He just changes his number."

"And it's the same message?"

"Kind of. Weird stuff." She held out her phone. The latest message read, "Proverbs 13:15."

Danny stared at it for a moment. "A quote," he said.

"I don't understand."

"It's a Bible quote. Proverbs is an Old Testament Book." He was already looking it up. "'The way of transgressors is hard.'"

"What does that mean?"

"It means you should talk to the cops."

She shook her head. "I can't. Paul will be upset I didn't tell him. He'll—"

"Would he prefer you dead?" Danny took her by the shoulders. "Because people who get these little messages have a way of ending up dead."

She slid her arms around him, and he realized she was sobbing now. So he held her, patting her back, and murmuring nonsense until her shaking subsided. If nothing else, he made a good towel. At length, Michelle pulled back and gave him a wan smile.

"So I just made a fool of myself."

"No. But you do need to talk to the cops. My brother Kevin is a Philly detective. I can take you to see him. He'll be discreet. I promise."

"All right." She wiped her face and sniffed. "I must look like hell. I'm going to run to the ladies room and pull myself together," she said without looking up. "Will you wait here?"

"Of course."

She twisted the tissue until it began to pull apart. "I never forgot you, Danny. Never." She leaned over and kissed him on the lips, and then she was up and hurrying across the lobby.

*

Fifteen minutes later, Danny had made a call to Kevin and was still waiting in the lobby when his phone vibrated.

It was a text from Michelle that read, "Sorry, Danny. Drowning in a river of tears."

He shoved his phone into his pocket and ran to the reception desk. "I need someone to check the ladies room," he said to the startled woman.

"I beg your pardon?"

"My friend went into the bathroom fifteen minutes ago, and I think there's a problem. Please."

"I need to call security."

"Please. Right now."

She waved a guard who stood discreetly near the entrance. "Charlie, this gentleman says his friend went into the ladies room and didn't come out. I need you to come with me."

The guard raised his eyebrows slightly but followed. Danny tagged along behind. Bathrooms in hotels could be dangerous. He knew from experience.

They walked in, and he heard the receptionist give a small gasp. "Charlie, call the police."

He pushed past the guard. Michelle sprawled on the floor, her neck twisted at an unnatural angle, her forehead bleeding where she must have hit it against the sink. Her purse lay open on the ground beside her, its contents strewn on the marble floor. The iPhone with its gold case was missing.

32

A pigeon landed on the window ledge and settled in as Alex stared at her blank computer screen. She typed, "City Council met today and did nothing." Then she looked at her notes and sighed. The council members had bickered for a while. No fistfights though.

Her editor, Tim Gluckman, walked up and dropped a file on her desk. "Yo, Burton, stop daydreaming. You need to get down to Penn's Landing. Senator Harlan and Congressman Crossman are making some kind of announcement along with . . ." He scanned a piece of paper. "Oh, yeah, the mayor."

She looked at him, left eyebrow raised in question. "About?"

"A new interstate development initiative. It's all about jobs, you know." He grinned, and she knew he absolutely believed it was not at all about jobs. "Go sniff around and see what's up."

"You don't believe in interstate development?"

"Not when those two are involved."

He was probably right. Alex leaned back and stared out the window for a moment before she started to pull up information about the new project. Her cell phone rang.

"Burton," she said.

"Ms. Burton, it's Rachel. Rachel Jeffords."

Alex sat up straight and grabbed a pen. "Mrs. Jeffords. What can I do for you?"

"I was wondering if we could meet. You said you wanted to talk about Jenna yesterday?"

"Yes. Yes, I would."

"Because I changed my mind."

"That's wonderful, I'm so glad. But why if you don't mind me asking?"

Rachel hesitated. "Well, you're a woman, so I thought you'd understand. About Jenna, I mean. Why she was special. So you'll come today?"

Alex looked up at the clock. Even if she got this damn article finished, she had to be out the door in an hour for the second press conference. "I have a press event this afternoon. Tomorrow might be better. I'll head out tomorrow morning."

Rachel hesitated. "Oh, tomorrow? Well, I guess that's fine. You just get here when you can. It's a little hard to find. I'll give you directions. Please."

Alex wrote down the address and directions carefully, but she didn't think she'd have a problem. Straight out 30 West, then turn right. That wasn't so hard, and she had a decent sense of direction. She tucked the directions into her purse and went back to her article.

Across the newsroom, she heard Eric Thompson talking about something at the Ritz Carlton, but she paid it no mind. She wanted to get this article put to bed ASAP. She'd deal with Robert Harlan and George Crossman, and tomorrow, first thing, she'd be out the door and on her way to Lancaster.

33

Kevin slumped in his desk chair and listened to the bustling squad room. Phones were ringing, and voices chattered around him. He heard the rapid fire of Detective Patterson's fingers on her keyboard, and he could smell the aroma of fresh coffee wafting toward him. His gut ached as he ruminated about the call from Danny this morning, and he paused to take a swig of Maalox.

"Could you maybe apologize to Alex?" Danny had said. "You really hurt her feelings."

"Jesus Christ. Didn't we already have this conversation? It's the black thing, isn't it?"

"No, it's the you-acting-like-an-asshole thing."

"That's one hell of a way to ask for my help."

Danny had sighed, the way he always did, and Kevin had pictured him taking a moment to cool down. It had taken him two beats, but Danny had said, "You're right. I'm sorry. I'm trying to figure out this whole Greg Moss situation. His death may have been tied to that senior week party, or it may have been about his ties to a land development company named Cromoca Partners. I can't make the pieces fit together."

"And you're looking for a connection."

"I'm looking for anything that ties them together."

"Maybe there is no connection. Maybe it's one or the other."

"Maybe, but I still have to figure it out."

Given Danny's disdain for cops in general, Kevin hadn't pointed out that it was a police matter. It wouldn't have made any difference. Theresa liked to call Danny "Pighead," though she felt free to apply that name to both of them. Their sister had inherited the Ryan tendency for trash talk.

"I'll see what I can do, but don't get your hopes up. Tell me what you know about a cop named Ollie Deacon. He was in my class."

"Killed on the job?"

"No. I don't think so. South Philly kid. Made the wall of honor at the Shamrock."

"And this is connected to Greg Moss?"

"I don't know. Maybe." Danny paused and then added, "Did Eliot have anything to say about that tongue?"

"Nothing relevant," Kevin said. "I'd say it points to a different killer, but this is one screwed-up case. Who the hell knows?"

Long after he had hung up on Danny, Kevin had listened to the chaos in the squad room as he pretended to read the file on his desk. He stared at the coffee cup Kelly had made him for Father's Day years ago. She had drawn him as a big stick figure holding her hand. She gave them both oversized grins and put them inside a heart. Kevin used to be her hero. Now he was just another asshole. Danny was the cool guy.

"Watch after your brother," Ma would say to Kevin when she was lying in her sickbed. "You're my sweet, strong boy."

She'd looked like a wax doll, and he'd trembled when he took her cold hand in his. He'd wanted her to get up and tell him it would be all right, that of course she'd be better in time to make the pumpkin pies for Thanksgiving. She'd always made a special little pie just for him because he'd always stayed to help her in the kitchen.

The old man and Junior had always mocked him. They'd said he was doing women's work. Danny would be hiding someplace with his face in a book, and Theresa would always be locked in her room with the hall phone. But Kevin would help Gran and Ma measure out the spices and crack the eggs. He'd wash the pans, clean the floor—anything to be closer to her, to breathe in her warm scent of rosewater and fresh-washed linen, baked bread and something indefinable. That familiar scent had been buried with her.

Now he sat here in the grimy squad room, pushing papers and sucking down Maalox, to what end? Junior was dead. Theresa tolerated him, and Danny? Who knew what Danny really felt. They had a connection, but it had never been easy. Certainly it had never been what Ma had wanted, but all he could do was soldier on.

Kevin shoved his files aside and began to search through the records for Ollie Deacon. The file wasn't hard to find. It might be a cold case, but Deacon was a brother in blue. It never stopped being a priority. Deacon had been hit by two shots. The first bullet penetrated the liver. The kill shot was a direct blast to the heart. The perp used a nine millimeter. Eyewitnesses had described the killer as a stocky black male, a stocky white male, and a clown, though one guy thought it might have been a woman with red hair. So much for eyewitness testimony. Ollie had been shot right outside his home. No security footage available.

"Kevin." Jake appeared at the front of his desk and dropped a file in front of him. "A little paperwork on your friend Ted Eliot. It's interesting."

"Incriminating?"

"Weird. He was working in Camden proper for about six years. Good record. Fine upstanding cop. Commendations up the wazoo."

Kevin frowned. "Not helpful."

"Right. So he gets hurt on a domestic. Nothing earthshattering. He got shoved down a flight of steps and fucked up his back. Bad. He's out for six weeks. Comes back. Continues, but—here's where it gets interesting—his production starts to drop off. A lot. Eventually, he goes out on extended leave supposedly for his back. It turns out he's got a fractured vertebrae."

"And this is important why?"

Jake shrugged. "My guy says the hot rumor is Eliot had a substance problem, but nothing was ever proved. He went out on long-term disability. He then comes back a year later, and with his glowing recommendations, everything's just peachy. He's been a straight arrow for the last three years."

"But something happened."

"Something happened." Jake pointed to the file. "Look at that. It's so perfectly clean it sparkles. He's got connections somewhere, Kev. My guy doesn't know where, but they're heavy duty, so watch your back."

"You think he's dirty?"

Jake pointed to the file. "I think he's fucked up, and that might be worse."

*

Kevin had finished reading the ridiculous file on Ted Eliot and was busy with Ollie Deacon when his phone buzzed.

"Ryan," he said.

"Kevin? It's Ted Eliot."

Kevin reached for his bottle of Maalox. This was going to be interesting.

"I assume you're calling about the ballistics?" Kevin took a swig of Maalox and grimaced.

"I had to browbeat our lab guy, but here's the info you wanted. The gun that killed Greg Moss was a nine millimeter. We recovered the bullet. Nate Pulaski, Christopher Soldano, and Richard Farnasi were all killed by someone using a nine millimeter. Bullets and casings were recovered for all three murders, but if it was the same gun, someone changed the barrel. We can't get a ballistics match on any of them, so there may or may not be a connection. What's your thought here?"

Kevin wasn't about to tell Eliot that Danny was trying to make some strange, possibly nonexistent, connection to a twenty-year-old murder. Danny didn't need any more suspicion thrown his way. "We have a cold case here that might be connected. The victim was shot in the heart by a perp using a nine millimeter."

"All we can say is all these murders were committed by someone using a nine millimeter. All the victims were shot in the heart."

Kevin took another swallow of Maalox from the bottle on his desk. "Damnit, I was hoping we'd have something more to connect these murders. Any texts?"

"That would be helpful, but if there were texts, nobody noted them, except for Pulaski. He mentioned something about a Bible verse." Eliot's voice cracked out each word. "They were all shot in the heart. Point blank. However, at least three of them had other wounds. And well, you know about Moss."

"Not enough to pull in the FBI at this point."

"Not yet, but it raises a red flag. Like I said, I don't know if they were all getting text messages, but you should warn your brother."

Kevin sighed. As if he didn't know Danny's propensity for painting a target on his back. "Believe me, he knows how serious this is."

"This information is for you only," Eliot said. "One cop to another."

"Don't worry," Kevin said. "And there's no connection beyond high school?"

It was Eliot's turn to pause. At last he said, "Not so far as we can see."

"No chance it could be connected to Greg Moss's development activities?"

Kevin swore Eliot dropped his phone, but his voice sounded calm enough when he said, "Not that I know of."

"How about his client parties?"

"What parties are you talking about?"

"Are we going to play games, Detective?"

"Who told you about Greg's parties?" Eliot's voice went from neutral to semistrangled in about two seconds. *Interesting.*

"Do you think I'm going to give up a confidential source? Why don't you tell me what you know?"

"I beg your pardon?"

"It's been a shitty morning, and I don't feel like playing games. Tell me about your connection to Greg Moss."

"Wait. You trying to jam me up, Ryan?"

Kevin took a breath. Not quite the reaction he expected. Maybe this whole thing had nothing to do with Danny's high school days. He was grasping at straws here, but he had to sound more confident than he was. "I need information. If you've got it, you need to talk to me. One cop to another."

"Do I have a choice?"

"I'm assuming you want to solve this case." When Eliot didn't answer, Kevin added, "Meet me this side of the river. Famous Deli on Fourth. One thirty." Kevin figured the restaurant was a spot that was well populated enough that Eliot couldn't pull anything if he were so inclined.

Be safe was his motto.

Long after he hung up, Kevin sat with his bottle of Maalox. What to do? This whole case had just bent in a very unpleasant direction. This either led back to the past or forked into a very new and unpleasant direction.

"Déjà vu all over again," he said.

If only the feds were taking over; Kevin had a few contacts who would keep him informed. But there wasn't enough evidence to draw in the FBI. All they had was a series of peculiar murders and a very questionable cop. Sometimes his brother got it right.

Kevin looked back at Ollie Deacon's file. The detective who originally caught the case was Vic Ross, but he was out on call. Something about a dead woman at the Ritz Carlton. Kevin would have to wait until he got back with Newgate. At least that was one murder that didn't involve his brother. Kevin turned back to Ollie Deacon's file.

34

Danny sat with his head in his hands and waited for the cops to finish with his phone. Somehow he had a feeling he wasn't getting it back anytime soon, but it was easier to focus on the phone than to think about Michelle lying on the floor of the bathroom in her white dress. She'd hit her head on one of the porcelain sinks by chance or design, leaving a fairly horrific dent in the side of her skull.

Michelle had been placed in a body bag and discreetly wheeled out of a service entrance. The CSU people were processing the scene.

He looked up and stared around the lobby, wondering if someone was watching him now. He hoped so. Danny hoped whoever was watching recognized that killing Michelle was pointless. "I'm still going to find you," he said. One of the cops glanced around.

Michelle hadn't been part of Greg's group. She hadn't even been inside Greg's house that night. Her only connection to anyone in that house was through Danny. Was that what made her a target? And why was her murder so vicious?

The guys in his class had been shot, but the women were singled out for particularly horrible retribution. Jenna was burned. Barb was almost asphyxiated. And now Michelle.

Did the murderer think that Michelle and Barb knew something about that night? And what about Jenna? Had she seen something? How could the murderer have known Michelle was meeting him at the Ritz Carlton? Nobody knew about that, not even Alex.

The police were getting the security footage, and maybe Kevin could get him in to see the tape. For now, all he could do was keep digging. He could do that much for Michelle.

"Mr. Ryan? I'm Detective Newgate." The bald detective hovered over him. "How're you holding up there?"

Danny shrugged. He was the goddamn angel of death. Women beware. He said, "She was going to meet her mother at one down at HUP. Her mother's a nurse. Rita Perry."

"Can she ID the body?"

"Yeah. She can."

A few hours ago, Michelle had been a person. Now she was "the body" in a black plastic bag. The detective put a hand on Danny's shoulder. He had big square hands and looked in decent shape, like maybe he was once a lineman. His shaved head gleamed like polished mahogany, and flickers of light danced around it. Danny blinked.

"You sure you're all right? You look kind of shook up."

"I'm okay. I'll be okay." If he kept telling himself that, it would become true. Maybe. "I know Michelle's mother. Would it help if I went out to Penn to talk to her?"

Newgate sighed. "I know you want to help, but you need to let us handle this right now, Mr. Ryan."

Danny understood that Newgate wanted to protect him. It was difficult enough to get news about the death of a loved one from a cop. He knew all about that. Danny also knew Rita Perry's wrath would be substantial, but he didn't want to shield himself. He deserved it.

"Hey, you're Kevin Ryan's brother, aren't you?" Newgate said.

"I am, yeah."

Newgate gave the thumbs up to the other detective, and for a moment he regarded Danny with something akin to bemusement.

"You can go, Mr. Ryan. You're not a suspect. You are a witness, however, so I'll ask you not to leave the area. We also will have to hold onto your phone. Sorry about that. I'll give you a receipt, but I wouldn't count on getting it back any time soon."

"Yeah, I know the routine."

"I guess you do." Newgate handed him a receipt with a little flourish. "I'm gonna ask you not to approach Mrs. Perry on your own. You let us take care of that. You want to talk to her later, that's your right. But right now, you let the police handle the situation. You understand?"

Danny nodded.

Newgate patted him on the back. "Good. You take care of yourself, Mr. Ryan."

35

A slight breeze stirred the air as the small crowd of press gathered around the staging area at Penn's Landing. Sun sparkled off the Delaware River, and Alex watched a bright-red motorboat cut through the water. Across the river, Camden actually looked inviting. Everything depended on perspective.

The mayor had arrived, along with two city councilmen and three state reps, when a silver Jaguar pulled up. Congressman George Crossman stepped out. Alex had seen him a few times on television and in the paper, of course, though she didn't handle Jersey politics. In person, the congressman looked better than his photos: tall, trim, blond, with a good square jaw. In his sleek gray suit he seemed to almost radiate light as he bounced up the steps, smiling. *Wow.* Talk about movie-star looks. He was probably in his late fifties, but he didn't look it. Plastic surgery? Good genes?

Senator Robert Harlan's limo pulled up at last. He waited until his driver opened his door and then slowly emerged. White-haired, tanned, he had an electric presence, and Alex could almost feel the heat of his dark eyes scanning the crowd before he began his slow ascent. The senator wore his usual navy suit with a crisp, pale-blue shirt and a bright-red tie. He grasped his cane, though he barely leaned on it. He didn't quite smile but surveyed the assembled crowd with a studied disinterest. He was the king. Everyone was here at his leisure.

Alex couldn't take her eyes off him.

The mayor began to talk about the new initiative that would bring federal money to the Philadelphia–Camden area and was thanking the senator and congressman for their efforts.

"In these partisan times, it's really gratifying to see that two of our most prestigious representatives from the US Senate and House of Representatives have come together for the good of the region," the mayor was saying. "Their bold initiative will bring hundreds jobs to the area. Good-paying jobs!"

The press conference droned on. Congressman Crossman thanked the mayor, Senator Harlan, and some fellow named Eldon Jones, a slim black guy who was the president of Cromoca Partners LLP. That name again. The company that was buying and selling property in the cities of Philadelphia and Camden. Interesting. Alex circled the name in her notes. She took a picture with her cell phone and nudged Santos.

"Make sure you get a few close ups of Eldon Jones," she said.

"Already done." He moved a little closer and aimed. "Tell Danny I got a juicy close-up of his buddy the senator. He looks pretty good."

Alex smiled. She pushed to the front of the crowd. "Senator Harlan," she called. "What's the deal with Cromoca Partners?"

The senator turned and pinned her with his gaze. It was like being hit by a laser, and Alex held up her notebook against her chest in defense.

"Cromoca owns the land we wish to develop, and they are selling it at a very reasonable price. They are working with us toward a greater good, Miss?"

"Burton. Ms. Alex Burton."

"Yes, Ms. Burton. From the *Sentinel*. Because Cromoca has agreed to sell the land at a much-reduced cost to the cities of Camden and Philadelphia, we will be able to build new sites for light manufacturing as well as for condominiums and recreational use."

"But this is prime real estate, sir. Why are they selling it at a reduced price?"

"It is in the public interest," the senator said.

"How much in the public interest? What's the incentive?" As Alex scribbled "cheap land?" in her notebook, the congressman stepped in.

"It sounds a little too good to be true, but it isn't. Cromoca owns land that we wish to buy. They have agreed to sell it, and we will develop it with federal assistance. We share a common goal, which is a stronger Camden and Philadelphia. Cromoca owns other properties in the area that they are planning to develop. If the area improves, it's good for business."

"Why these properties? Where are they located? What condition are they in?"

"They are scattered throughout the area," Eldon James said as he stepped up to the microphone. "Several parcels are in prime locations, particularly those along the Camden waterfront."

"How can Cromoca afford this?"

The congressman smiled. "Cromoca is being a responsible corporate citizen. They aren't selling at a loss. Moreover, this venture is about bringing jobs, restoring our cities, and rebuilding infrastructure, isn't it?"

This made no sense. Nobody sold millions of dollars' worth of land at a very reduced cost just to be a good corporate citizen. Even if they weren't selling at a loss and even if they were developing land nearby, Cromoca wasn't making much profit. Certainly tax breaks were involved, but even so, it didn't add up, not for the amount of property involved. Something was amiss.

"Could you be more specific about where the properties located?" Alex called.

"You'll be getting a list at a later date," Congressman Crossman said.

Alex rocked back on her heels. The congressman reminded her of someone, but she couldn't quite think of whom. He dressed well. He and the senator could have had a dress-off. Those were two high-profiling show ponies.

She started to follow up, but someone from the *Business Journal* cut her off, and after that nobody would acknowledge her. Why would they? The business press was lobbing softballs.

When she got back to her cubicle, she started to put together her piece, but something nagged her. Cromoca Partners LLP. That seemed odd. She was about to put it aside for later, but instead she walked over to Steve Chen's cubicle. The business reporter was still laboring away at some piece about rising interest rates and consumer confidence.

"Steve? I need a favor."

He glanced up and grinned. "I knew this day would come."

She rolled her eyes. He was cute behind his nerd glasses, but ten years too young. "Please. I was down at a press conference with the mayor and some other luminaries—"

"The big Philly–Camden initiative?"

"That's the one." She appreciated a guy who kept up on current events. "A name came up. Cromoca Partners LLP. You ever hear of them?"

He frowned. "Cromoca. Cromoca. Oh, yeah. Been buying up land in Camden and South Jersey."

"They're now selling properties cheap for that new business initiative. Real cheap."

"Did they say where?"

"No, but what would be the incentive?"

Steve frowned. "Well, tax breaks for one. Cromoca might be selling property in return for a cheap long-term lease."

"Why would they do that?"

"The property might be attached to a larger parcel of federal or state land. It might become part of a larger project. Who knows? Also, I don't know what properties are being sold so I don't know what, if any, environmental impact studies have been completed." He looked at her. "You need to find out where these properties are."

"Could properties be sold without environmental impact studies?"

He nodded. "They could. Probably not all the properties, because it would raise too many red flags, but they might sneak in some. They use an 'As Is, Where Is' clause. Say you have a property that might have some problem—maybe PCB contamination—you sell it and set a fast-closing date with an 'As Is, Where Is' clause, which means the people you sell it to buy the property as it is without doing any due diligence and hope for the best. They might get a great piece of land, or they might get a boatload of PCBs."

"Isn't that illegal?"

He shrugged. "The owner can claim ignorance. If you get caught, you're screwed, but otherwise? It's buyer beware."

"So we don't know if Cromoca is planning on selling questionable property to the city."

"They probably won't attempt to do it in Philly. There are just too many rules and regulations. But in Camden? It's a poor city with a majority African American population. Therefore . . ."

"Therefore, nobody gives a shit." Alex sighed. "If you were a realtor, you'd be able to scope out property easily."

"Especially property that looked good on the surface, but you'd have to be careful. As a realtor, you have to disclose everything you know about the property you're selling, or you're liable."

Alex nodded when the magnitude of the Camden–Philly initiative hit her. In a huge project, it would be possible to hide questionable properties for a while given the pace of government. "That's the thing, Steve. You have to disclose everything if you know. What if you claim to know nothing?"

"It's tricky. You might get away with it, or you could get in a lot of trouble. Depends on who you sold to."

Alex let his words sink in.

"Depending on who you sold to, you could get dead."

36

Kevin was already seated at a window table at the Famous Fourth Street Deli when he saw Ted Eliot turn onto Bainbridge and find a parking spot at the end of the block. Kevin had chosen the place because it was a popular eatery among tourists and those who enjoyed giant sandwiches filled with pastrami or turkey or ham so huge you'd have to unhinge your jaw like a snake to take a bite. That guaranteed it would be crowded.

Danny had introduced him to Famous Deli. It was a political hangout on election day, but Kevin didn't care about that. Let Danny socialize with the politicians and their egos. He lived in the real world and dealt with the sad problems that entailed. Kevin eyed the pastrami on rye that a waiter plopped down at the next table and decided that would be his lunch. Fuck the diet.

Kevin turned back to the window. Eliot had come alone as far as Kevin could tell. He strolled toward the restaurant with his hands in his pockets, trying to appear nonchalant, but Kevin knew that behind those mirrored shades, Eliot was scoping out the area. That's what you did when you were entering unfriendly territory. He watched Eliot make his way past the takeout aisle and move toward the back of the restaurant. A waiter led him to the table.

"Detective Ryan," Eliot said.

Kevin looked up. "Detective. Have a seat."

"I only came today because I felt like I owed you an explanation."

"Oh?" Kevin almost smiled. This promised to be interesting. "Would it have anything to do with the late Greg Moss?"

"It would."

"Is there any reason you didn't say anything at the beginning of this investigation?"

"Like what?"

"Like you might have information that would be useful to solving Greg Moss's goddamn murder."

Eliot made a sour face, and they both paused to order coffee and sandwiches when the waiter reappeared. Kevin ordered his pastrami while Eliot went for the turkey breast.

"I knew Greg. I didn't say anything because it didn't seem to be relevant."

"It didn't seem to be relevant?" Kevin held up his hand. "Don't tell me everyone knew Greg Moss, because I'll call bullshit on you. Tell me what's really going on. You dress like you stepped out of some New York showroom. You got on a real expensive watch I had to look up. Those shoes of yours are handmade Italian jobs. What the fuck are you doing playin' police?"

"I'm not playing at anything. I became a cop because of my father."

"Your father was a cop?"

Eliot shook his head. "My father is Congressman George Crossman."

"Jesus Christ. Are you kidding?" Even Kevin had heard of George Crossman, the majority whip. Was this going to turn out to be another one of those kinky sex cases after all? Danny sure could pick 'em. "What's with the name?"

"I took my mom's maiden name after the divorce. She went back to New York to get on with her causes."

"So why aren't you using your family connections to do something more lucrative than police work?"

"Yeah, I often ask myself that. I could have. I won't bore you with my good intentions, but it just didn't work out."

Kevin digested that information as the waiter set down two cups of coffee. It didn't compute. Here was a guy who had everything. Money, looks, connections, and he chose to become a cop. Who did that kind of thing?

"I don't understand. How you go from being you to being a Camden cop?"

Eliot gave him a bitter smile and held up his hands in a weary gesture. Kevin had often seen Danny use the same gesture. It was somewhere between a shrug and a dismissal, as if he was tired of trying to contemplate the answer, or maybe for him, there was no answer. Whatever had driven Ted Eliot away from his father and into the Camden PD wasn't something he cared to discuss, which made it very, very personal indeed.

"Why don't you ask something relevant?" Eliot said.

"Okay. How did you meet Greg?"

Eliot poured some cream into his cup and stirred. Delaying. Kevin watched patiently. At this point, it was important not to jump on this guy. Let him feel comfortable. Kevin could almost see the weight pressing down on Eliot.

"I needed a house. Greg was recommended. It wasn't anything big or secret. He knew who I was. Knew I wouldn't have trouble getting a mortgage, that sort of thing. He used to throw parties for privileged clients."

"So he knew you were a cop?"

Eliot looked out of the window. "Yeah. And he knew who my parents were."

Kevin nodded. Eliot had more to say, and Kevin didn't want to let on that he was fishing here. "So did he ask you for favors?"

"I'm not like my father, okay? King of the Hill? Master of Favors? Or my brother and sister, for that matter. I was a cop, but a good one, you know? I took it seriously. Doesn't get more serious than Camden. Then I got hurt on the job. Screwed up my back—I won't bore you with the details."

Kevin was trying to work out what Eliot wasn't saying. He knew how his story ended. It was a quick slide from popping one oxy to numb the pain to gulping five or six or ten a day. Once you couldn't get enough pills, where did you go? Kevin didn't want to hear the story of Eliot's sad life. He had enough sad stories of his own. He just needed to know what was relevant.

"So you developed a habit?"

"I was in pain," Eliot said. "I fell down a flight of steps and cracked a vertebra in my back. The doctors thought it was just a herniated disc. You know, rest for a few days and it'll get better. And it kind of did. But then I really screwed it up it chasing a perp."

"So you were taking pills?"

"It was the only way to manage the pain, but the pills weren't enough. I . . . I just . . . it got bad. Greg said he could help. I don't even remember how it all happened. I just ran into him, and he was like, 'You look awful. What's the matter?' And I ended up at one of his parties."

"And what? You started using?"

"Not much at first. Just enough to get by, but I saw a lot of shit go down. Prostitutes, drugs. I looked the other way, yeah. Because no one was getting hurt. It was all consenting adults. I mean, I was fucked up."

Kevin nodded. He did understand the daily parade of horrors that slowly pulverized you. He'd looked the other way not so long ago to protect his family. It still made him sick. Against his will, he felt for Eliot. Somehow he doubted that his meeting with Greg Moss had been an accident. "So what was your drug?"

"Heroin. Didn't mainline. Shot up between my toes. I thought I had it under control. Just enough to keep myself, I don't know—what's that Pink Floyd song—'Comfortably Numb'? That was me. It was pretty much a nightmare, but I got into a program. Got straight. My father pulled strings. It's the only time I ever asked him for a favor. I'm not proud of it, but I've stayed straight since."

"Did you stay in contact with Greg?"

"Just marginally. He understood. He was fine with it. He wasn't a pusher. I guess more like a facilitator. I don't know. He was a decent guy. He drove me to goddamn rehab."

"But a dealer." A dealer who knew all about Ted Eliot's addiction and probably had proof.

"He wasn't a dealer, but his partner was. Maybe more of a trafficker."

"You know his partner?"

"No."

"This person was involved with Cromoca Partners as well?"

"I don't know. I only know Greg was into different things."

"And then he died."

Eliot paused and took a breath, and Kevin saw something in that pause. It shifted before he could put a name to it, but Kevin filed it away. He'd consider it later.

"And I catch the case," Eliot was saying. "At first I thought no big deal, but then I thought maybe your brother was investigating because he knew something about Greg and his parties. I thought maybe someone killed Greg to shut him up."

"But now you don't?"

"I never ran into any of these dead guys at any of his parties."

Kevin slid him a photo of Barb Capozzi. "How about her? Does she look familiar?"

Eliot picked up the photo, his face turning pale. "Barb? She's part of this? I know she catered the parties. She was Greg's ex."

"Is that all?"

"Let's just say she was good at recruiting."

"She brought in the girls."

Eliot shrugged. "Barb was one of those people who had connections. She and Greg both. She just knew how to bring people together. Get clients what they wanted."

"They were dealing a lot of dope?"

"Not exactly dealing, but if Greg was closing a deal with a major developer, he might spring for a casino weekend and top it off with a party at his shore house in Wildwood. Greg didn't live large on paper. He was careful, but he had money. A lot of money. Most of his property was tied up in LLPs and holding companies that were in offshore accounts."

"So Greg the Saint wasn't such a saint."

"Greg was a genuinely nice guy, but he was a player. I'm sure of that."

"And Barb?"

"I don't know." Eliot shook his head. "Barb catered parties, but she wasn't a dealer. She didn't have anything to do with the drugs. No, Greg had a partner. They went way back."

"Back as far as high school?"

"At least."

"But you don't have a clue who he is? He never made an appearance?"

"If he did, Greg never introduced us. But whoever he is, he's big time."

"If this got out, you could be in a world of hurt," Kevin said.

"In the larger scheme, that doesn't really matter, does it?" Eliot gave him a tired smile. "If this guy is a high school buddy, your brother may be the only person who can ID him."

37

The morning was barely over, and the day had already turned surreal. Danny couldn't get the image of Michelle out of his mind. Whoever had killed her wanted to make sure that Danny always remembered her as a victim. That creep had stalked her online and harassed her.

There was a certain petty vindictiveness to it that reminded him of high school bullies and their chosen prey. The relentless taunting. The pack mentality that led tormentors to swoop in on their victims like rabid animals and tear them apart, emotionally, if not physically.

For Valentine's Day, Jenna had given him a copy of her opus, *Jenny's First Love*, which she'd signed and bound in a red cover. When she'd handed it to him in the middle of the cafeteria and kissed him to the jeers of Frank Greer and his band of cohorts, Danny had stood, unable to move. He'd spent high school trying to fly under the radar only to have Jenna shine a bright spotlight on him. But he'd pulled on his armor.

He took *Jenny's First Love* to his lunch table and read passages aloud in a breathless voice that sent his friends into spasms of laughter. It was only after lunch when he saw Jenna in the hall that the weight of his own cruelty smacked him.

"I think you should give this to someone who deserves it," he'd said, holding the book out to her. He didn't want to tell her he felt like shit.

She'd surprised him by smiling. "Oh, Danny. Aren't you sweet! You do deserve this. I wouldn't have written it if it weren't for you." She'd squeezed his arm and walked away.

Danny had kept that damn book, though he had no idea what had happened to it. Poor Jenna. She deserved better than to die like a trapped animal in a house fire.

Now Danny headed for the city morgue. When he'd covered the crime beat, he'd spent a fair amount of time hanging around the morgue. Bodies had never bothered him until he'd been forced to identify Beth and Conor after the accident in Chester County. Sometimes he still dreamed of Conor lying still and white on the table. Sometimes the lingering odor of formalin seemed to coat his skin and fill his nostrils until he thought he was drowning.

He parked and took a few deep breaths, forcing air into his lungs, ignoring the shredding pain in his chest, before venturing into the building.

Rita Perry sat waiting, perched on the edge of her seat, her eyes dry, her mouth compressed in a grim line. She gripped her purse against her lap and stared at the door leading into the main autopsy room. For the moment, her police minder seemed to have disappeared.

"Mrs. Perry. Rita," he said. "I'm so sorry."

"They said you were with her," Rita said. Her face was expressionless and gray.

"She wanted to talk to me. I met her at the Ritz Carlton."

"Why didn't you stay away from her?" The words hissed out like steam, burning him with their intensity.

"I—she asked me. How could I say no?"

He wished he could roll time backward, but that was impossible. The "if onlys" of his life had grown into a mountain of refuse. All those bright, shiny promises lay stripped and abandoned.

Rita's eyes filled with tears. "She was so happy. She had the perfect life."

Maybe Michelle *had* found the perfect life. She'd seemed so brittle when he'd met her, so on edge, but he understood that. She was a South Philly girl who had cast herself into the perfect Connecticut housewife and mother. She'd earned her degree from a prestigious school and had a high-achieving husband and an attractive family. The American Dream. She hadn't wanted to jeopardize that.

Danny knew all about that dream.

"Rita, she called me. She was afraid."

Rita bent over, small strangled noises coming from her throat as she fought to hold back her tears, and Danny sat beside her. He put his arm around her, and she beat her fists against his chest until the bitter, silent tears finally came.

A policewoman stepped into the room. She looked at Danny in alarm for a moment, but Danny waved her off as he held Rita and rocked her as if she were a child.

"My baby," Rita said. "My beautiful baby."

"I know."

"Will you take me home? That policewoman was going to, but I don't want her. At least you knew Michelle," she said, and he nodded.

"Yes. Of course."

The policewoman came to take Rita to identify Michelle's body. When Rita returned, her shoulders were slumped, but she had stopped crying. She twisted the tissue in her hands as if she were strangling it.

"They cleaned her up and combed her hair, so you couldn't see where she hit her head so much." Rita's lips were white, and her body trembled like she had palsy. "She looked asleep."

Danny put his arm around Rita's quaking shoulders. "I'm glad." He knew it didn't matter what they had done to Michelle. He'd seen her lying on the floor of the bathroom. It would have taken a miracle to make her look like she was sleeping. Maybe grief allowed Rita to imagine Michelle as she had been, to reassemble her. Danny hoped so. The policewoman handed him a cup of water, and he offered it to Rita. "Let's sit down for a minute so you can get your bearings."

"I don't want to sit anymore. Not here. Not in this place. I don't want to think about her in this place."

"No. I know you don't. I'll take you home."

Danny drove Rita back to South Philly and sat with her in her spotless living room. This house, just two blocks from his old home, was a shrine to Michelle.

Her high school graduation photo sat next to Rita's Blessed Mother statue along with Michelle's baby shoes, which had been lovingly dipped in bronze. The flowered walls were decorated with plaster plates featuring Michelle's handprints and a succession of photographs from birth to high school graduation. A portrait of Michelle on her wedding day with her new nose and blonder hair sat behind the blue sofa. Danny shuddered a little.

He was surprised that Rita had bothered to keep any pictures of the two of them together, but she had kept a whole album of senior prom photographs that sat on the coffee table.

"You kept this," he said.

"Well, you did make a nice couple at prom," Rita said. "She was very happy that night." She peeled a photograph out of the book. "Here, you take one. So you remember."

It gave him a peculiar jolt to see his younger self in his rented black tux. He was looking at a familiar stranger with a baby face and a shy smile. Would Conor have looked like that when he got older, or would he have developed his mother's sharper features? Danny stared down at the photograph, his chest aching. Michelle had worn that white gown with gold beads to the prom that night, and she really had looked like an angel. If she'd hurt him, it didn't matter. He had loved her, adored her, and it broke his heart all over again. He spent a few long hours with Rita until her sister arrived, and then he slipped away, promising to come to the funeral.

Lights had stopped flickering in front of his eyes by the time he drove down the expressway, but his head felt like a kickball. He drove slowly, watching the taillights stream red in front of him, relieved that traffic was light. By the time he reached his house, he almost tripped on the envelope on the back steps. He tossed it on the kitchen table, threw the dead bolt, and grabbed a bottle of water.

Danny wanted drugs. He popped a foil packet, knowing it was too late. The gremlins in his head were wielding pickaxes tonight. He grabbed two Valium and swallowed them. There was a bottle of something on the counter. He couldn't make out the label, but he figured it was for pain. He swallowed three pills and pulled out an ice pack. He still had syringes of Imitrex, and he rooted through the kitchen cabinets, but he couldn't find the cartridges. Danny wanted to ram his head through the refrigerator or lay it on the chopping board and hack it off.

For a moment he had a brief vision of Smokes Winston strung out on heroin. Strung out but mostly pain free. He could use a speed ball right now. He had other painkillers upstairs, but his legs didn't seem to be working. Danny stumbled into the living room and fell onto the sofa. He dropped the ice pack on the floor but couldn't find it in the dark. It didn't matter.

Something was definitely wrong with him. His brain wasn't working because his heart was broken beyond repair. He was everyone's friend and nobody's. Maybe when Conor died, he took the last spark of real feeling Danny had to give. Christ, maybe he needed to start drinking. A bottle of scotch with a morphine chaser.

If Alex were around, he would have talked to her. He needed her, and that had to end. He wasn't going to be responsible for breaking up her marriage and ruining her life. Maybe she'd already reached that conclusion on her own and had run away as fast as she could.

Danny could still hear Rita crying, "My baby. My beautiful baby." Or maybe he was the one who was crying as he curled into himself, lost on his own dark shore.

The pain in his head began to recede in tiny increments, and a blanket of warmth spread over him. Somewhere close by Conor whispered, "I'm here, Dad. I'm here."

"Please," Danny said. "Let me come with you."

Conor leaned close. "You will."

For those that love are sad. Someone wrote that, but he couldn't remember who anymore. Danny let himself slip into the tide and wash away.

38

Alex headed out Route 30 West toward Lancaster. She'd thought about inviting Danny to join her, but Rachel Jeffords had asked her to come alone. Rachel had said she felt more comfortable talking to another woman.

Alex understood.

She'd deliberately left the packet of information about Cromoca Partners on Danny's doorstep last night without bothering to knock, and she'd left at eight this morning because she knew Danny was not an early riser. She'd stopped at Nudie's for breakfast and indulged. Usually it was coffee and yogurt, but today Alex had devoured a short stack of gingerbread pancakes with a side of bacon. She'd just finished her last bite when she remembered she'd given up bacon a year ago.

She'd eaten Danny's favorite breakfast item. What the hell was wrong with her?

Danny and she had always gotten along, but that was friendship. Okay, maybe they did understand each other well enough to complete each other's thoughts, but only sometimes. He did have those blue eyes. Sad eyes, like they'd seen a lot and understood pain. He had a way of looking at you like you like your story was essential to him, which was, of course, why people liked talking to him. But hell, who didn't like a man who wanted to listen?

And the man could kiss. It wasn't the weed. Her toes curled when she thought about his mouth on hers. You could tell a lot by the way a man kissed—whether he shoved his tongue in or teased you or found that perfect combination. And damn, if someone hadn't been there watching them—and maybe it was just some kid—she would have ended up in his bed. No doubt about that.

Would she have regretted it? Well, hell, not the sex. That would have been great, but there were other considerations.

She didn't know if she was ready to throw away her life with Sam. Twelve years was a long time, and they were mostly good years. She liked to think that Sam was yin to her yang. If she was all flash and heat, he was cool and serene. She liked having that safe place with him. Didn't she?

Miami hung between them. Sam had been trying to save a man's life and had been arrested for his efforts. She had a right to challenge the fat cop who dragged him out of the bathroom in cuffs. She had a right to scream at the cop who slid his hand between her legs, checking for weapons. Sam believed she'd made a bad situation worse. She believed he'd allowed himself to be bullied. Now they stewed in their unspoken anger. They directed it at each other. They couldn't seem to find a middle ground.

There was the baby issue, too. Sam wanted a son. She wasn't ready, and she wasn't sure she ever would be. She could barely manage herself, much less another human.

"Daniel and his wife had a child, and they both maintained their careers," Sam had said.

"He had a column. It's different. I'm just a reporter. And they had a nanny."

"So hire a nanny."

She still wasn't ready.

She and Sam lived like polite strangers, saying all the right things without speaking any truths and dancing around each other instead of moving in rhythm.

Alex turned off a side road that ran along the Susquehanna River and pulled over to the shoulder to check her directions.

Thick, dark woods spread out on both sides of the road, though she could see the glint of the water here and there. She shivered a little. The trees were tall enough to blot out most of the sun.

She considered sending a text to Danny but figured she'd surprise him. After all, this might prove to be nothing, but if she found out something big, well, she just wanted to see his face. That smile. She shouldn't have needed his approval so much, but approval came her way grudgingly these days. Alex continued down the road until she came to a mailbox shaped like a rooster. It had a large number four painted on it in green, and she made a right onto the long gravel driveway.

The woods seemed to swallow her, and she stopped. Maybe she would send that text. She held up her phone. No service. That was stupid. She considered turning around, but shook off her unease. Rachel Jeffords was a sixty-year-old woman. How threatening could she be?

At the end of the driveway, a dark-green ranch house squatted. A flagstone path decorated on each side with bright-red ceramic toadstools and little brown toads twisted from the driveway. Resin elves peeked out from behind a large pine tree, and plastic daisy pinwheels of bright-pink, yellow, and purple protruded from the ground and spun lazily in the slight breeze.

Alex blinked. Rachel Jeffords's home was peculiar but whimsical. Nothing she couldn't handle. She pulled up in front of the house and parked. As she unbuckled her seat belt, she saw the curtains in the front room twitch. Alex paused as the hair on the back of her neck prickled. She turned off her cell phone and shoved it deep inside the cushions of the passenger's seat. If something happened—and she didn't expect anything would— the cops could trace her using the phone's GPS. It wasn't the first time she'd done it.

She hesitated a moment longer. This was silly. There was nothing here but an older woman with a story to tell. Alex got out of the car and headed to the house.

39

Danny opened his left and then his right eye and then shut them against the brightness of the sun slanting through the windows. For a moment, he tried to remember where he was. His head felt detached from his body, and he reached up to make sure he was still in one piece. He started to push himself up and had to lie back when nausea seized him. Jesus, what the hell had he taken last night?

He sat up more slowly this time and assessed. He'd been sleeping on the living room sofa wrapped in a throw. Danny retrieved an icepack from the floor and wandered into the kitchen, trying to determine what had happened last night beside the headache.

It was a jumble of images, none of which made much sense. He'd dreamed of Conor, a more grown-up version of Conor. His mind tried to fill in a face, but he could only see a shadow hovering over him. A dream brought on by his night with Rita Perry, and Christ, it was a week from Conor's birthday. The drugs pushed all those memories to the surface.

Danny couldn't remember what he had taken, except it was a lot. Maybe he was going to end up like Smokes Winston. He needed a shower and some coffee.

A manila envelope lay half open on the kitchen table. He glanced down at the papers spilling out of the envelope. Information on Cromoca. Had he opened it? He must have started to look at it and then given up. Now he saw there were site maps outlining properties acquired by Cromoca in the past fifteen years. The acquisitions were mainly in New Jersey, but there were a number in South Philadelphia, including the land where the Shamrock used to be located, a large parcel in his old neighborhood where a new townhouse development had been built, and several parcels in Northern Liberties.

Was it significant? Possibly.

He checked his phone. One text from Kevin: *Call me. ASAP.*

Danny looked around on the kitchen counter as he dialed. What the hell had he taken? He just saw the usual. The Maxalt and Valium. He could have sworn he took something else, but his memory was wrapped in cotton. Maybe it was the pain. Maybe he was losing his mind.

"Ryan," Kevin said.

"It's me."

"Listen, I'm on my way out, but I want you to do me a favor and stay the hell home today."

"Somebody's in a good mood." Danny poured water into the coffeemaker.

"I'm not shitting you, Danny. At least stay away from Ted Eliot."

"I wasn't planning to hang out in Camden today, but okay. Will you tell me why?"

Silence.

"Come on, Kevin. Don't make me guess."

Kevin sighed, and Danny could almost see him reaching for his Maalox. "Ted Eliot's old man is Congressman George Crossman. And George Crossman is asshole buddies with—"

"Robert Harlan."

"So maybe Greg Moss's death had more to do with land deals than high school. I don't know for sure, but for now, promise me you won't go near Eliot on your own."

"You think he's involved."

Kevin didn't answer right away. At length, he said, "I think there's a possibility he knows more than he's saying."

"Okay. I'll stay away from Ted Eliot." It was an easy promise to make. For now. He had other leads to pursue. It was after nine, and he needed to get moving.

*

Danny drove up the Lincoln Drive, passing under the span of the Henry Avenue Bridge, its great Roman arches looming over the twisting road. In the bright sun, the bridge seemed more picturesque than threatening, but Danny could never drive under the suicide bridge without a chill passing through him. Today it was more like a deep shudder.

He headed to photographer Al Frederick's house in Mt. Airy, the middle-class section of Northwest Philly, known for its mixed-race, liberal population. Not as upper middle class as Chestnut Hill, its immediate neighbor to the north, nor as working poor as Germantown, its neighbor to the south, Mt. Airy struck just the right balance on paper, if not in fact.

"Say it out loud, we're liberal and proud," Kevin would always say as he drove through Mt. Airy on his way home to the more working class Roxborough. These days, Danny didn't comment. It seemed Kevin carried a heavy load of disdain for people of all political persuasions. He was happiest when he could throw himself into his lounge chair and retreat from the world. Middle age was hitting Kevin hard, and it wasn't pretty to watch.

Danny found Al Frederick's large twin home not far from the Jewish Community Center. It was a slightly dilapidated, three-story affair surrounded by a wooden fence and overgrown shrubs. A pot of bleeding hearts hung from the porch, and the scent of lily of the valley filled the air. Danny rang the doorbell and waited.

"Hold on. Hold on."

Danny heard the familiar raspy voice coming from the side of the house before Al appeared. A tall, thin fellow with a shock of white hair and sharp dark eyes that peered at him from under deep-gray brows, he walked with the rolling gait of a man who had spent his life in the saddle. As far as Danny knew, Al had been born and raised in the city, probably in this house, and had never come closer to a horse than an old western movie. Spook, hell. Al looked more like a goblin. He raised the Leica hanging around his neck to snap Danny's picture.

"Daniel Ryan. I can't believe it," he said. "I thought you'd moved on from these parts."

He held out a hand, and Danny shook it. "How are you, Al?"

"Can't complain. I take pictures of nature now. It's a little quieter." Al patted his camera. "Come on. Darkroom's in the back. You want coffee? Soda?"

"I'm fine," Danny said.

"You look like you could use a shot of bourbon."

Danny followed Al around the side of the house to a back entrance and then down a set of cracked concrete stairs to the basement. The front half of it had been converted to a darkroom, but the back half was filled with glass cases containing Al's beloved camera collection, which included a Leica I from 1927. That camera alone was probably worth millions, yet it sat in the basement of this run-down home in Mt. Airy next to a set of carefully labeled flat file drawers.

Over the years, Al had photographed the faces the city preferred to forget: the junkies and homeless, the denizens of seedy bars and strip clubs, the beaten and abused. The murdered. The faces that brought Danny's stories to life.

On the walls hung a variety of photographs Danny stopped to examine. Some of them were all too familiar. Al had photographed the Sandman victims—or as much as the police would allow. The sites, the eerie aftermaths where the victims' ghosts walked. A blossom of blood on the sidewalk where Jane Doe Five had been discovered. It glistened in the sun and trickled down to the gutter—beautiful and horrific.

Al had a distinctive way of framing a shot. He'd snapped a series of photographs of Amy Johanson leaping to her death off the Henry Avenue Bridge, her fragile body arced like an acrobat against the cloudless sky all the way down to the crumpled heap of the girl lying broken in the rocky creek, her blood rushing away in the muddy water. Danny had never seen the whole series before, and he stared at the photographs in a sort of horrified fascination. Amy Johanson had been Danny's first feature at the *Sentinel,* and Al's last three shots were of him leaning over the bridge, his face contorted in a helpless cry of horror and despair. Al had used a zoom lens, and the photos should have been out of focus, but they weren't. Danny looked away and clenched his fists. He had no desire to see more bodies.

"Those bother you?" Al asked.

"It was a long time ago," he said, like he didn't mind Al stealing a bit of his soul.

"It was an ugly scene. You did a nice piece. Front page, if I remember right."

"How do you know where to stand? How to frame it?"

Al shrugged. "I don't always. Sometimes I'm just in the right place. Most everyone was on the bridge that day. I went down below. If she hadn't jumped, I wouldn't have gotten those shots."

"So you got lucky."

"I generally guessed where to get the best shot right more than I guessed wrong." Al held up a folder of photographs, and Danny wondered whether all those great shots ate a little of Al's soul. "Here, take a look. Those pictures you wanted of the Jeffords house fire. These are the best of the bunch, but I have more." He spread them out on a light table.

Danny came over, and Al handed him a magnifying glass.

"This is the best shot. I enlarged the crowds. I can go larger if you need me to, but we're going to start to lose detail."

Danny looked over the photo in its normal view. In it, a firefighter consoled Mrs. Jeffords. Her head bowed down, and his arm curled around her. Her left hand clutched at her turquoise dress, but in the shot, it was slightly blurred. Too bad. He wanted to get a clearer view of her ring. It looked like a Claddagh ring. Danny wasn't sure it mattered, but it was a detail.

Behind the figures in the photograph, three homes burned, and a crowd was gathered on the sidewalk. Danny stared at Mrs. Jeffords. What was the worst thing in the world that could happen to a parent? Losing a child. No question there.

Danny laid the enlarged crowd shots around the photograph. He wasn't sure who or what he was looking for. Al took these photos in the time before Andy's citizens with cellphones took over. People looked stunned, curious, and unfamiliar. Then he saw the face at the edge of the crowd.

"Al, can you blow just this part up?" Danny held up the photo.

Al looked at it and nodded. "The resolution is going to decrease as it gets larger, but I can play with it. You got something?"

"Maybe."

The face in the crowd belonged to Frank Greer.

40

"Mrs. Jeffords, thank you so much for meeting me."
Alex reached out to grasp the pudgy hand of the
woman before her. Short and round, Rachel Jeffords had the pale skin of a person who didn't go out in the sun
coupled with long dark hair and light-blue eyes. She was surprisingly youthful for a woman near sixty, but Alex figured if
you avoided the sun and hid in your house, your skin probably
would remain in decent shape. Rachel had squeezed herself into
a bright-orange spandex top and white skirt about three sizes too
small. Her body shivered like a Jell-O mold when she walked.

Alex tried not to stare as she followed Rachel into the green
ranch house. The floors were covered in dark oak, and the overstuffed furniture was pale green and yellow. A mustard-yellow
rug covered the floor. Almost every inch of the dark-green walls
was covered with embroidered pictures of flowers and kittens
and puppies, and Alex could hear the scrabbling of who-knewwhat creatures on the roof. In the corner, a cuckoo clock ticked,
and dust motes floated in the floral-scented air.

"Thank you for coming," Rachel said in a soft, girlish voice.
"You came a long way. Let me get you something to drink. Iced
tea? Soda? Water?"

"Iced tea is fine. Thanks."

"I bet you don't eat a thing," Rachel said.

"Oh, I eat a lot. I just can't sit still," Alex said, thinking of the pancakes she had eaten earlier. "I guess I burn it off." She hoped that was the right thing to say. "You sure do look young, Mrs. Jeffords. You have such great skin."

Rachel was like fresh bread dough. She was white and pasty and threatened to pop out of that orange top at any moment. Alex forced a giant smile. She needed to stop thinking.

"Aren't you sweet," Rachel tittered and batted her eyelashes. "Let me go get refreshments."

Alex took a breath and wandered around the living room. She was too hyped. She needed to relax. Pay attention. Here and there were photographs: a baby in a white christening gown, a dark-haired boy of maybe two with fat cheeks and big blue eyes, the same boy at five in a soccer uniform, and older in a succession of Christmas photos. In the bookcase sat piles of typewritten pages, a bunch of romance novels, and at least twenty copies of Danny's book on class in America. Weird. That book had come out almost ten years ago.

A pink, cloth-covered photo album sat in the bookcase, and Alex pulled it out. She nearly dropped it. On the front page was a photograph of Jenna packed into a scarlet satin prom gown and next to her stood much younger Danny in a white tuxedo. Something looked off about the photograph, and then Alex realized that Danny's face had been photoshopped onto another boy's body.

Jenna had been slimmed, but the result had twisted her body out of proportion. Her face was thinner, but her head seemed too small for her body. In her yearbook photo, her eyes looked sleepy; here they seemed too wide and the small mole under her left eye was gone. She clutched a bouquet of red carnations and white baby's breath, and Alex noted the gold Claddagh ring she wore on her left hand, the heart facing outward. Jenna had been substantially altered, but the swan never emerged.

Alex stared at the photo. Something about it bothered her. Not just the twisted body. Something . . .

When she heard footsteps, Alex shoved the album back into place.

Rachel appeared in the doorway with a tray of beautifully iced sugar cookies, Tastykake Butterscotch Krimpets, and two glasses of iced tea. Lemons and sugar packets were neatly arranged beside the glasses. It was the picture of creepy domestic tranquility. Alex wondered what went on in Rachel's mind.

Why the hell has she constructed some fantasy about her daughter and Danny?

"I don't get so much company these days," Rachel said. "Please sit."

Alex perched on a chair. "Your little boy is adorable," she said. "Your son?"

Rachel nodded. "He's my sweetheart." She paused. "I don't have much family left."

Should I ask about the father? "I thought Jenna was an only child. I must have got my facts wrong."

Rachel blushed, and her mouth turned down slightly. "His father and I haven't been in touch, but that's about to change. I hope."

"I'm sorry. It's not my business. I'm really here about Jenna. I hate to come out here and put you through all that again," Alex said. "It's just that we think Jenna's death might be part of something larger."

"What do you mean?"

"Well, could Jenna have seen something in the neighborhood? Would anyone have had reason to do harm to her?"

"Jenna? Oh, no. Everyone loved her."

Alex cleared her throat. She wasn't sure everybody loved Jenna, but Rachel was entitled to her reconstructed memory. "I'm looking into a development company called Cromoca Partners. They might have had something to do with the fire that killed Jenna. Does that sound familiar?"

"Cromoca? It sounds like a dance. I'm doing the Cromoca!" Rachel giggled and waved her arms. "I never heard of them."

"I'm working with another reporter. We're trying to trace Cromoca Partners." Alex took a sip of tea. This place was strange as all hell. Something about that photograph. Something about that little boy. Something about Rachel. Alex's mouth felt dry, and she swallowed more tea. She was sitting in the nuthouse with the Head Walnut. This was going to be harder than she'd anticipated.

"Oh," Rachel said. "I thought you were working alone. May I ask who you're working with?"

Alex took another swallow. "It's actually a weird coincidence. You might even remember him. Dan Ryan? I think Jenna went to school with him."

Rachel's face softened. "Danny." She leaned closer. "My Jenna was very close with Danny Ryan."

"Was she?" Alex considered her options. "Well, Danny remembers Jenna very fondly. He said she wanted to be a writer."

"Isn't that sweet? He remembers that? I always knew there was something special between them. You know he was her first love. Isn't that amazing?"

Alex grasped her glass in both hands and then gulped the rest of her tea. "Her first love? That is interesting."

"Oh, yes. He took her to her senior prom. They were a beautiful couple."

"Well, Danny and I, we, uh, didn't discuss that. We're, like I said, trying to get some information about Cromoca and Jenna's death, of course."

What the hell is this? That wasn't Danny in the original photo. Alex was pretty sure Danny Ryan had never worn a white tux in his life—even to a high school prom. The kid in that photo was built along square lines with thick, short-fingered hands. Danny was slim-built with narrow hips and fine bones, and his hands—she knew all about his hands. Alex took a breath when the room seemed to tilt for a moment. Her own hands shook when she placed the glass back on the coaster. For a moment the glass seemed to split into two before it came back together, and she blinked.

"I'm sorry. Did I make you uncomfortable? Would you like more tea?"

"I—no, thanks. I—" Alex stared at Rachel and tried to force her mind to work. It made no sense. Something was wrong. Rachel seemed far away, her voice traveling down a great tin funnel. She stared at her. At the Claddagh ring on her left hand, the heart turned outward.

"Do you like my ring?" Rachel asked.

"It's very pretty."

"My first and only love gave it to me, but you knew that, didn't you?" Rachel's voice seemed to be slowing down, or maybe there was something wrong with her hearing. Alex just nodded.

"Are you all right, dear? You look pale."

"I'm . . . fine." Alex pushed on the arm of the chair, trying to stand, but her legs buckled beneath her.

"Oh, my," Rachel said. "I think you'd better have a rest."

No. No. No. Alex didn't want a rest. She wanted to get the hell out, but she couldn't force her legs to obey. She sank down on her knees. The cuckoo clock loomed over her, ticking, but it sounded like it was scolding her: *tsk, tsk, tsk.* The yellow rug smelled vaguely of mold and something more unpleasant. Alex watched Rachel's head bob over her like a giant party balloon.

Something was wrong with the picture.

"You. You're . . ."

"Goodnight, Alex."

Rachel held the tray in her hands, and Alex heard a rush of air before it crashed against her face.

41

Danny sped up Delaware Avenue, two photographs on the seat beside him. This afternoon, he needed to confront Frank before the bastard disappeared. Alex was right: this tangle of circumstance went back to Jenna Jeffords's murder. Somehow. He just hadn't quite figured out the how and the why, but he would. Frank was going to help him—whether he wanted to or not.

When he pulled into the scrapyard, Frank's red Caddy sat in its space, and Danny gave it the finger. "Scrap you, you bastard," he said.

He marched into the office. "I want to see Frank. Now," he said to the receptionist. Her mouth dropped open in a red O, and he walked past her. "Just tell him I'm here."

"You can't. He'll be pissed," she called after him.

"I don't care."

The door at the end of the hall opened one second before he reached it, and Frank stood glaring at him. "What the fuck do you want?"

"Answers, Frank!" Danny held up the photographs. "What were you doing at Jenna Jeffords house the day it blew up?"

*

Frank waved Danny into his office, his face a mask of disgust. "Jenna Jeffords? Are you shitting me?"

Danny pointed to the photo. "Jenna Jeffords. Her house blew up. Remember? And look who's in the crowd."

"And based on a photograph of me in a crowd, you think I blew up her house? Jesus Christ, Ryan. It's a good thing you didn't pursue law as a career." Frank sat down behind his desk. He leaned back in his chair, trying to look unconcerned, but Danny saw the way he clenched and unclenched his fists. The muscle under Frank's left eye looked like it was pulsing to an electric current.

"Jenna Jeffords. Why would I want to kill that cow?" Frank said.

"I don't know. Why would you? Come on, Frank. Tell me what happened at that party. It was over twenty years ago."

"As I recall, Greg threw a party, and a lot of people showed up."

"And they're getting killed off." Danny sat on the edge of Frank's desk. "Do you want to be the next victim?"

"Do you?" Frank leaned forward. "Get the fuck off my desk. Take your goddamn photos and get out of my office."

"Not until you tell me about that party."

"Fuck you and the party."

Danny took a breath. They were going in circles, and it needed to end. "Not until you tell me what happened to Jenna at the party."

It was a guess, but Danny could see he had hit a nerve. Frank turned ashen, but he pointed to the door. "Get out."

"Did you kill her to shut her up?"

Frank was on his feet. "I didn't kill her. I lived on the next block, you moron. My mom still lives right there. Why the hell would I kill her?"

"Because something happened at Greg's house!"

"Nothing happened!"

"Yeah, Frank, it did. Because people are dying, and every one of them was at that party."

"The only thing happened at Greg's house was Jumbo Jen pulled a train. Okay? You got it? She wanted to get laid. She. Wanted. It."

Danny grabbed the edge of the desk and leaned closer. He wanted to kill Frank Greer. "I don't believe you."

"Oh, no? Well, you know who she was hoping would be the caboose? You know who she was calling for? 'Where's Danny? I want Danny.'"

"You're a lying piece of shit."

Frank reached across the desk, grabbed Danny by the shirt, and pulled him close. Danny could smell the metallic grit that coated him and tried to pull away, but Frank shook him like he was made of rags.

"You goddamn self-righteous asshole!" Ribbons of spit hit Danny in the face as Frank's eyes turned flat and dead, but Danny saw a horrible sort of truth there. Frank's version of the truth. "She was hoping for you, Danny Depp, you fuckin' pretty boy faggot. You with your goddamn Barbie doll wife and little clone son. It used to make me sick to see you in the paper, you useless piece of shit. They probably killed themselves to get away from you."

Frank grabbed Danny's shirt tighter, and Danny's brain began to fill with red. He groped on the desk until his fingers closed around the marble paperweight. Then he smashed it into the left side of Frank's head. Frank let go of Danny's shirt and dropped to the floor, knocking his chin on the desk as he fell, and Danny walked around the desk to stand over him. Frank stared up, dazed. Danny clutched the paperweight, his breath coming fast and hard. He wanted to smash the cold weight into Frank's temple, and he could see from the way Frank cringed back that he was afraid.

Danny could hear the old man whispering, "Do it."

But he wasn't his father.

"Who fucked Jenna Jeffords?"

Frank groaned and touched his head. A trickle of blood ran down from his scalp, but Danny figured he'd live. The Frank Greers of the world were survivors.

He kicked Frank and said, "Pulaski? Farnasi? You? I want names, Frank."

"I'm fucking bleeding. You probably cracked my skull."

"Cry me a river. Names. The Awesome Eleven?"

"Who?" Frank hunched over like a wounded animal, and Danny gripped the paperweight tighter. Animals were most dangerous when wounded.

"You heard me."

"Yeah, I guess. Pulaski. Farnasi. Stan. Chris Soldano. Some others."

"And you. Don't forget you. Who else?"

"I don't remember. Okay? We were high. On your dope. Jenna liked that goddamn dope. It set her free. She wanted to fuck, fuck, fuck."

"Did Greg do her?"

"Not Greg. He was boning Barb Capozzi."

"How about Ollie?"

"Ollie? Maybe. Yeah. I guess."

"So you gangbang Jenna—"

"She wanted it," Frank said.

"She was high. How the hell did she know what she wanted?"

"We were all fuckin' high. She never said stop. She never filed a report with the cops. She never did nothin'."

"It looks like someone's doing something now."

Frank coughed. "Fuck you, Ryan." Blood was running down the side of Frank's head in a stream now, and he stared at Danny with flat eyes, gauging the distance. Danny was careful to keep space between them and not turn his back.

"Do you know who blew up Jenna's house?"

"No. I'm telling you. I had nothing to do with it. I didn't even know she lived there until it happened. That block is part of them new townhomes. That's all I know."

"The townhouses your friends at Cromoca built?"

"How the fuck do I know? They were built twenty years ago."

"You lived right around the corner."

Frank turned white. "I don't know. I had other things to worry about back then. I gotta get help, you sonofabitch. I could die."

"We couldn't get that lucky," Danny said. "I'm leaving now, Frank. Better get your scalp looked at, though I'm not sure it matters."

Frank glared at him. "Oh?"

"If there's a hit parade, and there seems to be, you're on it."

Frank wiped his hand against his head, smearing the blood. He sucked air through his teeth, and Danny could see the kid who liked gouging out the eyes of live frogs before he slowly dismembered them. Frank Greer, the human predator.

Danny glanced at the photograph on the wall of Frank, Stan's old man, and Congressman George Crossman. Did that matter, or was it just a loose thread?

"I think you'd better watch your back, Frank. Or maybe get out of town," Danny said. Greg Moss, friend to all, was part of something big and dirty. Something that went beyond a revenge killing.

"I think you've got it wrong," Frank said. "I'm not going anywhere. Now get the fuck out and don't come back, or I guarantee, you'll be the next victim."

42

Kevin tapped on the door to Barb Capozzi's hospital room. She was sitting up in bed, hair brushed and, if he wasn't mistaken, wearing lipstick. Though she still wore a hospital gown and her neck was bandaged, she managed to look put together. Not a bad achievement for a woman who'd almost died of anaphylactic shock.

Lots of flower arrangements stood on the window sill—big ones with balloons, baskets, a vase of roses. A *Sentinel* lay on the bed, and CNN flashed mute images on the TV. Kevin noted the small black suitcase beside the bed. Barb was ready to get out. She was frowning over her cell phone but looked up when he entered.

"Are you allowed to use that here?" Kevin asked.

She tucked the phone against her side. "I don't know. Nobody said I couldn't. I know you, don't I?" Her voice still sounded a bit hoarse, but it enhanced the natural seductive quality. She could have done phone sex. Maybe she had.

"I don't think so." Kevin started to fumble for his ID as she assessed him.

"I never forget a face. You're Kevin Ryan. We went to the same high school. I know your brother."

"And you're Barb Capozzi," Kevin said, holding out his ID.

She widened her dark eyes and gave him a coy smile. "Am I under arrest?"

He didn't return the smile and kept his face neutral. "I'm hoping you'll answer some questions for me. I had an interesting conversation with Ted Eliot about your friend Greg Moss."

She didn't freeze up, didn't get hostile. She just gazed up at him as if she were trying to determine how much he knew and how much she needed to say.

"Is Ted in trouble?" she asked at last.

"I don't know. He's an addict."

"And he got clean. It's been tough for him. His family's a nightmare. All Ted's ever wanted was to not be part of that world. I know it sounds weird, but he's a decent guy."

"Is he?" Kevin pulled out a chair and sat. "He likes his fancy clothes. That stupid watch."

She laughed. "He is a peacock. But he doesn't usually wear the watch. He must have forgotten." She held up her hand and pointed her finger at her temple. "He can be a little dense at times. He grew up in a goddamn mansion, for Chrissake. Of course, his father practically disowned him. No wonder he wanted to pretend to be someone else, right?"

"Dad didn't approve of his life choices?"

"To say the least. I guess that's why Ted joined the Camden PD. Trying to be all macho. What an idiot."

"Is that how he ended up at Greg's parties?"

"He was in serious pain. Hooked on oxy, you know? Heroin is an easy fix for that. Plus, he met people."

"Prostitutes," Kevin said.

"He met other guys." Barb gave him a look that challenged him to make a remark. "Cops can be such assholes. Most of the guys at Greg's parties were rich. A few were in the closet, too. But he finally met someone who wasn't an asshole. Drew's sweet. He wasn't really part of the whole party scene. He talked Ted into getting straight. Well, you know what I mean."

"So good for Ted. He got clean and found true love."

Barb pursed her lips. "You don't believe in love? Or is that just for heteros?"

Kevin suppressed his sigh. That's right. He was the asshole. "I believe in love, and to be honest, I hope Ted Eliot is happy as hell in a house with a white picket fence. I just don't give a shit unless it has bearing on this case. I want to know about Greg and his parties. If he's important, I need to know about Drew. I want to know what your deal is, Barb. I want to know about Greg's partner, and I want to know about Cromoca."

She blew out a slow breath and ran her tongue over her lips. "That's a lot of information. I could call my lawyer."

"Someone's after you. Maybe it's connected to Greg's parties. Maybe it's not."

"I'll talk to you as a source. If you try to arrest me, I'll deny everything."

Kevin considered. He might need her testimony. Greg Moss was dead. She definitely was tied into the party scene, but did the parties tie into Greg's death? Was it worth losing her as a possible accessory? If it saved his brother, then yes.

"I'm not recording you. I'm not talking to you as a suspect," he said. "I'm trying to connect the dots."

"Look. I know people. That's my job. I cater parties. Okay? I just got my real estate license. Yeah, I introduced people to Greg, and he introduced people to me. I catered his parties. I helped provide entertainment."

"Entertainment?"

"Escorts." She hesitated. "The women were working girls, but very high-end. Like you think Philly's a dead town, but it isn't. Lots of upscale escorts. There were girls from Atlantic City and New York, too. Nobody underaged. No sex slaves."

"You'd swear to that?"

"Yes, but I'm not going to court."

"A lot of dope changed hands?"

"Yeah. Mostly blow, but they were moving heroin and pills, too. Lot of X. The old guys needed their little blue pills, so it was available. And trust me, you aren't going to get anywhere going after the people who went to those parties."

Kevin swallowed. That sounded familiar. "Greg's clients paid to get in. Is that how it worked?"

"Something like that. If they wanted a full package—dope and sex. Some guys got comped because they were major customers. Some made extra arrangements with the women on the side. It was pretty free form."

"Do you know how Greg brought in the drugs?"

"Greg had a partner. He took at least half of the profits."

"Did you ever meet him?"

She shook her head. "He never came to the parties, but I know Greg and he were old friends. Greg only did business with old friends."

"Like high school friends?"

"Yeah." Barb sighed. "Greg could never let go of anyone, you know. So whoever this guy was, your brother knows him."

Kevin perked up. It was a slim lead, but still a lead. "Why do you say that?"

"Greg said so. His partner knew your brother, said he was a good guy."

Kevin clenched his fists. Greg's drug dealing partner thought Danny was a good guy, which meant he was probably an associate of Vic Ceriano. On the other hand, maybe Theresa knew him. Their sister knew most of the lowlifes in the city. That was something. A shred of something.

"What about Cromoca?"

She hesitated. "Cromoca is just a property acquisition company. It buys land and sells it. Nothing illegal."

"Nothing illegal?" Kevin gave a harsh laugh. People always said that when they hid behind these goddamn corporate fronts. Nothing illegal, his ass. "Who's making a profit, Barb?"

"I don't know. I don't know who the partners are. Greg never told me."

She made eye contact and spoke directly, but Kevin didn't believe her. She held herself rigid, her lips pursed. She was holding something back. He either pushed her or let it slide. For now, he chose the latter.

"So what are you going to do?" Barb asked.

"Nothing for the moment." Kevin leaned a little closer. His size tended to intimidate people. Barb Capozzi didn't lean back, but he watched her pulse begin to notch up. Good. She was nervous. "But let me tell you something. If you didn't spike your own drink—"

"Are you crazy? I almost died! I'm not even supposed to touch naproxen with my hands."

Her pulse was hammering now. Fear? Anger? Both? She looked genuine enough, but sometimes the best liars seemed the sincerest.

"Look," she said. "If I tell you something that has bearing, could you maybe stop hassling me?"

"Something like what?"

"At senior week, at Greg's, there was this one night. He had this insane party with excellent dope, and things got out of control."

"This isn't anything new, Barb."

She played with her cell phone, running her fingers around the edge of it, almost but not quite pressing the button to turn it on. Kevin waited. She was testing his patience, but with witnesses, he knew how the game worked.

"This girl got gangbanged."

"What girl?"

"Jenna Jeffords."

"So? Nothing I can do about it now. She's dead." But it gave him a place to start, and maybe it tied into whoever was texting Danny. "Who was involved?"

"I don't know everyone. Frank Greer. Stan Riordan. Rick. Nate. Chris. Not Greg, though there were probably others."

Kevin took a breath before he asked the next question. "Danny?"

She shook her head. "Danny never came in the house."

"Okay. Write the names down."

"It won't—you won't use my name?"

"No."

"There's something else." Barb reached for Kevin's arm, and he stared at the bruises left by the IV on the pale flesh of her hand, not wanting to look into her eyes. "I don't know if it's true, but I heard Jenna got pregnant."

"And then she was killed in that fire."

Barb shrugged. "I guess."

Kevin needed his Maalox. This case was insane. "All right, Barb. I suggest you watch your back, and don't think about leaving town. I might need to talk to you again." He reached into his pocket and pulled out his card case. "Here, take my card. It's got my cell phone. If you think of anything, you call me. If you see something, you call me. If something doesn't seem right, you—"

"I got it. Call you." She gave him a bitter smile. "And you'll be my protector?"

"Something like that."

"I sure hope you carry a great big gun."

Kevin shoved the case back into his pocket. "Just call."

43

Alex's head throbbed, and she thought she could hear the *tsk, tsk, tsk* of a cuckoo clock. But that was wrong. That was a bad dream where she'd been in a green living room with a crazy woman. She opened her eyes and let out a small sob. She was lying on her side on a cold dirt floor that smelled vaguely rotten, like old vegetation, her hands duct taped behind her back. Her knees and ankles were taped as well. Something thick and sour and cottony had been stuffed into her mouth and taped in place.

She took a deep breath, and the cotton fibers mixed with the smell of feet choked her. She had to relax. She tried again. It was a little better. It was important to be calm. Try to get her bearings. If only her head didn't hurt so much. Then she remembered Rachel offering her iced tea. Standing over her. Smacking her with that goddamn tray.

Calm. She had to stay calm. Crazy Rachel who believed Danny and Jenna were in love. Crazy Rachel who photoshopped a prom picture to make it look like Danny and Jenna had been prom dates.

Where did Rachel get that photograph? What other photos were in that album? If only Alex had texted Danny and told him where she was going this morning. He would have come after her.

Now she was on her own. In a hole. Dim light filtered through an opening in a corner of the room, just enough to turn the gloom dark gray.

Alex closed her eyes. In the distance she thought she could hear the sound of water, so the river wasn't too far. That meant the earth would probably be soft. Maybe this was some kind of boathouse? No, the river didn't sound close enough. The air was dense and close but not overwhelmingly hot. She was underground. How far was she from that crazy house?

The walls appeared to be cement block though the floor was dirt, and the ceiling was braced and held up by jacks in three spots. It wasn't particularly reassuring. Whoever had built the foundation for this—whatever it was—had done a terrible job of it.

The floorboards overhead squeaked as heavy footsteps approached. Alex curled into a ball as a door above her opened. Footsteps trod down wood steps. A flashlight shone in her face, and she turned her head.

"You look good like that," a male voice said. Young. Alex tried to see his face, but the light shone in her eyes. "All trussed up like a Christmas turkey." He ripped the tape off Alex's mouth and pulled out the gag. Then he yanked her upright.

"Be nice now, dear." Rachel's voice.

"Rachel, please. Let me go. I don't understand why you're keeping me here," Alex said. Her voice came out in a froggy croak as she worked to get saliva back into her mouth.

The man said, "Keep that light shining in her face, Ma." He held Alex with one hand and pulled out a bottle of water with another. "Sit still." He let go of her to open the bottle, and she slumped sideways. He jerked her back up and threw some water in her face. "I said, sit still. Now drink." He held the bottle to Alex's mouth, forcing her to swallow. She choked, and water slopped down her front. "Stupid black bitch."

"Fuck you!" Alex screamed the words as loud as she could.

He poured the rest of the bottle of water over her head. "You think screaming will help? Who's gonna hear you? The raccoons?

We own twenty acres. Nobody's gonna hear you." He dropped another bottle on the ground. "That's all you get till tomorrow, so make it last. Have fun getting it open."

"Oh, now, honey. There's no need to be so mean. Ms. Burton, I'm going to leave you these nice sandwiches. I think you can eat them if you just lie down on your stomach." Rachel set down a paper plate with two peanut butter and jelly sandwiches.

"Rachel, please." Terror made her voice crack. Alex tried to see past the glaring light, but their faces blended into the darkness.

The man let go of Alex so quickly, she dropped back onto the wet dirt.

"Jesus Christ. Be nice to her if you want, Ma. She's the one your precious Danny was trying fuck the other night. Remember that. She's nothin' but a Ho-Ho-Ho." He gave Alex a kick in the stomach, not hard enough to do any real damage, but enough to knock the wind out of her. "You're a wicked Jezebel."

Alex couldn't answer. If she did, he'd come at her again, but if he touched her, she'd hurt him. Somehow. She didn't care what it cost her.

Alex glanced up. Rachel had let the light droop again, and she could see the man now. He was young, in his teens or early twenties, with wavy dark hair. She bet he had a pair of bright-blue eyes. He was the boy in the photographs. She was sure of it. She lowered her gaze before he caught her staring.

Rachel said, "You should be nicer anyway. She's our guest." She opened the second water bottle. "Here, you'd better drink a little."

She eased Alex up and held her until she'd swallowed enough water to ease her thirst.

"Okay, Ma. Be nice, but she's untrustworthy."

Rachel ignored him. "Now you can rest." When she let go, Alex slumped over, and it occurred to her that there might be something in the water. Poison? It was too late now.

The boy just chuckled. "Let's let our guest eat her snack." He paused at the foot of the steps. "If you get lonely, you can howl." He was still laughing when he and Rachel closed the door.

Alex lay with her face pressed against the cool mud. The smell of peanut butter made her stomach rumble, but she couldn't force herself to move closer. "I'm not afraid," she said aloud. Something brushed past her, and she gasped. "It's dark. I can deal," she said after catching her breath.

She couldn't just lie there. He might come back. He'd hurt her if he came back alone. His hatred had been a living thing, like a black cloud of stinging bees. He'd been watching Danny and her the other night. That was enough to make her skin crawl.

She'd messed up, and now she was paying for it. Mama always said she was too headstrong, too damn stubborn.

"You want what you want now, and there's no compromising with you," she'd say. "You're just so too full of yourself. You'll pay for that."

Wasn't that what Sam always said? "You don't listen enough, Alex. I don't understand how you can be a good reporter when you don't want to listen."

Tears boiled in Alex's eyes. She was a screw-up. That's why she still toiled in relative obscurity. She pushed and pushed, but she didn't have the knack for drawing people out. Her parents would shake their heads, ever so gently. Never wanting to give offense. It always pissed her off. She was always the squeaky wheel while her sister, Thea, was a perfect lady. Thea should have married Sam. By now, they'd have two perfect kids and a dog, and she'd run his house and cook his dinner, and they'd have a perfect life.

Screw them all.

Alex started wiggling and twisting. At least Danny liked her the way she was. He told her she had fire. If she was going to die here, at least she'd kissed him, even if she'd told him they couldn't do it again. If she got out, she'd do more than kiss him. And she wasn't sorry. If she got out. God, she had to get out.

Alex managed to push her body through the circle of her arms and gave a shout of triumph. All that yoga was good for something. Now at least her hands were in front of her.

She picked and peeled away the duct tape that bound her knees and then her ankles. Maybe she'd be able to catch Rachel and that boy off guard when they returned.

The boy. He called Rachel "Ma." Of course, Rachel was clearly missing a few marbles. That photograph. Something about that photograph bothered her, aside from the fact that Rachel had done a piss-poor job of altering it. Damn.

Of course, Rachel probably didn't understand technology that well. She'd come out here and hidden away. Why?

How much did anybody know about Rachel Jeffords? Did she have family? Alex tried to remember, but her thoughts were turning wispy, like a fog rolling in. Rachel must have had some family. Somewhere. Why did she choose to hide out here with that horrible kid? Where did he come from?

Was he Jenna's brother?

Not her brother. The revelation came to Alex like a clap of thunder. *Oh, shit.* She was wearing that same damn Claddagh ring. It couldn't be, but it would explain why Rachel looked so young. Something happened at that beach house all right, and Alex had to tell Danny. She had to get the hell out of this hole in the ground. Alex started to stand, but she toppled over into the mud. There must have been something in the water they'd given her, and she fought to stay awake. She had to fight. She had to get out.

Jenna Jeffords hadn't died in that fire. Her mother had. Jenna'd switched places with Rachel, and nobody had figured it out, until today.

"I'm not afraid," Alex shouted. "I'm getting out." She tried to push herself up again, but her elbows buckled. Tears slid down her cheeks, and she rolled onto her back. "I'm awake. I'm awake. I'm awake." She said it over and over until the darkness took her.

44

D anny cruised down Delaware Avenue toward the old neighborhood, turning right on Tasker and heading down Second Street. He wasn't trying to remember the good old days in living color. He wanted to check out Jenna Jeffords's old home. It was gone, of course. According to Alex's site map, the property was owned by a Henry Chang, and it was no longer a redbrick row house. The entire block was part of a larger development of townhomes that was slightly more upscale than the surrounding neighborhood. This was Cromoca Partners' first major development in Philadelphia.

Danny parked and got out. He took a picture of Henry Chang's house and accessed the homes facing the development. Redbrick rows, a few with Blessed Mother statues in the front windows, which probably meant they belonged to older folks. It was a warm afternoon, and Danny figured the owners might be coming out to enjoy the sun.

He saw a woman in a blue sundress. Blonde, in her sixties, and built like a fire hydrant, she frowned when he approached and asked if she knew anything about the new townhouses. She stepped back from him and shook her head. Even after he pulled out his press ID, she eyed him like he might be a serial killer, so Danny stood back and let her go on. A pair of teenagers shrugged and said they were

new to the area, and an older man was so deaf, he couldn't understand what Danny was asking.

Danny wasn't deterred. He walked down to the end of the
block where two older women in bright sundresses sat watching
him from their white vinyl beach chairs.

"Hi there," he said and gave them his best smile.

A thin woman with tight auburn curls and skin like leather
looked him up and down and said in a gravely smoker's voice, "Hi
yourself, doll. I'm Midgie Santangelo. You're not from around here."

"Used to be. I lived up past Sigel, right off of Third. Dan
Ryan." Danny held out his press pass. "I'm working on a story for
the *Sentinel* about changing neighborhoods."

"Changing neighborhoods? Ooh boy. We seen lots of changes
here. Haven't we, Florie?" She smoothed down her lime-green
dress and nudged her friend.

"Sure have, Midgie." The other woman, heavier set with black
hair, nodded and winked. Her voice was slightly higher pitched
but no less gravely. She wore bright-yellow, and as she gestured
with her hands, her bright-pink nails sparkled in the sun. "I'm
Floretta Giacomo, but you can call me Florie. Would ya like some
lemonade, hon? Have some lemonade."

"I thought we knew everyone from around here, but I don't
remember you," Midgie said. "What'd you say your name was?"

"Dan Ryan. I went to Furness, but I haven't lived here for a
while."

"Hmm. That name's familiar," Florie said. "Oh, wait, Midgie!
I remember. Little Danny Ryan. His daddy was a policeman."
Florie waved her hand, and her pink nails glittered. "Didn't you
grow up handsome?"

"Oh, my God! That Danny Ryan! Now you're a big news
writer. Have you got a girlfriend?" Midgie leaned closer, her red
curls bobbing.

Both women cackled now, and Florie waved her hand
toward the front steps. "Go grab a chair, hon. Have some lemonade. You look like you could use a little sun. Just grab that
pitcher and a cup."

Danny knew the neighborhood well enough that he couldn't just ask questions without socializing. He handed Florie the pitcher, grabbed a plastic cup, and pulled an extra chair from the side of the house.

Midgie and Florie exchanged a look before Florie poured him a glass of lemonade. When the two women smiled and nodded at him, Danny took a swallow and almost choked. It was little more than lemon-flavored vodka. He smiled. "Thanks," he said, clearing his throat. "Just what I needed. Maybe you could tell me something about the townhouses across the street."

"Oh. Them townhouses," Midgie said and gave him a conspiratorial wink. "That was something. If you get my drift."

Danny leaned a little closer and pulled out his notebook. "I take it there was something unusual about them."

"Unusual? Oh, yeah. What a scandal that was. That crumb bum, Tim Rosina. What a crook," Florie said, wrinkling her nose as if she smelled something bad.

"Tim Rosina?" Danny blinked at her. Jesus, someone else was involved in this rat's nest.

"Oh, that man. You probably don't remember Tim, but he was a big-time builder back in the seventies and eighties and early nineties. Had all kinds of political connections." Florie took a long swallow of lemonade. "Drink up, honey. Don't be shy. We got plenty."

Danny took another small sip. "It's great, Florie."

"Aren't you sweet? Such a nice young man." Florie patted his arm, and Midgie frowned.

"Stop flirting, Florie. Tell the man what he needs to know. I bet you want to hear about the fires." Midgie nodded her head for emphasis.

"Fires? There were multiple fires?"

"Oh, yeah. I mean not here. There was only two in this neighborhood. Three years apart." Midgie frowned, remembering. "The first one was in the late eighties. Mrs. Sullivan's house. They said she was smoking in bed and whoosh! Gone. Just like that."

"Took out four other houses," Flora added. "That was awful."

"I don't remember," Danny said.

"Oh, honey, you probably weren't even born," Midgie said. She pinched his cheek. "So cute. No one died, but the houses were gone. So much was going on in this neighborhood anyway. Lots of turnover. People moving out. All kinds of changes."

"Anyway. Tim Rosina and his partner bought up all them houses and planned this big development." Florie's eyes twinkled with glee. "And guess what?"

Danny leaned forward. "What? Someone wouldn't sell?"

"Oh, no," Midgie said. "Everyone sold. He was paying top dollar. If anyone was reluctant, I guess accidents could be arranged, if you know what I mean. No. The thing is, Tim up and dropped dead. Heart attack."

"Heart attack? When did that happen?"

"Heart attack." Florie blessed herself. "It was the Hand of God, or whatever. I guess in the early nineties. Construction had finally started, and Tim was sitting on the crapper when he took the big one. You know? But his partners took over, 'cause the houses got built."

"Do you remember the name of his partners?"

"I don't remember," Florie said. "I think they were Mexican. Don't you think, Midgie?"

"Mexican?" Danny wasn't sure if he had wasted his time or not. He had half a cup of Florie's lemonade sloshing about in his stomach and Tim Rosina floating around his head. It wasn't much. Tim Rosina and the Mexicans. It sounded like a band. "Why do you think they were Mexican?"

"The name was definitely Mexican," Flora said. "Like that cockroach song."

"'La Cucaracha'? Could it have been Cromoca?"

"Yeah, something like that," Midgie agreed. "Plus, he had a sister. He left everything to his sister."

"His sister? Do you remember her name?"

"Sure. She used to do real estate. Livvy Capozzi. Well, she was all la-di-da. Olivia Capozzi, if you please. She made a bunch of money. Had a house down the shore and a condo in Florida. She lives in Florida now. A real piece of work."

"And she had a daughter?"

"Oh, yeah. She sure did. Barbie Capozzi. Ooh la la. Real looker. I guess she took over for Livvy. I don't know. She wasn't a realtor, but she was real tight with Ernie Moss's boy—can't remember his name, but he was a big real estate guy."

"Tell him the real scandal," Florie said. "The real scandal is that Tim Rosina was helping people scam the insurance companies by setting fire to their houses. Of course, no one ever proved nothing."

"How was he doing that, Florie?" Danny prodded.

Florie shook her head, and she looked at Danny with narrowed eyes. "There's rumors he could make it happen. That's all I heard." She grasped his hand. "You're going to write about us, aren't you? I don't want you to use my real name."

"Is there reason to be afraid?" Danny leaned closer.

"I don't know, dollface," Midgie said. "But rumors are rumors." She glanced up as a couple came out from a house down the street. The man stopped to pick up deck chairs, and the woman carried a large green plastic pitcher in one hand and a basket in the other.

"Midgie, Florie," the woman called. "Do you have company?"

Danny started to stand, but Midgie pulled him down in the seat. "Oh, no, don't leave. Here come Sal and Rita Gentille. They'll know more than we do. You just sit for a little while. You'll find out everything you want to know about Tim Rosina."

*

The world had turned indigo, and the moon slashed a sharp grin across the sky by the time Danny pulled into his driveway. Still no message from Alex. He sat on the back steps and breathed in the scent of roses and honeysuckle as he watched the fireflies glitter in his backyard. There was too much floating around inside his head right now, and he needed to clear it. At least here in the quiet of his yard he could think.

He'd let Midgie feed him a plate of baked ziti before he left South Philly, because he was pretty sure he would have driven off the road if he hadn't. Midgie and Flora and their neighbors had given him great chunks of undiluted gossip. He needed to process the information he'd learned, to put the pieces in place.

Danny wasn't sure how much of the gossip was true or useful, but it seemed that Tim Rosina and his partners were acquiring property in South Philly by running insurance scams starting in the eighties, if not earlier. Rosina left his money to his sister, Olivia Capozzi, whose daughter happened to be Barb Capozzi, Greg Moss's ex-girlfriend. South Philly was a very small world. Or it used to be.

Rosina had certainly bought the Jeffords' old home, so it was possible that he had arranged for the gas leak to occur. His so-called partners may have been cockroaches, but they weren't Mexican. They were Cromoca Partners.

Danny paged back through his notes. Tim Rosina had been quite a character. He'd dated half of South Philly, according to Florie and Midgie. His "Saturday Night Girls." Danny had two whole pages of names. Rosina's special favorites got cars and fur jackets. The others got dinner and a movie. Danny shuddered. He knew some of those women. Susie Farnasi, Ricky's mom. Amanda Fernwyler, his eighth grade math teacher. Annie Gretske, Ray's mom. Danny wondered who had been regulars and who had been dinner, movie, and sex dates.

He needed to talk to Alex.

Danny wasn't sure if Alex was working on a story for the paper or on something that pertained to Jenna Jeffords. Or maybe she was angry with him. He texted her again. As he waited for her to answer, he stood and went into the house to reexamine the package of information she'd given him.

Between the vodka and the sun, his right eye was beginning to throb, and he grabbed a foil packet before he had a repeat of last night. He swallowed the pill with water, wandered into the pantry, and began to open cupboards. Boxes of tea. Two containers of coffee. Whole wheat crackers. Christ, he did need to go shopping.

Danny stared at the odd little markings on the wall. The little word puzzles. It was stupid to think Mr. Rebus would have left an obvious clue. The puzzles were a distraction. He glanced at the image of the exploding pie, the only puzzle that made no sense, though it really looked more like a mushroom with light rays coming off it. A magic mushroom.

He'd checked the oven, but there was nothing inside—pies or otherwise. Exploding pie. Magic mushroom. Then it struck him. The picture was neither a mushroom nor a pie. It was a keyhole, and he'd been looking in the wrong oven.

He walked to the bread oven and felt inside. Tucked along the right wall was a small indentation. When he slipped his fingers inside, he grasped a small key, which he pulled out.

The key must open something in the pantry. The walls were smooth, but he began to check the cabinets, moving counter-clockwise from the fireplace. He reached the cabinet almost directly opposite and opened the doors. He was pushing aside the few cans of soup and boxes of tea when he saw the tiny key-hole in back. When he fitted the key, he heard a tiny snick, and the cabinet swung forward.

Danny now faced a small room with a sloping ceiling, clearly under the front steps. In the light that spilled in from the pantry, he saw a black leather chair wedged into a corner and a Tiffany lamp that sat on a small round table with a marble top. Narrow bookcases lined the walls. When he stepped inside, Danny realized the bookcases were filled with leather-bound books. He pulled some out at random. They were signed first editions: *The Great Gatsby, Look Homeward, Angel, Ulysses*, so many others.

Mr. Rebus had left him a small fortune in rare books. Danny was about to reach for what appeared to be an original *Vanity Fair* when he saw the plastic bag on the floor. He opened it to find empty bags of chips and beer cans.

What in the living hell was this? It couldn't be old refuse from Mr. Rebus. This was fresh, judging by the sell-by date on one of the bags of chips. There were still trickles of beer left in a couple of the cans.

Jesus Christ. Someone had gotten into his house and hidden in this room. Watching and waiting.

"Hello."

Danny dropped the plastic bag and spun around. A thin shape stood silhouetted in the doorway, and Danny recognized him from the Shamrock, from Northern Liberties. The young guy in the hoodie.

"Who are you?"

The kid lifted a gun, and he pointed it at Danny. "You don't recognize me? I guess you wouldn't, but I know all about you. Dad."

45

Kevin sat at his dining room table filling out index cards, careful to slide a catalogue onto the oak surface before he started writing. They didn't use the dining room much, except for holidays. The dining area was small, almost part of the living room, and the big china closet pushed back against the wall took up a lot of space. They used the server to collect school photos, trophies, and the kids' art. He looked around. Crap covered every horizontal surface—magazines, school shit, candy wrappers.

That's how you could tell they were poor. Danny's house was neat, and his expensive furniture didn't have weird spots. Danny didn't have to worry about damaging his one nice table because if he did, he could just buy another. Kevin pushed against the gnawing unease in his stomach.

Some days, Kevin tried to imagine what life would have been like if he had told the old man to go to hell and taken a chance on Penn State. Would he have carved a path like Danny had? He might have made the NFL, or he might have blown out his knee.

What the hell was the matter with him? What was the point in looking back? It was this goddamn case. Traveling into Danny's past inevitably pulled Kevin down that well-worn road, and he didn't like it. He had enough memories of the good old days to last him forever.

Kevin turned back to his cards. He thought better when he could write things out on cards and line them up in order. It helped him keep his facts straight. That was how Danny used to prep him for history tests. Everything on index cards. Memorize a date and a fact. Put it on a card and line it up. At the time, it made him feel stupid, but it worked. Maybe Danny should have been a teacher. If nothing else, he'd always been patient.

Now Kevin laid out the facts of this case and tried to decide what mattered and what he could discard. Greg Moss's mysterious partner bothered him. If he was a high school acquaintance, he could be tied in with the murders in some way, and yet from what Barb said, this guy was a businessman. Why kill the guy who was making you money? That made zero sense.

That brought him back to the party at the shore. Barb said the girl, Jenna Jeffords, had been gang-raped. Barb mentioned Frank Greer as a participant. Not surprising. In addition to being an ex-con, the sleazy asshole had gotten caught up in three domestic complaints, though the women had all dropped the charges.

Three different women. Three different complaints. This guy definitely needed a hard look.

Kevin stared at the list of names of Danny's high school acquaintances. How many of these kids did Danny know anyway? Danny had shed high school like a butterfly sheds its cocoon and emerged as someone new and improved, but he always did have that gift for reinventing himself.

"Your brother has a high bullshit factor," the old man would say as he sucked down yet another Dewar's in the gloom of the Shamrock. "Maybe he should stop pretending he's somethin' special and remember he's just a fuckin' hack."

You could always count on Tommy Ryan to put you in your place.

Kevin wrote down one more name: Ted Eliot. The cop was tied to Greg Moss. He'd been a customer. He was clean now but vulnerable. Maybe Greg had something on him. Greg's murder seemed like the others, and yet he was the only one who had been mutilated. Why cut out his tongue? As a warning? Out of rage? As a distraction? Something about it was off.

Kevin yawned. His indigestion was bad tonight. Maybe he did need to cut back on some of the fried shit. The trouble was, he always ended up rolling out of the house last minute in the morning because getting to sleep was a bitch and getting up was a chore. On the job, who had time to eat regular food?

He glanced at the clock. It was twenty past eleven, and Kelly was late. Her curfew was eleven, and he wasn't letting her slide on this. Rules were rules. He clenched and unclenched his fists.

She was just like Danny with her "I'm a rebel" attitude. If she couldn't stick to her curfew, she wasn't going on any trip to Costa Rica. He didn't care what Jean said. He might be the dummy of the family, but hell, he was her goddamn father.

Kevin stood and began to pace. His stomach was on fire, the pain pressing up against his chest. All he needed was an ulcer. Some Maalox would calm his stomach, but his bottle was down in the rec room. He lumbered to the stairs and stomped down.

Damnit. He jammed his foot against one of the twins' hockey sticks, and he bit back a curse. Sean and Mike lay sprawled on the leather couch asleep, some dumbassed slasher movie flickering on the TV. Kevin grabbed his Maalox and shuffled back up the steps, hanging onto the railing with his right hand as he swilled the thick liquid. It didn't seem to be working. Everything hurt tonight.

He'd reached the top of the stairs, puffing for breath, when the kitchen door clicked open and then shut. Tentative footsteps padded across the floor, and he faced Kelly, who stood, shoes in hand, blinking at him.

The smoldering flame in his stomach erupted into a raging fire around his heart. Oh, Jesus, she was killing him.

Her eyes grew wide as Kevin started to say, "Where the hell have you been?" But he couldn't force the words. The Maalox bottle slipped from his fingers and plopped to the floor with a wet splat. His ears rang like a warning bell.

Flatline. Flatline.

"Dad? Dad? Daddy?"

Kevin reached out for her. Somehow he missed, and the floor crashed up against his face. The banshee was wailing, and he shut his eyes, trying to remember the Act of Contrition.

46

"So what're you going to do? Kill me?" Danny assessed the kid and gauged the distance. If the kid pulled the trigger, he probably wouldn't miss. They stood less than twelve feet apart, and the gun pointing at him wasn't shaking. Danny figured the kid knew how to use it.

"Why would I do that?" the kid asked.

"You tell me."

"I figured it was time we met."

"You should clean up after yourself."

"You're so dumb, you never knew I was sitting in there. You didn't even know about it until tonight. For a reporter, you aren't too smart."

"So how did you figure it out?"

The kid puffed out his chest. "'Cause I am smart. I'm a genius. My mom told me."

"Clearly, you're not my son," Danny said. He looked around the room for something to throw. A book. The lamp. He'd have to move fast. This kid held the gun steady enough, but the fingers of his left hand twitched.

"I started watching the old man when I found out you were buying the place."

"But how could you know I was buying this house?"

"I been watching you for a while. Mom said it was time."

"Time for what?"

"Time." The kid gestured with his gun. "Come out now, or I'll shoot you and leave you in here to bleed out."

"Someone will find me."

The kid laughed. "You think so? Someone like your hot little reporter friend? Guess again."

Danny swallowed. "Where is she? Where's Alex?"

"Let's just say her welfare depends on your cooperation. Now, are you coming?"

Danny walked out into the pantry. This kid had Alex someplace. But why? What the hell was going on? His phone began to ring.

"Do you mind if I answer?" he asked.

"No tricks."

He checked the caller ID. It was Kelly. Something was wrong.

"Ryan," he said after he picked up.

Her words came out in a rush. "Oh, my God! Uncle Dan, Dad had a heart attack they're taking him to the hospital right now can you come?" Danny gripped the phone against his cheek. Ice was filling his veins, and his heart was drumming, trying to force some warmth into his body. He caught his breath and angled away from the kid.

"Hey, Kelly. I can't talk right now. How about I call you back?"

"Didn't you hear me? Dad had a heart attack. They're taking him to HUP. It's really bad. We need you."

"Okay. I understand. Tell your mom Uncle Daniel will be there when he can." It was a stupid thing to say, but he couldn't tell her he was standing with some lunatic who was calling him "Dad." Maybe she'd figure something was wrong. Or not. Who besides Kevin knew their code?

If you ever need me, you call and say Daniel needs his brother. You understand? Except Kevin wasn't there to hear him.

"Are you listening?" Her voice rose an octave.

"Are you?" Danny said.

The kid grabbed the phone from his hand and slammed it down. "Talk time's over. What's the matter, Dad? Family problems?"

"Go to hell." Danny had to get away from this kid.

"You can close up that little room there. It was real convenient, I gotta say." The kid waved his gun at Danny. It was a Glock. Nine-millimeter semiautomatic. "Go ahead. Close it up."

Danny pushed the cupboard back in place. He tried to steady his hands. Would Kelly figure out something was wrong, or would she think he was being an asshole? Did it matter? And Kevin. *Oh, Jesus, Kevin.* Danny couldn't catch his breath. His lungs were ripping apart.

"I was almost living in there, and you never noticed. You really should lock your doors," the kid sneered.

"Who the hell are you?"

The kid smirked at him. "I already told you, Dad. We got things to do. Where shall we start?"

"What kind of things? Where's Alex?"

The kid smiled at him. His lips curved up, but his eyes remained cold and dead. "In a nice safe place. For now."

"Why do you keep calling me 'Dad'?"

"Because you are."

"I only had one child, and he's dead."

"Jenna Jeffords is my mom."

"What? Jenna is dead."

"No."

Danny swallowed. It all began to take shape now. The party. The yells and whoops. The loud music and chanting. The song. It kept playing over and over. And he could hear it now—"Shut 'Em Down," Public Enemy's hip-hop howl about racial inequality. He was holding Michelle on the porch as she sat on his lap. A hot land breeze that night made it feel unseasonably warm, and her skin tasted salty and sweet. They were making out, and something was happening just beyond the wall. Something.

"I never slept with Jenna," Danny said.

"You were her boyfriend."

Danny shook his head. "No."

The kid grabbed a stainless steel bowl and slammed it into the side of Danny's head. "Liar." The bowl clattered to the floor as Danny dropped to his knees, blood running down the side of his face, and he thought of Frank Greer. *Everything comes back to bite you. Everything comes back.*

Fuck this little bastard.

Danny grabbed the kid's leg, and he crashed sideways, the gun sliding across the floor of the pantry. Danny scrambled for the gun. The kid was faster, but Danny snatched the bowl and smashed it down on the kid's hand before he could grab the gun. He launched himself onto the kid's back, and they rolled across the floor, grunting and kicking and punching.

Danny grabbed the kid by his hair, jerking his head back, ready to pound it into the ceramic tile. The kid was sinewy and fast, though, and he twisted, landing a solid knee to Danny's stomach. Gasping, Danny doubled over, his grip loosening. The kid pulled free, and Danny hurled himself toward him when he heard the pop. Like a firecracker.

It took him a second to realize the bullet had torn through his left side. Blood began to stain his shirt, and he stared at it, almost uncomprehending. Then he lay back on the cool floor, his heart pounding against his throat.

"Fuck," the kid said. He stood and reached into a drawer and pulled out a towel that he dropped onto Danny's chest. "No more games, Dad. We have places to go. Get up or get dead."

47

ed Eliot sat back on his sofa and stared at the unopened bottle of Chivas sitting on the black lacquer coffee table. He didn't know when everything had careened out of control, but his life had broken free of the rails and was plunging down a steep cliff. Again. He didn't know how to get it back.

He was lucky he'd been the one to get the call when Dan Ryan found Greg's body.

Of course, they could trace Greg's phone through his service provider. They'd get a list of numbers called. His, for instance. Greg had his number, but he'd been up front with the captain about it. He'd bought his house through Greg Moss. He'd even offered to step aside on the case if the captain thought there was a conflict. So far that hadn't happened.

He needed to produce a suspect. He needed someone who tied Greg's death to this weird rash of killings.

His meeting with Kevin Ryan convinced him that he didn't have much time. Ryan seemed like a decent enough guy, but he wasn't going to cut any slack. You could sense it. Worse, he seemed like a fairly meticulous investigator. Ted had exhausted his options.

He gazed around the living room. He'd started to build a life here with Andrew. A small island of peace. They'd filled the house with good furniture. White sofas with striking asymmetrical white chairs. A deep-purple rug covered the blond wood floor. They had travelled up to New York to buy a couple of decent paintings for the walls, and he'd been happy for a while.

The awful demons had started to recede. If his father disapproved, he didn't much care anymore. His mother seemed charmed by his new life. It was a start. Now he needed to eliminate all traces of the past.

He put his head in his hands. He hadn't meant for things to get out of control, but Greg kept pushing him about the information he needed. "You owe me" hung over every request even if Greg never said the words. The chain grew longer and heavier every day. And there was no escape.

His phone rang, and he stared at the DC number. He considered letting it go to voice mail, but grabbed it. "Eliot," he said.

"You know who this is?"

"Why are you calling, Dad?"

"We need to meet. I have some things to discuss with you."

"Jesus Christ." Ted ran a shaking hand against his forehead. Oh, Christ. "Dad, this isn't the best time . . ."

"I'm sending a car."

Ted sighed. He wished he hadn't answered the phone, but it was too late. It was too late the day he met Greg Moss. This probably wouldn't end well, but he'd already made a series of bad choices. He was glad now for the trip to LA that had taken Andrew out of town for the last few days.

"I'll be here," he said.

48

She was kissing him. They were sitting on those cold back steps kissing, and his hand was sliding up her thigh to cup her bare ass. Then she realized she had nothing on, and when she opened her eyes it wasn't Danny at all, it was that horrible boy. Jenna's boy.

Alex tried to scream, but he pressed his hand over her mouth and began to push her down, down into the dirt until she was suffocating. Bugs were crawling over her body. Inside her. In her hair.

"Wicked Jezebel. Wicked Jezebel," he said.

Alex woke with a start. Just a dream.

The room was dark gray, and she could see a small hole in a corner of the ceiling in the far wall where a thin finger of pale light pointed through. Not trusting herself to stand, she dragged herself over to the wall. Here the uneven floor sloped up, and the ceiling was barely six feet high. The cement was crumbling, and she was able to poke a larger hole in the foundation.

"Let there be light," she said when a medium chunk of cement fell on the floor, barely missing her skull.

She looked at the duct tape wrapped around her wrists. The cement had an edge. She might be able to cut through it if she could hold onto that piece of cement just right. If it didn't crumble. If she had time.

She was thirsty, but she didn't dare touch the water Jenna had left her. The sandwiches were covered with ants. Dead ones. Alex stopped sawing. Jenna had tried to kill her. It wasn't a huge surprise. It probably meant she'd be back to make sure she'd succeeded. How much time did that leave her?

Alex began to saw with renewed vigor. "Got to get out. Got to get out," she said as she struggled to pull her wrists apart. The tape was just beginning to fray, and she was already pouring sweat. The cement crumbled into several pieces too small to be useful.

"Damn it! Damn it!"

Her mouth tasted like it was filled with glue. She was strong enough to stand, though, and she went to the wall. The foundation was jagged in spots and she angled herself so she could rub the duct tape against the broken edge of wall. Her skin was rubbing off as well, but she didn't care. A little more tape frayed, and she tried to pull her wrists apart, cursing.

Halfway there, she heard what sounded like a door squeaking open, and she yanked herself from the wall, pulling off a medium chunk of cement as she landed on the floor. Slow, heavy footsteps creaked overhead. Alex stared for a hot second at the hole in the wall. It wasn't huge, but she was pretty sure she could squeeze herself through it. Maybe. She didn't know what she'd find on the other side, but it had to be better than sitting here waiting for crazy Jenna or her evil son.

She clambered onto the broken foundation. Using her bound hands like a scoop, she tunneled up through the dirt like a mole, ducking her face away as the earth tumbled down on her. It smelled damp and loamy, but air and freedom were just beyond her frantic hands. Keys rattled in the lock as she pushed up toward the light.

49

Danny slumped back in the passenger seat, his head pressed against the window. Dawn was breaking over Philadelphia, the violet sky just paling to lavender as they skirted the Delaware River. He tried to collect his thoughts as they flitted before him, but he was swimming in an ocean inside his mind. He could capture nothing. Kevin was at HUP, and Alex... Christ knew where she was. Danny fought to keep his eyes open.

He glanced over at the boy driving him. A kid in his early twenties, skinny as a snake and twice as mean. Last night, he'd poured a bottle of rubbing alcohol on Danny's gunshot wound and sewed it shut with black thread. When the rubbing alcohol ran out, he'd used a bottle of Stoli. He'd slapped some gauze pads on Danny's left side and taped them. He'd also force fed Danny enough vodka to keep him off balance.

"You'll live for the moment," the kid had said. "I didn't hit anything important."

"Where did you get your training, Nurse Ratched?" Danny had asked, but the kid had just scowled at him.

"Move, or I'll give you a permanent disability, old man." He'd grabbed Danny's cell phone from the kitchen table.

The kid's rough medicine had worked, more or less. Danny's wound was only seeping a little, though his left side throbbed like a bad toothache. Danny wasn't sure how much blood he'd lost. There'd been a fair amount on the pantry floor. His jeans were stiff with it, and his discarded white shirt had been soaked. The kid was right: the bullet hadn't hit anything vital. Still, it was better to pretend he was in worse shape than he was. Hell, he didn't want to know whether he was in bad shape or not. He shivered in his black T-shirt as the air conditioner blasted him, but he didn't ask the kid to turn it down. It kept him awake.

They passed the airport, heading north on 95, and Danny watched a jet rise into the air. Not so long ago—time had become a fuzzy concept—he'd held Alex right on this roadway. If only he'd been smart and not smoked that dope. If only he hadn't touched Alex on the back steps, Jenna and her crazy son wouldn't have made her a target.

"Hey," he said to the kid, more to shut out his thoughts than to make conversation. "Do you have a name?"

"Why?"

"Do you want me to call you 'shithead'?"

The kid slanted him a look, then shrugged. "Johnny."

Christ. He could have predicted it. Who was Jenna's favorite actor of all time?

"Why do you think I'm your father?"

"Mom told me."

"We should get paternity tests done. Why don't we stop at HUP?"

"Like that's gonna happen. Dad."

"Why not? I'm B positive. Are you? Have you ever had blood drawn? Did you ever ask your mother?"

"You're an asshole."

"Why did you have to hurt Alex? She's not part of anything. She didn't go to high school with your mother."

"You were messing around with her. She's a goddamn whore."

"She's not a whore."

"'Happy is the man whom God correcteth.'"

"Excuse me?"

"It's from the Bible. Don't you ever read the Bible?"

Danny stared at him in disbelief. Johnny was throwing this bullshit at him like some kind of Holy goddamn Roller.

"Sure, when I'm looking for a quote. It makes me sound self-righteous."

"You're a blasphemer."

"And you kill people. What does that make you?"

"I'm doing holy work. Cleansing the earth of sinners."

"You're murdering women."

"No. I didn't mean . . . I got upset. With the one in the bathroom, I was going to bring her home with me." Johnny gave him another glance, his eyes looking a touch unfocused. "But the others. Those bastards raped my mother. She could have miscarried. You should have stopped them."

"Kid, I didn't know what was happening to your mother."

"Stop lying!"

"I'm not lying. I didn't know. I was with another girl."

"Shut up! Shut up!"

Danny tried to put himself inside this kid, tried to picture growing up with Jenna, her mind unhinged by whatever had happened, maybe taking it out on her child. He knew all about that.

"Michelle Perry never did anything to your mother," Danny said. "You should have stayed away from her. You didn't need to 'cleanse' Barbara Capozzi."

Johnny shook his head. "You're kidding, right? If it wasn't for Babs, my mom wouldn't have been raped. She invited her to Greg's. I cleansed her the way she deserved. Besides, she was mean to my mom. She laughed at her. Called her names. And the other one was your whore, asshole."

"Michelle wasn't a whore, for Christ's sake."

"What do you know?" Johnny turned up the radio. KYW blasted the five-day forecast and then turned to a sports update.

"So why did you kill Greg Moss? He didn't touch your mom."

"I didn't kill Greg. I wanted to save him. He didn't hurt my mom, but he provided a den of sin. But mom said he was nice, so I sent him Bible verses so he'd repent. The others I pronounced

246

sentence on. If you read the texts, you'd understand. They were totally different."

"What?" Danny turned to look at him in surprise. "But he was shot just like the others. I got a text."

"I didn't kill him, and I didn't text you. You weren't supposed to get any messages until it was time. Until the wedding."

"What the hell are you talking about?"

"You're going to marry Mom, and then she'll be happy, and we'll be a family."

"In what alternative universe?"

Johnny glared at him. "I told you! Shut up. Shut up. Shut up!"

"Will you tell me where we're going?"

"You'll find out."

Danny slouched down farther in his seat. Nothing made sense. He was on a road trip to hell with a delusional kid who believed he was his father. Waiting at the other end was Jenna Jeffords, who was waiting to play his blushing bride. Worse, he was losing strength with every passing minute.

If Johnny didn't kill Greg Moss, who did? Danny tried to get his mind to function, but he couldn't force the pieces together. There was no reason for Johnny Jeffords to lie about murdering Greg when he'd easily admitted to killing Michelle and trying to kill Barb.

What was he missing? He had forgotten something important. Kevin had warned him to stay away from Ted Eliot, but they never had a chance to talk about it. There was a connection, though. The realtor on the make and the cop with too much money. Did they have a falling out? Was Eliot providing Greg with some kind of privileged information?

That scenario made sense. If Greg had something on the cop and the cop got tired of jumping to Greg's whistle, maybe he lost his temper. It would be easy to set up the crime scene—except for the tongue, which was pretty weird. Eliot could then take Greg's computer and cell phone and toss them just in case there was anything incriminating.

It made more sense than anything else Danny could come up with. Now all he had to do was prove it.

They had passed Lincoln Financial Field and were passing the Delaware Avenue exit. Danny considered lunging across the seat and grabbing for Johnny's arm, but it wouldn't accomplish much beyond sending the car careening out of control across multiple lanes of traffic. He could take his chances on throwing himself out of the car, but they were travelling at close to eighty. It was early, a little after five thirty, but that didn't mean he wouldn't get squashed by a passing eighteen-wheeler or worse.

In any case, it didn't much matter where he ended up. It wasn't going to be pleasant. He needed to focus on staying in one piece for Kevin. For Alex. If it wasn't already too late.

50

Alex pushed her arms up toward the light like a swimmer emerging from dark water, dragging her body up, up until her head popped out of the dirt. She coughed and pulled herself forward, kicking her legs to widen the hole, knowing she had seconds to get free. Something grasped at her foot, and she tried to kick it away.

Please, please. Oh, dear God. She had to get free, but a hand clamped around her ankle. It pulled her back down into the darkness, and she landed in a heap on the dirt floor, staring up at Jenna, who was resplendent in a sparkling white dress. Her dark hair was caught up in a twist and woven through with sparkling rhinestone beads save for one long curl that hung over her right shoulder. She could have been an ornament for her own front lawn.

Jenna clamped her right hand on her hip. "Where do you think you're going?"

"Please, Jenna. I can't stand the dark. Let me go." She started to reach out, but Jenna slapped her hand away.

"Don't touch me. You're disgusting." Jenna brushed the front of her dress. "Do you want to ruin my wedding dress? That was really stupid, Alex. Now I can't trust you."

"You can. You can." Alex shrank back against the wall. "Your wedding dress? I'm so sorry. It's—you're so beautiful. Please. I got scared when I woke up and saw the sandwiches were poisoned."

"Poisoned?"

"All those ants are dead."

Jenna gave a grim laugh. "The sandwiches aren't poisoned, stupid. They're drugged. You were supposed to eat them and sleep till Johnny got back."

Alex looked up at Jenna, her mind racing. Jenna held a heavy flashlight in her right hand, but no gun. She might have one in the bag she carried over her shoulder, but at the moment, she wasn't pointing it in Alex's direction.

"Why don't you tell me about Johnny?" Alex said.

"What do you mean?"

"Your story. I'd still like to hear it."

Jenna shook her head. "I just said that to get you out here."

"I know, but since I'm here, can't you at least humor me?"

Jenna glared at her with narrowed eyes for a long moment. "You don't really care."

"Yes. I do. I came here for a story. At least let me hear it. The real story." Alex swallowed a few times to force saliva into her mouth. She was filthy and thirsty, and she had to delay her because Jenna might club her with that big flashlight.

"Danny Ryan was my first love."

"Oh, Jenna, I know Danny. He'd never have left you if he knew you had his child. He had a little boy. His name was Conor, and he died a few years ago. Please tell me what happened."

Jenna's face grew pinched, and she rocked back and forth.

"I know it must have been difficult for you," Alex said.

"Danny was my first love. That doesn't mean he loved me back. That bitch Michelle got in the way." Jenna's voice was flat and bitter. "No one loved me back. You know what they called me? Jumbo Jen. Mouth breather. Swamp creature. You know what that's like?" She sneered at Alex. "No. You don't know. I'll bet you were one of them."

How did one reply to the truth? Jenna was right. Alex had been popular, athletic, and smart mouthed. Less proper than her sister, she was a good-time girl, never at a loss for words. Always the center of attention. Now this crazy woman was focused on her, and Alex needed to calm her. She needed to draw her out, like a reverse Scheherazade, and keep her spinning tales.

"Tell me how it was," Alex said. "Woman to woman."

Jenna stared at her. "You don't care about me."

"That's not true. I'm a reporter. I write stories. I want to hear your story. Why did you like Danny? At least tell me that."

That was an easy question. Jenna's tight face relaxed, and for a moment she looked girlish again. In love. Alex shivered.

"Danny was nice to me," Jenna said. "We worked on the newspaper together, but he also wrote these beautiful stories in English class. I mean, he wrote that juvie essay, but he wrote other things, too. I bet you didn't know that he used to write made-up stories. Heartbreaking stories. Like everyone expected he'd be this big novelist—not that being a columnist is a letdown or anything, but you know?" Jenna sighed and patted the front of her dress over her heart. "And he wasn't stuck up about it, so basically he was just sweet and kind."

"Yeah. He is." One of Danny's greatest assets was the way he insinuated himself with people, got them to feel comfortable and reveal those little insights he'd share with his readers. Was it real? Sometimes.

"But didn't you go to the prom with another boy?"

"I paid him." Jenna sighed and a tear rolled down her cheek. "Ollie. A hundred dollars. Half in advance because I knew if I paid the whole thing, he'd screw me and ask someone else."

"But prom was okay, right?" Alex edged back against the wall. Jenna was all sorts of crazy, but once she'd been a girl with hopes and dreams. How much abuse did you have to suffer before you became that swamp creature, especially if you were broken to begin with?

Jenna shrugged. "If you mean, did they dump a bucket of pig's blood on me—which they didn't—then sure, prom was okay. I starved myself for two months and lost twenty pounds. But Danny was with that bitch Michelle Perry, and she was gorgeous in this sparkly dress, and they looked like they belonged in a movie. And I just wanted him to dance with me—like in a movie where the popular guy finally notices the plain girl. But he didn't."

"But I'm sure you looked beautiful, too."

"No, I didn't. I looked like a big red whale." Jenna's face contorted into something between a frown and a grimace. "I lost twenty pounds. But it didn't matter. Everyone still laughed at me."

"Oh, Jenna. I know kids can be awful. But—"

"No buts about it, they were awful. And Danny didn't even notice me. He should have. He really should have."

"Maybe he was, uh, distracted?"

"By Miss Perfect-I'm-So-Smart-and-Skinny-and-Wonderful? You bet he was. She dumped him, you know."

Alex didn't know, and she didn't want to know. Or maybe she did. What was wrong with her? "Jenna, won't you untie my hands? They really hurt. I promise I won't run."

"You have to earn my trust."

"How do I do that?"

"We'll see. Maybe if you're a good bridesmaid."

Jesus. What hell did that mean? She couldn't really believe that she could force Danny to marry her, but Jenna was swaying and humming. Alex would have taken a chance and hurled a piece of the cement at her head, but she wasn't sure she could move fast enough to evade that flashlight.

"At least tell me why you went to Greg's house," Alex said.

"I went to Greg Moss's house because I lost ten more pounds, and Barb said I should come because I looked so glam. I knew Danny would be there, and I thought maybe Michelle wouldn't because her mom was so we're-better-than-everyone. I was as skinny as I ever was in my life. I was just stupid."

"No, you were just young."

"Barb invited me, so I guess I should have known better. Danny wasn't even there when I walked in, but Ollie was. My prom date. Ollie. And he just ignored me. So I got drunk and high, and I thought, why not? I've never been laid. I probably never will get laid. Why not?"

Alex rubbed her head, trying to comprehend what Jenna was telling her. "But why would you want to be around those guys? They were such creeps."

"I don't know. I don't know. I just wanted to be wanted . . . for once." Jenna was crying now. "You don't know. That song. I still hear it. 'Shut 'Em Down.' They kept playing it and playing it. And Frank went first. I had this halter top, and he said I had the biggest tits he'd ever seen. And he just pulled off my shorts and pulled my legs so far apart I thought he broke them.

"I thought it would make me popular, but I was . . . the room smelled like animals. Frank stuck his fingers in me. Then he fucked me. Just like I asked.

"And it hurt. It really hurt, and I wanted it to stop, but they wouldn't. They just kept coming. And that room. It was dark and hot. And Frank kept shouting, 'She loves it.' But I didn't. I wanted them to stop. I just—I couldn't say it."

Alex's blood was pounding. She wanted to hate this pathetic woman, but she couldn't. Jenna Jeffords was a sad specimen. She had been degraded in the worst manner possible.

"Ricky put a pillow over my head 'cause he said I was too ugly to fuck otherwise. He had a little dick, and he made me suck it. Stan was last. He couldn't get it up, so he jerked off on me."

"Oh, Jenna. Why didn't you report it?"

Jenna looked at her without expression. "Report it? It was my fault. I asked for it. I said I wanted to fuck. I didn't stop them."

"It wasn't right," Alex said. "What they did wasn't right."

"I thought about burning down the house. I wanted them to burn," Jenna said. "But I didn't know how. Then, well, you know the rest. I couldn't tell Johnny about how he got here, so I told him a story. It was a nice story."

"He's been killing people to keep that story real."

Jenna banged the flashlight against her palm. "I told him the truth. Okay?"

"What do you mean?"

"After Danny's family died, I knew it was a sign. I knew he thought I was dead, so I, too, would be reborn. I told Johnny what happened, and I told him he could help me clean the slate."

"Clean the slate?"

"Once all the bad ones were gone, everything would be okay again."

"But it's not okay. Don't you understand?" Alex bit her lip to shut herself up when Jenna frowned.

"Danny should have noticed me."

"Tell me about the fire. Please."

"Mother was angry when she found out I was pregnant. She called me names. She wanted me to get an abortion, but I couldn't abort Danny's baby."

Jenna patted her stomach, and Alex let her words sink in. A few moments ago Jenna had seemed completely lucid. Now she had slipped back into fantasyland. It wasn't possible that Danny would have taken advantage of Jenna. The man Alex knew simply wasn't capable of it. The horrible little voice in her head laughed at her. *It's because Jenna's so ugly.* Alex wanted to stop up her ears. No. She knew Danny. He just wouldn't.

She stared at Jenna in panic. "But it's . . . Tell me about the fire. Did Frank set it?"

"Frank? He'd never be that useful. The funny thing is I probably would have run away from home with the household money or something, but the Angel came to me."

"Who came to you?"

Jenna gave her a sly smile. "I can't say."

"Why not?"

"I don't know. Maybe he's not even around anymore. He worked for a guy in South Philly. He helped people."

"Your angel helped people?"

"He built pretty houses for people."

"Do you know who this guy was?"

Jenna shrugged.

"Who set the fires?"

Jenna giggled. "I told you. The Angel."

"Jenna, please."

"He's probably gone by now, but he made a lot of old, ugly places disappear, and then beautiful, new places appeared. I guess people thought he was dumb, just like people thought I was ugly. But he was special, just like me and Danny."

"You knew him?"

Jenna nodded. "Ask Danny if he remembers the Angel. I know he does." She sniffed and blinked as if she just remembered something. "You're a naughty Jezebel, aren't you? You don't fool me, though. You've been trying to slow me down, but we have a wedding to prepare for, and you're going to look beautiful in my red dress."

51

The shredder at G and R Scrap stood silent, and only a black Chevy pickup was parked in the lot when Johnny pulled up to the curb. The gate was unlocked, and Danny recognized an oh-shit inevitability to the situation that made his stomach turn over.

"Did you call Frank Greer?" he asked.

Johnny smirked at him. "No. You did. You texted him. Pretty funny, huh?"

"Hilarious. If you think Frank is going to sit by calmly and let you shoot him, you're an idiot. Maybe he isn't even here. I don't see his car."

"We'll see. Get out of the car and walk to the scale. I'll be right behind you, and I've got a gun. When you see Greer, you tell him I want to talk."

"Talk about what?"

"You just tell him."

The humid air was cloying and thick with dust when Danny opened the door and walked down the gravel driveway toward the scale. He could try running, but he doubted he'd get far. Either Frank or Johnny would open fire. He was like a duck in a shooting gallery. On the other hand, Frank wasn't an idiot.

The road curved to the left, and Danny knew Frank would be watching him approach. Frank wouldn't have a clear line of sight to the road, so he wouldn't see Johnny if he came through the parking lot.

The pink clouds were starting to break the horizon, and Danny held up a hand to shield his eyes. Frank's red Caddy was parked to the side of the trailer, close to the shredder. Danny could see the big scale the trucks pulled onto ahead, and the scale house across from it. It was little more than a broken-down trailer with a wide door and a single window. A camera mounted on the window pointed at the scale. Inside was a video recorder, but Danny couldn't tell if it was running or not. Danny paused and looked back. Nothing. He stood alone. Johnny had cut through the parking lot.

"What the hell do you want, Ryan?" Frank's voice came from the vicinity of the scale house, but he didn't show himself.

Danny looked around. Frank was either inside or pressed against its jutting outer edge.

"Remember that chat we had yesterday?" Danny called. "I think your past is calling."

"What the fuck are you talking about?"

"Your past would like a word or two."

It didn't occur to Danny until the words left his mouth that he might be speaking the truth, but it made a kind of sense. Frank and he were of a similar height and build. They were both dark-haired and blue-eyed. One of them had sex with Jenna Jeffords and was a sociopath. Did the tendency run in families? Maybe it did, especially if Jenna was in the mix.

"Shut up, Ryan," Frank said. Danny could see him now through the filthy window of the scale house. Frank wasn't alone.

"Let's all introduce ourselves," Danny said.

"Let's not," Frank said. "You take that kid and get the fuck off my property. Or we can stand here till the rest of the guys roll in to work. That'll be in about forty minutes. Your choice."

Danny glanced back. The boy had disappeared. *Shit.* He now understood his role: decoy. "Frank," he said. "You better watch—"

A shot pinged the ground right in front of his feet, and he jumped backward. The second shot winged his left calf, and he dropped to the gravel. A third shot whistled past, and Danny realized Johnny must have slipped around the back of the trailer.

Frank started to shout. "Get down! Get down! That goddamn bastard's back here."

Danny heard more shots, but he didn't move. His side was burning. When he twisted and fell, the crude stitches must have torn, and his blood began to seep through his T-shirt at a faster pace. He was at least a pint low by now. That was pretty funny. He thought about making a break for the car, but the effort seemed too great. He lay in the gravel, staring up at the lightening sky.

52

Ted Eliot was pleading for his life.

"Look, you don't understand the pressure I'm under. I can't keep giving up all this information. The brass is starting to get suspicious."

"We need to know what Vice is looking into."

"I don't work Vice. You know how difficult it is for me to get this?"

"You're a smart guy, Ted. You can do it. I mean, think how much worse it would be for you if they saw you on tape, stoned out of your head, getting blown by a tranny hooker. Right?" Greg started to laugh, and Ted jerked awake. Despite the air conditioning, his shirt clung to him.

His good buddy, Greg Moss. When had it all had spun out of control? Bad enough that Greg had wanted confidential police information. Worse, he wanted Ted to start feeding him clients, friends of his mother.

"I want to get into the New York real estate market," Greg had informed him.

"You don't just get into it," Ted had replied.

"I know. You need connections. Rich connections. Like your family. I can show them a good time. Don't pretend they don't party."

"You're crazy if you think you can tap into that, even with my mother's help."

"No. I'm good at getting people what they want."

Ted didn't know he was going to kill Greg until that night. He'd surrendered most of his dignity. He wasn't offering up his family. He'd pulled out his Glock and pointed it at Greg.

"Go upstairs," he'd said.

"Is this something kinky?"

"Just go. When you get to the bedroom, strip down to your boxers."

"You know I'm straight, Ted, but if you pay me enough . . ."

Something had taken over Ted's mind. He walked behind Greg, made him strip down and sit in the middle of the bed. Greg was still taunting him when Ted shot him point blank in the heart. Greg fell back neatly on the bed as if he were sleeping.

He didn't know why he cut out Greg's tongue. He didn't know why he sent that text to Danny Ryan, except Greg had mentioned the weird texts he'd been getting. The friends who had died. Greg had asked him to see if any complaints had been filed in Wildwood in June of 1992. There hadn't been anything, but it gave Ted a hint of something. He thought it would point attention away from the sex parties, and he knew that date would make Ryan look in a completely new direction. Should he have anticipated that a crime had been committed? Ted no longer knew or cared.

The car pulled to a stop with a slight jerk. Early dawn was breaking over Georgetown, and he recognized his father's redbrick townhouse at once. He took a breath and let it out slowly before he exited the car and walked to the green front door. It opened before he could knock.

He followed the silent maid down the quiet hallway, appreciating, in spite of his feelings, his father's taste in colonial furnishings. The blue carpeting set off the rich mahogany furniture, the large grandfather clock ticked away in the corner, and his father's office was a showcase for his massive library of American literature, history, and law. Nobody could accuse Congressman

George Crossman of being an illiterate when it came to the finer points of constitutional law. An authentic copy of the Constitution sat preserved under glass in the holy sanctum of the congressman's office.

Now his father stood up as Ted entered. The congressman was freshly shaved, showered, and dressed in an impeccable gray suit with a white shirt and pink tie. His tan was a perfect bronze, and it set off his blue eyes and dazzling smile. He was freshly Botoxed and, if Ted wasn't mistaken, had recently undergone a little eyelid surgery. In a few years, his father would look younger than he did.

"Ted," his father said, holding out his hand.

"Sir." Ted shoved his hands into his pockets. It was easier to think of him as the congressman than as his father. "Is there a reason for this meeting?"

"I've been concerned about you. This case you've been working. Your mother asked me to check on you."

That was a lie, but Ted admired the ease with which it flowed from his father's lips. If his mother had been concerned, she would have called him herself.

"I'm flattered. What's so urgent that you had to see me face-to-face?"

"This murder investigation. This Greg Moss case."

Ted sank down on the blue brocade sofa facing the fireplace. "What's your interest in Greg Moss? Business or personal?"

His father sighed and sat across from him. "All right. You know, Greg was helping us negotiate that land deal. It will impact the Philadelphia–Camden area. We were looking to acquire property for state and local development, and he had a company willing to work with us. His death was inconvenient."

"Inconvenient?"

His father waved his hand. "Do you have any leads?"

"As far as I know, it was done by someone with a tie to his high school days."

"High school? Are you certain?"

"It looks that way. He was shot with a nine-millimeter semi-automatic. So were several other victims. We can't necessarily tie the victims together, but it looks like a similar shooter. All the victims were in the same high school class. Apparently, they all were receiving text messages. It was a very strange situation."

"And you don't have a suspect?"

"We're working on it."

"How about that reporter? Any connection to the murders?"

"Doubtful. He's not a viable suspect."

"But he's involved."

Ted gauged his father's interest. It was weirdly high. That was both interesting and unnerving. The last thing he needed was his father poking around this investigation. He said, "Dan Ryan is only a witness. We're hoping to reach a satisfactory conclusion to the case soon."

"What about the woman? Alex Burton? She's a pain in my ass."

"I expect she's doing her job."

"I'd like her to disappear."

Eliot shrugged. "That's not my department. I'm not your trained baboon. I don't make people disappear. I said I would keep you apprised of new developments. There are none."

"I wasn't suggesting—"

"I think you were."

"Let's try this again." His father clasped his hands together and leaned forward. "You, you're well? You've been able to carry on?"

Ted shifted in his seat and looked away. "Is this the real reason you brought me all this way? To ask questions you could have asked over the phone?"

His father smiled. "Ted, we're on the verge of making an enormous investment in the area. It will bring jobs and—"

"Please. What's your end of the whole thing? This must mean something to you or you wouldn't have me sitting in your house."

"That's unkind."

"That's true."

His father sighed as if grievously wounded. As if that were possible. He said, "I have a small stake in the development. It's important that it be done right."

A small stake? His father never had a small stake in anything. Whatever he was involved in had to be big. As Greg always said, he liked making connections. It was a partnership sealed in hell.

"Greg was your partner."

"Something like that."

"How something?"

His father smiled his wide constituent smile and brushed a nonexistent piece of lint off of his trousers. "We were connected," he said. "That's all you need to know."

That's all he wanted to know. In the end, Ted didn't care about his father's deals and connections. He wanted to get out of this house and as far away from his father's world as possible. He said, "Greg's death wasn't connected to your deal, as far as I can see. So you can rest safe."

"You're sure that it won't come back to bite me?"

"I'm sure it had nothing to do with your business."

"That's what I wanted to hear."

"Am I free to go?"

"You're welcome to stay for breakfast."

"You'll understand if I decline."

His father nodded. "I'll have my driver take you back at once."

Ted stood. Only his father would drive him down to Washington for a ten-minute conversation because he was either too paranoid or too smart to talk on the phone. He wanted to go home, stand under a hot shower, and scald himself.

"And Ted," his father added, "I don't suppose I need to remind you that this conversation never happened."

"What conversation?"

*

Congressman Crossman stood by the window and watched the car with his son inside pull away. Ted had looked gaunt, and his eyes were ringed with dark shadows. His lifestyle was catching up with him, or maybe he had something weighing on his mind. It was hard to be sure.

"So the prodigal son returned. What do you think?"

Crossman turned to assess Senator Robert Harlan. The older man stood in the doorway, a steaming cup of black coffee in his hand. His black eyes were, as always, cold and calculating, like those of a hawk or a vulture. Crossman hadn't gotten involved with the nasty business that had sullied Harlan a few years ago. He'd heard the chatter about the child porn ring. Harlan wasn't personally involved—or so he'd said—but he'd invested money in some dubious clubs. It was enough to destroy his presidential ambitions. Nothing mucked you up faster than whispers about child abuse. There was no way around that bad press.

"I think there isn't going to be much of an investigation into Greg Moss's business dealings. This murder seems connected to a serial killer, as I told you. If it was something else, Ted would tell me."

"Would he? You're not that close." Harlan paused to sip his coffee, his lips curling in what was close to a sneer. "Why do you have such faith? What's changed in your relationship?"

"I got Ted his job. I've covered up for him and pulled strings. If there were a problem, he'd tell me. He has a sense of survival."

"Indeed." Harlan crossed the room, a little slowly, and sat on the sofa. "Survival. Yes. I suppose that's a motivating force, but I know Daniel Ryan. If there's dirt to be found, he'll dig it up."

"Your son-in-law?"

"Former." Harlan practically hissed the words, and Crossman watched his eyes turn to black tunnels. *Christ almighty.* He never wanted anyone to look at him with that amount of malice. A shudder passed through him.

"Don't worry about that. I'm telling you. The cops say it's some deranged serial killer. Maybe Ryan's the one doing the killing. You never know."

"No. We couldn't get that lucky. It would be nice if he were to accidentally step in front of a bullet though."

"He's not important, Bob. He's not going to play a role in this investigation. He might end up dead himself."

"We can only hope." Harlan set down the coffee cup on the Chippendale table and leaned back against the brocade cushions. "Don't let this get out of control. Do you understand?"

"Everything is under control."

53

Two more shots rang out. They were followed by a shout and three more shots, but these weren't coming at him. They were coming from inside the scale house. Danny stared up at the sky. He wasn't dead yet. Blood soaked the leg of his jeans, but the bullet appeared to have grazed the skin instead of lodging in his leg. It ached, but he'd live.

He had to get out of the line of fire. He took a deep breath.

Pull yourself together, Ryan.

Danny pushed himself into a crouch and gauged the distance between the scale and the side of the scale house. Less than fifteen feet. He could do that. His heart was pumping. Then he heard voices. Johnny must have made it into the scale house while he was napping in the sun.

"What's on the intake belt this morning, Frank? Nothing? Gotta fix that."

Johnny was dragging Frank outside, and Danny could see Frank's left arm dangling as if it were broken. Blood leaked from his left shoulder, painting the yellow fabric of his polo shirt scarlet. The left side of his head was bandaged from where Danny had hit him yesterday, and he sported a black eye.

"Ryan," Frank shouted, "tell this little shit to let me go!"

"Let's get things fired up, right?" Johnny pointed his gun at Frank. "Let's get the shredder rolling, Frank. Nothing like getting an early start." He looked at Danny. "Isn't that right, Dad?"

"What the hell are you doing?" Danny said.

"Get up." Johnny pointed the gun at him, and Danny struggled to his feet. "Move, Dad."

Danny walked with them to the shredder, trying to process what was happening. There had to be something he could do. Frank tried to pull away, but Johnny twisted his left arm hard enough that Frank went down on his knees. He didn't try to resist any longer.

The control panel sat above the machine, housed in a glass-enclosed booth. "You first, Dad." Danny pulled himself up the steps while Johnny dragged Frank up behind him. "Turn it on," Johnny said.

Frank turned on the motor, and the shredder rumbled to life. The intake belt gave a quick lurch and then began to roll up toward the top of the shredder, ready to feed mashed cars and chunks of metal to the hungry machine.

"What the hell do you think you're doing?" Frank shouted.

Johnny turned on him, his eyes gleaming. "Come on. We need to make a deposit." He looked at Danny and pointed the gun. "Move."

Danny said nothing. He walked with Johnny and Frank back to the scale house.

"No games," Johnny said to Frank.

Frank didn't appear to be in any kind of shape to fight. He was losing blood too fast. Danny didn't think he'd ever seen Frank look so helpless. Together, he and Frank made half a person.

Danny went with them into the scale house. Lying on the floor next to one of the big scales was a thin guy with the jack of spades tattooed on his bicep. The back of his head was blown away. Bits of brain and skull fragments covered the floor.

"Wrap his head in something," Johnny said.

Danny shook his head. "It's a little late, don't you think?"

"Mom doesn't like a dirty floor."

Danny exchanged a glance with Frank, whose eyes darted around the room. Danny knew he was looking for a weapon. He followed Frank's frantic gaze. There had to be something. In the huge wire baskets were bits of metal. On the pretext of looking for some kind of covering, he palmed a sharp piece of copper pipe and slid it in his pocket. It was small, but it would have to do. "Who the hell is this?" Danny asked.

"Mark Piscone." Frank's voice was a weak monotone. He found a filthy piece of oil cloth, and Danny helped tie it around what was left of the guy's head.

"Take him to Frank's car," Johnny said. He gestured with the gun.

Together, Frank and Danny managed to drag Mark Piscone's body to the car and throw him in the trunk. Before they could shut the trunk, Johnny tossed in a propane canister.

"This is an expensive goddamn car," Frank said. "Jesus Christ."

"Too bad," Johnny said. "Here's how it works. You see that machine right there?" He pointed to a large construction vehicle with an arm that ended in a metal claw. "That's called a grappler. Right, Frank?"

"So what?"

"Give me the keys. I know you got the keys to everything." He grabbed Frank's ring from his fingers and pulled him to the side of the car. "You look tired, Frank. You should sit down." He opened the door to the back seat and shoved Frank inside.

"What the fuck?" Frank started to grab the door, but Johnny grabbed him by the neck and leaned over him. He shot Frank first in the left kneecap and then the right.

Frank began to howl. "Who sent you? I told Crossman I'd keep my mouth shut about the land. I don't care about the arsenic. What the fuck is this?"

Danny tried to grab the gun, but the kid clubbed him on the side of the head.

"Jesus Christ, you can't do this!" Danny cried.

"Sure I can. They're childproof locks." Johnny smacked Danny again, then hit the ignition button through the open front window. He slammed the door shut. Danny could hear Frank screaming.

"Jesus Christ. I wasn't gonna to talk! Tell Crossman! I wasn't tryin' to jam him!"

"It's not about Crossman! It's about my mother. You raped my mother! Jenna Jeffords!" Johnny leaned in and fired another shot at Frank, who slumped over, whimpering.

Frank's mouth dropped open, and he stared at Johnny with a mix of revulsion and horror. "I didn't rape her!"

Johnny grabbed Danny and pulled him to the grappler before he climbed in. "Watch this." He turned the ignition, and the machine rumbled beneath them. Danny could hear Frank wailing.

Danny shouted, "Jesus Christ, let him out. What the hell are you doing?" He ran toward Frank's Caddy.

"I don't care about land. I care about my mom." Johnny guided the grappler over to the car and dropped the claw before Danny could reach it. It grabbed the Caddy in its steel jaws, and Johnny pressed a lever. The car swung up in the air, and he dropped it on the intake ramp.

Frank was struggling to free himself, but he had no strength. When Danny tried to jump onto the intake ramp, Johnny fired a shot that nearly grazed him.

"I'll put the next shot through your stomach, Dad."

The car was nearly at the top of the shredder. "I didn't rape her. Your mom wanted it. I could be your father!" Frank was shouting.

"'Woe unto them that call evil good and good evil'!" Johnny yelled.

Danny ran to the booth and tried to grab the shredder controls, but Johnny was on him. He clubbed him once more with the butt of his gun, knocking him to the ground. "No!"

Frank's screams were barely audible over the roar of the shredder as the car tipped inside. The propane tank exploded. The machine rumbled and belched as it digested the car and what was left of its contents. Danny closed his eyes. He'd just helped Johnny Jeffords commit murder.

"Move." The kid had him by the arm again. "It's time to go see Mom."

"I think you just killed your father."

"'Fools make mock at sin.'"

"Did you look at him?"

Johnny raised his arm as if he was going to club him again but turned away. "Just get moving."

Danny glanced back at the shredder. The sun had cleared the horizon, but he was shaking with cold. This kid. This crazy god-damn kid. Danny reached into his back pocket for the piece of copper and leapt up, driving the pipe toward Johnny's throat, but the kid deflected his arm. The copper shank tumbled onto the platform, and Johnny beat Danny with his gun until he sank to his knees.

"Stupid move, Dad. Now I can't trust you."

"You aren't my son," Danny managed to say.

"Fuck you."

Danny's right eye had swollen shut, and he stumbled as Johnny dragged him back toward the car. Then he thought about Alex. He had to pull himself together for her. It didn't matter what happened to him. He had to help Alex.

54

Alex edged back toward the wall, heart pounding. Jenna didn't move, but she watched with a sort of dispassionate amusement. In her right hand, Jenna gripped the large black flashlight, ready to club Alex should she get any ideas about running. Did she have any other weapons hidden? Alex tried to assess. Could she overpower Jenna? Possibly, but Jenna outweighed her by more than a hundred pounds. It could be an advantage or disadvantage. Maybe Jenna wouldn't want to muss her wedding gown.

"Here. Put this on," Jenna said. She pulled a red satin dress out of her bag and threw it at Alex. She recognized the dress. It was the same one Jenna wore in the prom photo.

"I think you should let me go. Before it's too late." Alex kept her voice even and glared at Jenna, trying to keep herself calm. She couldn't show weakness. She had to seem confident, like she knew she was going to be rescued. She had to believe it or she'd fall apart. "Please, Jenna." Alex tried to make herself as small as she could. If Jenna got near her, Alex could kick out and maybe knock the heavier woman off balance. It was a crap plan, but that was all she had.

She wished her head didn't ache so much. Her mouth tasted like it was full of old socks. The tape had loosened on her wrists, but it still bound them together. Alex didn't know how much longer she could fend Jenna off.

"Don't make me hurt you, Alex. Put on the dress."

"But I'm so dirty."

"You shouldn't have tried to get out."

"I can't with my hands tapped."

When Jenna took a step toward her, Alex cringed a little.

"Lie on the ground," Jenna said. "Put your arms above your head and don't move."

Alex considered charging Jenna, but she still felt unsteady. She lay on the ground and held up her arms. She felt a quick tug and heard the sound of metal snipping through the tape before she realized Jenna was cutting her hands free with a pair of scissors.

Jenna stepped back. "Okay. Get changed."

Alex stripped out of her clothing and stepped into the red dress, her hands clumsy and swollen. She managed to pull it up, though, and fasten the halter top. It hung on her, the upper half ballooning away from her body, the hem too short. She might as well have been naked for all the coverage the dress provided.

"Bitch," Jenna said. "You're too skinny! Get back down on the ground where you belong."

Alex tensed, keeping her eyes on Jenna. Was it worth trying to keep Jenna talking? She had to try. "Why did you kill Ollie Deacon?"

"Ollie Deacon?" Jenna rocked back and forth. "What difference does it make?"

"Why him and not Frank Greer?"

Jenna scowled and tapped the flashlight against her hand. "I know what you're doing. You're wasting my time."

"I'm trying to understand. Tell me why you killed Ollie."

Alex watched Jenna, the way she rocked back and forth, tapping her flashlight. She wanted to get on with whatever she planned to do, but a part of her wanted to talk. Maybe she hadn't ever talked about all of this—the prom, the kids, her anger and hurt. Jenna had crossed a line, but maybe she had been forced over it. Cruelty could easily break a fragile mind.

"Tell me, Jenna," she said.

Jenna smacked the flashlight down against her hand. "I had to pay him to go to the prom, and he didn't even buy me flowers." *Smack.* The flashlight came down on her palm again. "I mean, I got him a boutonnière, and he couldn't even get me a lousy wrist corsage. He was there that night, and he just got fucking stoned. Ollie Deacon was a useless piece of shit." *Smack. Smack.*

"He became a cop."

"He was a lousy cop, too. I followed him for a week, and he didn't even notice me. He deserved to get shot."

"You must have been pretty clever."

Jenna glared at Alex, her eyes wide and furious. Crazy eyes. Alex waited for them to turn into cartoon pinwheels, but they remained focused and malevolent.

"I didn't have to be clever. I'm fat." *Smack.* "When you're fat, people look right past you like you don't deserve to be there. Nobody noticed me. I shot Ollie on a street corner right in front of his house, and six people said I was a black guy. How do you like that? Do I look black to you? Somebody even thought I was a clown." *Smack. Smack.*

So much for eye witnesses. Alex wanted to be outraged, but right now, she couldn't manage it. All she could do was huddle with her back against the wall and wait for Jenna to come to her.

"Is that how you killed the other guys? You just went up to them and shot them?"

"I didn't kill them. Johnny did. I helped, though. We followed them. Some of them for weeks. Nate. Ricky. Chris. They were so stupid."

"You were clever."

"I didn't have to be clever. You know why it was so easy to become my mother? Because she was an old, fat woman." *Smack. Smack. Smack.* "All I had to do was cut my hair and change the color. I put on her dress and played with some makeup, and it was so easy. They didn't even check the bones because who would believe it? My mother was only thirty-five anyway."

"You killed your own mother."

"My mother was a bitch. I couldn't do anything right. It was always, 'If you'd just eat salad, Jenna,' or 'Don't wear that, Jenna. It makes you look chunky.' Like I didn't already know that."

"Maybe she was just trying to help."

"Maybe she was just being a bitch. She made fun of my stories. She always was after me to do something practical. Everything I did was wrong!" *Smack.* Alex thought Jenna would break her hand with that flashlight.

"I don't understand. You killed your mom. You killed Ollie. Why did you wait to kill the others?"

Jenna blinked. "Isn't it obvious? Danny's wife died."

"I don't understand."

"He thought I was dead. So when I heard about his wife and little boy, I knew it was a sign. We needed a clean slate. We could start all over again out here. Together forever. With our son. Our beautiful boy."

"Wow." Alex tried to comprehend what Jenna was telling her. "I don't know what to say."

"Of course I had to tell Johnny about what happened that night. It upset him something fierce, because I raised our son right."

"I'll bet you were a wonderful mom," Alex said.

Jenna caressed the flashlight. The red faded from her cheeks, and she patted her hair. She was still scowling, but she looked less fierce, as if the storm was passing.

"I *was* a wonderful mother. I did everything for my Johnny. Everything. He still nurses, you know. Still sleeps with me. We have an unbreakable bond. Completely unbreakable. He'd do anything for me. He loves his mommy."

Alex shuddered but gave her a tentative smile. "I bet he does. So why don't we sit here and talk until he gets back?"

"Oh, I don't think so. We have to get ready, but I don't think I can trust you."

"What do you mean?"

"Well, I can't keep you down here any longer," Jenna said.

Alex didn't wait to hear any more. She launched herself at Jenna, knocking the larger woman backward. All she had to do was get to the top of the stairs and out of the upstairs door. Alex took the stairs two at a time until she came to the top. The door was locked.

Hurling herself against the door, Alex screamed, "Help me!" She pounded it with her fists and rammed it with her shoulder again and again until she collapsed on the top step. When she looked down, Jenna stood at the foot of the stairs watching her with that strange smile. She patted the flashlight against her left hand.

"You're pretty funny, Alex. Where do you think you're going? Do you think I'd be so dumb that I'd leave the door unlocked?"

"Please." Alex's throat was raw.

"'Please, please, please,'" Jenna said. "I'm not gonna hurt you. Unless you keep doing stupid shit. I need you."

"Need me. For what?"

"You're gonna be my maid of honor, of course."

"What?" Alex's legs were trembling. Jenna wasn't kidding. She really believed she was getting married. Jenna continued to regard her with a cool, amused smile.

"You should be flattered, Alex. It's a great honor, you know. I don't even like you."

"Who's the lucky groom?"

"You have to ask?"

Alex nodded. Yeah, she had to ask, though she knew the answer.

"It's Danny. We're going to get married as soon as he gets here."

"Danny!" Alex almost started to laugh but realized tears were blurring her eyes. It was too bizarre the way Jenna veered in and out of reality. "How do you know he's even coming?"

"Our boy is going to bring him home, and we'll be a family. At last. It'll be a happy ending. A beautiful ending." Jenna frowned and put her hands on her hips. "Now you have to cooperate, because I have a lot to do and not much time."

"And if I don't?"

"I'll kill you," Jenna said in a matter-of-fact voice. "So let's not make this unpleasant. I have a wedding to plan!"

55

Despite the early morning traffic on the Washington Belt-way, Ted Eliot was back home by nine o'clock. He'd already called in sick. Now all he wanted was to crash for the rest of the day and night.

He wished he could go back two weeks and start over, though that was surely not long enough. He needed years, not weeks. How did you erase a mountain of bad decisions? He'd wanted to get away from his father, and now he was tethered to him tighter than ever.

But there was something more going on. Something was wrong about those properties—at least some of them. There was some kind of cover-up going on.

Ted dragged himself up his front walk and unlocked his door. He didn't care about his father's schemes. He had no interest in exposing him for the fraud he was. Ted didn't want to play any role in his father's life at all. He wanted to get away.

He stepped inside, and someone grabbed his arms from behind. Cuffs snapped on his wrists as a bag dropped over his head.

"Hello, Ted," said a soft voice. "We have things to discuss. Have a seat."

Ted struggled to stand, but strong hands shoved him back into the chair.

"Who are you?" he said. He couldn't see anything with the bag that smelled like old cigars tied over his head. His neck itched, and he could hear his heart rattling. What was this new insanity?

"We need to talk about Greg Moss," said the voice.

"Greg Moss?" Ted's bowels went cold.

"Tell me who killed Greg."

"We think he was murdered by someone he knew from high school."

"Was he? Was he really? What happened to his phone? His computer?"

Ted swallowed. No one knew about the phone and computer disappearing. It was privileged information. Only someone connected to the case could know about it.

"Who are you?"

"Right now, I'm the person asking the questions. All you have to do is answer."

"Who sent you?"

"What did I tell you? I'm asking the questions, Ted. Let's not make this more unpleasant than it has to be."

If this guy was willing to break into a cop's house, things could get nasty indeed. Ted didn't want proof of intent. He could hear the determination in the speaker's silky voice.

"His phone and computer were gone. But we know he was getting messages before he was murdered. Weird messages. Bible quotes. He told people. We believe the other victims were getting similar messages."

"What else?"

"He was shot with a nine-millimeter semi. I'm betting a Glock because they're common and light. All the other vics were shot with a nine millimeter."

"The Glock's a cop gun."

Ted swallowed hard. "It's a common gun. Lighter than some other models."

"And it matches the gun used to kill the other victims."

"The model is the same. We don't know if it was the same gun. We can't make a ballistics match for any of the victims."

"I see."

Ted listened to the ensuing silence. The person behind him shifted, the floorboards protesting slightly, and he became aware of the heavy breathing growing uncomfortably close. Ted was sweating, the rank smell of stogies filling his nostrils. He had been running all his life, trying to be something; he could no longer remember what. He no longer cared.

"And Dan Ryan. Is he a part of this?" The voice spoke with a strange urgency.

"No. He just stumbled into it."

"Are you sure?"

"Yes. He wasn't involved."

He heard the voice give an audible sigh. Of relief or frustration? Ted wasn't sure.

"And Frank Greer?"

Ted almost jumped. "Frank Greer? I don't know Frank Greer."

"That's kind of hard to believe. Greg said you were going to help him with people like Frank."

"What? No. Greg and I were friends, but that was a while back. I got straight. He never—"

"He never asked for a favor?"

Of course he had. Over and over. Favors on favors until Ted reached his breaking point. *Wasn't that what you said when you finally snapped? You reached your breaking point? Sorry, old friend, but I've made one too many compromises.*

"Yes. I did him favors. But he never asked for anything . . . major."

"Are you sure about that?"

"He wasn't stupid."

But Greg was greedy, and once he got his claws into something, he never let go. Ted took a breath. Was this person going to shoot him? Did it matter? Did he care?

Again, that suffocating silence. Ted closed his eyes. In a way, he would welcome permanent quiet. This had become too much of a burden to carry.

At length, there was another deep sigh.

"Okay, Ted. I'm choosing to believe you for the moment. I hope it's not a mistake. For both our sakes. I'm gonna unlock those cuffs and put you in the closet for now. Pretty ironic, huh? Don't disappoint me."

Ted heard the click of the key turning in the lock as the cuffs slipped off his wrists. He was propelled out of his seat, into the hall closet, and shoved in among the coats. By the time he had managed to yank the bag off his head, his inquisitor had gone. Like magic. He didn't know who he was or where he had come from.

All he knew for certain was that he was a very dangerous man.

And he could easily make Ted disappear.

56

"We're here, Dad."

Danny didn't answer. He stared up from the trunk at Johnny Jeffords and tried to get his bearings. He was soaked with sweat. The trunk was like a small tin oven, and he had been cooked on the drive to wherever they were. Swaying evergreens rose up around them, and the sky had grown overcast. Strange things peered at him from behind the trees. He cowered back until he realized the figures were resin elves. *What the hell is this place?*

"You look like shit, Dad." Johnny reached out a hand to pull him out of the trunk. Danny shook his head, trying to clear it. He needed to regain his faculties. He needed to find Alex.

"I hope love is blind. Mom's been waiting a long time to see you."

"Your mom's a psycho, just like you." He couldn't summon the wit to parry with this kid. He could barely put one foot in front of the other.

"You better be nice to my mom, because I've got your friend."

"If you hurt Alex, I'll kill you." Even he didn't believe his rasping voice.

The trees shivered and swayed, and Danny blinked at the brightly colored pinwheels spinning in the air. As they approached a dark-green ranch house, he stared at the red ceramic toadstools and elves that littered the front lawn and hid behind trees. Yard junk, Beth would have called it. Eccentric, he would have countered if he were feeling kinder. He wasn't feeling kind, but the fog in his head was lifting as the air cooled his body. Thunder growled in the west, and Danny could smell rain in the air.

Johnny ushered him into the house, and Danny looked around for any sign of Alex. But there was nothing. It was a simple ranch house, decorated in yellow and green and smelling of floral air freshener. Danny heard a cuckoo clock ticking in the cluttered living room.

"Your mother doesn't seem to be at home," he said, staring at the paintings and embroideries of big-eyed puppies, kittens, and children that adorned the living room walls. It was Jenna Jeffords's precious world where romance novels came true—at least in her own mind. Disney tunes should have been playing in the background to complete the ambiance.

"Come on," Johnny said.

"Interesting artwork," Danny said.

"Mom did the paint-by-numbers herself."

The cuckoo clock chimed the hour, and two fat wooden children emerged from one miniature door to chase a black-and-white puppy around into another. Danny stood gaping. It earned him another smack on the side of the head as Johnny dragged him out to the kitchen. He pulled a bottle of water from the refrigerator.

"You drink some first," Danny said.

"Don't be stupid. It's still sealed."

"You first, Son."

Johnny twisted off the cap and downed half of the bottle. He wiped his mouth. "Less for you now," he said and handed it to Danny.

"Thank you."

Johnny squinted at him, maybe to see if Danny was being sarcastic. When he realized Danny was sincere, Johnny actually smiled. He pulled out a second bottle. "You better take this."

His mouth was parched, and the cold water brought tears to his eyes, but Danny sipped from the bottle, not wanting to cramp up. He needed to stay alert.

Johnny led him out the back door, and they set off down a dirt path. The wind was rising, and the dark clouds were rolling in, obscuring the sun. A fat drop of rain plopped down, followed by another and another.

"Where are we going?" Danny asked.

Johnny pushed him in the back. "To find Mom."

"What about Alex? Is she alive?"

"Last time I saw her."

The rain was falling in sheets by the time they reached a clearing where a dark-green utility shed stood. Beyond them, the river churned and bubbled, its brown water filled with debris. The thunder now seemed to roll across the sky as lightning flashed in shining forks.

Danny was soaked once again, but he didn't care. It felt good against his blistered skin.

"In here." Johnny pushed him toward the utility shed.

Were they keeping Alex in this metal shack? It had no windows, and when Johnny opened the door, heat blasted out. A bolt of lightning illuminated the inside for a moment. Danny glimpsed old rakes and a riding mower, as well as a few brooms and saws. A wall had been constructed inside the shed with a heavy-looking metal door.

"Open the door," Johnny said. He pulled out a small flashlight from his back pocket and trained it on the door. He handed Danny a set of keys.

Danny fumbled with the lock. "You're keeping her here? Like a goddamn animal?" He pushed open the door and stared down the steps.

In the dim light, Danny could see that Jenna Jeffords lay on her back at the foot of the stairs, tangled in what appeared to be a wedding dress. She looked up at Danny, lips white and eyes glazed. When Johnny nudged him in the back with his gun, Danny took a cautious step down into the dank cellar.

Jenna's lips were trembling. "You came," she said. "I knew you would."

"Jesus Christ. What happened here?" Danny tried to take in his surroundings. Water poured through a hole in the corner of the cellar, puddling on the dirt floor. He couldn't see Alex. Where the hell was she?

"My leg is broken, or maybe it's my hip," Jenna said. "We fell down the steps."

"Where is Alex?"

Jenna sighed. "Gone."

Danny knelt beside her. "What do you mean gone?"

"She ran away. Left me here."

"Goddamn bitch. I'll kill her!" Johnny shouted, and Danny grabbed his arm.

"No. Call nine-one-one. Get an ambulance for your mother."

He could only hope that Alex had found a telephone and a way out of this place. Outside, the storm was raging, and he wondered if the foundation for the shed would hold. The metal groaned in the wind.

"This doesn't seem too stable," he said to Johnny. "This whole shed could collapse."

"I don't want to die in a hole," Jenna sobbed.

"Fuck!" Johnny banged his fist against the railing.

"Call for help," Danny said.

"How could you let her get away, Ma?"

Danny grabbed the kid's arm. "We need to get your mother out of here. Do you understand that?"

Johnny stared at him with wide, unfocused eyes. "We got unfinished business, Ma. It won't be right if we don't finish."

Jenna clutched Danny's hand. "You came back to me," she said.

He wanted to pull away, but the horror that was Jenna Jeffords held him to the spot. If he stayed, maybe it bought Alex time. "What happened here, Jenna?"

"Ma! We need to take care of business!"

"She doesn't need to do anything. She needs help!"

Johnny leaned close for a moment. "Don't worry, Ma. I'll call for an ambulance. Then I'm gonna find that bitch." He took off up the stairs, and Danny heard the door slam. Now he was trapped.

"Jenna," he said. "Do you have a phone?"

"No service down here," she said. "But at least we're together. Do you like my gown? It's just like Michelle's prom dress. I thought it would be beautiful for the wedding."

"Oh, Christ, Jenna. This whole goddamn building is going to collapse."

"We'll be like Romeo and Juliet."

The side of the shed seemed to lift slightly and settle as the wind caught it, and one of the jacks supporting the floor tilted and slid sidewise. The hole in the side of the foundation had opened into a gash and water gushed through. It sounded as if a freight train was bearing down on them. The shed moaned and swayed as the wind picked up volume.

The side of the shed gave a final moan and began to collapse in on itself. Danny saw the ceiling begin to buckle and dragged Jenna toward the stairs. As the ceiling gave way, he wedged both of them as close as possible to the stairs and closed his eyes.

57

From inside Jenna's ranch house, Alex had watched Johnny Jeffords drag Danny down the dirt path to the shed. She didn't know how much time she had. She gave a quick glance at the balled-up prom dress on the bathroom floor and shuddered.

It was still pouring rain, but the wind had died down somewhat. Alex was pretty sure a tornado had touched down close by, because she had never seen the sky turn that copper color or heard wind howl with that force. For a few moments, she'd thought the house was going to lift up and swirl into the angry sky. She'd hidden herself in the master bathroom of the creepy house, crouching in a pink ceramic tub until the wind subsided.

Alex heard sirens in the distance.

She'd already called 9-1-1 and was torn about what to do next. She didn't want to wait in this house any longer than necessary. She could get out. She'd found her purse in what she supposed was Jenna's bedroom, a pink-and-white lacy boudoir covered with needle-pointed sentiments straight out of clichéland—"Every day is special because you're alive"—and the same dreary pictures of kittens and puppies. On Jenna's nightstand was the same altered prom photo. It made Alex's skin crawl.

Alex couldn't go searching in a prom dress. She found a stretched-out yellow spandex shirt in Jenna's drawer and a pair of men's running shorts. They were dark blue and didn't hang down to her knees, so she figured they belonged to Johnny. Alex looked at Jenna's shoes, every pair a size six. She found a pair of Johnny's running shoes and put on two pairs of socks.

Alex glanced in the mirror. No time to do anything with her filthy self.

She found her car keys and figured her car was in the garage. There was nothing to keep her from leaving, except she knew Danny was out there. She took her purse to the garage where her car stood waiting for her. Her phone was still tucked under the passenger's seat, and when she pulled it out and turned it on, she had one bar of service and almost a full battery. She found a flashlight, some rope, a baseball bat, and some gardening shears. Maybe she'd need them; maybe she wouldn't. It wouldn't hurt to go prepared.

*

When she reached the clearing, Alex stared at the space where the shed had stood. The thing had collapsed inward. She ran to the edge, sliding in the mud, and peered over.

Wood flooring and beams stuck out, as did jagged pieces of aluminum siding that looked to have been crumpled by a large fist. A riding mower sat upside down in the mud thirty feet away, and two rakes stuck out of the edge of the hole at right angles. She grabbed one and leaned as far as she could over the hole.

"Danny?"

She tried to remember where the stairs would have been and moved to her right. It was a mess of twisted metal, concrete, and mud down there. Rain was pouring into the hole.

"Danny?"

If she had enough rope, she could climb down at least partway. She wasn't going to leave him in that hole. No matter what.

"Danny. I've got rope and a light. I'm gonna climb down."

The silence terrified her. *What if . . .*

A tree stood ten feet from the hole, and Alex tied the rope to it. She tied the other end to her waist and stood by the rakes. The river was swollen, already starting to overflow. If it got much higher, the ground would be completely underwater.

"Ryan," she called. "Can you hear me?" She wished she could whistle. Maybe he'd hear a whistle. Going over the edge of this hole seemed a little foolhardy. Did it matter? Was now a good time to remember she was afraid of heights? Was climbing down the same as climbing up?

Just do it.

She sat on the edge. A sheet of metal jutted out. She could grasp it and work her way down. The rain made the metal slippery and hard to hold onto, and she had to keep the rope from getting tangled. Slowly she began to ease her way down into the darkness. The metal groaned.

"Ryan? Where are you?"

In the gray light, she could see a pool of water filled with debris. She didn't know how deep it was, but it seemed to be in the center of the room. What if he was trapped underwater? She fumbled for the flashlight.

"Danny?"

She thought she heard someone call her name.

"Danny?"

She let go of the metal piece and lowered herself straight down.

The water was cold, slimy, and knee deep. She shuddered and shined the flashlight around the room. The shed had collapsed in toward the middle, though pieces of debris lay all about in the water. Alex picked her way through the cement blocks and broken wood.

"Ryan!"

"Alex!"

His voice came from her right, and it occurred to her he probably hadn't been able hear her over the pouring rain and groaning metal when she was above ground. A piece of the floor had crashed down and cut the room in half.

"I'm going to see if I can find a way around this. Are you okay?" Alex called.

"Jenna's hurt pretty bad. I think her legs are crushed."

"I called nine-one-one. Can you see my flashlight?"

"Alex, it isn't stable in here."

"To hell with that. Where are you? Are you hurt? Can you see my goddamn flashlight or not?"

"I can see it."

She could almost feel him take a breath, and she willed him to hang on.

58

D anny supported Jenna's head in his lap and tried to slide closer to the steps. He couldn't see much in the gloom, but he could tell from the groaning of the metal and the fallen debris that the ceiling had collapsed. The cellar was flooding. He could hear water rushing uncomfortably close, though the water was only a few inches deep in the area where he and Jenna sat. When the ceiling had come down, Jenna's legs had been crushed, pinning her to the ground. Somehow the shock had kept her from processing the pain, or maybe her back was more damaged than either of them realized.

He watched the thin beam of Alex's flashlight at the far end of the room. She squeezed herself though a crevice, untied a rope from her waist, and picked her way across the floor. She was covered with muck, her clothes were torn, and she had never looked so beautiful.

"Ryan." She ran the beam of the light over Jenna and him. "Are you hurt? Oh, man. The only way out is up the side of the wall on the other side."

Jenna began to wail. "I can't get out. I can't get out. This is your fault," she said to Alex.

"My fault?" Alex gave her a grim smile. "You and your nutball son created this little hideaway. How is this is my fault?"

Jenna clutched Danny's hand. "Please don't leave me here in the dark. I'm so afraid."

"Help is coming," Alex said. She leaned closer and touched Danny's face. "Jesus, Ryan. Someone beat the hell out of you. Your face is blacker than mine."

Danny was pretty sure he looked worse than he felt. His lap was soaked with blood, but he wasn't sure how much was his and how much was Jenna's. He suspected she was in far worse shape than he was, though his thoughts seemed to be running on a ten-second delay. "It's not a big deal. I'm a little beat-up, but I'll live. I'm okay otherwise."

"Not down here. You'll get some kind of flesh-eating bacteria. You'd better come with me. You'll be lucky if you just get off with a concussion."

Jenna whimpered and clutched his arm tighter. Danny didn't know how much longer she had before the shock wore off and the pain set in. If she were lucky, Jenna would pass out, but her prospects seemed pretty grim. Danny wasn't sure how much faith Jenna should put in luck.

"You can't just sit here," Alex said. "This place is going to flood."

"I can't leave her alone," Danny said. Too many people had let Jenna suffer alone.

"So maybe you like me a little," Jenna said.

He leaned his head back against the wall and looked up at Alex. She shook her head.

"We were meant to be together," Jenna said.

Maybe this was how things ended: trapped in a flooding basement with a poor deluded woman who lived in a fantasy world surrounded by resin elves and plastic flowers and a malignant psychopath of a son.

"Jesus, Daniel! Are you insane?" Alex smacked his shoulder.

From far away, he heard what sounded like voices shouting. The voices grew closer, and suddenly the bright glare of a flashlight sliced through the darkness, and Alex bounced up.

"Now at least I don't have to hit you on the head and drag you," she said.

He started to smile, but stopped when he saw the look in her eyes. As she turned away, he saw the pair of gardening shears jammed in her back pocket. If it came down to it, he had no doubt that Alex would have done what she had to do, no matter what the cost.

59

There wasn't going to be a happy ending. Not for Ma, anyway. Or maybe there was. She was buried under the rubble of that shed with her true love.

Johnny Jeffords maneuvered his car to the side road off Delaware Avenue that looped back to G and R Scrap. Overhead, cars zoomed past on the I-95 bridge. Clueless people in their stupid cars. He wanted to pull out his Glock and take a few shots, but he was on a mission.

He'd taken Ma's car just in case that bitch reporter managed to get to the police. Normally, Ma would have kept her car in the garage, but they'd stowed the reporter's car there. Alex Burton. He wished he'd had a chance to make her pay for hurting Ma. He should have taken the time to look for her, but he was too agitated. It was hard to think straight. He had to concentrate.

He'd deal with the reporter later.

Right now, he had this job to complete. He had to deal with the final name on his list. Stan Riordan. The big, dumb water boy. Frank Greer's buddy. Johnny knew all about him, and he knew just where to find him.

He pulled across from G and R Scrap. It was getting ready to close for the day. Time to get acquainted with Stan Riordan.

60

It had only taken the firefighters a half hour to free Danny and Jenna and Alex from the cellar, and they emerged from the darkness, blinking in the glaring gray, rain still spitting down. Alex stood talking with a policewoman. Danny overheard the EMT say Jenna had no pulse in her feet before they loaded her onto an ambulance.

It took almost an hour for Danny to convince the emergency personnel to release them.

"You need to come into the hospital to get checked out," one of the EMTs said. "We can't just let you go."

Danny shook his head. "I'm fine. Most of the blood is Jenna's, and we really need to get back to Philly."

"Your face looks like someone tap danced on it."

"It always looks that way," Danny said. He gritted his teeth against the pain in his side and told the police to look for Johnny Jeffords. His car was still on the property, so he figured the kid must have taken off on foot.

Alex waited without comment. When they finally made their exit, she let him use her phone to call Jean.

Kevin had survived his heart surgery and was resting in the ICU. Danny promised to be there soon. If Jean was angry, she didn't show it. Maybe she was too exhausted. He should have been there instead of wallowing in the mud with Jenna, and yet he couldn't have left her in the dark.

It wasn't until they were finally on the road back that Alex lit into him.

"Are you insane, Ryan? What the hell were you thinking? Sitting with that crazy woman!"

"But Jenna was kind of pathetic, don't you think?"

"Jenna killed people."

"I know."

"So if you were writing her story, you'd say that it wasn't her fault?"

"No. I wouldn't say that. But she was tormented and bullied, and she wasn't stable to begin with. I think it broke her."

"So the moral of the story is to be careful who you bully, because it might come back to bite you on the ass?" Alex considered for a moment. "I didn't bully her."

"I'm not sure it mattered."

"And look at you. That kid of hers beat the crap out of you. He killed Greg Moss. He killed who knows how many others. Christ knows where he went."

"He didn't kill Greg Moss."

Alex put up her hand. "What do you mean?"

"He tried to kill Barb. He did kill Michelle Perry—you don't even know about that one yet. The point is, he confessed. I was there when he killed Frank Greer and his friend Mark Piscone. He killed the others, too—Ricky Farnasi, Nate Pulaski, and Chris Soldano. But he didn't kill Greg."

"And you know this because?"

"He told me."

"And you believe him?"

"Why confess to everything else and lie about Greg? He said he was trying to save him. I know it doesn't make sense. But this kid doesn't make sense. He's as crazy as his mother."

"But you've got somebody you like for Greg Moss's murder."

Danny nodded. "What if you were a guy who was getting squeezed by Greg Moss, and you were also close to someone working with him, someone who wanted you to keep an eye on Greg because he didn't trust him one hundred percent?"

"And you were stuck because both of them had something on you?"

"Exactly."

"Are you thinking about the mysterious partner?"

"I'm thinking about a cop."

"Wait." Alex shook her head. "I don't believe it. You're thinking about Officer Friendly. But I don't get it. Why?"

"Because he knew Greg. He had a substance problem that Greg knew about and held over his head. Because his father is Congressman George Crossman. He was the man in the middle. Plus, Kevin warned me to stay away from him."

"George Crossman." Alex said nothing for a few moments. She digested the information, tightening and loosening her hands on the steering wheel. "That's a lonely place to be. Talk about a river of tears."

"I don't have any proof."

"It makes sense though. He would have known Greg well enough to have heard about the texts, but maybe he didn't know what exactly they said."

"He wanted to get Greg off his back, and what better way than to try to tie his murder into the high school killings? But he needed to make sure someone made the connection."

"He knows Greg has been talking to you and makes sure he texts you to get you involved. The tongue's a little kinky."

She looked over at Danny, her face streaked with mud and her hair standing straight up in spots. She smiled, the connection sizzling. When she reached for his hand, he grasped it.

They had reached the outskirts of Exton, and Alex headed toward 202. The storm had already passed through here, though it seemed to have only grazed the area. Dark clouds drifted well to the north.

"Do you think we have time to wash up?" Alex asked. "You're still bleeding."

"I think we can take a few minutes to clean up. I might be out of alcohol."

"You're a hot mess, Ryan."

"I know. You like it though."

"I called Sam and left a message. He hasn't called me back."

"He might not have gotten the message yet. He was worried about you."

"Yeah, well we need to—"

Alex's phone buzzed. She grabbed it out of her cup holder. "Burton. What? You think what? When? Okay. Will do. Thanks."

When she disconnected, she turned to Danny. "Johnny Jeffords isn't on the property. He took Jenna's car. I just got a call from one of the cops from the scene at Jenna's, and he was sort of insistent that we seek out shelter because Johnny just might be looking for us."

"Maybe."

"Maybe as in you don't want police protection? Because we could head straight to the hospital. Or maybe you have something else in mind."

"Maybe as in I think I know where he's headed," Danny said.

"Damnit, I wish I'd had those goddamn garden shears when he was in the basement. Where are we going?" Alex asked.

"You drop me at home. You don't need to get in the middle of this."

"Oh, no, you are not doing this to me. We're in this together, Ryan. You tell me where to drive, or I stop right here on the side of the road." She held the phone in her left hand. "And no. You get no phone privileges. You can barely see, much less drive."

"Jesus, Alex. This isn't a game."

"I know that. So we're either a team or we're not."

Danny wasn't sure how he'd explain to Sam if something happened to Alex, but he nodded. "All right. You win. We need to get to South Philly. We're going to the original G and R Scrap yard. I think Johnny Jeffords is going after Stan Riordan."

"The water boy?"

"The caboose on the train."

"I think we need some backup on this, Ryan."

"I know. I'm going to call Ted Eliot. It's his case. If you give me the phone."

"Kind of risky, don't you think? Considering you think he's a killer himself."

"I'm going to call Kevin's partner, too. There's at least ten Philly cops camped out at HUP. I just hope this kid's predictable."

"I guess we'll find out." Alex handed him the phone.

61

It was after seven when they neared the South Philly scrapyard. Alex parked across from the yard behind a pile of concrete blocks. Danny led her down a narrow road. The chain link fence was still open, though the trucks had stopped rumbling into the yard for the day. Overhead, traffic whizzed by, though the worst of rush hour had passed.

"I hope I haven't screwed this up, too."

"This isn't your fault," Alex said. "Whatever happens."

He couldn't answer. He'd guessed wrong on so much of this case.

They slipped into the parking lot, and Danny saw a bright-red Mazda convertible with the license plate "COOL GRL." It stood near a van. He grabbed Alex's arm.

"Oh, Lord," Alex said.

"Call Jake Martinelli. Tell him we found Johnny Jeffords, and find out how far out he is," he said.

She took the phone, and he was creeping closer to the main office when he heard a scream. It was followed by a shot.

Johnny Jeffords came running out of the scale house holding a gun. Danny waited until he was just past the corner of the building where he and Alex were crouched and threw himself on Johnny.

Danny had surprise going for him, but Johnny had manic strength. He twisted and bucked until they were rolling in the dirt and gravel, flailing and punching. Johnny's nose looked smashed, and blood flowed down his face, but he bared his teeth in a sort of grimace and spat before he rammed his fist into Danny's left side. Danny gasped as pain clawed up his side and tried to kick at Johnny, but he was losing strength. He grabbed a handful of gravel and tossed it in the kid's face, but Johnny grabbed his arm and slammed it down.

"Fuck you, you sonofabitch!" Johnny gave him another vicious punch. He grabbed his gun. "I shoulda killed you back at Ma's. Worthless piece of shit!" He smacked the butt of the gun into Danny's cheekbone. "I'm gonna kill you. Then I'm gonna take your sweet little friend, and I'm gonna kill her, too. Real slow." Johnny pulled himself to his knees and knelt on Danny's chest. "I'd make you watch, but—"

"Drop the gun!"

Johnny started to aim the gun. Danny heard a boom, and Johnny's chest blew apart in a spray of red. He fell down beside Danny, arms spread apart. The gun lay beside his hand.

"Police. Move very slowly."

Danny sat up slowly, trying to force air into his lungs, as he watched the figure in the perfectly cut navy-blue suit walk toward him. He started to stand and then thought the better of it.

"Don't move," Ted Eliot said. "You look like you'll fall over."

"Detective Eliot," Danny said. "It's such a nice evening, I'd thought I'd take a minute to enjoy the quiet."

"My partner is with Ms. Burton. She's all right."

"Thank you. In a few minutes, this place will be crawling with Philly cops."

"It might be helpful if you were to testify that I identified myself before I shot."

"Given the situation, you might have read him his rights and I wouldn't have heard you."

"I might have." Eliot held out his hand. He wasn't wearing a watch. "I'm going to report that this was Greg Moss's killer. It will be my last act as a Camden County detective. Will you have a problem with that?"

Danny let the detective help him to his feet. From somewhere, he could hear the faint strains of Public Enemy's "Shut 'Em Down" drifting on the evening air from the scale house. It brought back memories of a night long ago. A pool of blood spread out from Johnny Jeffords's prone body.

Reporters wrote facts, but Danny was no longer sure what the facts were. Was Greg Moss a good guy or a bad guy? Was he both? Was Ted Eliot acting out of selfish motives or not? Because Danny was reasonably sure Eliot had pulled the trigger on Greg Moss. It wasn't about land deals or money. It was about self-preservation. And Danny himself had helped Johnny Jeffords kill Frank Greer. Hadn't he?

Did the pursuit of good justify bad deeds? Maybe all the sinners really were saints and vice versa.

Once you killed, did it become easier to kill again? Danny didn't know. He didn't want to find out.

Danny could hear sirens in the distance, and he knew they didn't have much time.

"Cromoca. Were you involved?" Danny asked.

"No. I wasn't part of it beyond the obvious. But there are some who are involved who know you. They might not have your best interests at heart."

"But you aren't one of them."

Eliot shook his head and gave him a wry smile. "I'm not one of them."

Police cars were streaming down the side road toward the scrapyard.

"You'd better check on Stan and the other poor bastard in the scale house," Danny said. "They're probably not doing too well, if they're even still breathing."

Eliot nodded. "You better get your side checked out, Ryan."

"I'll do that."

"Are we square?"

Danny considered. Ted Eliot had murdered a blackmailer who was going to profit from the sale of poisoned land, but he'd saved Danny's life. Did that balance out? Danny was in no position to play God.

"We're square," he said.

62

The nurse behind the receiving desk at HUP looked up in surprise when Danny walked off the elevator. Alex had dropped him at the emergency entrance.

The smell of antiseptic assaulted him, and he kept his eyes on the beige rubber tile floor.

"Excuse me, sir? Are you all right?" The nurse's voice cut into his thoughts.

Danny looked up. "I'm looking for Kevin Ryan. I understand he's been moved to the ICU?"

"Sir, are you all right?"

"Kevin Ryan." Danny gritted his teeth. It felt as though flames were searing his insides. "I'm his brother."

"Your name, sir?"

"Dan Ryan."

"The family lounge is at the end of the hall."

Danny forced himself to give her a grim smile. "Thank you."

The nurse started to approach them. "Sir, you're bleeding. You need help."

"No."

He turned down the hall to the waiting area. When he reached the doorway, he saw Jean, Kelly, Mike, Sean, and TJ huddled together in a miserable knot in the corner. His family. It was all he had.

"Jean," he said, and she gave a cry of distress. Then she was on her feet, wrapping her arms around him, leading them to the sofa, into their circle, his family.

She looked at his battered face. "Oh, my God, Danny, what happened?"

Jean fumbled in her purse for tissues, and he stilled her hands. He was breaking under the pain of her concern, the affection of these kids hovering around him. His voice shook when he said, "It doesn't matter. I'm okay. Tell me about Kevin."

*

Danny sat with Jean and the kids, waiting for Kevin. Waiting for him to wake up. Every few hours, a new group of cops would wander in to hug Jean and talk to the kids. It was a second family. The blue line was very real.

A tall, thin doctor walked into the room, and Danny went to Jean's side to place his hand on her shoulder. His heart seemed to have lodged in his throat, and he had to let Jean speak as Kelly edged under his arm. The twins crowded in like oversized puppies, and TJ wedged between his brothers. They all huddled together, surrounded by Kevin's cop family, waiting for the doctor to speak.

"Mrs. Ryan, your husband is stable. That's a good sign."

He began to talk about the myocardial infarction that had shut down Kevin's heart and the ten-hour surgery needed to repair the valves, and the whole time, Danny patted Jean like she was a pet retriever while Kelly cried against his chest. His family was together. For now.

"Hey, man." Kevin's partner was leaning over him. "You need to get looked at, buddy."

Danny started to protest, but someone pushed him into a wheelchair, and he was too tired to argue. He had a vague memory of someone wheeling him down a hallway before he let himself drift off to sleep.

*

When Danny opened his eyes, he was lying in a hospital bed, hooked up to an IV. He would have jumped out of bed, but he wasn't sure his legs would support him if he stood. Danny tried to move his arms, but they seemed to be tied down. A second IV line on the back of his left hand had been capped. He'd been transfused recently. *Jesus Christ.* His clothes were gone.

His pulse shot up from fifty-eight to ninety. His blood pressure went from ninety over sixty to one thirty over ninety.

"Oh, hell," he said. "I hate hospitals."

"You're awake." The voice came from a figure who sat in a chair by the side of the bed. Danny couldn't make out the face in the dark, but the soft, low voice was familiar.

"I'm awake. Who are you?"

"It doesn't matter."

"I think it does."

The figure shifted in the seat, and Danny watched him steeple his fingers in front of his face. "Maybe it's better for you to think of me as a dream."

Danny tried to feel around for the nurse's call button. He had no idea what time it was. The door was shut, and only a faint band of light crept under the frame.

"There's no need to panic. I'm not here to hurt you."

"That's a relief. Why are you here?"

"Greg Moss was my partner. Let's just say I have a vested interest in his unfortunate passing."

Danny closed his eyes and tried to remember the voice. "We knew each other in high school?"

"I need you to tell me who killed Greg and why."

Danny heard the threat in the soft voice. There was no reason he shouldn't tell the truth about Ted Eliot, but he knew he wouldn't. Eliot had been trapped and saw a way out. Danny didn't condone murder, but he knew the cop would have to live with himself, and that would be hard enough.

"A kid named Johnny Jeffords," Danny said. "His mother was Jenna Jeffords. You must remember Jenna. Jumbo Jen. Swamp Creature Jen. She attended a summer party at Greg's house and pulled a train."

Danny knew he sounded as hard and crude as Frank. He wanted to do something to provoke a reaction. Maybe this asshole had been one of the guys who'd been at Greg's party. Maybe he was Johnny Jeffords's father.

"And what part of the train were you?"

"I wasn't on board, but thanks for asking."

The figure sighed. "Poor deluded Jenna. She loved you."

"I didn't ask for that."

"True. But all the same, being the class reject. It warps you."

"Were you at Greg's party?"

"No, but rejects learn a lot of hard truths. Fairy tales don't come true. Fat girls don't become Barbies, and reject kids end up in juvie or worse because that's the way it is."

"You were a reject who ended up in juvie?"

Danny tried to click through names of every person he knew who'd gone to juvie. His brain moved at a slug's pace, but it came to him at last. Ray Gretske. He'd been selling dope to Ray under the I-95 overpass the night they were both busted. The night he went to juvie courtesy of his father. Lesson learned, and he wrote his essay. That goddamn essay. It hung around his neck like an albatross.

"Ray Gretske," he said. "You were helping Tim Rosina. Why?"

"I got busted for possession summer before my senior year. A misdemeanor, but I still did six months in juvie. Then I got busted again, and I was looking at serious time. Tim pulled some strings. I don't know how. So I did him some favors. Why not? Anyway, my mother was one of Tim's 'Saturday Night Girls.' At least he took care of us. Unlike some of her other friends. It didn't matter. In the end, he left everything to his sister, Olivia. Some people have all the luck, right? So maybe fairy tales do come true, huh?" Ray patted Danny's arm. "I could kill you right here, you know. Inject enough morphine into your line, and you'd flat line. Maybe they'd save you. Maybe not."

Danny's pulse began to edge up again. Where the hell was that nurse's call button? Did it matter?

"Don't worry. I never forget anyone who was nice to me." Ray folded his hands, almost as if he were praying. "That bullet just missed your intestines. You might have gotten sepsis, but you didn't. You are a lucky man. So do yourself a favor—watch your back, especially if you're going to go digging into Cromoca Partners."

"Cromoca Partners," Danny said. "They're selling poisoned land as part of that big federal initiative. Greg knew about it. The congressman knows, and so does Senator Harlan. It won't stay a secret for long. I'm not the only one who's onto it."

"Cromoca doesn't matter. Not to me. It mattered to Greg because he got greedy. That's what gets you in the end. Know your limits. Don't take more than you need. Besides, Cromoca is just a small part of a larger picture."

"What are you talking about?"

"I'm afraid that's all I'm talking about. I will repeat my advice: watch your back. You've made some interesting enemies, Daniel Ryan."

"Interesting advice coming from a drug dealer."

"You would think so, but I do know my limits. I've always been careful. I can thank your father for that."

Now he knew he must be dreaming. "My father? My father never gave a damn about anyone."

"Not true. He helped me get my record expunged. Now I'm a ghost. Or better yet, an Angel, or an Alien, if you like."

Ray stood, and Danny could tell he was dressed in scrubs. "It's time for you to go to sleep, Danny. Tomorrow this will be a dream. Or maybe it won't. Either way, it doesn't matter."

It took a second for Danny to realize that Ray held a syringe and was injecting the contents into his IV. He tried to move, but he was held fast to the bed. He opened his mouth to cry out, but the drugs flooded his system, drowning his screams in the onslaught.

63

Alex took special care to French braid her long hair and enclose the ends in a gold clip. She slid into a brilliant tangerine dress that clung in all the right places and spent time applying just the right amount of makeup. Nothing covered up the bruise on her left cheek or the scrapes on her arms and legs. She stared at herself in the mirror.

Sam had already left.

Last night their discussion had been painful.

"Alex, this investigation could have killed you. Surely you understand that. I don't see why you drove out to that house by yourself. No column is worth this."

"Yeah. I saw how worried you were. You called at least once."

Sam had only shaken his head. "I thought you had decided to leave me. I thought you needed time to think. Even Daniel didn't know where you were."

"Wait! You thought I'd just leave without telling you?" She'd been grateful for the water dripping down from her wet hair. It covered the tears. She told herself they were angry tears; she always cried when she was angry. It was a good distraction from the solid lump in her throat. "I can't believe you think so little of me."

"Oh, Alex. Maybe we need to stop pretending with each other."

Alex wasn't sure that they had reached any decisions, except that they had a problem. They could fix it if only she quit her job and got pregnant. She walked to the bed, grabbed a throw pillow, and stuffed it under her dress. Then she walked back to the mirror. She wasn't feeling the joy.

He was right. He made much more money than she did. His career was booming. A "total package," one of the senior staff had said at the last cocktail party they attended—smart, handsome, articulate. What did they expect? But she would always clench her teeth and smile. That was Sam: a wonderful show poodle. Alex had learned to dress sedately and keep her mouth closed, to be an asset.

She tossed the pillow back on the bed. She was tired of being an asset. She had opinions and a big mouth. He'd have to deal with it, or she'd deal with him. But not now. She had too much to get done this morning.

*

Three hours later, Alex had stopped by Danny's house to pick him up some clean clothes and shoes. She'd gathered the information and site maps detailing Cromoca Partners' land holdings along with Danny's personal notes. After checking in at the paper, she'd made her way toward the hospital and was now heading up to his room.

She'd checked in on Kevin, who was still in the ICU but slowly gaining strength. That was good enough.

Alex tapped on the door of Danny's room. It was private, which made life easier. She peeked around the door to make sure the nurses weren't doing anything embarrassing, but he was lying asleep, still in restraints, hooked up to slowly beeping monitors and oxygen. He was still getting IV liquids, though they'd stopped transfusing him, and he was still on a catheter. She eyed the collection bag hanging on the side of the bed.

That little bastard Johnny Jeffords had beat the crap out of him. The right side of Danny's face was the color of an eggplant, his eye a slit inside the swollen flesh, but asleep, he looked ten years younger, maybe because the tension was gone. Alex stood beside the bed and fished into the bag she'd brought from his house.

"Okay, Ryan. I'm just fumbling around here. I brought you some clothes. I'll hang them up for you so you don't have to walk out in that hospital gown. And I brought notes on Cromoca and your notebook, but that's for when you feel better. For now, I thought maybe you'd like to have this by your bed."

She pulled a photo of Danny and Conor out of the bag. It was a close-up of the two of them at a kid-sized table working on a puzzle. Danny had that giant smile as he hugged Conor close. He looked so alive, and she wondered if he'd ever look that way again.

Fumbling in the bag, Alex pulled out a long piece of black jet. She'd found it on his nightstand, so maybe it was important. She set in front of the photograph. Old ladies wore jet beads. She'd have to remember to look up jet. Did it have some kind of significance? Maybe it had a special meaning for him.

Alex pulled a green chair closer to the side of the bed and settled into it. Opening her laptop, she started to go over her files.

"Alex."

She almost jumped out of her chair at the sound of his groggy whisper. "Hey, you're awake. I was getting worried about you." She took his hand and leaned close.

"Someone was in here last night."

His eyes were sleepy and unfocused, but she could see him trying to get his thoughts together. Alex patted his hand.

"How could someone get in here? There're security cameras all over."

"Someone was here last night. He warned me about Cromoca. He told me who Tim Rosina's sister was."

"Olivia Capozzi," Alex said.

"How did you know that?"

"It's in your notes. I can't read a lot of your writing, but I can read names."

"Oh, Jesus, you're right. I did know. But I still spoke to someone last night."

SARAH CAIN

"I think maybe you were just trying to remember your notes. Think about it. Why would someone who didn't want you to look into Cromoca come and give you information about Cromoca? It doesn't make sense." She settled back in the chair. "We are going to write this story. It's going to be an asskicker."

"No, someone was here. Cromoca is part of something bigger."

"Bigger than what?"

"I . . . I don't know."

She smoothed his hair. "Okay, baby. I'll have them check the tapes. Right now." She paused and handed him the piece of jet. "What is this?"

"Don't laugh?"

"I won't laugh."

"It's supposed to protect you from harm and heal grief. I don't think it works too well."

She kissed his forehead. "I'll have them check those tapes."

*

Alex wasn't surprised when Kevin Ryan's partner, Jake, reported two hours later that no one had been caught on tape entering Danny's room, though he did admit that the room was at an odd angle to the security camera.

"It's possible someone could get in and out, but you'd really have to know the layout. And why would you sneak into someone's room just to chat?"

"I don't know."

"Did he say he was threatened?"

"He said they had a discussion. It was weird."

"He was pretty snowed under. You have a lot of weird dreams when you're that doped up."

"He said the guy was wearing scrubs. Could you just double-check?" She gave him a wide smile. "I'd really appreciate it."

He winked at her. "You know how to play it, don't you?"

"Will you do it?"

He slipped her his card. "Absolutely. If you need anything else, you call me."

"Thanks, Jake. I'll do just that." Alex knew when to be diplomatic.

64

Ray Gretske lay on a floating lounger and drifted in a gentle rocking glide on the surface of his rooftop pool. From here, he could look out and see the ocean without the disturbance of small children and other people. He enjoyed his serenity.

He heard the footsteps tramping up the wooden steps and tensed long before he stared up at the beefy man who loomed over him.

"Well?" Ray said.

"The police have closed the investigation into Greg Moss's murder. They caught the guy. Some loser named Johnny Jeffords. He killed a bunch of people."

"Do you have names?"

"Frank Greer. Stan Riordan. Len Piscone. Mark Piscone. A chick name Michelle Martin. Plus a bunch before that. The guy was some kind of nut job."

"Indeed. Do the police have a motive?"

"Like being crazy ain't enough?"

Ray looked up and cocked an eyebrow. "No. I'm afraid not."

"Well, if there was another motive, I didn't hear it. He was crazy, and he had a crazy mother."

"What about the detective?"

"Eliot? He's the guy who brought Jeffords down at some South Philly scrapyard. Jeffords was in the act of beating the crap outta some guy."

"A bad character."

"A real scumbag."

"Was any mention made about Cromoca Partners?"

"Not specific-like. But some reporters been asking questions about Cromoca."

"What reporters?"

"A woman from the *Sentinel* named Burton. Your friend Ryan. A couple guys from Camden."

Ray pushed the float to the side of the pool and hauled himself out. He wrapped himself in a white robe and stared out toward the ocean. On the beach, the sunbathers were just beginning to gather in force, and he looked away in disgust.

"I'd build a wall, but then I couldn't see the ocean," he said. "Well, it seems that I picked the right time to unload Cromoca. I had hopes for it, but I'm afraid I was played on that one. Fools selling poisoned ground. Of course they were going to be found out. They got greedy. Let them sink or swim on their own. I think it may be time for a vacation. I dislike the Jersey Shore in the middle of summer. Do we have anything on the schedule that I have to handle?"

"No, sir."

"Very good. Deal with the congressman. Tell him I'm not interested in acquiring any new partners. He'll be annoyed, no doubt, but I'm not getting involved with that situation. Maybe we'll leak something to the Burton woman about Cromoca. That will be fun. That will make those Washington idiots dance and jump. Not too much yet, just enough to make them uncomfortable."

"Anything else?"

"No. I'm taking a nap. Make sure I'm not disturbed."

"What about the cop?"

Ray looked back over the ocean. He doubted that this Johnny Jeffords character had killed Greg. He was reasonably sure Ted

Eliot got tired of his leash. It was always a possibility. Greg had gotten greedy.

Maybe Eliot had done him a favor. Ray always knew that one day he would have to make changes, and now seemed as good a time as any. He had learned long ago that the only way to survive was to fly under the radar. Let people think less of you. It always worked.

Cromoca was a small strand of a very large financial web filled with dangerous spiders. He'd always been careful to keep his finances separate and under cover.

In any case, now was a good time to disappear permanently.

He looked back at his associate. "Oh, I think we'll let Mr. Eliot go in peace. I've never been one to hold grudges."

65

When he was finally allowed to see Kevin, Danny barely controlled his horror at the sight of his gray-faced brother lying amid the monitors. His face was obscured by an oxygen mask, the blood pressure cuff tightened and loosened, and some monitor beeped. Two bags hung from the IV pole. Kevin had been in the hospital for a week, and he already seemed diminished.

"Hey, Kev," he said.

Kevin rolled his eyes open with some effort. "Look shitty," he said, his voice slurred.

Danny swallowed. Kevin sounded broken, and now it was his turn to play the stronger brother. He leaned close. "You look shitty, too."

"Asshole." Kevin moved his hand slightly, and Danny took it. Kevin's big square hand felt cold, and it looked so pale against his own.

"I know. I know. You need to get better so you can keep me in line."

"Jean?"

"I'll look out for her and the kids. Till you're up and around."

Kevin nodded and shut his eyes. Danny kissed the top of his head. "You hang in there, Kev." He didn't say, "Please don't leave me," but he wanted to. He wanted to throw his arms around Kevin and beg him to get up, bat him on the head, and tell him everything would be all right. Life didn't work that way.

Kevin said, "Tired."

"I'll let you rest, for now." Danny squeezed Kevin's hand. "Hey? I love you, Kev."

Kevin was asleep.

*

When he left Kevin's room, Danny smelled his sister, Theresa, before he saw her. She'd always bathed in heavy-duty perfume that made his eyes water, and it comingled with the aroma of too many cigarettes. But she looked better than she had in years. Theresa had spent over thirty thousand of his dollars to repair her teeth and a few thousand more to upgrade her wardrobe.

She'd gone back to her natural brunette and wore a leopard-print dress with a gold scarf, which might have looked good if Theresa had any curves left. Years of drug addiction had left her looking hollowed out. Still, she persevered, clacking down the hall in her scarlet four-inch platforms.

"Yo, Danny. You see Kevin? I came to see him, and no one will let me in."

"He's asleep, Theresa."

"I think Jean told them not to let me in. Like I'd bother him or somethin'. Jeez, I'm his goddamn sister, y'know?"

"He's very weak right now. I'm not sure his heart could take the sight of you."

"Fuck you."

"I meant you look great."

She patted her hair with one hand and tapped her long red fingernails on the back of a chair with the other. "Well, I drove here from South Philly, and I had to park. It ain't cheap, y'know?"

Danny sighed. "I'll take care of the parking."

"I'm glad I caught you anyways. I've run short."

"Aren't you working?"

Theresa folded her arms and cocked her head. "Please, how much do you think being the office manager at a dental office pays? My insurance is crap. You're rich. You can fork over some bucks."

Danny heard the scratch of resentment in her voice. Theresa had led a hard and fast life. Now everyone was paying for it. He'd die with her hand in his pocket and her voice in his ear whispering, "You owe me."

"You want my help? You can help me," Danny said. "My associate and I are writing a story. We need some background. You help us, I'll pay you."

Theresa narrowed her eyes. "Sure, I'll help."

"You talk to her. If she thinks you're useful, I'll pay you."

"You're an SOB."

Danny took her by the arm. "We're meeting in the cafeteria. I'll introduce you. Her name is Alex Burton, and she doesn't deal well with bullshit."

*

"It's not like Vic forced them kids to sell dope. Ask Danny," Theresa sat back in her plastic seat and drank black coffee while she checked out the mostly empty cafeteria. The scent of burgers and Italian dressing filled the room. "Where are the goddamn doctors? Don't they eat?"

"We missed the lunch rush," Danny said. "Are you trolling for a date?"

"Go to hell, Danny." Theresa glanced at Alex, as if trying to gauge whether or not she had a sympathetic audience. She sighed when she saw the stony look on Alex's face.

"Who were some of the kids who sold drugs for Vic?" Alex asked.

"I don't see why it matters now. Most of 'em are dead, and it's not like you can persecute Vic."

"You mean prosecute," Alex said.

"No." Theresa slammed down her cup and glared at Danny. "I mean persecute. 'Cause that's what he does. Persecutes me."

"You look like you're doing pretty well." Alex pointed to Theresa's purse. "That's a Celine bag, and it looks authentic."

Theresa pursed her lips. "I deserve some perks. I work hard."

"If you want perks, you better earn them."

"I can walk away right now."

"And I can get another lowlife source a lot cheaper."

Theresa turned away from Alex and leaned closer to Danny. "You let her talk to me that way? I'm your sister."

"I told you Alex doesn't like bullshit."

Theresa folded her arms. "Vic took care of you good."

Danny pinched the bridge of his nose. He wasn't going to argue with Theresa about the merits of the man who tried to introduce him to the joys of Mexican brown when he was fourteen. "Makes the pain go away," Vic had said. "Stairway to heaven." He'd been just smart enough to understand that nothing Vic was pushing made the pain go away.

"Just tell us about the kids who worked for Vic and anything you might know about Tim Rosina," he said.

"It's gonna cost you," Theresa said.

Danny exchanged a look with Alex. "Like I didn't know that already."

*

"And what have we learned from this?" Alex leaned back in the plastic cafeteria chair and waved toward their notepads, the stacks of coffee cups, and the empty bags of potato chips and peanut butter cups. Danny had handed Theresa five twenties and promised to transfer an unnamed five-figure sum into her checking account before she tottered off. He hoped she was heading home instead of upstairs to torment Jean.

"Families are fun?" he said.

She patted his hand. "As if we needed that lesson. Hang around and I'll introduce you to mine."

"We learned that Vic Ceriano took lots of kids under his moldy wings and taught them to sell drugs. Among other things," Danny said. Vic Ceriano was a modern-day Fagin.

"And among those kids was your old buddy Ray Gretske."

"Whose mother was one of Tim Rosina's 'Saturday Night Girls.'"

Danny shook his head. "Ray was going to be thrown into juvie for pushing drugs to kids, but Tim Rosina pulled some strings. In return, Ray did some little favors for Tim."

"Like burn down some houses."

Danny nodded. He didn't mention that Ray had already pretty much confirmed what Theresa said. He should have. Ray was a drug dealer. He'd torched houses as a kid. But he'd never been malicious. Maybe he would have turned bad on his own, but Danny had given him an assist. Ray had called him a lucky man. Danny wasn't sure whether he was lucky or cursed.

"Maybe you could leave Ray's name out of this article. We don't have any definite proof he burned houses."

"He might be Greg Moss's missing business partner. Why do you want to protect him?"

Danny shrugged. "Ray wasn't a bad guy. He had a really screwed-up life. And my sister and her boyfriend made it worse."

"So you feel guilty?"

"I don't know. Write what you can prove."

Alex sat up straight. "Wait. Did Ray have a nickname? Jenna remembered someone called the Angel."

"The Alien. Because he always seemed like he was in another world."

"She called him the Angel. She was really definite about it."

"She called him by name?"

"No."

"So? It could have been anyone in Vic's merry band of delinquents. She believed I was her boyfriend. She was definite about that, too."

Alex nodded, though she seemed unconvinced. "Maybe they're both right. Maybe to Jenna he seemed like an angel."

"Well, she's in rehab in Lancaster. She lost both legs from the knees down. They're keeping her there until she goes to trial for the murder of Ollie Deacon and your kidnapping and a whole host of other charges. You should go talk to her."

Alex shuddered. "You know this because?"

"I've seen her." Danny looked away.

Jenna had finally gotten her wish. She had slimmed down, but her white flesh sagged against her bones, making her look drawn and haggard. Poor Jenna Jeffords would never be a swan. "I'm still wearing my Claddagh ring," she'd said, and he'd shuddered, even as he'd mouthed some sort of banality. She'd drift in and out of reality as if her brain had some kind of broken switch. When he sat in the small room with Jenna, Danny struggled to breathe. It was only when he was driving home that he could pity the poor soul lying in the hospital bed. What a coward he was.

"Would she talk to me?" Alex asked.

"Maybe. I don't know. She asked for me. She doesn't get much company."

Alex squeezed his arm. "It's not your fault. Try to remember that."

Isn't it? Danny didn't know. Had he somehow led Jenna on? Made her believe he cared about her? He hadn't wanted to be like his father, like his brother Junior. He'd tried to be kind, but he'd never been a saint. Christ, he'd peddled dope. What did that make him? You couldn't go back because you always saw the past through the prism of your present. You were never that person you imagined you were.

Alex watched with sympathetic eyes. He wasn't any kind of hero, and she didn't seem to mind. "In any case," he said, "you have a huge story about political corruption, land development, and profiteering. And that's just the beginning. Play it right and you might get a Pulitzer nod."

"What do you mean *I* have a story?"

Danny leaned back in the chair and closed his eyes. He knew it was going to be hard to explain. He wasn't quite sure he understood himself. "I watched you when you were grilling my sister, digging into the background, just going through my notes— you've got the fire, Alex. You want to slay the dragons. Right the wrongs. And that's a wonderful thing. You need that." He sat up and shrugged.

Alex wrapped her arms around her chest. "But you don't."

He shook his head. "I'm tired."

"So you're just going to walk away?"

"I talked to Tim Gluckman, your managing editor. I'm going to do a piece for the magazine about Jenna and high school bullying. I know it's been done to death, but I feel like I owe her."

"You do realize she and her son tried to kill you."

He nodded and watched her try to puzzle it out. "I know. But somebody should still tell her story. She was a sad case."

"And then what? You head off into the sunset?"

"I don't know. I haven't thought that far ahead."

"What does that even mean?" Alex's eyes narrowed in anger, and Danny knew anything he said would be used against him. He didn't want to have to explain that he needed to walk away before he hurt her, too.

"It's time for me to move on."

"You trying to be noble, Ryan? Or maybe you just don't like black women?"

"Jesus Christ, Alex. You're still married, and every woman I've loved I've managed to get killed."

"So are you telling me you love me?"

"I'm telling you I care about you more than I should."

"What does that even mean?"

"It means you're married, and I—"

"Don't you dare tell me you're still in love with your wife."

He almost smiled at the ferocity in her eyes. How could he begin to tell her about Kate, who still claimed a small but very real corner of his heart? Maybe he needed to admit he loved a ghost, but she was gone. Life kept rolling forward, and the woman glaring across the table at him was vibrant and real. He reached out to take her hand. They stood on equal ground, and he didn't want to screw it up.

"I'm not still in love with Beth," he said.

"So that leaves us?"

"Moving forward?"

"Together?"

"You have some loose ends to tie up, don't you think?"

Alex sighed. "Loose ends are a bitch."

"Can we work out those loose ends?"

"Oh, baby." She leaned close enough that her lips were a breath away from his. "We can work out anything."

66

By late August, Alex had gathered a huge amount of background for the exposé on Cromoca. It had been tentatively set to break the second week in September, but the deadline kept getting pushed back.

"It's a cesspool," she'd told Danny when they last met for dinner. She was glowing.

She and Sam hadn't officially separated, though he had leased an apartment in West Philly near the hospital, and she still lived out in Devon. She was working almost round the clock to pull the article together, but she and Danny had head-banging sessions at least four times a week.

He looked forward to them.

Danny stood on the Penn Charter soccer field on a warm afternoon watching Kelly practice for preseason. She'd had a growth spurt and now stood at a rangy five eight, her long dark hair pulled back into a tight braid as she ran sprints.

"She's fast," Danny said to Kevin.

Since June, Kevin had lost nearly fifty pounds and was working on losing another fifty. His color was better, and he could jog a quarter mile without running out of breath. He barely complained when Jean fed him his broiled chicken and broccoli or salmon and asparagus, though he looked ready to cry at the tiny vanilla birthday cupcake she served him a few weeks ago.

Small steps.

"Kelly's a good kid. Helps her mom. It's been tough," Kevin said. He ran a hand against his face. "What a thing. Right? Heart attack. I was too dumb to know what was happening."

"Lots of people don't know. You had a lot on your mind. You've got a great scar," Danny said.

Kevin grunted, but Danny watched him relax slightly, walking to the bleachers to sit. Danny sat beside him. In the next field, some younger boys were practicing, and he turned to watch. Conor would have been eight now, younger than these boys, but no less enthusiastic. Just getting ready to start third grade. Danny pushed his fist against his chest. Would the pain ever go away? Maybe when his heart stopped beating.

"Oh, here, this came for you. It was mailed to our house. Guess whoever sent it didn't have your new address."

Kevin handed Danny a beige envelope. The kind people used to send before they stopped writing letters. Danny opened the envelope and pulled out a photograph and a single sheet of paper with a note was scrawled on it:

Here I am enjoying my new life. As you can see, everything is fine. Hope to meet again someday soon. All the best.

The photograph was of John Novell, the detective who'd saved his life eighteen months ago. He stood in front of an expanse of glass in a pair of khaki shorts and a white polo shirt, a Marlins baseball cap on his head and a pair of sunglasses covering his eyes.

Danny squinted at the picture. Reflected in the glass was the woman taking the photograph. She was small and wore a flowing white dress and a sun hat. He would have sworn she was Linda Cohen, who had, up until last year, owned the *Sentinel*. Seated behind them on a low stone wall was a light-haired woman holding a small child. She rested her chin on the child's head, and Danny was absolutely positive the woman was Kate Reid. The woman he had loved. The woman he had believed was dead.

Kevin looked at him and frowned. "What the hell is the matter?"

Danny handed him the photograph.

"Mother of God," Kevin said. "Get rid of this."

"But you know what this means."

He looked at the envelope. The return address was Los Angeles. It was postmarked June.

"It means nothing," Kevin said. "It's been sitting in my junk pile for well over a month. Let it go."

"But Kate's alive. She's alive!"

Kevin caught him by the arms and gave him a little shake. "Listen to me. It's taken you damn near three years—three years!—to get your life back together. Don't throw it away because you think you see something in a photograph. For Christ's sake, Danny."

"She's holding a child. It could be mine."

"It could be the goddamn postman's. It might not even be Kate. Look, she's blonde. Let it go. Let her go. Don't be an idiot. For once in your life, throw that goddamn thing away and move on."

"I don't know if I can."

"You've spent too much time looking back. Move on."

Danny placed the note and photograph back into the envelope. On the field, the girls were starting to go through their drills, and he watched Kelly raise her fist in the air and shout. She glanced around and waved at the bleachers. Kevin waved back.

Danny's heart beat against his throat. Alex was expecting him for dinner, where they were going to review her notes. He had an article to finish, and his life was threatening to come apart. Again.

A lifetime ago, Kate had given him a deep-sworn vow. She'd walked away, and he believed he'd closed the door between them. But he'd never locked it.

The old familiar faces were waiting. Should he stay or go?

Acknowledgments

As always, I am very grateful to so many people for their support.

First and always, thank you to my wonderful husband, Howard, who was not only supportive throughout this whole adventure but also a source of fascinating information about the scrap industry and, of course, the ins and outs of local government. Thank you as well to my three terrific children, Alexandra, Michael, and Mary, who both inspire me and make me a proud mama in every way, every day. I am so lucky to have such an amazing family whom I adore beyond reason.

Thank you to my wonderful writing women: the fantastic and fabulous Julie Duffy (of Story-A-Day), the multitalented and multifaceted Lorinda Lende, and my darling supernova of a writer (and friend) Maria Hazen-Lewis (who has patiently held my hand and listened to my moaning and groaning for far too long). They were my critiquers, coaches, and all-around writing buddies. I would never have gotten through the manuscript without these women by my side. They are amazing writers, generous with their time, friendship, and guidance. I love you all, and I believe it's time to start planning field trips (with margaritas)!

Thank you to my dear Michelle Massey, who has been a cheerleader and supportive beyond reason. I love you. You are the best. Never doubt it.

Thank you to Thea Kotroba and the staff of the recently closed Chester County Book Company. This lovely store was a warm and welcoming place to discover books and a grand supporter of local authors. It will be sorely missed.

Thank you to the Main Line Writers, who are a warm and welcoming group that, under the leadership of Gary Zenker, provides a home for aspiring and published writers. It is a lovely group of people who are generous, talented, and kind.

Thank you always to my agent, Renée C. Fountain, who got me started and who has always been there for me.

Thank you to Matt Martz and the crew at Crooked Lane Books for their help and editorial assistance in getting the story right, with a particular shout-out to Heather Boak and Sarah Poppe for their time and assistance and to amazing cover designers Andy Ruggirello, who worked on *The 8th Circle*, and Melanie Sun, who designed *One by One*.

I'd also like to thank Dana Kaye and Julia Borcherts for their hard work publicizing the book. You are the dynamic duo.

Finally, thank you to those who came to readings, book signings, and other events and who took the time to comment on the novel. I appreciated every one of your thoughts and our discussions. Follow me at http://sarahcain.author.com or on Facebook or Twitter.